THE
REDWOOD PALACE

M. K. HUTCHINS

Appropriate for Teens, Intriguing to Adults

Immortal Works LLC
1505 Glenrose Drive
Salt Lake City, Utah 84104
Tel: (385) 202-0116

Cover Art by Ashley Literski
http://strangedevotion.wixsite.com/strangedesigns

ISBN 978-1-7339085-3-5 (Paperback)

AISN B07T2TC9RW (Kindle Edition)

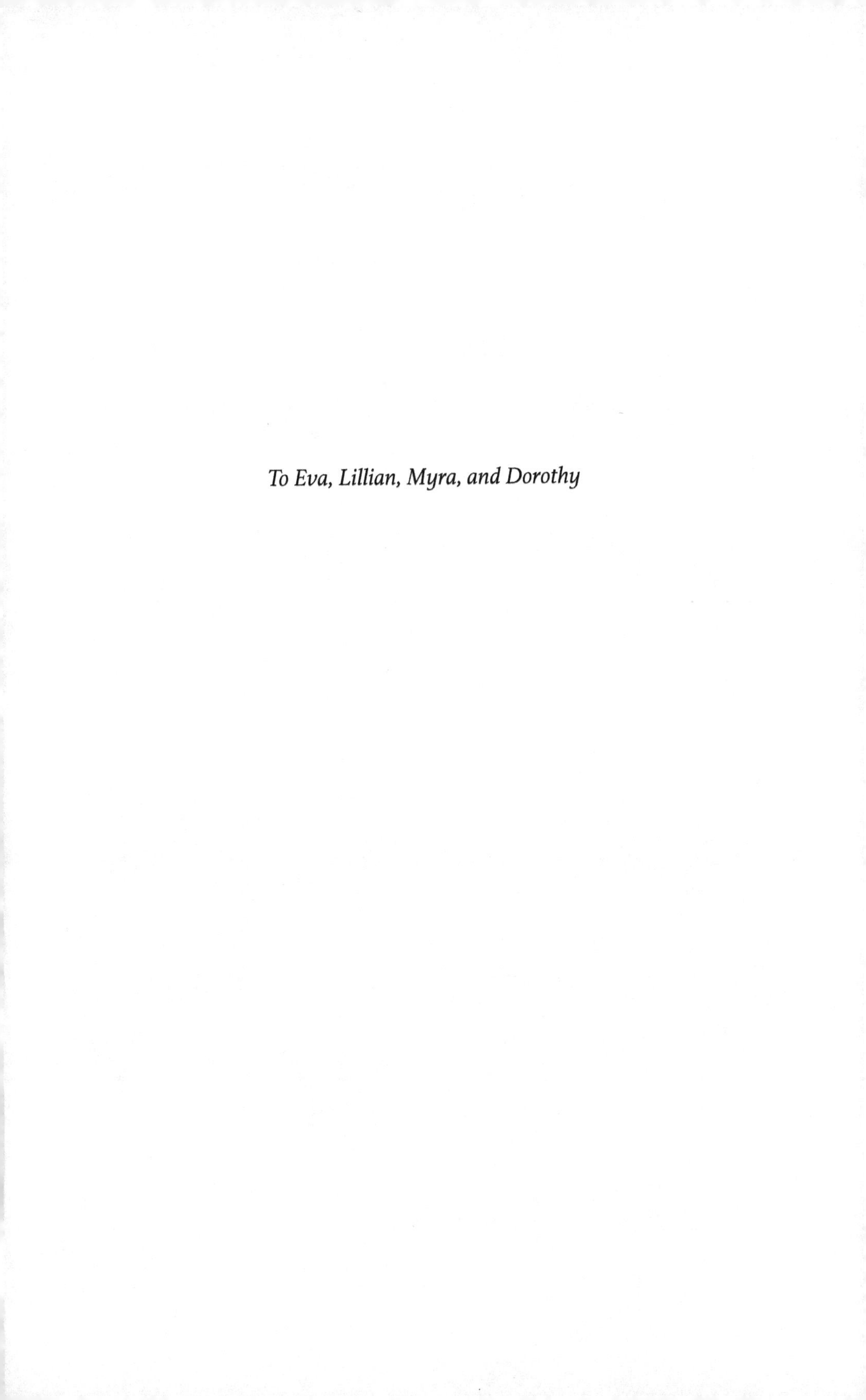

To Eva, Lillian, Myra, and Dorothy

CHAPTER ONE

Given that old Grandmother Sandpiper had fallen in her fire again, Father and I abandoned our regular route and hurried toward her house. He carried the bag of bandages and salves; I carried my satchel of cooking instruments and herbs.

"Iris said her arm is the worst of it. What'll she need for that, Plum?" Father asked. Even jogging down a lane, he tested me. Maybe it was force of habit.

"Parsnips or kale will target the arm. Adding fish skin, vegetable peelings, hedgehog mushrooms, or onion will further target her skin. She'll need sour for strength, which will dull the pain, and sweet for endurance to help her heal."

With how fast we were moving, I was grateful for the cool afternoon spring breeze on the back of my neck.

"Ah, you make me feel old. Have you learned all I have to teach you?"

"You'd be disappointed if I answered falsely, and now you bemoan that I answered well. Is it possible to please you?" I teased, a bit short of breath. Teasing helped me swallow the sour worry in the back of my throat.

"I'm allowed to be cantankerous in my old age."

"When you reach old age, I might agree with you."

Sandpiper's house came into view—we'd made good time. Both of us ran up the three creaking steps of Sandpiper's porch, then Father called through the door, "Sandpiper! We're here! May we come in?"

"Of course, of course," she replied, her voice muffled and tired.

She cradled her arm against her chest, so I couldn't see how bad the injury was. But the inside of her one-room house was worse than last time we'd come. It reeked of mice droppings and soot. Ashes from the hearth had spilled over the floor next to her crumpled mattress and bedding. Her lovely circular table, made from the cross-cut of a mid-sized redwood, was stained with bits of yesterday's hotpot.

"I'm so glad you came." Sandpiper was ancient—older than my nana had been. She gave a shaky bow, then nearly toppled over as she tried to sit on her own rush mat. Father dashed forward and caught her.

He gave me a look, and without further prompting, I opened all the shutters, letting in some light and spring air.

"Your children need to take better care of you than this," Father said.

Her wrinkled, sagging face was as proud as any queen's. "I thought you'd come to treat my burn, not meddle in my affairs."

She stuck her arm out. She'd clumsily wrapped it in a dirty dish-towel. Poor woman. Father was right—she needed more help from her children.

He gently unwrapped the towel, revealing a raw, red wound the size of my fist. Bad, but it could have been worse. Much worse.

"Plum, get the crock heating with some water while I clean this." He pulled out a flask of diluted vinegar from his satchel.

"Can't you just bandage it?" Sandpiper eyed the canteen suspiciously. "I'm not so young I'll believe you when you say it won't hurt a bit."

I opened Sandpiper's clay crock, but the smell of cold, moldering soup wafted out. How long had it sat there?

Sandpiper rubbed the back of her neck and mumbled an embarrassed apology. While she was distracted, Father dampened one of his clean rags with the vinegar.

"Hold still," Father said.

I tried to give Sandpiper what dignity I could by hurrying outside with the crock, but thanks to the open windows, I still heard her cursing my father's Ancestors for his existence.

Twice, I scrubbed the crock with sand, then rinsed it with water from her rain bucket. A clean crock is the foundation of cooking. Nothing tastes good with dirt in it. I scooped a cup of fresh water into the clean vessel then stepped back inside.

Father and Sandpiper sat across from each other on her moldering rush mat.

"But it will heal? If I'm careful not to bother it for a while?" Sandpiper asked.

I pulled my favorite obsidian knife from my bag, unwrapped the rabbit skin protecting it, then grabbed a dried fish from Sandpiper's pantry.

"Sandpiper, you need to talk to your children. I can't do that for you." Father folded the dishrag she'd used for a bandage and set it aside. "Did they forget that you raised them, fed them, clothed them? It's their turn."

Given the state of her home, it had been their turn for some time.

She bristled. "You might be yellow-ranked, but don't lecture me. I'm still older than you. My children don't want me to bother them. They've made that clear."

She managed to keep the pride in her voice as she said that. I wished her willpower alone could change reality and make it so. Carefully, I scraped just the fish's skin into the crock.

"They might feel differently if they knew you'd burned your arm tending the fire."

She glared at my father, like she was debating throwing us out. Hastily, I finished prepping the food. I added a drizzle of sour-sweet blackberry molasses, then chopped up a parsnip and tossed it in. A pinch of salt and a thin slice of ginger followed, for balance. I shoved it onto the coals—I'd taste and reseason after it simmered.

Then I grabbed a broom.

"Stop that!" Sandpiper snapped at me. "You're a chef, not a maid."

"I'm a very proud chef. I'm afraid I have to sweep," I said with a melodramatic sigh.

My father gave me a quiet, encouraging smile.

"That doesn't make sense," Sandpiper said.

"Of course it does. If you trip over something on the floor and bruise your hip, or get a cough because the air's bad, what will happen to me? People will say I must not be good at cooking, because, why, Plum visited Grandmother Sandpiper the other day and now she's worse off than before."

"Rubbish. You're as good a chef as your father, and anyone who says otherwise hasn't tried your food."

I shrugged. "Rumors burn through small towns like flames through chaff. Besides, a chef is supposed to support health and longevity. If I can do that while I wait for the crock to simmer, shouldn't I?"

She shook her head, but the tight lines around her eyes and mouth were already softening. "You're going to marry into that former Master Chef's family in Westbank, aren't you? Then you'll be an even better chef."

My stomach fluttered and my cheeks burned. Maybe. Maybe Sorrel's father would accept the proposal my father had written. Then I could read their vast recipe library and use their greenhouse gardens. "You just proved my point about rumors and small towns. How'd you know that?"

Sandpiper smiled, prim and smug at the same time.

"Fine, fine, keep your secrets. I'm just glad we've agreed that if you don't like me sweeping your floor, you'll have to talk to your children about helping you, instead."

Sandpiper reluctantly nodded—she'd do it. Good.

"I can't believe you look so calm about it," Sandpiper said. "I'd be in knots if I was waiting for a response."

I swept the crumbs and dust out the front door. "Well, the courier's still a week out from Clamsriver. Not much point in working myself up now, is there?"

My father hurried to the hearth. His voice sounded oddly tight. "How's that soup coming?"

"Courier's supposed to come tomorrow," Sandpiper said. "Who told you Elek would take so long?"

The bottom of my stomach dropped away. Tomorrow? *Tomorrow?*

My father sampled the broth. "Perfectly seasoned, as always, Plum," he said, far too innocently.

I pursed my lips. I couldn't question him here with Sandpiper listening.

"WHY DIDN'T YOU TELL ME?" I demanded outside. We stood behind Sandpiper's house, away from the road, where only her pen of ducks could eavesdrop.

The spring wind wasn't cold, but goosebumps still ran up my arms.

"Because I knew you'd fret. Master Chef Yarrow's response might not come tomorrow."

He left unspoken another possibility: it might not be good news.

"Maybe I shouldn't have written Chef Yarrow in the first place. He's green-ranked, Plum. I don't know how he'll take my suggestion."

I fiddled with the ends of my sleeves—they draped half-way to my elbow. Yellow-ranked sleeves, a rank below Green. The rank of an honored citizen able to hold a number of lesser offices. Like that of village chef.

Father squeezed my shoulder. "Sandpiper's right. You're a brilliant chef, and if Yarrow turns you down as a daughter-in-law, he's a fool."

"Is he a fool?" I asked. Father had served under him in his youth, when he worked as an apprentice in the palace kitchens.

"I hope not. But there's nothing we can do now but wait."

FOR THE REST of the day, I could think of little but the coming letter. I made sweet cranberry tea for Amari, who was expecting her fourth child next month. Then Father grilled sweet slices of acorn squash, right on the coals, for Hifal's cough. We aided a dozen houses before evening, then briefly stopped at a dozen more to taste their suppers and adjust the seasonings.

We'd nearly reached the porch of our house when someone screamed—it came from the gardens. Father and I ran.

Mother lay sprawled on her side in the garden, trying to push herself upright with one arm and failing.

Father reached her first. "What happened?"

"My back..." She winced in pain, struggling through the words. "It seized up again."

My stomach churned. Last time—three days ago—she'd promised us she wouldn't push herself.

Fear and worry lined Father's face. "You can't heal if you don't give yourself time to recover."

"I just had a few things to do," she protested weakly.

What a hypocrite I was—I'd silently criticized Sandpiper's children for not taking care of her, and here my own mother was lying in the mud. Father helped her sit, then the two of us lifted her upright.

"You're supposed to let Dami do the hard work," Father said. I wasn't sure if he was chiding her or apologizing for her poor health.

He didn't bother asking where Dami was. My sister often ran off in the middle of the day. I glanced at the mighty redwood forest that bordered our home, but of course I didn't catch any glimpse of her in the shadows of those giants. She knew how to hide better than that.

"It was important," Mother protested as we helped her up the porch. She loved that garden; anything wrong within its boundaries was a crisis.

"*You* are important," Father insisted.

I slid the paper-backed, lattice-screen door open with one hand. Together, Father and I got her into her room and onto her mattress.

"I'll go cook," I offered. "You stay with her."

Father nodded. He trusted me.

It was early to harvest the rhubarb, but I cut a few slender stalks from the garden anyway, washed them, and took them into the kitchen. The warm, nutty aroma of buckwheat twined through the air, mixing with wood oil, ash, and dried herbs. The shelves of knives and crocks stood as neat and clean as we'd left them.

I simmered up some thin-sliced sweet-and-sour rhubarb and delivered it to Mother. I stayed long enough to see the pain disappear from her face, then returned to make a simple hotpot for Father and me.

I needed the familiar, soothing movements of cooking. I tossed dried peas and smoked trout into a large crock. Both ingredients mildly targeted the torso, making this a good dish for already healthy people. My parents had considered hiring a girl from the village to help Mother, but they were too proud to actually do it. Especially with Dami at home and capable of the work.

After the hotpot simmered, I tasted it. Not balanced yet. I sprinkled in some dried parsley, letting its bright acidity bring out the best of the peas and trout.

When I left, if Sorrel agreed to marry me, I'd have to convince my parents that saving Mother's back was more important than saving face. Father would be working longer days without me to assist him.

I poured the first ladle of hotpot into the loveliest bowl in our home—white clay glazed with brilliant buttercups. I brought it to Father, and he placed it in our family shrine for our Ancestors. Then the two of us ate in the kitchen.

We didn't speak much—a comment here or there about the food and the cool spring weather. I couldn't tell if he was thinking about

Dami, Mother, or my possible engagement. My thoughts swirled between all three.

When he went to bed, the shadowy blue of twilight blanketed the sky. I stepped out into the garden to see what Mother had been doing. Weeding. Of course. She loved these plants, from the humble radishes to the glorious azaleas she'd carefully transplanted from the forest. Mother was perceptive-of-touch, and gardening had always been a tactile joy for her. She loved her plants almost as much as her children.

I knelt in the mud and finished her work. Still no sign of Dami.

PRE-DAWN DARKNESS CLUNG between the redwood trees, thick and syrupy as blackberry molasses. I stood on the porch, rubbing my chill fingers together, looking out in the direction the courier would come from, if he came today. My stomach felt like over-kneaded dough. Down the road in the village, bits of hearth light shone through the windows like stars fallen to the earth.

Most days, I'd just be waking up now, but I couldn't sleep. I'd already hauled four buckets of water from our well, started a crock of buckwheat on the hearth, and scrubbed the kitchen. Twice.

Half an hour until sunup. Plenty of time to busy myself setting up a picnic for breakfast. Fresh air might do Mother good, after yesterday.

I headed to the kitchen and started a crock of salmonberry tea with a few dried rosehips thrown in. A warm drink would be welcome on a morning like this, and it might ease my anxiety— salmonberries and rosehips both targeted the stomach, and sweet granted endurance.

Time to lay out the picnic. I wrestled our low table off its tightly-woven thrush mat, then carried the mat outside and spread it on the broadest part of our porch. It wasn't my fault that the broadest part also faced the road.

Heading back to the kitchen, I ran into Dami. Her lush, obsidian-black hair hung like a curtain, half-obscuring her face. Strong-of-arm, she carried our table flat on one hand.

"You're awake," I said, surprised. I didn't know how late she'd come home.

Dami yawned. "You're in the way."

I stepped back. Dami plopped the table down on the mat like it was as light as a basket of bluebells. That polished, circular slab of redwood probably weighed twice as much as me.

"Thank you." I wondered how to diplomatically tell her about Mother's collapse. Not that such problems in the past had convinced her to worry about Mother, let alone help. "You couldn't sleep either?"

"Nope. Who broke and told you the courier's due today?"

I flinched. Apparently Father had enlisted the family's help in his conspiracy.

But Dami wasn't waiting for my answer—she glowered at the empty road into Clamsriver. She looked like something out of a painting, with her moon-round face and dark eyes scorning the world. "Stupid courier."

Dami had been on the waiting list to become a palace servant for three years; we'd gotten word a month ago that she was next. But she might still have months to wait. I laid a hand on her shoulder. "The palace *will* send a courier with a summons for you eventually. Don't worry."

She yanked away from me. "You're lucky, Plum."

"Pardon?"

"With your birthgift. You've had everything handed to you. Easy."

Easy? I rubbed the calluses on my hands from scrubbing crocks and the scars from a half-dozen old knife wounds and burns. Yes, my birthgift—perceptive-of-taste-and-smell—gave me an advantage in cooking, but I'd toiled for my accomplishments.

"You think I don't deserve him. You think Sorrel should turn me down." My stomach churned, thinking of all the things I could learn about cooking at his home. I needed that calming salmonberry tea.

"No. I'm bored of watching you fret. Sorrel should accept you. You were born to be a great chef," she grumbled.

Didn't I spend every day training and working with Father in the village, while she traipsed about the forest? I bit back my accusations. I should talk to Dami while she was willing to talk. "Are you worried about your post?"

"They accept yellow- and green-ranked girls for service. You think yellows like me won't get the dirtiest tasks?"

"They might not," I tried to cheer her, though Dami was probably right. "You've never seen the Redwood Palace. You might love serving there."

"Serve at the palace." Dami wrinkled her nose. The hazy pre-dawn light did nothing to soften her expression. "Fetch this, fetch that. Wash this, wash that. It's all so menial."

I'd assumed my restless sister was eager to see a bit more of the world and live in the capitol. This post was perfect for her.

"Most jobs *are* menial, most of the time. The better part of cooking is scrubbing crocks and cleaning parsnips." I tried to make it sound boring, even though I loved scrubbing vegetables.

"What you do *matters*."

I couldn't argue with that. The last thing a mother ate before delivery determined her child's birthgift. The perfect bite could endow an infant with remarkable abilities. A careless dish could leave the baby crippled, or worse.

Even when births weren't in question, proper food could heal the body or balance the soul. Everyone needed to eat, even the Ancestors. What could be more important than cooking?

"Maybe the work isn't exciting, but aren't you excited to travel?"

She snorted.

"Well, then think of the tax exemption you've granted Father for being on the list. Thanks to you, he's bought every home in Clamsriver a decent crock." I gestured toward the clustered thatch homes of the village. "You've helped so many families already."

"The villagers can rot for all I care. Maybe I'll stay with the trees." Her face was stone-serious.

I stared at her. "Dami, you can't abandon your post."

A breeze rustled through the garden. "You always mix up *can't* with *shouldn't.*"

"Father would have to pay the back-taxes." I didn't have to say the rest aloud—that Father didn't have any savings. A chef's duty was to increase the health and longevity of others; Father generously shared his skills and his salary toward that end.

Dami shrugged. "Our parents are smart. They'll find a way to pay it back."

"Even if that were true, they'd suffer horribly in the meantime."

Dami glared at me. "None of you ever care about what I want. *My* happiness."

"You could be happy after plunging your family into ruin?" I asked.

"The world isn't as simple as you think it is, Plum. Food doesn't always make everything better."

I winced. Food was my world. But that didn't mean I was stupid. "Your agreement with the palace is for two years. You can leave after that, if you like. Is that really so horrible?"

She folded her arms and leaned back against one of the log pillars supporting the eaves over the porch. "I was supposed to be a soldier."

I gawked. "Is your brain boiling between your ears? A soldier? You know plenty of those don't come home, right?"

"Plum, you're usually better-spoken than this," Dami sneered. "I'm not sure if I should be hurt or proud that your insipid little mouth can be rude."

She wanted to rile me up. I stepped closer and kept my voice calm. "You do remember the girl they hung in Meadowind six months ago, the one who tried to join the army? It's treason to lie to your officer in wartime, even about your gender."

Dami shrugged.

I put a hand on her shoulder and turned her toward me. "Promise me you won't do something that reckless."

It seemed like something she might do.

"Fine. I promise. I'll be boring like you for the rest of my life."

I swallowed my annoyance and managed not to snap at her for that one.

"But you can't tell me Father wasn't hoping I'd be a soldier when he cooked for my birthgift. Vinegary kale. Strong-of-arm. He thought I'd be a boy."

"I'm glad you're not, with the war on." Battles raged on the opposite border of Rowak, but we'd felt its effects here. Five Clamsriver boys had already joined their Ancestors.

"What's a soldier in peacetime? I could be *helping*—fighting for Rowak and its citizens."

"And now you're one for helping." I shook my head. "You're a puzzle of contradictions, sister."

Dami glowered. "I'd rather have blunt and insulting than a nicely-worded lecture, Plum. Mother loves all this work, or she wouldn't keep doing it."

"We found Mother *collapsed* in the garden yesterday."

"Her fault," Dami said, not a trace of guilt on her face.

"Why are you so convinced that being a soldier is more honorable than being a daughter? Mother's a citizen, too. Help her."

Sunrise glowed at the tips of the trees behind Dami, the exact rich, amber color of good duck stock.

"I'm going back to bed." Dami stomped past me and disappeared into the house.

The morning spring air felt cold on the back of my neck. I finished setting up our picnic alone.

CHAPTER TWO

L ong shadows stretched from the forest, but dawn scoured the sky to a powder-blue. Father, Mother, Dami, and I knelt around the table, eating steamed buckwheat drizzled with sweet-and-sour blackberry molasses.

Dami wouldn't look at me. She barely looked at her food.

"Sweetheart, you should eat," Mother encouraged Dami. "It'll improve your disposition. You can't be muttering and slouching when you're at the Redwood Palace. What would your Ancestors think?"

"I'm sure they have better things to do than nag me," she mumbled, so only I could hear.

How could she say such a thing, with Nana gone to the Ancestors just this autumn? Dami straightened her back, but she didn't smile.

I poured my parents tea to give myself something to do other than shout at Dami.

Father sipped his tea, then raised an eyebrow at me. "Sweet salmonberry. Not anxious about anything, are we, Plum?"

"Of course not." I nervously balled my hands in my skirt. A courier carrying my fate in his satchel might arrive any moment.

Father chuckled and poured me a cup. I took it respectfully with both hands and sipped.

Sweet, sour, and spice, rounded out with a touch of salt. It stilled my writhing innards. For the first time all morning, I took a deep, calm breath. The air smelled of so many familiar things. The old wood of our house. Dew on our sprawling vegetable garden. Spicy redwood bark and sweet forget-me-nots from the forest beyond.

"Look!" Mother pointed down the path at the courier strolling our way.

My pulse pounded in my throat, but the tea kept my stomach calm. The conflicting sensations left me dizzy. He was coming here. With my letter?

I clenched my fists in my skirt under the table, then made myself stretch them flat. I smoothed my skirt and folded my hands neatly on my lap, but I couldn't keep them from quivering.

Dami rolled her eyes at me. I didn't care.

I recognize the courier as he strode up our porch steps—Elek. He grinned, front two teeth missing, his skin wrinkled like old leather. It always made me smile in turn.

"Good morning, Elek," Father said. "May we offer you some buckwheat?"

"Ah, smells lovely, that does. I'd be happy to take a bowl from you." He didn't offer up any letters from his satchel, but he flicked me a glance, a mischievous crinkle around his eyes.

He *did* have my letter. I forgot not to clench my skirt.

Elek laughed as he sat at the table. "Ah, I shouldn't tease you! It's hard to be a young thing, feeling like every moment's as long as a year. Let's see. I do believe I brought more than my appetite to this table."

He made a show of rummaging through his envelopes. Most were plain, undyed cloth, but bright embroidery decorated a handful of them. One of those would be mine, wouldn't it? Already, the mild tea was wearing off. All his rummaging wrung out my insides like an old dish towel. I took another sip.

At last, Elek held one aloft. Too fine for my letter—purple and amber brocade, a royal envelope. "Ah, let's see. This is for Dami."

Dami snatched it from him and shoved it under the table, but everyone had already seen the royal colors.

"It's from the palace! Open it," Mother urged her.

I stared at my hands, swallowing the lump in my throat. Nothing for me. And a letter for Dami that she strangely dreaded.

Mother craned her neck trying to glimpse the envelope again. "You'll make such good connections, serving in the Redwood Palace! Perhaps you'll even increase your rank, if you serve remarkably."

"You think I'll scrub floors so brilliantly they'll promote me to Green?"

"Dami!" Mother scolded, horrified.

My sister dropped the unopened letter on the ground and stalked off toward the woods. I pursed my lips. Following her right now was useless—better to wait until she'd had a moment to cool.

Mother opened the envelope, shaking her head. "It's as I thought —she's to report to the palace in seven days."

Father quietly apologized to Elek for Dami's rudeness, but Elek waved it away. "I can hold nothing against a house that prepares— and shares—such an excellent breakfast. Perhaps my other letter will be more cheering."

He pulled a finely woven envelope embroidered with blueberry shrubs and ginger flowers from his satchel.

I jerked upright. "Elek, don't tease me anymore. Is that for me?"

"It is."

He passed me the envelope. This had to be from Sorrel of Westbank. I could shortly be learning the finest cooking methods, with access to the best ingredients. My Yellow-ranked sleeves itched against my arm. Did his family think me beneath them?

"Aren't you going to open it?" Elek asked. "Now you're teasing me."

I felt like I teetered on the edge of a cliff. I couldn't put the letter back once I'd read it. This moment held hope, possibility. The next might bring rejection.

I slipped the fine paper from its sheath and unfolded it.

"I am pleased to accept..."

I got no further before closing my eyes. *Accept.* Hand shaking, I passed the letter to Father. "Please read it out."

Father's voice stayed smooth.

I AM PLEASED to accept your proposal to arrange a wedding between Green-ranked Sorrel of Westbank and Yellow-ranked Plum of Clamsriver. In two week's time, we will come to your home for the formal engagement ceremony.

I will admit, old friend, it was my inclination to decline your offer. But when Sorrel heard of it, he was overjoyed at the prospect of marrying a chef —someone who already loves what he loves. I am a soft father who spoils his children, I'm afraid. I couldn't refuse my son's pleas.

I am delighted that I'll be seeing you again soon. My son, on the other hand, is disappointed that I insisted on propriety, and didn't allow him to come to your Plum right away. Instead, he is cleaning and rearranging his rooms for his new bride. Usually I cannot drag him out of the kitchens. This marriage is not what I'd planned, but my son is extraordinarily happy, and I thank you for that.

SORREL WANTED ME. He'd pleaded and argued for me. And I'd meet him in two weeks!

I had to agree with Sorrel and not his father—it would have been better if he'd come right away. If he were standing here, right now.

Elek thumped the table. "Fine news! Fine news!" He packed in another spoonful of buckwheat.

"Good news all around," Mother said, glancing into the woods, a worried line between her brows.

I stood before she could. "Stay, Mother. I know you'll want to hear the news from the front. I'll find Dami."

"Thank you." She nodded her appreciation.

Father turned to Elek. "*Is there any war news?*"

"There might be. Could you dish me up another bowl?"

I STROLLED BENEATH THE REDWOODS. They shot skyward, impossibly taller than any building. On the ground, shade-loving ferns unfurled for spring.

Dami wasn't sitting on her favorite log—a crumbling old thing half-covered in moss and frilly, inedible mushrooms. I sat on it anyway, waiting, my feet dangling.

I watched ants crawling through dead tree needles and sprouting plants. The air tasted of loam, mixed with the brightness of buttercups in bloom somewhere nearby.

But Dami didn't come to talk to me. Maybe that was just as well. It felt cruel to have good news when she'd gotten ill. And I still couldn't think of anything new to encourage her about her post.

I stared up at the branches splayed against the sky. We'd gotten along so well as children. When had we become so different?

When I returned to our house, Mother knelt in the garden, weeding around staked-up raspberry canes.

"Mother! You have to rest!" How had she found more weeds?

Stiffly, slowly, she turned and smiled up at me. "Your father just headed into the village. If you run, you'll catch him before he gets to Sandpiper's house."

I faltered. I should take care of Mother first—but what could I do? Father and I used to treat her daily with pickled rhubarb, but deadening her pain only made her work harder and hurt her back again. Sweet rhubarb would help her actually heal, but she never rested long enough for it to work."

"Your sister will be along to help me shortly. Go on."

Dami wouldn't be along shortly. She never was.

I managed to pull Mother away from the garden and sit her inside with some spinning, but I knew she wouldn't stay there long.

"I'll help you today," I offered.

"Nonsense! Your father needs you. You don't have long now to aide him; I'm not sure what he'll do without you. As your mother, I insist you go. Now. Or I'll chase you out, Plum. I promise I will."

She had before. I sighed, bowed respectfully to her, and hurried down the road.

AFTER A LONG DAY working alongside Father, I slipped into the room I shared with Dami. I untied my skirt, hung it on its peg, then unrolled our mattress and plopped onto it. Usually I found the fresh scent of the mattress' pine bough stuffing comforting. Not today.

I should be daydreaming about Sorrel, but guilt gnawed at my marrow. I was Dami's older sister. I was supposed to watch out for her, care for her. And I'd failed. Miserably.

The porch steps creaked and the front door slid open, then closed. Dami's footsteps followed. My throat tightened. What could I say?

But she didn't enter my room. She went to our parents'.

"Now that we're ready to sleep, you finally deign to come home?" Father demanded.

Mother's voice was much softer. "She's just nervous about her letter. Isn't that right, sweetheart?"

Mother always was quick to forgive.

Dami snorted.

"I'm so proud of you," Mother continued encouragingly. "It's such a great opportunity for you to make connections in Rowak."

"Thanks for making me wish I was red-ranked," Dami snapped. Rank determined which government posts a person could hold, from Purple—the ruling rank—down to the dishonored Red, who couldn't take any posts. "Then you couldn't toss me away to be a servant."

Dami always abandoned us—not the other way around.

Father's voice reverberated through the wall. "You can spite me and hate me, but you will not talk to your mother that way."

Dami ignored his ire and casually asked, "Did Sorrel accept Plum?"

Mother's voice came out tentative and soft. "Are you jealous?"

"Jealous!" Dami laughed. "You treat her worse than you treat me! Hawking her off as a wife to some man you've never met, just because he's a chef. Plum might be cold and completely fixated on cooking, but even she deserves more consideration than that."

I curled the blanket tight against my chest. Cold?

"It's what Plum wants," Father said sternly.

I pressed my ear hard against the wooden wall.

"Maybe right *now* she thinks that. She's been oblivious to everything but cooking for years, ever since Grandma's health turned. And now that she's finally dead, Plum's *obsessive*. Let your daughter grieve. She might actually care about, I dunno, someone who might love her if you gave her a moment to catch her breath."

I dug my fingernails into my blanket. Of course I cared if he loved me. But who except a chef would? I wasn't eternally forgiving and patient like Mother. I wasn't fearless and beautiful like Dami. I wasn't half as charitable as my father. I was a cook—nothing more, nothing less.

Sorrel could respect my skills. Respect me. Love me? I imagined us sitting close together, pouring over recipes, or picking herbs in the garden, or squabbling adorably over how much salt should go in a hotpot. With him, I had a chance to not only grow my skills, but to be really, truly, happy.

"Plum cooks when she's stressed or sorrowing. It's good for her," Father defended me. I whispered a silent prayer of thanks. He understood.

"Maybe you should take note then that *all* she does is cook. Ancestors above, I told her I was mad about my post and you know what she suggested to make it all better? Come with her to Clam-sriver and watch some cooking!"

I winced.

"She's naïve and dull and it's cruel of you to throw her to some other family when she's obviously not ready to get married," Dami continued.

I closed my eyes tight. This is why I needed to—had to—marry a chef. Some other man might speak about me the way Dami did now. Find my skill and my dedication unseemly instead of admirable.

"Your mother spent today packing your things for your trip to the palace. You should thank her. You leave in the morning," Father said. "I know you don't believe me, but I do hope that your time there goes well."

"You mean you hope I'll marry well so me and my husband can come back and take care of you when you're as old and delusional as Grandma was."

She shouldn't say things like that about Nana.

"Sorrel's a first son. He can't leave his parents' home for this one. A second or third son would be lucky to marry you and inherit this house. You have great prospects, and yet you deride us for putting you in the position to make the most of them," Father chided.

"Yes, *you* put me in this position!"

Mother cut in. "Perhaps we should all go to sleep," she said. "I feel our conversation is not at its best with the day fading away."

Dami stomped out.

I rolled back onto my pillow. Dami was leaving tomorrow. How had I not realized that? We had little time to reconcile, especially when we understood each other so poorly. I'd tried to cheer her and made her furious. She'd bluntly defended me to our parents, but it wasn't a defense I wanted.

I listened to her hang up her skirt, then sit on the mattress next to me.

"Dami?" I began.

"Shut your annoying face. I don't want to talk to you."

"Fine!" I snapped. "I don't want to talk to you, either!"

She sat, silently brooding. I rolled away from her and hogged the covers around myself.

I never did hear her lay down. When I woke, my feet were cold and weak morning light glowed through our fabric-backed lattice window. Perhaps Mother was right—perhaps we could talk better in the morning. Our last morning together.

I rolled over to see if Dami was still sleep. On her pillow lay her shorn-off braid. The rest of her was gone.

CHAPTER THREE

As I stared at her hair, cold foreboding prickled my skin. Had she cut her own hair, or had someone done that to her?

Her sandals were gone, but her skirt lay crumpled on the floor. Her dress, too. Without a person in it, it was a just a rectangle, woven and sewn to the proper width for the shoulder seams to drape to yellow-ranked length. Usually Dami and I helped each other with our skirts in the morning, so the dress fabric hung the right way over each other's waistband.

I hastily knotted on my skirt, skipped folding up my mattress, and jogged to the kitchens, hoping Father was already up. My mouth tasted stale and sour. How could I tell him his daughter was missing?

The kitchen was empty. The counters lay clean, bare, unused. The clay crocks sat neatly on their shelves, next to the knives and four well-oiled maple cutting boards. The brick hearth held only ashes.

I headed to my parent's room. Their door—a wooden lattice backed with fabric—did little to muffle their voices.

"... find Dami?" Mother asked.

"I don't know. But I have to try."

Eavesdropping made my ears burn. I knocked.

The door slid open. Father stepped out, scuffed traveling boots tucked under his arm. His skin hung a decade older on his face, flabby and lifeless as duck skin peeled from its carcass. He opened his mouth to say something, then gave up and sighed.

Mother still sat on her mattress, one hand pressed to her back.

"What happened?" I asked.

Father shifted his grip on the boots. "When I woke this morning, someone had rummaged through my things and stolen my spare clothes. Then I peeked into your room and saw Dami's hair. I have to go look for her. I don't know what trouble she's gotten into now."

Cut hair. Men's clothes. My stomach sank. "I do."

Mother and Father stared at me.

"Yesterday... yesterday she talked about how she should have been a soldier. I think she's run off to join the army."

Mother stared. "Dami wouldn't be so reckless."

But her protests rang hollow. Dami was *exactly* that reckless.

"I have to stop her before she reaches Meadowind," Father said. Meadowind hosted our nearest recruitment camp. He hurried past me, accidently knocking me against the wall. Father didn't notice, didn't apologize.

Mother groaned and twisted on her mattress. I knelt by her side and tucked pillows under her back. "Stay calm, Mother. You'll make yourself ill."

"Don't you know what could happen if Dami joins the army?"

Of course I did. Lying to officers during war was treason. They'd hang her for pretending to be a boy. I couldn't say anything to blunt that reality. I fetched Mother's brush and combed her hair in long, smooth strokes, then braided it into a simple knot at the base of her head.

She relaxed slightly. She tried to rise, but I waved a hand. "I'll take care of you. Don't worry. You'll feel better after breakfast."

"Ah, Plum." She squeezed my hand. "Thank you."

I left her to haul in wood and build up the coals. As I worked, I whispered a small prayer to our Ancestors. *Let us be wrong. Let Dami be doing something else, something less foolish.*

I got the tinder flaming, then added the wood piece by piece. Father would return with Dami. All would be well. I should just cook for Mother.

I mulled over the four basic tastes. Spicy to enhance perception. Salty to encourage agility. Sour to bring strength. Sweet to provide endurance. Regardless of the prominent flavor, a dish became more potent when balanced and backed up by the other flavors—even the subtle natural saltiness of celery or a sour note of chopped dandelion greens. Wildly unbalanced, one-note dishes could actually harm the body

Mother suffered physical pain and heartsickness. Sour would dull the pain; sweet would ease her heartache. I couldn't harvest more rhubarb without hurting the plant, the asparagus wasn't ready to harvest, and we were out of dried lobster mushrooms. I'd have to settle for targeting her torso and muscles—rutabagas and dried apricots would work well enough.

I needed something for her soul, too. Using beets might make the dish too sweet, but Father had given away the last of our hazelnuts, so I'd just have to season carefully.

I fetched what I needed from the cellar, then washed everything thoroughly. I wasn't about to let a bit of dirt flatten the dish. I nestled the beets in the coals, then put a few moon-yellow slivers of rutabaga and strips of dried apricots into a small crock with a splash of brine from the bottom of a jar of pickled fennel. After that, I put on a crock of buckwheat. We'd need it for lunch and supper.

With everything cooking, I tromped down to the well and back several times, bringing in today's water.

By then the beets had fully roasted. I fished them out and rubbed them all over with a towel to remove the skin and reveal the gem-like interior. I sliced them into rounds, then fanned them prettily on a glazed plate. For some kinds of meals, presentation wasn't crucial, but the eyes feed the soul, too. I dipped a spoon into the crock with the rutabagas and apricots. Sweet and tangy—and the rutabagas were meltingly soft. I added a pinch of salt to bring out the flavors. I tasted again. Perfect. But sweet-and-sour rhubarb with chopped hazelnuts would have been better. I sighed. Sorrel probably had abundant rhubarb in his greenhouse already.

I poured the apricot-rutabaga stew over the beets and took it to Mother.

She'd curled onto her side, not moving at all. She had to be in horrible pain.

I gave her the plate.

"It's lovely, little blossom." A shaky smile touched her lips. She ate. Almost at once she stopped quivering. When she finished, she stood without so much as a grunt.

"Mother." I gave her a stern look. "You'll hurt worse tomorrow if you run around today. Do you want me to butcher your rhubarb plants trying to take care of you?"

She laughed, a happy sound, almost like a simmering crock. "Scolding your elders! You sound like your nana, you know."

Just hearing someone mention her left my insides hollow. Good food promoted longevity, but no amount of cooking could bring back the dead. "You should be a good child then," I replied. "Rest."

"I'll just take a little look around the garden."

She'd immobilize herself before lunch. "How about I fetch the mending for you?"

Mother shrugged but didn't protest. I sat and worked with her. Occasionally, her stitches faltered. Her brow pinched. Dami, Father, the recruitment camp at Meadowind. Sweet beets weren't stronger than a mother's worry.

I bit my lip and tried not to mirror her expressions. Should I have said something different yesterday? Or warned my parents of Dami's soldier-talk? I didn't think she'd actually risk her life and toss an enormous debt on her father.

I told Mother cheerful stories about Amari's children to pass the time. Mother laughed, but the sound died too quickly into silence. I couldn't make either of us stop glancing at the door for signs of Father.

After an hour, I checked on the buckwheat. A tad overcooked, but still good. My aching stomach reminded me I'd skipped breakfast. I dished up a bowl, then scraped the rest into a basin to cool slightly. Buckwheat doesn't target any part of the body, but it would give me sustenance.

The daily task of making buckwheat branches was unnervingly normal—unlike everything else today. I mashed the grains, then shaped them around skewers and grilled them over hot coals. The insides stayed chewy, but the outsides crisped. Buckwheat branches were easy to haul around—the standard lunch of working people. Any leftovers could be softened in the evening hotpot.

I laid all my pretty branches in a basket, covered them with a towel, and returned to Mother's side. Every creak of wood or whisper of wind made us jump. We laughed nervously at each other, like we didn't know who the other was listening for.

Let them both come back safe, I prayed.

Lonely old Hifal came around noon, wondering why we hadn't been by to treat his cough. I cooked him a quick bite, made polite apologies about Father and some important business, then saw him to the road. Today was not a day for visitors.

I'd begun a dipping sauce for the branches for lunch when Father arrived. Mother and I both ran to greet him in the hall. He'd left his boots on the porch, but somehow, he still trailed mud inside. I winced at the mess—I'd have to handle that quickly or Mother would get to it—but my stomach turned to stone when I saw his face: gray and limp. Like his words. "I can't help her."

"You found Dami?" Mother asked.

Father nodded. He trudged into his room and slumped against the wall. "She was already inside the camp, in uniform, drilling. There's nothing we can do for her."

Mother tried to hide her sob behind her hands. Her mending lay crumpled, forgotten on the floor. I stared at Father, feeling hollow inside, waiting for different words to come out of his mouth.

Dami would die on the battlefield, or she'd die when someone uncovered her treason.

Father's voice sounded as empty as I felt. "Dami's supposed to report to the palace in seven days."

The issue of the back-taxes hung thick in the air—taxes we didn't have the amber to pay. My throat tightened. Did Dami think she lived alone in this world? That her actions affected no one else? "We'll have to take out a loan from the officials in Meadowind," I said. "We'll have to start charging the villagers. Eventually..."

Mother shook her head and the words died on my lips. Father looked like old dishwashing water.

"Clamsriver is poor, Plum," Mother said. "I know you smell the good hotpots simmering on their hearths, but this war has cost them. Do you know how high the tax rate has soared these past three years?"

"N-not exactly."

"We have more to pay back than Clamsriver can give. They'd loan us a blanket if we needed it, but they don't have amber to spare."

"Then... maybe we should tell the palace that Dami died." The words tasted tart on my tongue. It could be true all too soon.

Mother sadly shook her head. "We'd still owe the taxes. King Alder is already persuading the Purple-Blue Council to change the exemption for being on the list at all. No one expected a three-year wait... but with the war dragging on, servants are staying much longer than their mandatory two years."

Father squeezed Mother's hand, his eyes apologetic. "We'll have to sell the house."

My insides wobbled. This land, where our Ancestors' ashes lay?

"*If* we can find someone to sell it to," Mother said. The common, orange-ranked citizens of Clamsriver couldn't own a building of yellow-ranked size. "Perhaps we can convince a wealthy official to buy it as a hunting lodge."

A hunting lodge, empty most of the year. An official wouldn't care for my nana, anyway. She'd be left to wander this world as a Hungry Ghost. "And where will you live?"

"Hifal has room and he'd enjoy the company," Father said. Two of Hifal's sons died in the war; their widows had returned to their own villages. "We'll have to put up a good face until after your official engagement, Plum. You'll be comfortable, at least."

I didn't want to be comfortable while my parents and Ancestors suffered. I bit my lip. "Sorrel's father... might he buy our house? His younger sons might want their own home."

A brother-in-law might care for my Ancestors.

"Chef Yarrow is one of the best chefs in Rowak, but what little wealth he has, he's poured into his library and greenhouses. If he were a richer, more ambitious man, he wouldn't have accepted a yellow-ranked woman for a daughter-in-law."

Even though Father spoke in a listless monotone, the words stung.

Mother cut in, voice soft. "We have to tell the Royal House that Dami died. If they're insulted she abandoned her post, we could be demoted to Orange-rank."

An orange-ranked citizen couldn't hold the post Father had. He'd lose his work, his salary. And he wouldn't be permitted to own this house, either. Nausea coursed through me.

Father's face drooped. "You're right. We'll draft a letter informing them of her death and sell the house. Quickly."

Mother nodded, the matter settled. Before I could stop her, she started scrubbing furiously at the mud, as if that could sap her grief away.

Nana left to wander as a Hungry Ghost. My parents homeless.

"Won't the villagers ask about Dami? Where she went?" I asked.

Father paused; he hadn't considered that.

"If we say she died, they'll wonder why we didn't invite them all to the funeral. There will be questions. Especially since there's no body."

"It doesn't matter. We'll come up with an excuse."

"You think you'll be able to keep Hifal from sniffing out the truth if you're living with him?" I asked.

They glanced at each other and frowned.

I swallowed hard. I couldn't let Nana starve. "What if... Dami fulfilled her two years at the palace, anyway?"

Father couldn't meet my eyes. "She can't leave the training compound, little blossom. Her supervisors would notice."

"I know that." I felt like I'd eaten a basket of bad mushrooms. "But there's still a way."

I READ and re-read my acceptance letter. Penned by an actual former Master Chef, accepting me as a fellow cook. Sorrel and I were supposed to marry come summer, when the valerian flowers bloomed pale pink all through the meadows. His name danced like poetry on the page. A greenhouse with strawberries all year round. A library of recipes. Instruction from his incredibly talented father. A chef for a husband, a man who might love me as unconditionally as Nana had—not because we shared blood, but because we shared the name of *chef*.

If I already had all the skills I'd learn there, maybe Nana would still be alive.

I tore the letter into tiny pieces, my chest ready to crack like an unseasoned crock over hot coals. Per my instructions, Father had already written a letter to Sorrel's family, informing them that I'd rejected the proposal. I wouldn't be here in two weeks for the formal engagement and I couldn't delay for two years without arousing suspicions. My parents would tell anyone who asked that I was visiting my mother's relations. They lived nearly a weeks' journey away, on the northern border.

In the morning, I'd leave. Not for any relative's, but for the Redwood Palace. No one there had met Dami. I'd pass for her well enough, I hoped.

I'd always been the responsible one. I'd always tried to keep Dami out of trouble. Today, preserving her life meant giving up mine.

I let the bits of paper fall and scatter on the floor.

CHAPTER FOUR

F ather insisted on cooking me something besides buckwheat for breakfast before I left for the palace. He wouldn't let me help, either. He started by cleaning a basket of clams.

"How early did you get up this morning?" I asked. Digging for clams took time.

His weary smile belonged to a man two decades older. "Couldn't sleep. I figured you'd need a good meal."

Since clams are eaten whole, they target the entire body. They're no good for specific problems—say, swollen ankles or an upset stomach—but they're perfect for a healthy person starting a journey.

I still loved watching him work. He nestled a crock in the coals, then added wine, green garlic, and the clams. Father fussed over the pot, adding salt and a touch of maple syrup. Balancing spicy, salty, sour, and sweet perfectly would center my soul and grant me perception, agility, strength, and endurance.

It smelled amazing. If I were marrying Sorrel and moving to

Westbank, I could cook like this every day. My throat knotted. The engagement had been so *perfect*.

"Dami?"

I blinked. "She's... not here."

"That's *your* name now." Father tasted again, then put the lid on and let it simmer. "How old are you?"

"Sevente—" No. I dropped my eyes to the floor. "Fifteen."

"That's my Dami."

Dami ran away from home and in doing so, she'd erased me.

"What's your birthgift?" Father asked.

I froze. *Perceptive-of-taste-and-smell.* That edge allowed me to become a cook. But now I was Dami. *Strong-of-arm.* That's what the census records and Dami's application stated.

No one in the palace would trust me to cook. I'd have to pretend to know nothing about food.

I hadn't cried before, but I did now. Fat, sticky tears that made me feel no older than three. I tried to wipe them away, but of course Father saw.

He hugged me. "Oh, Plum."

Would that be the last time I heard anyone speak my name?

I composed myself. "I'm fine. Simply... tired."

And I'd be lucky to be simply tired by the time I left the palace. For two years, I'd be hauling water or doing laundry while pretending my birthgift made it easy. My back would be as bad as Mother's.

"Tired," Father echoed in a tone that told me he knew better. He banked the coals around the little crock, then tidied the counter. I loved this room. I loved the fire-stained brick hearth, the glowing wood walls, the row of obsidian knives and the shelf of carefully cleaned crocks.

Father's eyebrows pinched together. "I've always tried to do good. Always tried to increase my skills. I think we have the healthiest village in Rowak."

I nodded, the words washing over me.

"Even if some calamity left you orphaned, I knew the village would care for you. In so many ways, taking care of these people mattered to me more than storing up amber. I should have realized that amber mattered, too."

Was he *apologizing*? "Father, this isn't your fault."

It was Dami's. A coal of anger burned in my stomach. How could she do this to herself, to us? Throughout our lives, the sages teach, we are cared for and we take care of others. Grandparents care for infants. Parents work to support children and grandparents. Then the child becomes the parent, the parent the grandparent. The living feed and honor their Ancestors. And our Ancestors watch over all of us. Interdependence. That is how the world works.

Did Dami think she didn't belong to this world, to this family?

Father sighed. "If I'd been more careful with my salary, if I'd saved, then—"

"Stop!"

Father blinked at me. I never raised my voice.

I swallowed the knots in my throat and spoke calmly. "I won't let you blame yourself for Dami's actions."

"But I'll always regret that I couldn't protect you from them." Father wiped his eyes and hastily turned back to the crock. He fussed over it some minutes more, then poured the beautiful clams into a bowl. After a final taste-test, he topped it with fresh herbs and brought the steaming delight to me. "And I deserve plenty of guilt. You know if the Royal House discovers your deception, they'll execute you for your lies. I'm risking one daughter's life to preserve the other's."

OH, I knew my plan meant lying to the Royal House, but I'd thought only of Sorrel's library and greenhouses, of my ruined future. But of course. Lying to the Royal House, in wartime or not, was punishable by death.

Vertigo washed over me, despite Father's excellent meal. I

thanked him, then staggered into our shrine, the centermost room of our home.

The small shrine held a lacquered table, just big enough for the daily supper offering. Shelves filled the wall above it, decorated with redwood boughs and white ribbons. The preserved heads of my Ancestors, going back three generations, rested on the lowest shelves, with plaques standing in for Ancestors on the higher shelves. Those older heads lived with Father's relatives in Lillywhite. When we could, we made a pilgrimage to pay our respects.

I knelt. It seemed like only last week that we carried Nana's body to the sages in Meadowind. Mother, Father, Dami, and I prayed outside while they worked. The sages shaved her head to preserve her hair, then detached her head from her body and boiled it over and over until only a whitened skull remained. Then the sages layered special clay over the bone, shaping Nana's face. Dami and I each found a brown river stone for her eyes. We burned her body and scattered the ashes in a circle of redwood trees near our home.

I felt Nana so close when I said her name here, even though her head looked wrong. The skilled sages created a life-like face, but it wasn't hers. The clay wore a smooth, young smile with an elaborately braided cap of gray hair. Nana had sun-broiled skin with deep wrinkles, like old pine bark. Maybe after a few decades, her new clay skin would develop fine lines like wrinkles, as my great-great grandparents had.

"Nana." I'd never personally known anyone else on those shelves. I didn't know how to plead with them. Nana would hear me and relate everything to my other Ancestors. "I'm scared. I'm scared for you, for me, for my parents, for Dami. But you'll take care of us, right? Everyone is interdependent."

I felt no reassurance, just the familiar ache—that ache for Nana's honey-scented hand on my cheek.

"I suppose it's my turn to take care of you, now. I won't let you starve. I won't leave you to roam the world as a Hungry Ghost. You loved me too much, Nana, for me to let that happen to you."

FATHER PACKED me a bag with buckwheat branches, my spare dress, and a few amber chips and beads for the rest of the journey. I'd walk through Meadowind to Sandhead—a two day's journey. In Sandhead, I could buy a quick, two-day ride to the capital at a carter station. I might have to wait in Sandhead a day for the next westbound cart, but I'd make it to the palace on time. And no one that far west should recognize me.

Father tucked Dami's royal summons into the inside pocket of his best mantle, then draped it over my shoulders.

"I can't take this," I protested as he belted the mantle around me.

"It's yours," he said. "If nothing else, you'll be warm."

Mother cried and covered my face with kisses. "You come back safe. You promise to come back safe."

"I promise." The words tasted like raw flour. I couldn't promise anything.

Mother held me and stroked my hair, like I was little again. But I didn't mind. This might be the last time I saw her. "Two years. Two years and you can honorably step down from service. I'll see you then."

Father hugged me, nearly crushing my ribs. Mother kept crying. Father's face grew more and more pinched with guilt. My feet felt stuck to the floor, like sauce burnt onto a crock.

But delaying the journey would only make my parents hurt longer. They'd start to heal once I left.

I turned and headed down the path.

THE FOREST WAS Dami's domain, not mine. I picked wild herbs and mushrooms here, but neat, cultivated rows of turnips and strawberries were my delight. The redwoods reached almost higher than I could see. Ferns, moss, and pine needles blanketed the floor under them, dark and glossy in the trees' perpetual twilight shadows.

I ached to turn around. Instead, I munched on one of the branches Father had packed for me. The buckwheat itself was merely filling, but the sweet compote of parsnips, carrots, and rutabaga he'd piped into the hollow center of the branch gave my limbs and torso a touch of extra endurance.

And I needed that. One step in front of the other. Home behind. The Redwood Palace ahead. By now, Father had probably walked into the village. Given a courier the letter refusing my engagement to Sorrel.

That thought kept me walking forward. No wedding waited for me at home now. No Sorrel of Westbank. No greenhouse with strawberries. No library of recipes. No former Master Chef Yarrow for my father-in-law.

I couldn't mourn losing Sorrel, either. I was Dami. I'd never been engaged. I was strong-of-arm. I cared nothing for cooking now.

By midday I reached Meadowind. I should have kept going. Or I should have rested someplace else. But I sat on a hill, close to the training grounds. A few others lounged nearby—mostly girls giggling and pointing at the army recruits as they drilled.

I didn't laugh. I scanned the men. Each wore loose pants and a belted rectangular shirt that fell to the knee. Each wore an armband with some insignia on it. And each held a staff. An officer—distinguished by his bright armband—shouted instructions. The recruits clumsily tried to follow. Block. Swing. Block. Behind the shouting, arrows hissed and thunked, but I couldn't see the archery range.

A young man about my age grinned and plunked down next to me on the grass. He smelled like pine-needle soap. "Come to enjoy the view?"

"Just stopping a moment to eat."

"You look like you've been traveling. From out east?" His voice had a warmth to it, like smoked salt. He leaned back on his hands, flirting with the two-foot gap of space propriety demanded between young men and young women. His sleeves draped halfway to his elbows. Yellow-ranked, like me.

"I look exhausted, or I look strange?"

He laughed—an infectious sound. "Neither. I have to come here to keep an eye on my sister." He nodded at a clump of girls down the hill. "But I haven't seen you before. And usually girls gawk in bunches. You're interesting."

From his mouth, all of that sounded like a compliment. I stared down at my half-eaten branch and wished my traitor cheeks weren't burning.

"I'm Fir, by the way."

I swallowed my real name. "Dami."

"Dami." He grinned with those dazzling teeth. "That's a beautiful name. Here." Fir pulled out a thinwood box from the bag he carried. "Mother packed these for us, but since my sister's hardly paying attention, I'll share them with you."

He slid the lid off. Inside, dumplings sat on clean leaves.

"They're smoked salmon. Go ahead. Take one."

After a morning of walking, I didn't protest. The balance wasn't perfect—too much hotradish, ginger, and salt—but it was good for a home cook. Especially the light texture of the dough.

Fir ate one, then gave me another. I was turning it in my mouth, letting everything mix together, when the soldiers set down their staffs and rotated. New trainees replaced them.

I spotted Dami at once. At least that meant she hadn't been caught yet. A bruise darkened her cheekbone. From a fight? A training accident? She held her staff as well as any other trainee, eyes focused on the instructor.

I tightened my fists in my skirt. I wanted to yell at her. Wanted to make her understand what she'd done to the rest of us and what could happen to her. Her face showed no regret, only concentration as she drilled. She never glanced my way.

"You look intense. Those aren't settling with you?"

I'd forgotten all about Fir. "No, they're lovely. I..."

And I didn't have an explanation, so I flashed him a smile and took another dumpling. Fir took the last. Then he glanced at the clump of girls. "Drat. My sister wants to talk to me. It was a pleasure, Dami."

He winked and strolled away.

I watched him go. Would Sorrel have been like him? Easy to smile, eager to share? I'd never know.

I couldn't stay here and watch Dami train. I'd need two backpacks of soul-calming sweets for me to endure that. So I left Meadowind and tried not to think of the people I'd lost. Sorrel gone forever. My parents for at least two years. And Dami—would she survive? Would she come home if she did?

By dusk, I made it as far as Bobcat Run, the town between Meadowind and Sandhead. The sole wayhouse wasn't hard to locate. The aroma of broiled fish and pease porridge permeated the smoky, dim common room. My stomach rumbled. Those salmon dumplings seemed an eternity ago.

A double-chinned woman gave me a flat look. "You want a room, dinner, or both?"

"Both, please." I opened my bag. Where had that purse gone? I shoved my spare dress to the side.

The woman raised an impatient eyebrow.

"It's in here somewhere," I muttered, pulse pounding. I couldn't have lost the amber. I had to hire a ride tomorrow in Sandhead.

At last, I found the pouch under what remained of my branches. But my stomach sunk as I lifted it out. The weight and shape felt all wrong.

I opened it. The amber was gone. In its place rested a single dumpling wrapped in a clean leaf.

CHAPTER FIVE

"Trying to slip in a night for free?" The woman sneered, chins waggling.

My words stuck in my throat like uncooked dough. A few of the other patrons pointed and laughed, glossy bits of glazed carrots and broiled fish on their plates. I swallowed. "I... I was robbed."

Saying it out loud didn't make it less jarring. Fir was nothing but a polished thief. And I'd fallen for it.

"I don't care *why* you're out of amber. If you can't pay, you can't stay." She said the last line in a nasty sing-song—like she'd said it a hundred times before.

"But..." I stammered, mind reeling. "My father will reimburse you. Or maybe the palace. I'm headed to a post..."

Her glare silenced me. "Unless you're King Alder himself, I don't care. Fancy yellow-ranked people, always thinking they're so much better than everyone else!" She placed her hands on her hips as if to emphasize that her dress just covered her shoulders—orange-ranked.

"I've been robbed!" This had nothing to do with rank or trying to flaunt it.

"Do you have payment now? No? Then you don't get food or a room now, either. Shoo!" She reached for a broom.

I hurried out, hugging my bag to my chest. No amber. No hot food. No room. No fast, comfortable ride purchased at the carter station tomorrow.

If I returned to Clamsriver, Father might have a few more beads around, but going back would add at least two days to my travels. If I had to wait for a cart in Sandhead for a single day, I'd be late.

Would the palace dismiss me and fine Father for three years of unpaid taxes? I didn't know. I couldn't risk it. Walking was slower than riding, but surely not slower than two days' wasted time.

I ate Fir's salmon dumpling. Even if he left it to mock me, it was food.

I SLEPT POORLY against the damp wood wall of the inn and woke covered in frigid spring dew. After downing my last buckwheat branch for breakfast, I shook out my skirt and walked. At least the road sloped gently downhill as I headed away from the mountains. Sometimes it cut through the dense redwood forest, sometimes through meadows or fields.

By late afternoon, I noticed more and more jays—scavengers that enjoyed scraps left by people. Sure enough, I soon crossed into a small town. My mouth watered at the aroma of early spring greens and salted fish. I navigated my way through the children playing in the green around the well and filled my water skin. A pair of men chatted next to one of the houses. Maybe I could ask them for a meal.

A girl my age with a jug on her hip came toward the well. Even better.

"Excuse me, but is there... is there anywhere here to stay?" I fumbled. I made a horrible beggar. "I've lost most of my things, but

I'd be willing to work for a meal and a night's shelter. I'm good at... at scrubbing pots and such," I finished lamely. I couldn't go around proclaiming to be a decent cook; someone might take note of me.

Her expression soured. "Not tonight, I'm afraid."

My empty stomach twisted, trying to pull my innards into my sandals. "Oh."

"Usually we're a hotpot of hospitality," she apologized, "but there are some returning veterans coming this way. We're supposed to house them tonight."

What was one more? "Surely there's plenty of extra work, then."

"Have you heard much news about the war?"

I paused. They didn't send women as camp cooks, so I'd never paid much attention.

The girl filled her jug as she talked. "Not too long ago, some soldiers heading down to the front stopped at Hidet. A traveler like you showed up, just staying the night. She slit their commander's throat before running off. Now, you don't look like one of those Bloodmarrows to me, but if I were you, I wouldn't want to be sharing a bowl with a soldier if you're a stranger here."

"I don't even know what a Bloodmarrow is." It sounded familiar, but I couldn't place it.

"People say they're Vengeful Ghosts controlled by the Shoreed for their evil ends. Wherever they go, folks die and disappear." She eyed me suspiciously.

The Shoreed didn't have an army of ghosts at their disposal. A well-trained spy had killed the poor commander. I fumbled for my papers. "Would this be enough to prove myself?"

"Serving at the palace. That's pretty. Maybe with that, you'll find someone in town willing to risk feeding you." She walked away.

Apparently, she wasn't willing.

A little boy ran up to me, hands all grubby from play. He handed me a pair of dried, tart yellow plums. "Here! You're hungry, right?"

"Yes. Thank you."

He beamed at me, front two teeth missing. "Mother always tries to get me to eat those. Better you than me."

He scurried off as fast as he'd come.

I munched gratefully on my namesake as I walked. Plums target the muscles. The simple snack gave me a moment of pain-free limbs before my aches settled back in.

A commander killed in his sleep. Did his family already have word that he was returning alive and whole? Did he have children waiting, eager to hug their father? The redwoods blocked out the sun above me, chilling the air. I tied Father's mantle shut, wishing it hung down further than my knees.

I heard the soldiers before I saw them. I ducked off the side of the road and lay flat behind the burled roots of a redwood. If they wouldn't be happy to see a lone stranger in a village, they wouldn't be any happier to see me here.

I'd expected a larger crowd. Three soldiers pulled the cart, with two walking alongside—all wearing armbands denoting active service. Eight men with veterans' armbands rode in the cart. Had all the veterans left a piece of themselves in the west? Feet, legs, arms, hands, fingers, eyes, ears—only one hadn't visibly lost anything, and he was retching over the side of the cart. Recipes for their various injuries rattled through my brain. I ached to cook for them, to use my skills to ease their pain and strengthen their souls.

Each veteran wore a polished piece of amber-studded wood on a thong around his neck. I couldn't see the details, but I'd bet my shoes that they were awards for their service.

One of the veterans looked even younger than me, about Dami's age. I hugged my mantle closer around me. I hoped she came home unharmed. I hoped she came home at all.

THAT NIGHT, I found a still-living redwood tree with its heartwood hollowed out
from uncounted, ancient fires. It made good shelter, but I still woke stiff, cold, and starving. Foraging would cure all three.

The forest provided curly fiddlehead ferns, wild onions, and a pair of gorgeous, earthy-sweet morels. Raw, however, all but the onion would harm instead of help me. The next village might loan me a hearth, even if they wouldn't feed me. I tucked my findings into my bag and continued down the road, cramming down one of the onions.

It didn't take long to realize I'd been thinking with my hollow gut instead of my head. Without any salt, vinegar, or honey to balance the raw onion, I'd consumed straight spiciness. The poorly-planned snack muted my senses—the very thing spiciness bolstered in well-balanced food. My vision blurred, my fingertips tingled, and the sounds of the forest dulled around me.

I stumbled over the undergrowth for the next ten minutes. Even when the ill-effects faded, I was dizzy and weak. I craved salt, badly. My stomach was right; I could use the agility and grace that saltiness brought.

At midday, I came across the ashes of a half-dozen campfires just off the road. Merchants? A column of soldiers headed west? I didn't know, but the coals were warm. I used a stick to gather everything into a pile, then scavenged for kindling.

I lay on the ground and blew gently. Ashes stirred and stung my eyes, but I didn't flinch. One of my dry sticks smoked, then another. Soon, a small fire licked at the new wood.

I staked two forked branches on either side of the fire, then threaded my fiddleheads and morels onto a third stick, which I rested on the first two. The remaining onions, skins on, went straight into the coals.

Then I struck out from the road to find more. A handful of cress later, I heard water—water!—and followed the sound until I stumbled across a small stream. It smelled cold and clean, spiced by the redwoods around it. I grabbed a rock and dug in the bank.

I muddied my dress, skinned my knee, and ended up soaked. Three small clams were my reward. Less than I would have liked, but I still scurried back to my fire and nestled them into the coals. I rinsed the cress with my clean flask of well-water, then dangled it over the coals until they wilted. I ate it with my fingers.

The clams popped open. I grabbed them, burning my fingers, and slurped down the juices and the packet of meat inside—sweet, ashy, salty.

No chef would call it satisfactory, but it was the best bite to ever grace my mouth. I devoured the meltingly-soft onions, sweetened and mellowed by the fire, alongside the fiddleheads and morels. After downing the rest of my water flask, I trekked onward.

I KEPT an eye out for bandits, but never spotted any. At least my sorry state signaled I had no amber to steal.

That afternoon, it seemed like a dozen carts passed me. Most of them had two large wheels nearly as tall as my shoulder supporting the cart bed, with a large cross-beam in front where two or three abreast could pull. Packages bulged under the oiled canvas on the merchants' carts, with the porters plodding against the cross-beam. The private passenger carts, with painted walls and curtained windows, moved at the same slow gait.

But not the carter's carts. These were open to the sky, with two long benches against the sides for passengers. And fast porters. Running, laughing, smiling, sweating porters. They tore down the hard-packed road as fast as they could without dumping passengers. Fresh porters would take over at the next carter station.

I watched one young woman riding such a cart, clutching the railing as she rode in wide-eyed wonder, hair streaming behind her.

That could have been me.

Instead, I trudged. I passed a carter station at dusk—a cheery, well-lit building with a few jays flitting about the roof. Within shouting distance of this place, I could sleep safely, if not comfortably. I waited until after sunset to fill my waterskin at their well. Then I curled up in some promising-looking ferns and pulled Father's mantle tight around me. I'd been a fool to tell him I wouldn't need it.

The next morning, it rained. Hard. I couldn't find wild onions—let alone anything else. Carts became scarce on the muddy road, replaced by wriggling worms and yellow slugs. I'd been right to walk instead of returning to Clamsriver for more amber. Not that being right stopped my legs from numbing or the rain from flooding my sandals.

Around midday, I spotted a trio of merchants and, Ancestors forgive me, I slipped onto the back of one of their carts to spare my numb feet. We hadn't gone an eighth of a mile before one of the porters noticed and knocked me into the mud.

My hip ached after that.

Near evening, I stumbled across a redwood circle—an opening where an enormous, ancestral redwood once stood, but had long since given itself back to the earth. A ring of new trees had shot up from its roots, now grown eight feet across each. I stepped inside, where the ground was damp instead of sopping.

We'd scattered Nana's ashes in a redwood circle like this, near our home. The trees themselves taught us so much about what we owed our Ancestors; they are the root that continues to give us life. Travelers and the poor alike used these sacred circles as shrines.

I had no food, so I poured out the last of my waterskin for Nana and prayed that she'd take well to what I could offer her. That she wouldn't become a Hungry Ghost. That I wouldn't lose her again, in the afterlife.

I slept well in the protection of those trees.

The next morning, the seventh since Dami's summons, blurred in my memory. Finding a fire, but no clams. Trudging. One foot after the other. Stomach trying to eat itself. Dry tongue glued to the roof of my mouth.

Passenger and cargo carts rattled past as I neared Askan-Wod, the capital. I thanked my Ancestors for a large, fairly safe road to travel on, that nothing worse than being tossed from a merchant's cart had happened. I wished I could thank them for real food, too.

By the time I reached the great gates of Askan-Wod, my head felt like a granite boulder—I didn't waste effort lifting my eyes from the road. I saw so many feet. Some bare, some in lovely suede slippers, most in sandals. A few with boots. Children, men, women. Their elbows jostled me. I clung to my bag and stumbled onward.

Merchants sold food from stalls. I smelled noodles with dark dipping sauces, fried fish, and coal-charred scallions. My innards groaned. If I'd had a single amber chip, I would have stopped and bought something salty to increase my agility. Right now, I felt as dexterous as a newborn chick. The relentless noise didn't help—so much noise. Shouting, laughter, hawking. The stagnant air reeked of sweat and sharp urine.

I missed mountains. I missed trees.

At least finding the Redwood Palace was simple. Up. Up to the center of Askan-Wod. My legs burned, but at last I reached the gates. Stout gates with heavy cross-beams.

An obsidian spearhead appeared in front of my face. I followed the haft down to a pair of thick hands, then up to a face. He was shouting at me. Something about beggars? But I wasn't begging.

I pulled my letter from its pocket inside my mantle and offered it respectfully with both hands. The guard frowned, mustache drooping. He shouted instructions inside.

A young woman appeared, maybe Dami's age. She had a no-nonsense face with strong cheekbones and a straight nose. Her voice rang out high and clear. "Shall I tell Blue Lady Egal you turned away a beckoned servant of the Royal House?"

"She's probably a thief," the guard said.

"What's your name?" the girl demanded. "I'd hate to give my lady the wrong name."

"Umm. Dami."

The gate groaned open. The girl took my arm. Her sleeves hung elegantly over her elbows—green-ranked. The bleached silhouette of an eagle decorated her fine, emerald green skirt. "Come along, then, Dami. You report to Lady Egal, the King's aunt and the Matron of the Household. I'm her gate servant."

My mind fuzzed. She was talking to me. I took a step forward, then another, letting my gaze settle on her feet. Despite the decorative braid running around her ankle, her sandals were sturdier than mine. I could have used sandals like that on this journey. I wouldn't mind having ten clean, manicured toes, either. She looked like she belonged in a palace.

Gravel crunched under my feet and I smelled gardens—buttercups, shooting stars, and blue-eyed grass. The lawn on either side of our path gleamed green.

I managed to glance up a few times. A multitude of gardens, hedges, and groves made it impossible to count all the exquisite buildings. The Redwood Palace felt like a town unto itself, but it was lusher and lovelier than any town I'd ever seen. Some of the porches were broader than my whole house. Perhaps this place had fallen here from the Ancestor's Realm. The peaked roofs boasted fine, black shingles. Carved birds, trees, and fish decorated the eaves—all supported by ubiquitous, whole-log pillars, painted or polished to a currant berry red. The lowest rank, the Red rank, was said to have blood on their hands—they were the children of criminals and traitors. But the Redwood Palace used red to show that this place was the heart—the lifeblood—of our nation.

At least if I hanged for my lies to the Royal House, I didn't have any children to be demoted to the red rank.

We climbed three stairs onto a porch, where a door servant let us into a sitting room that smelled almost like the forest. The wood still held its warm, spicy scent, and there was something else—stream violets? Yes, stream violets, with a hint of sharp cress.

"Nisaat, what have you brought me?" The voice reminded me of the glossy leaves of poison oak—beautiful, but promising pain.

Nisaat bowed, so I did as well. "This is Yellow-ranked Dami of Clamsriver. The servant you've been anticipating."

"This wretched creature?"

I lifted my eyes. Lady Egal was perhaps sixty, but she held herself like a beauty of decades younger. Her slate-gray hair granted her refinement; her dark eyes gave her presence. She sat behind a polished redwood desk.

"I... I was robbed," I croaked.

"Robbed." Lady Egal tilted her head to the side, inspecting me.

She held herself with such poise—was her birthgift of agility? She wore the handsomest dress I'd ever seen, a shimmering blue fabric draping to just above her wrists, a shade that perfectly matched her lapis lazuli earrings. Still, the dress paled in comparison to the woman wearing it.

I couldn't hold her gaze. I stared at my feet. "Yes, Lady Egal."

"Your nose is sunburned. Your face is rough."

I couldn't let her dismiss me. Reject me. "I journeyed here for six days, with no money and no food."

"Really?" Her tone held nothing but elegant scorn. "How did you survive?"

I fumbled out what details I could. When I finished, silence met me. I stared down at my dirty feet, indistinguishable from my equally grimy sandals. I bit my lip to keep myself from making fists in my skirt.

"Nisaat, fetch her application from the Hall of Records."

Nisaat bowed and hurried off. Lady Egal picked up her brush with one hand, held her sleeve back with the other, and continued writing like I wasn't there.

Aches ran through my marrow. Would it be rude to sit? Probably. No one had invited me to relax and the gleaming chairs with their lattice backs seemed too fine for my tattered self.

Nisaat returned with a single sheet of paper. Lady Egal lay her brush next to the inkstone and took it. "Recite your generations, Dami."

I started with my parents and recited backwards, the images of the clay-wrapped faces in my family shrine smiling at me. I knew these names as well as my own. When I reached my great-great-great grandfather and his obtainment of the Yellow rank through military service, she waved a hand. "That's sufficient. I believe your identity."

I bit my lip. My stomach rumbled loudly, then Lady Egal graced me with a regal glance of disgust. "You're not fit to be anyone's personal attendant. Or a door servant. I wouldn't trust you with laundry, or sewing, or maintaining the bathhouses. Fortunately for you, being strong-of-arm will make light the only work I can, in good conscience, entrust you with."

I winced. Lady Egal turned to Nisaat. "Take her to Hawak for whatever filthy jobs he has. Her manners are not fit to be seen by the Royal House."

CHAPTER SIX

Lady Egal gave Nisaat final instructions, something about having the laundry send a servant's dress to my room for me for tomorrow. Then Nisaat led me out of Lady Egal's apartments and over another path of fine white gravel.

"Your papers say you're strong-of-arm?"

The base of my skull throbbed. Her words drizzled slow as honey through my ears. "Yes. Strong-of-arm."

"Good! That'll be helpful for scrubbing crocks."

Scrubbing crocks. "We're... going to the kitchen?"

"Yes. Hawak's the Master Chef."

My pulse pounded, making me dizzier. I'd be by the food. I'd get to smell it. I stumbled, but Nisaat caught me. "Careful, there. You're not scared, are you?"

"Scared?" The word didn't make sense. Food wasn't frightening. Food was life. Food was art. Food was heartbreakingly beautiful.

I smelled the kitchens long before we reached them—roasting meat and stewing vegetables, thick and seductive in the air.

"The kitchen's haunted. But don't tell anyone *I* said that—I want to keep my post."

"H-haunted? With Bloodmarrows?" I asked, remembering the young woman's story about Vengeful Ghosts controlled by the Shoreed.

"Bloodmarrows were made up by soldiers to excuse their friends when they desert," Nisaat said with open disgust. "The kitchens are far more interesting. The story you told Lady Egal, about clams and sleeping outside carter stations, was that true?"

I nodded. How could the royal kitchens be haunted? I stumbled over a dip in the gravel.

"You're brave, then. You'll be fine." We passed a landscaped stand of spruce trees and ferns, then climbed another three-step porch. Nisaat opened the door.

Dizzy and weak, I managed to look up. It seemed like acres of polished granite counter stretched before me. Six hearths burned, each with crocks, spits, or smokers. Fresh salmon and sturgeon sprawled on the cutting boards. Baskets of young dandelion greens and heads of soft lettuce glistened from a recent wash—the latter had to be from a greenhouse. Scrubbed turnips and rutabagas were heaped in baskets, lustrous as a hoard of pearls and opals. A dozen young men bustled over everything.

"Master Hawak!" Nisaat called.

A middle-aged man strolled over, his face glowing with good health—the sign of an excellent chef. He was broad, from his shoulders to his hands to his face. He flicked me a glance. "I know she looks like a wild bear cub, but I do believe that mud-caked thing is a girl, Nisaat. I refuse to skin and roast her for you."

"Thanks, but I'm not that hungry. This is Yellow-ranked Dami of Clamsriver, the palace's newest servant. Lady Egal assigned her to scrub crocks."

"Looks like she could use a good scrub herself," Hawak chuckled.

I rubbed the side of my head. At any other time, I might have protested, but I itched with a patina of grime. The pounding in my head crept down along my neck. I didn't have the energy to argue, either.

"Run along Nisaat. I'll see to your cub."

Nisaat bowed and left, her well-made sandals hardly making a sound. Hawak folded his arms across his expansive chest. "Well, well. I'm Green-ranked Master Chef Hawak of Napil. This is my kitchen. The rest of these are my bungling apprentices. Do tell me if you can't distinguish them from the crocks."

He paused for me to laugh, but by the time I digested his joke, he'd continued.

"I have few rules. No stealing food. You'll be fed at meal times, not between. Understood?"

My stomach rumbled. I ached to snatch one dried apricot, one rabbit leg. But I hadn't come so far to get dishonorably dismissed on my first day. I'd survive until supper. I nodded.

"Good. One more rule: no rumors. No gossip. No speculation. No... *superstitions*." He'd lowered his voice and his broad face turned as hard and unforgiving as a first frost. "None at all. Do you understand?"

The apprentices seemed to stiffen, fear in their brows. Maybe this place *was* haunted. "Yes, Master Chef."

He frowned at me, then led me through the parade of smells to a sweltering corner stacked with clay crocks of all sizes and glazed bowls dripping with bits of leftovers. "You'll be washing these. Scrub them until they gleam like chalcedony. Most people don't realize it, but a clean pot is the foundation of good cooking."

My eyes prickled. I knew that.

I sat and picked up a crock crusted with a plum-rhubarb sauce. We scrubbed crocks at home with sand, but here they had salt—a whole bucket of salt, just for cleaning. The salt mines produced well, but it still seemed extravagant. I tossed a large pinch inside the crock and grabbed a rag.

I should be grateful. No one would notice a crock scrubber. No one would ask me too many questions. No one would discover I wasn't Dami.

I'd never cook here, but at least I'd be *near* the food. Not that I had the concentration to watch the apprentices and scrub crocks right now. My head felt like it floated above my body, with a string attaching the two.

"Dami!" Hawak shouted from across the kitchens. "You'll have those pots scrubbed by next year at that rate! Come here."

Bile rose in my throat. Hadn't I been scrubbing furiously?

I stood. My visions swarmed with dark spots.

Then everything turned black.

"Her pulse says she's dehydrated and underfed. What would you make her?" Hawak's booming voice echoed through my skull. I groaned.

"Elk and carrot hotpot?"

"No. Dewar?" Hawak called.

"Bean cakes with blueberry jam?" the apprentice offered.

Hawak sighed. He shifted. From the savory smells floating through the air, he'd just lifted a crock lid. He continued his lecture in a scholarly, pragmatic tone. "A lack of food and water leaves one in need of all things—perception, dexterity, strength, and endurance. The whole body is likewise in need of help, but heavy food will hurt a weak stomach. Stock, made from a whole duck or rabbit carcass, is the answer."

A spoonful of something warm dribbled into my mouth. Luscious and silky from the duck, with depth of flavor from sweet carrots, spicy garlic, and bright, sour parsley, it swirled around my tongue. Salt perfected the balance of all four flavors in that heavenly liquid.

I'd made thousands of broths and tasted thousands more. But none, not even my father's, could match the subtlety of this one. Tears budded in the corners of my eyes. I'd tasted perfection. And I couldn't ask Hawak how he'd made it, not without raising suspicions.

"Are you awake?" Hawak asked.

I opened my eyes, then wished I hadn't. All twelve apprentices stared down at me. I'd become Hawak's teaching moment. He strained the stock into a bowl, while ordering some of the apprentices to help me into a corner. They propped me against a bag of beans, then Hawak brought me a bowl of the amber liquid. "I thought you were lazy, not ill. I'm sorry."

I raised the spoon to my mouth and sipped. I wanted to burst with enthusiastic praise for this stock. I wanted to weep over Hawak's feet and beg him to teach me his techniques. But strong-of-arm Dami wouldn't know she tasted nothing short of a masterpiece, the culmination of decades of study.

I'd almost been daughter-in-law to a man with this kind of skill. "This is delicious."

"Well, I try," Hawak said with a grin fully aware of his mastery of our art. "When you've eaten half, I'll bring you a buckwheat branch to soak in the remaining stock. Your stomach will handle it by then."

As he stood, the door opened. *Fir.*

My spoon froze, halfway to my mouth. Except the thief didn't look like an unassuming boy from Meadowind anymore. His sleeves still indicated yellow-rank, but his hair was waxed into soft curves, the corners of his eyes touched with umber in the height of fashion.

"Ah, Hawak. Grandmother's feeling partial for a mint infusion."

I turned, trying to make myself small against the sacks of beans.

Hawak waved at one of the apprentices to handle it. Fir waited against the wall and stared at me, eyes hard. My arms prickled with gooseflesh. Tea tray in hand, he left without a word.

Hawak brought me the promised buckwheat branch.

"Who... was that?" Despite the stock, the question turned my mouth dry.

"Yellow-ranked Fir. He's the grandson of Blue Lady Egal, King Alder's first cousin once removed. But his mother married beneath herself. I'm sure if you want to gossip about his handsome features, you'll find plenty of company among the other servants."

I flushed. That wasn't what I meant at all. "I was just asking."

"Less asking, more eating. You still have crocks to scrub."

Hawak had some semblance of fairness, at least. He left me with a crock of stock, keeping warm on the ashes, more branches, and an admonition to take breaks.

I did, of course, still need to finish all the dishes before going to bed.

The kitchens seemed almost peaceful, once the apprentices retired. The various hearths glowed, like the sleepy eyes of watchful grandparents. The dim light left the edges of the counters blurred, the ceiling hidden. I could imagine myself chopping onions over there. Seasoning a freshly-filleted trout here. Preparing berry pudding in the height of summer there.

My scrubbing slowed. Why would Fir rob me? He wasn't poor and he had no reason to hate me.

My stomach turned icy. Not me, *Dami*. He'd asked my name and he'd been so happy to hear it. But he had no reason to hate her, either.

Unless she'd done more than mope when she disappeared into the woods.

I rubbed my eyes and paused for a ladle of the stock, hoping that would clear my mind. Its lulling warmth made my eyelids heavier. Maybe I could risk a nap on the grain bags? No. Better to finish. I couldn't afford to lose my post.

Father, Mother, Nana, Dami. They all depended on me.

The outside door rattled. Strange. "Hello?"

Hawak had mentioned another dishwasher I'd share a bedroom with—she had her half-day off today. When the sun set, I'd assumed she was sleeping elsewhere tonight, maybe with family in town. A dishwasher would knock, though, and the door kept rattling —furiously.

"Hello?" I stood, clutching my half-scrubbed crock, the closest weapon to hand. A crock could probably knock out a thief. Still, no answer. Just more banging. Was someone injured?

My hands turned clammy. The long shadows on the wall shifted as I crossed the room.

I cracked the door. It burst open, whacking my hand and knocking me onto my backside. Sharp pain shot down my still-bruised hip.

A ghost loomed above me.

Corpulent rolls of tar-black skin covered its massive body, supporting a diminutive head with a pin-prick of a slime-dripping mouth. It stood on two tiny, withered legs that seemed too small to support such girth. Two tiny, withered arms dangled from its chest, barely visible against the mounds of slime-coated fat.

I wished, for once, that I wasn't perceptive-of-taste-and-smell. It smelled like pickles gone bad and spoiled fish. It smelled like a deer's carcass, left to rot on the forest floor. It smelled like an old man had died and voided himself.

The ghost tilted its disproportionately small head to the side and considered me.

Some kinds of ghosts ate corpses. Maybe this one wasn't so particular as to require dead meat.

I hurled the crock.

It bounced off the mounds of fat and rolled to the floor. A well-made crock, not to break. The ghost pounced on it and slurped the half-scrubbed insides—tried to slurp the insides, anyway. That pin-prick mouth let nothing pass. Worse, its lips turned everything they sucked at into ooze. Sharp-scented, eggs-gone-bad ooze, thicker than the black slime that coated its body.

This was a Hungry Ghost, then. Not a Vengeful Ghost, or a Mournful Ghost, or a ghost with unfinished business, but some deceased spirit that could not rest for the famine burning in its belly. A belly regular food refused to fill.

It picked up the next crock and tried again, all interest in me gone.

I should have moved. I should have run. Gone to the room Hawak said I could sleep in and barred the door.

But I couldn't tear my eyes from the sea of fat, the way it rippled when the ghost moved. I couldn't breathe for all the stench in the air. I couldn't think.

I'd had a half-dozen crocks left to wash. The ghost didn't take long to lick them all into foulness. It shifted toward me, bringing its stench closer.

I gagged. And then I vomited broth and buckwheat all down my front.

It lowered its head and whined. Whimpered like a beaten dog. It looked from the stoves to me, clutching its huge belly. Its tiny eyes flashed in the firelight, but they weren't angry.

Sad. Sad and starving. *Feed me. Cook for me*, it seemed to plead. Its eyes were almost beautiful—a deep brown, like the bottom of a molasses pudding.

I shifted forward a step, then caught myself. Feed this thing? Feed it what, myself? I'd eaten everything Hawak left me.

Light shone in the outside doorway. A torch. I caught a glimpse of a young woman's hardened face and long hair. She swung the torch like a club, right into the ghost's back.

It howled with pain at the fire, jumped to the ceiling, and scurried upside down like a spider out into the night.

She smiled at me—a woman two or three years older than me with calloused hands and a plain, charcoal gray dress. "Welcome to the kitchens. I see you've met our ghost."

CHAPTER SEVEN

"You must be Dami. I'm Osem, the other crock-scrubber," she said, not getting any closer. She looked me and my vomit-splattered dress up and down. "Did laundry deliver you a dress?"

"I... umm... don't know." I vaguely remembered Lady Egal saying something about that to Nisaat, her gate servant.

Osem opened a door on the far side of the kitchens, near the stairway to the cellar. "It's here. But we should clean crocks first. Outside."

No sense in dirtying my only clean clothes. In the outside air, the crocks still reeked like something left in the sun for a week, but I could control my stomach. Each crock needed two scrubbings—I did the first round since I was already filthy. Osem folded her elbow-length, green-ranked sleeves on top of her shoulders and finished the work with practiced efficiency. Dami had been wrong about the yellow-ranked girls getting all the worst jobs.

"This sludge... it doesn't cause disease, does it?" Not that I'd asked in time for it to matter.

Osem shrugged. "The ghost rots the food, but it's just rot. Nothing us dish scrubbers can't handle, eh?"

"Right. You've seen the ghost before?"

"Oh, a few times. Enough to figure out it's scared of fire. You opened the door when it rattled, didn't you?"

"Ah, yes." I picked up another crock. The grime and water chilled my hands—there was nothing warm about scrubbing under a waning spring moon.

"Hungry Ghosts can't open closed doors. Not even a cupboard. Hawak learned that in his research and it's held true."

Someone might have mentioned that before leaving me alone in the kitchens. I passed Osem the last crock. "Why hasn't Hawak exorcised it?"

Part of exorcising a Hungry Ghost included cooking it a perfect meal. Surely a Master Chef like Hawak could handle the challenge.

"When he was busy researching, he relied on the apprentices to plan the menus. His Majesty noticed the change and commanded Hawak to stop."

I blinked as we hauled the cleaned crocks back inside. "His Majesty *wants* a ghost in the palace?"

"Oh, he doesn't believe it's real, since only apprentices saw it. Or maybe he doesn't like the idea that a Hungry Ghost *could* be in the Redwood Palace—he's a proud man."

I shook my head. Pride seemed a poor reason to avoid seeking out the truth. "I still can't believe how calmly you waved that torch."

"I'm not scared of our ghost, and I'm endurance-of-heart, too. Regular heartbeat. I don't panic easily, and I've never managed to faint."

Macerated strawberries for endurance-of-heart. I'd never heard of anyone with that gift.

"I know, I know. It's a bit odd. My father was sickly his whole life —as far as we could tell, because of his erratic pulse. My parents hoped this birthgift would keep me from inheriting his difficulties."

"That's *brilliant*. It seems to have worked?"

Osem nodded. "I was lucky. During Mother's pregnancy, the

Master Chef of that day—Master Chef Yarrow—visited my home town. He suggested it."

Former Master Chef Yarrow. Sorrel's father. I could have studied with him. I swallowed the lump in my throat, but it felt like swallowing ghost slime.

We stacked the clean crocks upside down on their shelves to dry. Work finished, Osem yawned, reminding me of how tired I was. My body throbbed all over, most of it sticky from cleaning.

Osem led me to the door by the stairway. The room inside barely fit two mattresses and a pair of blankets. Osem didn't quite slide the door shut so I could change by hearth light. I shoved my filthy dress under the empty basket and lay down.

By then, Osem was snoring like nothing had happened.

I tried to settle on my mattress, but this room smelled odd. The pine cuttings of our mattress were musty, the wood walls stale. Even from under the basket, I caught the acrid tang of my soiled dress. And, fainter still, I smelled the kitchens—ashes and herbs and well-oiled cutting boards I couldn't use.

HUNGRY GHOSTS PLAGUED MY DREAMS. Nana's sweet face shrank, her middle bloated, and her arms and legs withered until she was as putrid as the ghost who attacked me. That's what would happen to her, if no one cared for her—especially in this crucial first year after death. Without a daily offering in the shrine, she'd starve. She wouldn't ascend into her deserved rest with her Ancestors.

But the palace didn't lack food to offer the dead. Why would anyone be neglected? No, the palace shouldn't harbor any such ghosts.

My dreams shifted. People with too much lust for this world could also burn with hunger, regardless of the food offerings proffered them. Murderers, adulterers, and gluttons. All night they chased me. Some slashed at me with obsidian knives. Another caressed me and whispered nightmarish nonsense. Others tried to crack my ribs open, like I was a stubborn clam hiding a delectable interior.

I woke in a cold sweat.

If I were king, I wouldn't want to believe ghosts lived in my palace, either.

Osem didn't act like the ghost posed a physical threat. It wasn't a Vengeful Ghost, and it had seemed more interested in the crocks than devouring my internal organs. But I wasn't sure. I knew so little about ghosts of any kind.

I'd just keep the door shut. Even if it seemed impossible that something as flimsy as a door could keep the Hungry Ghost's bulk outside the kitchens.

Osem yawned, turned over, then nudged me with an elbow. "Are you awake yet, lazybones? We've got work to do."

Darkness swallowed our small room. It didn't feel like it could possibly be morning yet.

"The ghost didn't scare you, did it?" Osem cracked the door, letting in the hearth light. The natural lift of her eyebrows gave her a friendly, perpetually-laughing appearance. "Maybe if we work fast enough, Hawak will give us some time off to go to the baths. I mean no insult, but you need it."

Usually when people start something with "I mean no insult," they intend exactly that—but not Osem.

"Aren't you tired from being out after sunset? And then staying up to scrub all those crocks?" I asked.

She shrugged, offering no details on where she'd been. I followed her into the kitchens.

"We always get up before the apprentices and build the fires back up to full strength. Do you know how to tend a fire?"

My chest ached. I knew how to use every inch of this kitchen, from hearth to countertop. "Yes."

"Good. Start over there."

I blew on the coals and folded back in several unburnt ends of wood. Flames licked them up. Time to add more—but I frowned at the short stack of logs by the back door. "There's hardly any wood here."

"That falls to us, too." She snatched two buckwheat branches from a basket inside the cupboard and tossed me one.

I hesitated, despite its shiny, brown-broiled crust.

"We're *allowed* that for breakfast. I wasn't stealing." Osem imitated Hawak's robust voice: "For there will be no stealing in my kitchen!"

I couldn't help but smile. We munched the nutty branches as we walked into a cool, blue-black false dawn. The buildings, lawns, and gardens on either side of our gravel path rested peacefully—it seemed impossible that a ghost had roamed here last night.

Osem led me to a shed by the palace wall. "Half the palace gets their firewood from here. There's the pile of sacks."

We filled two up, stacked the split logs in the kitchen, then came back for another batch. The sky blushed pink. Birds called. At least I was used to getting up early. As we dumped out the wood, the apprentices staggered in, rubbing their bleary eyes.

After the fourth load, I groaned as I picked up the wood. My arms already ached from yesterday's scrubbing.

Osem blinked at me. "Aren't you strong-of-arm?"

I plastered a smile on my face and added a log to my sack, for show. "I'm just sleepy. That's all."

BY THE TIME we finished hauling wood, the apprentices had a heap of dirty dishes for us to clean. Hawak arrived to taste and re-season the breakfast dishes—buckwheat and a variety of sauces to go with them, pease porridge, easy-to-digest egg drop soup, and labor-intensive bean cakes. At home, we only made bean cakes for special occasions; the beans had to be ground into very fine flour, then whisked and whisked with hot water, then poured into molds and cooled. Only then could they be sliced and simmered in broth. Eating them for breakfast seemed ridiculously indulgent—but I guess this *was* the palace.

Hawak arrived with a smile and good-hearted laugh, but his demeanor soured as he rescued dish after dish from his apprentices' careless mistakes. By the time servants arrived to whisk trays off to royals, nobles, and other servants, he was scowling and swearing. I didn't blame him.

The servants returned with heaps of dirty dishes and the apprentices dove into lunch preparations. Hawak's mood didn't improve and I could smell why. One apprentice burned the honey. Another over-salted a soup—a hard mistake to recover from. The lanky one scorched the onions instead of sweating them.

I could cook better than that. How had these twelve bumbling young men gotten their places here? Family connections? Perhaps the number of chefs serving army units had left the country badly depleted of talent. But wouldn't the best cooks have first choice to work in the palace?

Come midday, one of them chopped a carrot into such uneven pieces that the littlest ones boiled to mush before the larger ones became tender. I gritted my teeth and scrubbed harder, despite the protesting ache in my arms.

"I know you're strong-of-arm and all, but don't break the crocks," Osem teased. "Still nervous about the ghost?"

The nearest apprentice glared at Osem. "Don't say things like that!"

"Like what?" one of the others asked.

The apprentice with a square jaw and thick hands gave the rest of them a hard look. The other apprentices shivered or flinched and skittered back to their work. They didn't look at each other after that.

"What—" I began, but Osem shook her head and mouthed, *later*.

We finished scrubbing crocks as the sun faded to a streak of egg-yolk orange on the horizon. The apprentices had long since retired.

"Too bad the baths are closed," Osem said, drying her hands on her skirt.

By now, dirt coated me like a second skin. At least the kitchen looked lovely—gleaming granite counters, polished redwood cupboards, well-swept hearths. It would be a mess again tomorrow. Or tonight, if we had a visitor. "Once the sun sets... will the ghost...?"

"It'll rattle the door, but given that all the crocks are clean and there's not much to smell in here, it'll give up soon. The Hungry Ghost will glean scraps from the city tonight."

"It goes into Askan-Wod?" The thought of that monster running past children's windows turned my stomach.

Osem shrugged. "I watched it go over the palace wall, once. Sometimes, on my half-day off, I've heard people complain about upturned slop troughs, but they always blame raccoons. You're not scared of the ghost, are you?"

With those crinkles around her eyes, I couldn't tell if she was teasing or not. "Of course I am! It doesn't belong in our world. It's *dead*. It should be exorcised."

"That's not happening."

I sat on one of the granite counters, marrow aching from my ankles to the base of my spine. "You said you'd tell me why the apprentices are all afraid."

"It's not because of the ghost. I told you how they asked Hawak to exorcize it?"

I nodded. I hadn't studied much about Hungry Ghosts with Father—we were too busy tending the living—but exorcisms weren't supposed to be an easy process. "And then the King told Hawak to stop, because the food got worse."

Osem sat next to me, feet dangling. Her face looked old in the dying light and the humor faded from her voice. "The apprentices all testified to King Alder about the ghost. This was in winter, when the sun set earlier, so they were around to see it. But His Majesty said the ghost wasn't real."

I didn't understand the heaviness in her words. She stared at me, mournful eyes waiting for a reaction.

"And then what happened?"

"Oh, Dami. The king said there was no ghost. That meant all the apprentices *lied* to him. The Purple-Blue Council agreed. Don't you know what happens when you lie to the king?"

My heart stopped, as sure as if a butcher had grabbed it. I was lying to the Royal House right now—I knew the punishment all too well.

"They all hanged from the city wall. The apprentices Hawak has now? They arrived ten weeks ago."

CHAPTER EIGHT

I didn't sleep well that night. The apprentices hadn't lied. They hadn't *tried* to deceive. The King could have given them a lesser punishment. A fine. A whipping. A dismissal.

His Majesty apparently did not believe in leniency. A cold, hard fear of being discovered lodged in the back of my throat.

Osem had continued, explaining that all the current apprentices were third or fourth sons—the only people desperate enough to fill the kitchen posts in the wake of the executions. Each of them was perceptive-of-taste-and-smell, but they'd either studied under poor tutors or none at all.

It made me wonder how Dami was doing—Dami, who'd had no training, before joining the army.

It was pure misery after that to watch the apprentices fail. If I were Plum instead of Dami, I could help them. It was too easy to imagine some badly-prepared meal sending all twelve of them over the walls.

But I couldn't risk it.

Over the next three days, every time we went to the woodpile, I picked up two more logs than Osem. My arms burned. They felt like wet noodles whenever I let them rest for a moment. But I couldn't be anything less than Dami, strong-of-arm. I told myself to ignore the cooking, but my soul wouldn't listen.

I ought to be chopping asparagus, washing crinkly kale, salting slippery duck hearts, and creating art from them. I didn't know if I was lovesick, or homesick, or mourning twelve dead men I'd never met, but all my meals tasted wrong because bile filled my throat.

My fourth day in the kitchens, Hawak waved us away after a simple lunch of buckwheat branches. "Go. Enjoy your half-day off."

I needed no further urging. Neither did Osem. We left the newly-dirtied crocks and stepped out into the midday sun. The lawn looked brighter, the rhododendrons pinker, the azaleas whiter.

"Where," I asked, "are the baths?" Dried sweat clung to me like a glove.

"Half of me wants to tease you and not tell."

I frowned.

Osem laughed. "But the *other* half longs to sleep in a fresh-smelling room. Too bad Lady Egal didn't send you to the baths, then to Hawak."

We passed a number of gardens on the way. I'd seen the wild one with spruce trees and ferns uncounted times while fetching wood, but most were new to me. Some boasted fountains, others held rambling paths, while more still were nothing but rugs of wildflowers and the butterflies they attracted. My heart wilted. Dami would have loved this—all this nature packed together, ready for exploring.

The bathhouse itself sat in the middle of a hedge garden—Osem said the leftover bath water drained to the plants. I followed her up the steps. Inside, high windows let in light and the perfume of orchids. The flowers had to be over the hedge; I didn't see them on the way in. Glorious blue tiles lined the floor of the single, large tub. A half-dozen women sat in the water, chatting, hair floating around them. Stools and buckets lined one wall, shelves of baskets the wall opposite.

Osem strolled toward the buckets. "These are for scrubbing up beforehand. Afterwards we can soak."

I glanced around. I wasn't used to being naked in front of others. "This... this is exclusively a women's bath, right?"

Osem laughed. She tossed her clothes to the floor, plunked down on a stool, and scrubbed from the head down with a piece of pumice she grabbed from a bucket.

Well, I couldn't stay filthy for the rest of my life. I slipped out of my gray dress and folded it on the floor. I grabbed a bucket, found the pumice, and scrubbed with my back to everyone else. I dumped a water-filled bucket over my head to rinse off the dirt, then slid into the clean bath.

Which, of course, was clear. My floating hair did little to cover me.

"You're from a small town, aren't you?" Osem asked, joining me. "No baths?"

"Me and my sister used a stretch of the river." We always hiked far downstream of the village. More than one young man had tried to spy on Dami.

Oddly, Osem's expression saddened, her laughing eyebrows turning down. "That must be nice. Having a sister. What's she like?"

I should have kept my mouth shut. "She's..." Did I describe Dami, or myself? "She's dedicated. To her profession. She works hard."

"Ah. No time for you, eh?"

"What? No, I..." Hadn't I always made time for Dami? Watched out for her?

If we kept at this conversation, I'd trip over my own lies. I changed the subject. "You don't have any sisters, then?"

Osem shrugged and fell silent. The water rippled softly around us; the other women kept chatting. Something about what birthgift Blue Lady Sulat, the king's sister, would try for her child. She wasn't due for a few months.

The silence between Osem and me stretched.

I had failing manners—just like Lady Egal accused me of. I couldn't keep up a conversation with my only friend in the palace.

A woman entered with a hamper and gathered up the clothes we'd discarded. Was she supposed to do that? I glanced at Osem.

"She's a servant of the Royal Household, too. Don't you see the gray dress?"

I'd thought gray dresses were popular, not a uniform.

"We're servants, but we're *royal* servants, Dami. Someone washes our clothes. Someone cares for the gardens. Someone," she winked at me, "even scrubs our dishes."

The laundress left, hamper on her hip.

"Lady Egal usually starts new servants off in the drudgery jobs, then moves them up to errand runners or personal servants."

Usually. I wasn't quite rude enough to ask Osem how long she'd been here. Long enough to witness the apprentices hanging—or had she learned about it later?

Osem got out, wrapped herself in a towel, and walked to the shelves full of baskets on the far wall. "The yellow-ranked width are over here, green over there," she pointed. "Take a spare. We can't come back until our next half-day off."

How would I survive the palace without Osem to instruct me? I pulled on a dress and grabbed an extra.

Osem then showed me the last of the baskets. Each held different-colored skirts. "The patterns and colors on these all indicate different positions... but we're dish-scrubbers." She grinned. "So we get plain ones. You'll be dismissed for dressing outside your place."

My eyes lingered over the colors—everything from scarlet to green to amber—decorated with a variety of patterns and animals. Osem picked up one the same color as our dresses. "Here, hold your arms up and I'll tie it on."

I couldn't help but think of Dami and our usual morning routine as I did so. When Osem finished, my dress draped neatly over my waistband.

I did the same for her. Osem looked so comfortable in that uniform, so at home.

"Thank you," I said. "For all your help." I hoped she knew I meant more than tying my skirt.

Osem wasn't one to gloat over others' gratitude. "Now I wish we could throw your mattress out, but we're not due for new cuttings until late next month. Want a tour of the gardens?"

"I'd love that!"

We strolled through a flower garden first, then past four servants rolling balls down a long, manicured spring-ball court. The red team was losing badly.

"We're all allowed to use these gardens?" I asked.

Osem nodded. "The King's garden around his Royal Bear House are walled-in and private, but here, officials send a servant ahead to clear us out if they want to be alone."

Dami loved spring-ball. She'd always challenge the boys in Clam-sriver, then play both the front and back tosses herself. I never understood the satisfaction she got from beating them—repeatedly. If a young man was confident and suave, she laughed all the harder when he trudged home moping.

"Is this a garden for women only? I haven't seen any men." It seemed odd—spring-ball at its most traditional played couple against couple.

"The palace servants are mostly women. Guards and soldiers aren't exactly getting much time off with a war on."

"Oh." Of course. I felt stupid for asking. I wished I knew which division Dami ended up in. Was she still training? Had she reached the field? Was she safe? I had no way to know. "I hope the war ends soon."

"I don't."

I stared at Osem.

She shook her head at me. "We're *losing*, Dami. If it ends now, well, there won't be a Rowak anymore. Askan-Wod would become a large city in Shoreed's realm. Shoreed started this over a simple land dispute, but they've already claimed that, and more. They're not going to stop until we're gone."

Despite the birdsong and the pink rhododendrons, I felt chill. I'd thought of our victory in terms of *when*, not *if*. My nation, my home, couldn't simply cease to exist.

"Speaking of men..." Osem nodded down the gravel path.

Nisaat, the gate servant who escorted me to Lady Egal's that first day, walked toward us along with a tall, broad-shouldered young man in a black military uniform with yellow-ranked sleeves. His hair swept low on his forehead, just above his eyes.

"Ah, Dami!" Nisaat smiled. She wore the same emerald green skirt with the bleached eagle, over a gray dress identical to Osem's. "I was afraid you'd left the palace for your half-day off."

The young man looked a little like Nisaat—same straight nose, same strong cheekbones. But his eyes were warmer and darker. Even when he bowed, he didn't stop staring at me. I couldn't tell if he was terrified or in awe of me, or how I'd earned such attention. He kept his left arm tucked behind his back—hiding what?

"No. I'm here." Though my face was growing warm. Who was this? Nisaat should have started with introductions.

"Going for a tour around the palace grounds?" Nisaat asked.

I pulled myself away from the gaze of the young man to glance at her. "Yes. Osem was taking me around."

"Ah! As it happens, I need Osem for a sudden, important task! Thankfully my cousin Bane here is an expert on the palace layout. Bane, Dami. Dami, Bane. Now you're introduced!" Nisaat hooked her elbow around Osem's and hurried down the path with her in tow. Osem flicked a glance at me and Bane, *giggled*, and let Nisaat pull her away.

"Nisaat!" Bane called after her, horrified. "You said—"

But the two of them were gone, with no signs of coming back.

How could Osem abandon me? The air was too thick and hot to breathe, with just the two of us staring at each other on an otherwise empty gravel path.

"I'm... I'm sorry," Bane fumbled. Even embarrassed, his baritone voice resonated. "Nisaat suggested we join you and Osem. I had no idea she'd..."

He glanced over his shoulder at them. As he did, I saw his left arm properly for the first time. It was amputated—empty from the elbow down. No wonder he wasn't on the front lines.

Recipes ran through my head—for swelling, for scabbing, for the injured soul. How recently had he lost his arm? The scars seemed well-healed, no longer pink, but I couldn't see them well at this angle.

"I won't hold you accountable for Nisaat's behavior."

"That's a relief." He managed a lopsided smile. "If you'd rather head back to the kitchens, I can direct you."

Into a kitchen where I wouldn't be able to make anything to ease his pain.

"Or... " He hesitated. "Would you like to continue with a tour?"

A pang ran through my chest. I didn't want his kindness. I wanted to make him a stew. Bane couldn't be older than twenty—so young to lose a limb.

He caught me staring at his arm. I flushed and glanced away down the path.

Despite my rudeness, he spoke gently. "I assure you, a missing hand won't compromise my ability to show you the palace grounds."

He wasn't asking for my pity. But that couldn't stop my soul from feeling it. "I was thinking about parsnips," I mumbled at the gravel.

"Parsnips?"

"The top half is good for treating amputations." The entire parsnip targeted the whole arm. Full-grown kale would work almost as well, but mature kale was hard to come by this early in spring, outside the palace greenhouses. "I'd caramelize them to bring out their sweetness and give you endurance."

He tilted his head to the side and peered at me. "You've learned a lot, scrubbing crocks. You must be very observant."

I bit my lip. Idiot, idiot! Of course I shouldn't know about cooking. "It's... well... Hawak is always lecturing his apprentices, and he's quite loud."

"In truth, I've eaten so many parsnips, I'm sick of them." He gave me a sad smile. "Here. The kitchens are this way."

"Oh, I..." I tucked a stray hair behind my ears. "I really would like a tour today. If, that is, you're still willing. I didn't mean to... give offense."

To stare and make an idiot of myself, I meant. I was used to analyzing injuries, not being polite about them.

He frowned. "Are you sure?"

"I'd be delighted if you'd do me the honor," I gushed.

Bane still seemed uncertain, but he gave me a handsome bow. "In that case, I'm at your disposal."

Bane walked a respectful two feet away from me, adjusting his longer gait to my stride. He brought me to a plum orchard first—a dozen trees with sculpted benches under them. The wind picked up and the tiny, white blossoms swirled through the air like snow.

Panic twisted deep in my throat. Was he mocking me? Did he know my real name?

But Bane's face remained calm. "Come autumn, the blue- and green-ranked officials like to sit on the benches here and enjoy plums. Servants and soldiers are forbidden to eat them, of course, but I like plum trees best in spring, anyway."

"They're lovely." Tiny flowers, destined to become sweet, purple jewels. "Every year, as a girl, I used to dance through plum blossoms."

Nana took me. She'd hold my hands and twirl through the petals with me. She was my guardian, friend, and playmate while Mother and Father worked.

Nana, I hope you're safe. Safe and fed.

I could picture all too clearly what Nana might look like, transformed into a Hungry Ghost.

"You sound sad," Bane said. "Is it not a good memory?"

I hesitated, but he smelled like juniper and smoke, a scent with brightness and depth, and somehow the words tumbled out of my mouth. "It's a memory of my nana. She passed, during the winter."

Dami would come with us, too, though she'd rather climb trees than spin under them and gaze up through the branches. Nana always chased her, muttering words I wasn't supposed to repeat.

"Oh. I'm... sorry," he fumbled.

Now we were both awkward again. What a horrible conversationalist I was. Bane bit the corner of his mouth. It made him look boyishly adorable, like he'd broken a vase and didn't know how to apologize enough.

I didn't let the silence stretch. "Could we move on to the next garden?"

"Of course! It's my favorite. Maybe it will cheer you, Dami."

As we walked, the fragrance of the blossoms lingered. *Call me Plum*, I wanted to say. *I'm so tired of hearing people call me Dami.*

I silently sighed. A silly, dangerous wish. I'd hear my own name again in two years, when I returned to my parents.

We turned around a hedge. A manicured lawn ran down to a pond. On the far bank, finches flitted between tall reeds. White pebbles blanketed the shore nearest us, matching the lazy clouds reflected on the water's surface.

I stopped and stared. "It looks like an opal embedded in mother-of-pearl."

"Oh, I don't love it just because it's beautiful. Come!"

He hurried down the lawn. I frowned. Would he throw me in the pond? I followed cautiously.

He picked up one of the rocks, smooth and circular. Facing the lake, he curled his forefinger around the edge, then cocked his wrist back and threw.

The rock danced across the pond, jumping from one spot to another, leaving a ring of ripples at each spot it touched. I couldn't tell if the rock sank into the water or made it to the other shore, but the concentric rings blended and mixed on the lake in mesmerizing patterns. "How did you *do* that?"

"Like this." He picked up another rock, gingerly held it, and tossed.

"You must be agile-of-hand."

"Strong-of-arm, actually."

Oh, how I ached to make him parsnips. I managed not to look at his missing limb. Someone with agile-of-hand might still be a scribe or artisan, but what use was one strong arm? "It skips because you throw it hard?"

"No. It has to be done gently."

I peered at him, confused.

Bane laughed. "Just because I'm *gifted* with strength doesn't mean I neglected everything else. I will never be as agile as some, but I can still learn agility, Dami. My legs have no gift, but I can run."

I picked up a rock, tried to hold it as he did, and threw. It plunked straight into the water. "Are you sure you're not double-gifted?"

An infant could receive two birthgifts, but chefs rarely tried. If the targeting ingredients weren't perfectly balanced against each other, the child ended up with little or no gift.

"You flatter me. No, there's a trick." He picked up another rock. "It has to spin. Toss it low and flat—you want a disk of spinning rock, barely kissing the surface of the water."

"Maybe I should leave this noble art to you." I glanced back up the lawn. "Will we get in trouble for this?"

"I haven't yet. Here." He handed me another rock, his amputated arm bent inward as if he were respectfully presenting it with two hands. "This is a good one."

My toss skipped once. Watching my stone float through the air— that was surreal, magical.

"Here. Go again."

We spent an hour like that, Bane mostly handing me rocks. At my best, I got four skips.

It sort of reminded me of Dami, when we were younger. Nana would rest against a boulder while we collected pinecones and arranged them in pretty patterns on the forest floor. The next day, they'd be mussed. Nana told us the Ancestors did it, though I'm pretty sure she knew it was squirrels, too.

But still, it felt like magic. It felt like watching rocks float.

Dami and I hadn't done that in years. I started going with Father into the village. Dami started hiding in the woods.

Eventually, Bane and I sat still and watched the ripples on the lake. I leaned back on both elbows; he leaned back on one.

"Are you sure you don't want me to get you some parsnips?" It was the wrong thing to ask, but I couldn't stop myself.

"Offering to steal from the kitchens for me? Hawak would be outraged."

I flustered. I itched to examine the amputation. Prod it with my fingers. Ask him if it hurt anywhere.

"Everyone worries about me. But you don't need to. I lost my arm battling at Rivergrass. I'm used to it, even if no one else is."

That had been one of the earliest battles—over three years ago. "You must have been a young soldier."

"Sixteen. And so excited. I'd trained my whole life, you know. Not just the hand-to-hand stuff that I naturally excelled at with my birthgift. I learned archery, javelin, the construction of siege engines... everything. I wanted to be a commander, one day."

No one would make him a commander now.

I almost offered him condolences but thought better of it. "Are you still glad you went?"

"Glad? No. Would I choose to do it again? Yes. Fighting... was different than I'd envisioned. Archers have it easiest. They can't see the face of the men they impale. But I served Rowak. I'm alive. And, Ancestors be praised, I have a post."

I glanced at the band around his arm—it showed a road zig-zagging down a stylized mountain. "I'm afraid I don't know what that insignia means."

"Ah. I'm a runner. A messenger. Lady Sulat uses me for dispatches in the palace and Askan-Wod."

"Lady Sulat..." It sounded like a name I should know.

"She's the Minister of Military Affairs—King Alder's sister and General Yuin's wife. She's expecting her second child in three months."

General Yuin, the hero of Rowak. *That* name I did know. "You speak her name with great admiration."

"She gave me a post when she could have abandoned me to what-ever fate brought. Not that ill-fate seems to bother you. Nisaat told me about your journey here."

I fidgeted, self-conscious.

"Braving the road... weren't you afraid of robbers?"

"Robbers? I had no money!"

"They still could have hurt you," he said, voice soft. I thought of the soldiers, the merchants, and the villagers' fear of Bloodmarrows and strangers. Maybe Nana had watched over me, seen me safely here.

"I did sleep near the carter stations, for some measure of safety." I shrugged. "I had to get to the palace, so I came."

"You'd make a good soldier."

"What?" I jerked upright, heart pounding. He *knew* about the real Dami. How could he know?

"I meant no insult," Bane said quickly. "You're just so dedicated to your position. And you're strong-of-arm. It's a good combination. I certainly wouldn't mistake you for a soldier, if you think I was calling you masculine."

The terror flowed out of me as quickly as it had come, leaving me cold and shaken. I hoped everyone *did* mistake Dami for a soldier. And she'd always been prettier than me. "Oh. Umm. Thank you."

"I was nervous to meet you, after hearing Nisaat's story," Bane admitted.

I had to laugh. "Me? Am I as terrifying as you'd imagined?"

"No. You're surprisingly easy to talk to." Bane smiled, and the warmth of it seemed to flow right into my bones. "It's almost time for supper, but I could walk you by the aviary, first."

"I'd like that." The words tumbled out of my mouth before I could stop myself. I ought to be hiding in the kitchens, not out in the palace lying about my identity to a young war veteran.

"Good. I'd hate for you to miss the aviary. There's a few messenger birds, plus hawks and eagles—not that anyone is going hunting with the war on."

As soon as we left the manicured pond, I smelled the tang of bird dung. Soon, chirps and coos filled the air.

"There."

The white-washed building boasted a lintel carved with falcons. Bane strolled up the steps; I followed a half-pace behind.

A guard in blue, not black, stood at the door. "The aviary is closed."

"We'll just look—I'm not trying to send a message."

The guard sneered and spat in Bane's face. "I won't open for military men unless they have *orders*."

I jerked half a step back. Why was he so rude? Bane clenched his hand. I glanced between the two of them, Bane furious, the guard smirking with both hands on his spear. I didn't care why they hated each other—it wasn't worth fighting and jeopardizing our posts.

"Let's go," I said, starting to follow my own advice. "I don't like birds, anyway."

Bane's shoulders slumped. He knew I was right.

As we turned to leave, the guard cracked the butt of his spear against Bane's shin, sending him tumbling down the stairs.

CHAPTER NINE

"Bane!"

I rushed after him. The guard behind me snickered, but he stayed put. I dropped into the habits I'd developed with Father. I knelt by Bane's side. He wasn't breathing right.

"Don't try to move." I pressed my fingers to his ribcage in a number of spots. "Does this send shooting pain?"

He shook his head and gently shifted away from my hand.

"I'm not going to hurt you. It looks like the air's knocked out of you. Let me look at your shin."

I reached for his pant leg, but he scuttled back and sat up, careful not to touch me. "It's just... bruised," he gasped, his breath coming back. "Please don't trouble yourself."

I pursed my lips, ready to give him a lecture on how to be a good patient, but managed to bite my tongue. "I'm trying to help. Someone ought to look at it."

"Then it ought to be Hawak, not a lovely young woman."

Oh. *Oh.* He was right, of course. We weren't family. We were close in age. He didn't know I was a trained chef. I hadn't thought twice about it—he was hurt.

"You should still get some sour duck feet from Hawak," I said, trying to sound professional to hide my embarrassment. "Or, if he won't get out delicacies, a salad of carrots and a dried stone fruit—plums or cherries would do, but apricots compliment carrots best."

Carrots targeted the leg; those fruits targeted muscles and would minimize bruising. Sour—strength—would ease the pain.

Bane tilted his head to the side, staring at me with his eyebrows frowning together.

Dami wouldn't know any of that. I coughed. "Like I said, Hawak is always lecturing the apprentices. It's hard not to pick things up."

Another guard in blue rounded the aviary. "What's going on here?"

The man who'd struck Bane leaned nonchalantly on his spear. "That idiot soldier came at me. But I've got it under control."

"Good."

What muck. I stood to give the guard the scolding of a lifetime, but Bane shook his head.

Maybe it was safer to let it go, but my throat burned. Striking an unarmed man, then laughing it away?

Bane got to his feet. His voice was still ragged but coming back. "You're right, Dami. We should go."

The real Dami would have taken a swing or two at the guard. She once broke a boy's nose for trying to kiss her. But I walked away with Bane, shame tightening in my chest.

The pair of guards chortled to themselves, but they stayed put. Bane's shoulders didn't relax until we sat on a cold stone bench in a nearby garden, a brick wall separating us from the aviary. It had to be a summer or autumn garden—there were no flowers, and the spindly branches of the shrubs only held dew-shaped leaf buds.

"Are you all right?" I asked.

"Nothing broken or bleeding, nothing to fuss about."

My indignation hadn't cooled, even if Bane's had. "He struck you. You're going to report him, aren't you?"

"The Palace Guard has never liked the military." He shook his head. "I'll be in more trouble than him if it's reported."

"You did nothing wrong!"

"I'm also a soldier. I should have prevented an attack—or dodged it. His officers would cheer if they heard a man in blue landed a strike on a soldier in black."

"That's... that's..." I spluttered like a lid on a boiling crock—I didn't have words for the stupidity.

Bane shrugged. "They guard the Redwood Palace. We fight wars. They train in comfort. We train in the mud. The Guard's jealous."

"Why are weaklings in charge of guarding the king?"

"Oh, they're not weak. They do nothing but guard, sleep, and practice. In a duel, they'd match most soldiers. But they live in the palace. They eat well. They sleep well. They're *soft*."

I rubbed the side of my head. I hadn't realized there was much of a difference between guards and soldiers until now, let alone their mutual animosity.

"It's getting late." Bane nodded at the sun, low on the western horizon. "Have I made you miss your meal at the servants' hall?"

"Hall?"

"Don't you eat there? Most servants who aren't someone's personal attendant do."

"Oh." I felt foolish for not realizing that. "I eat in the kitchens."

Had the apprentices left anything for me? I glanced at the position of the sun. They'd all be retired by now—I had maybe an hour until sunset.

Sunset. And then the Hungry Ghost would appear.

"Would you maybe like to eat in the city tonight?" He cleared his throat. "I mean, I know of a great noodle shop just outside the palace wall."

Osem might be adept at wielding a torch to get past the Hungry Ghost into the kitchens, but it wasn't a trick I fancied trying. I stood. "I have to go."

His soft smile disappeared. "Do you not like noodles? There are other food stands."

In the kitchen, it felt safe to talk about the Hungry Ghost. But out in the garden, anyone could be listening. "I'm sorry."

Bane nodded and let me leave without another word.

I JOGGED into a kitchen empty of people and full of everything else. The dying sunlight and smoldering hearths gleamed over the chaos: stacks of plates, a mountain of crocks, counters coated in flour or dripping some forgotten sauce onto the floor. The greasy smell of bear meat coated the air, but I couldn't find any leftover hotpot—except for what oozed between the bowls. I sniffed. Nicely seasoned with enough pickle brine to cut through the fat. But what a mess.

Was I supposed to clean this tonight? My stomach churned. I'd assumed the apprentices would scrub on our half-day off.

I wished Osem was here to tell me.

But if leaving these until morning meant losing my post, well, I couldn't risk that. I glanced at the basket of buckwheat branches on the counter, my stomach rumbling. Were those for me? I didn't know, so I regretfully left them alone.

I set a pair of crocks with clean water by the hearth and started washing with a half bucket of lukewarm water. A film of cold, congealed sauce coated all the lunch bowls. Could I finish these before sunset? Every creak in the kitchen made me jump—dreading the Ghost, hoping for Osem.

I longed for my stuffy, musty mattress in our small bedroom. Where was Osem, anyway? Not that she'd come home early on her last half-day off.

I ran out of salt and, cursing, stumbled through the cellar until I found more. When I came back into the kitchen, new stacks of bowls and platters awaited me, still warm from supper.

I felt like I'd swallowed vinegar. Of course servants would drop off more dishes as people finished their suppers.

Best to start on the fresh bowls, before they dried. At least I had crocks of warm water to work with now. I grabbed a crock, forgetting to protect my hands with a towel. Cursing, I jumped back.

The whole crocked toppled over, knocking into its fellow. The water from both ran, hissing into the coals.

I stood in a dimmed room, splattered with soot and hot water. A room a Hungry Ghost would shortly besiege. The vinegar in my throat swelled upwards.

"Nana," I whispered to the corners of the room, "do you hate me? Aren't you supposed to watch out for me?"

I could almost hear her voice in my head, the voice she used when I burned myself or cut my knuckles as I tried to perfect some new dish: *Oh, little blossom.*

The tears prickled the corners of my eyes. I wanted her here. I wanted to hug her, to see her crinkly-bark face. I wanted to be four years old again and know that nothing bad could happen because my nana held my hand.

No warm water, and now my cold water was filthy. I cracked the outside door. Threads of rhubarb-red sunset still streaked the horizon. If I hurried, I could make it. I grabbed a pair of buckets and took one step outside.

Something rattled in the mountain of dirty crocks.

For a brief, painfully hopeful moment, I thought Nana would appear. Then the rattling continued, and I came to my senses.

It was probably a rat.

I set down the buckets and grabbed a broom. The noise came from the center of the crocks. I shifted them around until I found the culprit—a brown-glazed thing with a clattering lid. How had a rat gotten itself stuck in there?

Gently, I toppled the crock over, and prepared to whack the creature senseless.

A snake shot out at me.

I stupidly threw the broom at it and scrambled onto the nearest counter, pulse pounding. The snake darted between the pots and struck. Its teeth hit wood. Then it tried again, but it couldn't reach over the top of the counter.

The snake coiled itself between my counter and the hearth, keeping warm. I tried to breathe regularly. To let my pulse slow. One snake. One me. I could handle this.

Then I noticed the dotted pattern on its back that marked it as a pit viper. Poisonous.

My throat swelled into a lump.

I doubted an uncommon snake somehow stumbled in here and trapped itself. But why, why would anyone trap an angry pit viper in a crock? All right, the angry part probably came after its imprisonment, but it hadn't put itself there.

The door creaked open, stirred by a gentle breeze. I hadn't closed it. I swore under my breath, but I couldn't reach the door. Not without jumping five feet over a burning hearth to another counter. I'd have to get rid of the snake first.

I couldn't spot any weapons. Crocks—clean or dirty—sat out of reach. The broom lay on the floor. A row of knives hung over the counter opposite me—another jump I couldn't make.

I stood, floured granite under my feet, and two lazy, reptilian eyes watching me. It showed no sign of falling asleep.

The door swayed. "Osem? Bane? Anyone? If you closed that, I'd be grateful."

Grateful to be shut in a room with a deadly pit viper. Dami would laugh until her ribs cracked if she ever heard this story.

No one answered. No one could hear me. I hugged my knees to my chest and glanced at the snake. It lifted its head, as if asking if I'd like to be bitten now.

I didn't move after that. My limbs prickled with the cold, spring night air. If I were strong-of-skin or endurance-of-blood, I might risk a bite.

The door slammed open, hitting the wall. I jerked upright, ready to warn the newcomer about the snake.

But the shape wasn't human. Outlined by moonlight in the doorway stood the Hungry Ghost.

CHAPTER TEN

The Hungry Ghost scrambled into the kitchen, its rolls of fat dragging on the floor. It tumbled over the crocks, its pinhole mouth turning all the burnt bits and uneaten sauce into a slime that reeked like overripe fruit and sharp urine.

I gagged as the foul ooze dribbled down the dishes, black and slick like molasses. The ghost's tiny, withered arms jerked frantically, desperate to shove more to the mouth that no food could pass.

The viper hid, slithering under my counter. I plugged my nose and breathed shallowly. Couldn't the snake have hid somewhere else? Anywhere else? Then I could have run to my room.

Soon enough the ghost destroyed every last drip of food not tucked behind a door—including the basket of buckwheat branches. Ooze dripped from its mouth, making it look oddly like an unwashed toddler. It blinked at me, then hung its head, beady eyes downcast. Almost like it was embarrassed.

The thing shuffled toward me, leaving a trail of its own filth. I stopped breathing altogether.

Then it whined piteously and shifted back.

"I'm not food. You can go now, please." I waved it toward the door.

It tried to wipe its bloated belly clean of its failed meal, but only dirtied its hands. The ravenous hunger subsided in its eyes, replaced with... what? Desperation?

The thing lowered itself to its belly in a mockery of a bow, its head and puny hands folded against its slime-coated girth.

I wished it wouldn't do that. I still had a snake to deal with tonight. "I don't know why you're still here."

The ghost swung its arms in a variety of movement, up and down, circling. I tilted my head to the side. It was pantomiming *cooking*.

"I know you're hungry, but if I get more food, your cursed mouth will turn it to slime."

The Hungry Ghost hung its head, tiny eyes wide—so pitiable. It *whimpered*.

"You don't want food?"

It pointed at me. It pantomimed cooking. Then it laid its head to the side, as if asleep.

"You want to rest. You want to be exorcised," I whispered.

The thing keened, high and sad.

"I... I can't..."

It pointed at me, then pretended to cook again.

Ancestors, this thing couldn't know my real birthgift, could it? Or did it just want someone, anyone, to save it?

"I can't help you."

Its whine grated against my ears.

"The king killed the last people who tried! Do you want me hanged? Do you think my family wouldn't suffer?" I ranted. "I'm just a dish scrubber. I can't even get down from this counter because someone left a snake in my crocks. I'm tired and hungry and I don't understand this place and I want to go home, but I can't!"

It stared at me, hands folded against its chest. Sympathy shone in its tiny eyes, as if saying *I want to go home, too.*

Ancestors help me, the only being I could speak honestly to was a Hungry Ghost.

It darted toward me.

I gasped and reached for a weapon that wasn't there, but it dove under the counter. It slurped the snake out like a long, spotted noodle. The snake writhed, alive, but stuck to the Hungry Ghost's mouth. Until the ghost snapped its spine with its spindly hands. The dead viper's skin dissolved against that pinprick mouth, sliding off bones that turned to sludge soon after.

I covered my nose and mouth with the front of my dress and stopped breathing. My head swam with the smell—rotted meat and old eggs. Pain prickled my skull.

The Hungry Ghost shuffled politely backwards, far enough away that I could breathe. It lowered its head and blubbered.

It reminded me of a girl from Clamsriver I treated one winter. Little Ryes was too young to wipe her nose. Snot and tears dribbled down her face for a month. Her mother cleaned her two dozen times a day, but she still perpetually wrung her hands, crying for someone to wash her face.

The ghost was like that. Dripping, miserable, unable to help itself.

My heart felt like someone had laced it onto a skewer. "I... I can't..."

It burbled mournfully.

Asking someone else to exorcise this ghost could bring the king's wrath. And I didn't know how to do it myself. Even if I did, I couldn't risk getting caught cooking. Nana, Dami, Father, Mother—they all depended on me to fulfill my two years in this post.

"I wish I could help. I do. But... but I have other loyalties first."

It picked up the basket the branches had been in. It pointed at the basket, then its mouth, then the basket again. Emphatically.

"You need to be fed branches?"

It shook its head, then pointed at the basket again.

"I don't understand."

It pointed at the basket, then itself.

A torch blazed in the doorway. The Hungry Ghost skittered onto the ceiling and somehow shot through the narrow opening above Osem's head. It disappeared into the night.

Osem stepped carefully around the mess, then blinked at me, still up on the counter. "Dami, how do you end up in such interesting places?"

"I was trying to clean the crocks."

Osem shook her head. "We're supposed to work extra-long tomorrow to catch up. Don't you know what time off means?"

WE COULDN'T LEAVE the kitchen filled with ghost-fouled crocks, so we took them outside. Osem worked with silent resolve, once more taking the second pass at all the dishes. I planned a hundred apologies, but they all choked and died in my throat.

I kept watch for more snakes, but thankfully no more appeared. The stars had moved considerably by the time we finished. We both stank like manure. Osem paused long enough to change into her spare dress, then collapsed on her mattress. In moments, her breathing relaxed into the deep rhythm of sleep.

My bones ached for rest, but my rumbling stomach and aching limbs kept me awake. If I reported the appearance of that snake, someone might investigate—and I couldn't risk an investigation with me at the center of it.

Surely snakes snuck in now and then, chasing the occasional mouse. I had to believe that.

I chewed my lip and tried to distract myself with everything Father had ever said about ghosts. A meal was one of the steps of exorcising a Hungry Ghost. If the ghost couldn't pass on due to neglect, their favorite food in life would free them. If the ghost remained because of their lusts for this world, they needed something to balance out their vices. Salted deer hoof tea, which increased the agility of your hands, could exorcise a greedy man. Did a dishonest man need a meal of endurance-of-tongue, or strength-of-tongue? I couldn't remember.

I drifted to sleep, coveting Sorrel's library. His father probably had a dozen manuscripts detailing the proper exorcism of ghosts.

THE NEXT MORNING, I woke to an apprentice cracking our door. "Nope. They're both in here!"

Osem and I both jerked awake and ran like mad to get the fires up, completely forgetting our skirts until, after our third run for wood, an apprentice chuckled at us.

When Hawak came in, he grumbled at the apprentices for being slow with breakfast, but they mercifully said nothing about the pair of dish scrubbers who'd overslept. Instead, Hawak commended us for getting up early to finish yesterday's work.

Perhaps the apprentices couldn't cook, but they were kind. More than ever I yearned to teach them, help them, but I kept my sleep-deprived head down and at my work.

Hawak thanked Osem and me with an especially good lunch—cold buckwheat noodles with julienned vegetables and a tangy, salty dipping sauce.

"Osem. I'm sorry. About last night and this morning..." After all she'd done for me, I'd failed to show her the respect and friendship she deserved.

She gave me a mock-stern look. "Serious crimes indeed, Dami! I'm afraid my forgiveness can only be granted on one condition."

I knew she was poking fun, but I bowed my head and meekly waited for my sentence.

Osem laughed. "Oh, Dami. I'm not mad. But I am deadly curious about what happened yesterday and I'm not above using your guilt to find out."

I stared down at my nutty-sweet noodles and fresh vegetables. The blue-eyed grass outside the kitchens, dotted with tiny flowers, gave the air a spring freshness. But that all seemed distant, with the memory of those two reptilian eyes staring at me, my pulse pounding in my throat. I couldn't report the snake. Why would anyone put it there on purpose? To attack me? To attack Osem? In daylight, the notion sounded paranoid, ludicrous.

Osem raised an eyebrow. "Bane was that unpleasant, eh?"

"Bane?" I jerked back.

"What did you think I was talking about?"

"Bane… Bane was…" Attacked. Thrown to the gravel. And he didn't want me to do anything about it.

"Ancestors, Dami, did he hurt you?" Osem asked, all teasing erased.

"No! Not at all."

Osem exhaled. "I wouldn't have left you with him if I'd thought him anything less than respectable… but you're positively ashen."

"You know him?"

"A little. I've served in the palace for two years; Bane's been around longer than that. Are you going to tell me what happened, or do I have to stay mad at you forever?"

I swallowed the noodles I was chewing. "You can't tell anyone."

"Do I look like a gossip?"

Not at all. I lowered my voice. "A Palace Guard attacked him."

Osem blinked, startled. "I didn't know about that."

Why should she know?

"Bane didn't report it, did he?" she asked.

"No. He said he'd be in trouble… Osem, you can't say anything."

She laughed. "Me? A dish scrubber? Not my place and I said I'd keep quiet. But I'm sad to hear it. This war… it's flamed the rivalry between the Palace Guard and the military. The Guard Captain, Blue-ranked Gano, doesn't discourage it. I bet he wants to set some new precedents about who gets jurisdiction inside the palace."

"He's making power grabs during a war?" That seemed incredibly unpatriotic.

"General Yuin's absent, even if his wife, Lady Sulat, isn't. War's full of upsets, changes. It's the perfect time for someone like Captain Gano to reposition himself. Maybe he thinks Lady Sulat won't notice since she's expecting."

Even after weeks here, I felt lost when it came to palace politics. "You're very knowledgeable."

"You pick these things up. Gano's hard to miss. Both politically and physically—he's ridiculously tall, and the military men are always telling jokes about his silly mustache." She shrugged. "Soldiers here seem to grumble about the guards more than they do the war."

The war. I pushed the noodles around my bowl, appetite waning. The longer the war went, the better chance Dami had of getting caught. Or killed.

"I didn't mean to make you mope." She gave me a mischievous grin. "Really, I want to know what you think of Bane."

"He was nice. Though I wish you hadn't run off like that. You could have both given me a tour."

Osem spluttered laughter into her noodles. "Wish I hadn't run off? Oh, Dami, you are a sweet little country girl, aren't you?"

I frowned. The question didn't sound like a compliment.

"Nisaat didn't bring him for a nice outing. She's trying to help him find a wife. He has no inheritance and no chance of advancement in the military now. At best, he'll keep his post as a messenger."

"You're making him sound calloused and calculating!"

"Ah-ha!" The crinkles around Osem's eyes deepened. "You think he's *very* nice, don't you?"

"Of course not." Even if I did, what then? I had secrets to keep. I couldn't take him back to Clamsriver and pretend I had two names.

My stomach swam. Dami—she would have liked Bane. Skipping rocks seemed like just her thing. She would have punched the teeth out of that Palace Guard, too, instead of uselessly prodding Bane's ribs. If she'd come, Father could have adopted Bane, left the two of them the house, and I'd be in Westbank with Sorrel.

My marrow ached. Why hadn't she come? Why had she abandoned all of us in the middle of the night?

I bit my lip. No, she hadn't abandoned us the day she joined the army. She'd done that long before—when she stayed in the woods and refused to admit that she was part of our family, when she refused to see that her choices impacted more than herself. At least with both of us gone, Mother would have less laundry. I hoped that saved her back.

"You're pensive for someone whose mind is made up." Osem ate, watching me out of the corner of her eye. "Bane will need a wife—and strong children to support him when he's no longer spry enough to be a messenger."

My gut twisted. "He flirts with all the new servants, doesn't he?"

"So he was flirting with you?" Osem grinned and continued before I could protest. "Nisaat dragged him out to meet people for the first two years after his injury, but he refused after that. It's been a year since he let Nisaat introduce him to someone. I wonder what she said about you, to change his mind?"

My cheeks burned. "He's not courting me."

"You should make sure he knows that."

I took my sandals off and wiggled my toes into the lawn. The coolness and the smell of earth was almost as centering as candied beets. "He has no reason to be interested in me."

Unless he knew about my lies. Unless he suspected. Then he could blackmail me into whatever he liked. He seemed too nice for such trickery, but Fir had been more charming still.

Osem laughed, a rich, rolling sound that somehow managed to be kind as well. "Do you want me to ask Nisaat about it?"

"No. I'm not interested," I mumbled into my noodles. I couldn't afford to be interested.

"But he is. He'll be at the kitchen door our next half-day off. I'd bet my post on it."

THAT EVENING, Osem and I crashed onto our mattresses as soon as possible for some much-needed sleep. At the end of the next day, my arms still ached, but in a good way. My muscles felt stronger. I wouldn't beat Dami in a wrestling match, but I could probably break a boy's nose.

"You're getting the hang of this, aren't you?" Osem asked that night in our dark, pine-musty room.

"I think so." At least with the dish scrubbing part. Bane, Fir,

Hungry Ghosts, and poisonous snakes were another matter. "You're not going to abandon me now that I'm half-competent, are you?"

Osem laughed. "What?"

"You've served your two years. You *could* go. I know a lot of girls don't—the palace is safe, a lot of the marriage prospects are off fighting..."

"I'm happy here."

"Good. Some people might get bored after two years." I'd be gone as soon as two years came, though not from boredom. I wanted to keep my neck.

"Three."

I blinked. "Three?"

"That's how long I've been here. Lady Sulat housed me for a year, until my name came through the list."

"Housed you?" I stared in her general direction, though I couldn't see her in the dark. "Your family must be important."

Osem's mattress rustled. "They weren't. Not terribly. We were the stewards of her lodge in Moonhill."

Moonhill. Near the western border with Shoreed. "That's... where the Shoreed first attacked."

"I know. I was there."

My words stuck in my throat. She said her family *wasn't* important, not that they *aren't*. "I'm... I'm sorry." Words weren't enough. "You must have left behind many loved ones."

"My parents, my siblings, my husband."

I managed a shaky whisper. "You were married?"

"For six short months. Goodnight, Dami."

Osem rolled over. I wanted to say something comforting, but what could I say? The silence of our tiny room leeched away the laughter than had echoed here.

Candied hazelnuts. Endurance to the soul. That's what I'd make Osem, if I could cook for her.

I woke in a morbid mood. Buckwheat branches for breakfast reminded me how insistently the Hungry Ghost had pointed at that basket.

Who had it been, before it died? A glutton for branches? That didn't seem right.

I spent the morning trying to puzzle out his gesture as I scrubbed cold broth residue off crocks. But its actions didn't make sense. Or I didn't know enough about Hungry Ghosts.

What had Osem's family been like? Her husband? I knew her father's heart had been weak, but that didn't tell me what kind of person he'd been, or what kind of relationship they'd had.

All morning, Osem acted like she'd said nothing of importance last night. But I ached for her as I smiled along with her jokes and jibes.

Not that we had time for talking after lunch. The apprentices shattered three crocks in quick succession—one hadn't dried from scrubbing and the other two were placed over the hottest coals without being warmed up. It left them behind schedule and Master Hawak in a foul mood. The char of burnt food mingled with that of sweet cakes. All my thoughts about the Hungry Ghost oozed out my ears like overly loose dough.

I was scrubbing someone's lunch bowl, head down, when Osem elbowed me.

"What?" I whispered.

Hawak bellowed at me. "Dami! I've called your name four times!"

I jerked to my feet and bowed.

"You're strong-of-arm. Come drag this bear into the butchery room—the apprentices hurt themselves last time."

I looked up. Sure enough, a dead bear lay near the inside door. A massive, sprawling bear. I wouldn't be able to budge it. "It's spring. Why do we keep getting bears?"

"Hungry bears who gorge on battlefields are wandering east, looking for more. Did you forget there's a war on?"

Blood crusted the bear's snout. I felt ill. Had that been some soldier's innards?

"Hurry up!" Hawak snapped.

An apprentice dropped and shattered a fourth crock, full of a bubbling hotpot, drawing Hawak's attention and a string of profanity.

I swallowed hard. I couldn't move that bear. Why had someone left it in the doorway, instead of bringing it all the way in? When I failed to budge it, they'd all know I'd lied. The king would hang me.

Why did I think I could be Dami? I wasn't her. I could only pretend. Poorly.

Each step forward felt like a century. Nana would end up a Hungry Ghost. My parents would be homeless, robbed of Father's post. Dami's lies would unravel.

I bit the inside of my lip, feet dragging like granite blocks as Hawak gave his oldest apprentice, the lanky Tanoak, instructions on butchering the creature. I prayed silently. *Nana, ancestors... we're all dependant on each other. I'm trying to help you, but I need your help, too.*

Nothing miraculous came to take the bear away, but a spluttering sound caught my ear—an over-boiling crock banked with white coals on the hearth closest to the bear. The image of Old Sandpiper's wound flashed across my memory.

My throat crusted over, like someone had filled it with burnt-on sauce. I couldn't pretend to be Dami.

But I could pretend to trip.

"Dami, before autumn comes!" Hawak's broad-chested voice cut through the kitchen clamor. He turned back to Tanoak.

My stomach buzzed. My heart tightened. But my marrow stayed calm. This was my best choice. And so, I had nothing to worry about. No need to fret. Nothing left to decide.

I stumbled over the smooth floor. I cried out and fell forward. My right hand landed on the warm lip of the brick hearth. My left I jammed onto the coals.

Before I felt the pain, I smelled my seared flesh.

I screamed. That, I didn't need to fake. I fell to the floor, shaking. Pain shot up my arm, then turned into a giddy light-headedness. I glanced at my hand. Bloated pink-red flesh—like one giant blister. No one would ask me to haul a bear carcass today. I laughed into my sobs.

"Dami! I said—" Hawak began, but then he turned. His face fell. "Tanoak! Dress some sorrel and fine-sliced onion in sour pickle brine. Now!"

Hawak picked me up like I weighed nothing and brought me to the side of the kitchen. He laid a compress over my palm. It burned cold, like fresh snow on bare skin.

"Clumsy girl," he muttered. "Don't you know you have to watch where you're walking in a kitchen?" He sounded more concerned than angry.

"I'm sorry."

I obediently ate Tanoak's salad. Coolness flowed down into my hand, taking the edge off the pain. A crisped fish skin chip with sorrel would be more effective, but we probably didn't have any fresh fish right now. Regardless, a burn this bad took time to heal.

I didn't know if Hawak had the apprentices do it, or if he sent for someone else, but by the time I finished eating, the bear carcass was gone, and the soft sounds of precise butchering drifted in from the other room.

CHAPTER ELEVEN

I wedged crocks between my knees and scrubbed them with my good hand. Osem washed faster than me, but I managed a fairer share of the work than I'd hoped. That evening, laying on our mattresses of musty pine boughs, she clucked over me like a mother hen. "You need to be *careful.*"

"I was." Not that I could explain why going to bed with a bandaged, throbbing hand was actually prudent.

Osem sighed. "First you're robbed, then I find you up on a counter with the door open, inviting in the Hungry Ghost, and now this. Dami, you're either cursed by your ancestors, or you're the *least* careful person I know."

"I didn't try to leave the door open," I defended myself, staring up at the darkness of our room. "The snake interfered."

Confused silence followed. Osem shifted on her mattress. "*Snake?*"

"A pit viper." I explained how I'd ended up on the counter, then laughed at myself. "I guess I'm not very lucky."

"You're not making that up, are you?"

"You think my life's dull enough I need to invent things?"

Osem sighed. "Dami, why didn't you tell me earlier?"

"It's just a snake." I squirmed on my mattress. I shouldn't have said anything. "It probably wandered in. I doubt I'm being stalked by sinister Bloodmarrows."

"Blood whats?" Osem asked.

I rolled over and explained what I'd heard the village woman say, about an army of Vengeful Ghosts controlled by the Shoreed who kidnapped and killed the people of Rowak.

"Dami, this is no time to laugh at superstition! You can't be calm about this. Deadly snakes don't just appear in the kitchen." Osem's mattress crinkled under her as she shifted. "Fir likes playing pranks on servants—sometimes he even makes them resign—but this seems beyond him."

Fir had already played a prank on me and it hadn't been harmless. I swallowed and tried to sound casual, but I couldn't stop my voice from jumping a pitch. "Fir?"

"Blue Lady Egal's grandson, King Alder's first cousin once removed. He's yellow-ranked, though—his mother married below herself. Now he lives off Lady Egal's generosity. No post. His brothers all joined the military, trying to advance themselves, but he loafs around here."

"Why doesn't he join the army?"

Osem shrugged. "He has no birthgift—maybe he's too scared to face gifted enemy soldiers? I don't know."

"No birthgift at all? Could his mother not swallow what the chef brought?" Vomiting during labor wasn't uncommon, but that didn't affect the gift.

"His mother tried for double-gifted, but the attending chef messed it up. When Fir was born, there was no birthglow around him."

"No indication of a birthgift at all?"

"None," Osem said. "Rather rash of the mom, hoping to get two."

"Not really." Parents sometimes asked Father to try for double-gifted with their later children. "If it succeeded, Fir's skills would benefit the entire family. Maybe even help him earn him Green rank. If it failed, well, he has siblings to watch over him."

Osem shifted on her mattress. "Hmm. I suppose so. In any case, usually I'd blame him. I think he harasses servants because he's bored."

"But he's tamer than this?"

"Oh, he's put snakes in people's beds before, but not *poisonous* ones. I think someone tried to kill you, Dami."

It sounded plausible when she said it. "Osem... you can't report this."

I should have watched my tongue better—it was too easy to talk around Osem.

"You sound scared."

"I am." The snake hadn't killed me, but an investigation with me at the center of it could easily send me to the noose.

"Why don't you want it reported?"

She sounded curious, not like she'd run off and report it herself. "I want to keep my post."

"No one would dismiss you over being attacked," Osem said. "But you're still right about saying nothing."

Now it was my turn to be confused and silent. I wished I could see her face properly in our dark room.

Osem continued, "If I wanted to kill someone and they started looking for me, I'd try *harder* before anyone figured it out."

"That's a cheerful thought."

Osem sighed. "Acting as if nothing happened will encourage the attacker to take his time. Maybe make him careless. I'll keep my ears open and see if I can't learn anything. In the meantime, make sure you're never alone, Dami. Stay with me, or Bane, or Hawak. It's not that hard to cover up one death as an accident. It's much harder to say the same about two or three."

DURING MY NEXT HALF-DAY OFF, I ran into Bane near the kitchens, on the path that skirted a natural-looking garden of spruce trees.

He fidgeted with an embroidered envelope, his brown eyes locked on mine. "Dami. I was hoping I'd see you during your time off."

"Oh." I flushed, suddenly glad Osem wasn't here to tease me. I tucked my hair behind my ear with my bad hand and winced.

He stepped a half step closer. "What happened?"

"Just a burn. Nothing some onion-sorrel salads won't fix in due time."

Bane blinked at me. "You really *are* learning a lot about cooking."

I silently cursed myself. I was horrible at being Dami around him.

"Well, I'm not deaf and I do work in a kitchen," I defended myself lamely. I shouldn't be talking to him—I didn't need another person to keep secrets from.

"You mean you're *clever* and you work in a kitchen." He smiled. "I'm sorry that I can't stay, though I'm glad I found you."

I blinked. I'd been sure he wanted to spend the afternoon together again.

"My schedule got changed," he explained. "I'm on duty right now. But I didn't want you to think I was avoiding you. I'd like to spend another half-day together, sometime."

"Sometime," I echoed, silently thanking my Ancestors that I didn't have to push him away or keep lying to him.

Bane smiled and bowed, his dark hair sweeping just over his eyes. Then he hurried down the path on his errand.

THE REST of the month passed peacefully. No more snakes appeared, at least, and Hawak granted Osem and me permission to tour the palace greenhouse. Parsely, carrots, snap peas! Their full leaves and stems made it look like summer had come. I couldn't touch them, or eat them, or cook with them, but *smelling* them made life easier.

My parents sent a letter, too—a painfully awkward one with mundane news from Clamsriver instead of the questions they wanted to ask. I spent a few chips of my wages to send an equally awkward reply. Mostly I told Mother about all the fresh food now filling the kitchens, then asked about her own plants.

My hand healed, bit by bit. The work didn't get easier, but it wasn't unpleasant with Osem there. Someone had to scrub the crocks, after all. Might as well be us. Watching the apprentices' mistakes made me itch to jump in, but by and large, the days passed smoothly. Sometimes I even overheard a tidbit of culinary wisdom from Hawak. Each lesson tasted better than our mountain's finest salt.

I could live like this until my two years ended. Until I could go back to being a real chef.

Really, only the nights were horrible. Osem and I kept the outside door shut, but the piteous whimpering of the Hungry Ghost cut through the wood and stabbed at me.

"Will it do that every night?" I asked in the still, quiet darkness of our room.

"Dunno. It never did this before you came. Maybe the snake you fed it gave it indigestion."

Or could the ghost somehow tell I was a chef?

"You... seemed to pick up on a lot of Hawak's research. Did you learn how to exorcise one?" I'd seen shadow-plays in Meadowind that featured all kind of ghosts—from Vengeful to Mothering to Hungry —but the exorcisms always happened in a moment with a wave of lights and no practical information.

"There are three steps, but I only heard the bit about cooking the meal," Osem said.

I bit my lip. I knew that much already.

"Let's see. Ravenous but never able to eat. Can't open closed doors. Oh. And at sunrise and sunset, they always return to the location where they died."

"Sunrise?" Ghosts existed at night.

"It's apparently uncommon, but some ghosts take human form during the day. Hawak's research didn't say if they could open doors in that form or not."

If our ghost was human during the day, it could ask for help directly. "Do you remember anything else?"

"No. But why are you so curious? It's not like you can cook a meal to exorcise our friend."

I needed that reminder. I couldn't do anything for the ghost without risking my post, my neck, and my family. I'd already asked too many questions.

The ghost let out a high-pitched whine. I sighed.

"You're not considering going out there and playing with it, are you? You have a knack for trouble without looking for more."

"I know. I just wish I could ease its suffering."

ONE MORNING when Hawak was teaching the apprentices how to grill green onions, Fir walked in. My neck stiffened and my pulse jumped.

But Fir didn't spare me a glance. He strode straight to Hawak, cutting him off mid-sentence. "You have to go, Hawak. She's getting worse."

"Tell Blue Lady Egal to send someone else. I'm the only one fit to run the kitchens."

Fir smirked. I hated how handsome he looked. "If the king's grandmother dies at the hands of one of these ducklings, you want it on your head?"

The apprentices unanimously glared at Fir.

"And if the king's father dies? That's no better," Hawak countered. I'd learned a little more about people in the palace. Last fall, the king's father fell deathly ill and abdicated the throne. The king's grandmother was ancient—nearing ninety. She'd lived at Sandhead taking care of her family's shrine ever since her husband died, some thirty years ago.

"You don't get to pick priorities, Hawak," Fir said.

I'd seen Hawak frustrated, and I'd seen him disappointed. But never angry like now, with his eyes pinched and his broad shoulders tight. "I don't know what you're playing at, but—"

"I'm not playing." He pulled a letter from his belt. "Blue Lady Egal and His Majesty discussed the matter this morning. He's *ordering* you to go tend to his dear, ailing grandmother—at once."

"King Former Fulsaan can't possibly concur."

"Too bad he abdicated." Fir nodded at the paper. "Look at the signatures. His Majesty insists you leave."

Hawak read, jaw clenched. "Get. Out."

Fir smiled roguishly. His soul must be filth, to look so charming while torturing Hawak. "Do you think I forged this seal? These are *His Majesty's* orders and—"

"And this is still my kitchen, whether I'm here or not. You're trespassing. Shall I call the Palace Guard?"

Fir stepped forward. "I am the grandson of a Lady! The great-grandson of a king! I will not be spoken to in this way."

"Last time I checked, you're a spoiled, yellow-ranked brat. Go complain to His Majesty. See if he cares that his Green Rank Master Chef has snubbed the youngest son of a lady who married below her rank."

Fir bristled. I wanted to cheer, but I bit my tongue and scrubbed a bowl with my good hand instead.

Hawak turned to an apprentice. "Tanoak, you're in charge while I'm gone. If you see this fox come around here, call the guard. Or save yourself the trouble and gut him on the spot. Your butchery work has greatly improved."

"Yes, sir," Tanoak replied, standing straight and tall as an ash tree.

Hawak stared Fir down until he stumbled out of the kitchen. Then Hawak threw his rag on the ground and swore.

HAWAK GAVE a brief speech to all of us about not letting the kitchen burn down during his absence. Barring any delays, the carter stations could get him to Sandhead in three days. His Majesty had ordered him to stay for at least ten, or longer if his grandmother hadn't recovered.

Sixteen days. That seemed like an eternity for the palace to be without Hawak. He left after lunch.

That afternoon, one of the apprentices burned three crocks of buckwheat, filling the kitchens with smoke. Another failed to whisk the bean cake dough properly and ended up with an inedible, lumpy mess. A third cut his finger and attempted to treat it with a quick sour thimbleberry tea that granted strength-of-heart, but that only made his wound bleed faster. He should have made endurance-of-skin to encourage clotting. The apprentices scrambled to remake their dishes as servants arrived to fetch platters for their masters' and fellows' supper.

Chaos reigned. Tanoak shouted himself hoarse—salal jam or honey-braised spinach stems would help, but time allowed no such luxury. Servants whined and complained at being made to wait, slowing the apprentices further.

I ached to stand, take charge of the kitchen, and make order from chaos. But of course I couldn't do that.

Without Hawak to monitor things, dishes seemed to dirty themselves at double the usual rate. My arms ached as I tried to keep up.

"Dami," Osem said, "we won't finish at this speed. C'mon, strong-of-arm."

"Strong-of-arm. Not endurance-of-arm. Though right now, I'd rather be lazy-of-everything," I muttered. The stew on the inside of this crock might as well be plaster.

Osem laughed. "If we're lucky, the King will revise his orders and send someone to fetch Hawak back before he reaches Sandhead."

"If we could send Fir away at the same time, then I'd feel better." Did he enjoy causing trouble? That couldn't be all. He was up to something.

Osem picked up the next crock—filthy, with hotpot bubbled up and burned onto the outside—and grabbed a handful of salt. "You're that upset about losing Hawak? He's married, you know. I'd stick with Bane."

No matter how hard I protested, Osem kept teasing me about him. I flustered. "Doesn't talking make us scrub slower?"

"But I enjoy it more." Her mouth tugged up in her about-to-tease-me smile. "Bane will be heartbroken if you abandon his affections to try and steal a married man."

I sighed. "This isn't about Bane."

And then I found myself explaining Fir's robbery in Meadowind. At least talking blocked out the pandemonium of the kitchens.

"You're sure it was him? Not someone who looks like him?"

I nodded and grabbed a clean rag.

Osem pursed her lips, serious for once. "It almost sounds like he wanted to make you late, get you dismissed—I mean, that almost happened. But then why not steal your letter?"

Could that have been his real goal? "My father tucked it into my mantle."

"Harder to find and harder to grab." Osem nodded thoughtfully. "The snake could have scared you away, or worse. The real question," Osem muttered, "is if you're the target. Given his history of tormenting servants... maybe he's trying to get someone on the waiting list *into* the palace. I underestimated him."

Had Osem always been this clever, or had living in the palace taught her to think like that? "Has anyone arrived, since me?"

"Not with the list moving so slow. Fir's pranks scared off everyone who wasn't determined to stay a long time ago."

I chewed those ideas over as I scrubbed. Fir couldn't have met Dami before—he'd believed me when I claimed to be her. His actions probably weren't personal. But how could getting rid of one servant justify trekking to Meadowind or planting the snake?

I didn't have time to contemplate. A servant with a black skirt, her hair sweaty and plastered to her forehead, burst into the kitchen. She leaned against the doorframe, panting. Her voice cut through the clamor, sharp as vinegar. "Lady Sulat has gone into labor."

Osem jerked upright. "She's at seven months!"

Tanoak froze, terrified.

"Still—" The servant paused to breathe. "The baby's coming. She needs a meal to determine the birthgift for the child, my prayers to the Ancestor that it lives."

Hawak had traveled a half-day already. A messenger couldn't fetch him back in time.

Mouth dry, I turned back to my pots. Tanoak would have to do his best.

"Does she need any calming infusion, in the meantime?" Tanoak asked.

The servant shook her head. "She took tea recently. Her first labor was fast—she needs a meal before the child comes."

"For what birthgift?" Tanoak asked.

"I... she just said to hurry."

Of course she didn't name anything. A premature child didn't need a gift, it needed a meal that would help it live. Strength, agility, senses, endurance—the unfortunate child couldn't lean any one direction. Its only hope at seeing tomorrow was a balanced soul, a balanced body, a meal of balanced flavor.

"Perception-of-eye. That's what the general himself has, correct? Good for archery or overseeing battles. We'll do that," Tanoak said.

The servant, oblivious, nodded and waited in the doorway. The other servants folded their arms and muttered about late meals—but thankfully they decided to wait in the hall.

Tanoak gathered bowls, cutting boards, and ingredients in his lanky arms. Huckleberries weren't in season, so he shouted at another apprentice to grab some dried blueberries from the cellar.

I gritted my teeth. I couldn't be Plum, couldn't be the girl who'd helped her father with two dozen deliveries. Dami would say nothing. Dami would scrub pots, because she didn't know better.

Tanoak grated hotradish.

All wrong. Lady Sulat needed the strength of a balanced meal as well to overcome whatever ill-fated complication caused this.

Tanoak's hands shook. His grating wasn't even—*and* he hadn't peeled the skin first. A muddy dish. The child would have no birthgift and it wouldn't matter, because it wouldn't survive the delivery.

I needed to stay quiet. I needed to do nothing. My life, my sister's life, my parent's wellbeing, and Nana's afterlife were all at risk.

But if I sat here and scrubbed crocks, that baby would die because I did nothing. My life wouldn't be worth saving.

I felt as woozy as I had when I put my hand in the coals. I hungered for some vinegared venison marrow to give my frame strength. Slowly, I set down the crock I'd been scrubbing. I stood and washed my hands. My injured palm shone pink now, the fresh, tender skin growing in nicely.

Osem gave me a strange look.

But I didn't know how to explain, so I didn't. Acid burning deep in my throat, I walked up to Tanoak, back as straight as I could make it.

"You're doing this wrong."

"Excuse me?" He looked at me like I'd sprouted leeks from my ears.

I took a deep breath. Tanoak and the other apprentices had shown me kindness, but none of them had any business cooking this meal. And I didn't have time to debate. "You're going to step aside. I am going to cook. I will not let your incompetence kill a baby."

CHAPTER TWELVE

I grabbed a polished stone bowl and cracked three eggs in. I whisked, hand whirring.

Tanoak gaped at me. So did the other apprentices. Proper whisking takes skill and practice to do it right, to do it fast. A skill I shouldn't have.

"Are there any fresh clams?" Eggs gently targeted the whole body —clams did the same and would boost the effect.

Tanoak shook his head.

"Is there any stock, made from a whole duck or rabbit carcass?"

"Here," one of the other apprentices said.

"Good. Place it on the table."

He did so. He seemed too shocked to do anything else. A spoonful at a time, I added the hot stock to the eggs, always whisking. Only a little stock. Too much too fast would cook the eggs and leave me with strings.

I tasted the mixture. Honey was too bright for these flavors. "Maple syrup. Scallions. And parsley."

Those ingredients would add sweet, spicy, and sour without overwhelming the dish. I added a bit of this, a bit of that, tasted, and adjusted again.

Tanoak seemed to have gathered himself out of shock. He frowned at me, taking charge. "I don't know what you're doing."

I dipped a spoon into the concoction, then handed it to him. His eyes lit up.

"*You* don't know what *you're* doing," I returned. Tanoak had no response for that.

I placed the bowl in the cooler dust of ashes and whisked furiously. The eggs needed to cook without scrambling.

The maid coughed. "Excuse me for interrupting, but she said it's urgent."

"And it's not finished." Raw goop would harm the baby, throwing its body and soul out of balance.

The mixture changed color and thickened. I found a clean bowl and poured the soft-set custard inside. I tasted it again. One more pinch of salt. Perfect. No need to garnish—I thrust it straight into the servant's hands. "Give Lady Sulat this."

She nodded politely and ran out.

A kitchenful of apprentices and one dish-scrubber stared at me. I coughed, mouth dry. I didn't have any explanation. "Excuse me."

I brushed past Tanoak and slid into my small room. Darkness mercifully swallowed me. No one knocked. The normal sounds of the kitchen—chopping, sizzling, stirring—gradually returned. Servants bustled in and out, retrieving long-awaited suppers.

While I cooked, I had nothing but concentration. Now my heart pounded. My palms sweated. My tender new skin smarted from being so carelessly used.

I wouldn't get to sit here forever. Too many people—apprentices and servants—had seen. Someone would come. Someone would ask questions. And when they did... how could I answer? I couldn't let this hurt my parents.

I wished I knelt at my family's shrine or in a redwood circle, where I could properly offer my Ancestors a bowl of good food. I wished Grandma was alive—she used to pray for me. She'd known a number of our ancestors when she was a child. She knew how to plead with them.

My voice creaked out, stiff as overworked dough. "I just want to keep my family alive."

The Ancestors prickled my soul. My plea rang false. I'd wanted to save an infant, too.

"I don't want this to fall on my parents' heads. Or Dami's."

Ah, but I could protect Dami, even if I couldn't save my parents from the back-taxes. I could lie. I'd tell them I was a street orphan. I'd jumped Dami on her way here, stolen her papers, and took her position. Given the state I arrived in, who would doubt it?

They'd execute me for lying to the Royal House. A fitting punishment given that I had, indeed, lied to them.

"The truth is," I whispered, insides numb, "I don't want to die, either."

No thoughts followed. My Ancestors couldn't grant me wisdom there.

"Please?"

Any sense of a presence outside myself disappeared. I sat alone in the tiny room. What would Sorrel think of me, if he could see me now? Would he be amused at his former bride-to-be's predicament? Sorrowful?

I wished I'd gotten to know him so I could at least picture a face, imagine a response.

I folded my hands in my lap and closed my eyes, letting the dark hollowness of the room swallow me. I had made the choice to come here—not Dami. And what did I have to fear? If I hanged, I could proudly tell Nana I'd done everything I could to take care of her. Maybe we'd be Hungry Ghosts together.

Someone knocked. I didn't answer. The door opened anyway, revealing the same polite servant in the black skirt with two not-so-timid, spear-carrying men behind her. They wore black uniforms—military soldiers, not Palace Guards.

"Lady Sulat requires your presence," the servant said, bowing.

The mother, at least, had survived the labor. I nodded and stood, though my legs felt as sturdy as soggy dumplings. Had something gone amiss with the child? Or was Lady Sulat following through with the inevitable questioning?

Maybe Lady Sulat always sent soldiers to fetch people, but she probably considered me a spy. An enemy in this drawn-out war.

The apprentices all watched me leave the kitchen. None smiled. Tanoak stood stiff as a soldier at a funeral. Only Osem wouldn't meet my eye, but washed crocks as if nothing had happened. She was good at that—at pretending talking about the Hungry Ghost meant nothing, at pretending that a dozen apprentices hadn't hanged this winter from the walls of Askan-Wod.

Well. I had my lie ready. Maybe the King would be generous and waive my parents' back-taxes. At least they'd keep their rank this way.

After we passed a number of spring-scented gardens, we reached a set of apartments much like others in the palace. The guards marched me up the porch steps, between two red-varnished pillars. Another guard held the door aside for us.

I barely glimpsed the sitting room—polished wood, rugs, and chairs—as the soldiers hurried me through another lattice door.

The curtains were drawn back from the bed's alcove. A single lamp burned on an end table. The place smelled of wood resin and herbed soap, but that didn't quite override the tang of birthing blood. Intricate carvings of flowers and birds adorned the bed, washing basin, and wardrobe. Their polished redwood shone darkly in the dim light.

Lady Sulat—who else could it be?—sat in the bed. She looked a few years shy of thirty. Despite her ashen pallor and sweat-slick skin, her face was composed. Almost as cold as Lady Egal's. The tiny infant in her arms nursed steadily.

The child had survived the birth. Whatever else happened now, I'd made the right choice to stop Tanoak.

The guards took positions at either side of the bed and the servant nudged me forward. The child's birthglow hadn't dissipated yet—the birth was less than an hour old, then.

Why would she bring me here so soon?

Then I saw the glow. The tones were muted, meaning the gift would be weak, but it spread from wrinkled head to tiny, perfect toes. My throat knotted. I'd managed not this-of-arms or that-of-foot, but I'd gifted his entire being.

And the colors. Muted, yellow, green, red, and white swirled over the newborn. Perception, agility, strength, and endurance. This infant was an All-of-All. A rare feat among chefs. Rarely *tried* among chefs.

I'd made an All-of-All. Perhaps I should have tried a little less hard with my cooking.

But I didn't mean that, not looking at the so-small child, half the size of other babies I'd helped with. With these gifts, the child would, Ancestors providing, grow old.

"Why," Lady Sulat began in a cool tone, "did you not inform the Redwood Palace in your application for a post that you are twice-gifted?"

I choked. I wasn't. "I'm... I'm..."

"Strong-of-Arm and Perceptive-of-Taste, yes, I can see that now," Lady Sulat continued, her tone firm.

"Umm." This wasn't what I'd expected. Looking at Lady Sulat's eyes, glossy as pools at midnight, she didn't believe a word of it, either. Why would she help me? Pretend my lie was one of omission instead of commission?

"Your father must have been quite talented, to balance sweet and spicy at just the right levels to grant you both gifts. And in a hotpot of... what would it be, for arms and tongue?"

"Parsnips and morels," I replied reflexively.

Her mouth quirked. I should have bumbled the question.

"My son is healthy, for one born so early. As an All-of-All, I have hope that he will continue strong. You have my thanks for this. Your post as a palace servant will shift from dish scrubber to part of my personal staff, where I may keep an eye on your talents."

So she wanted to watch me. Because she didn't trust me, or because I could be of use? However happy I'd be to skip scrubbing crocks, I'd miss Osem. I ignored the lump in my throat. I was still alive, surprisingly enough. I bowed, grateful. "Thank you."

Lady Sulat nodded, then turned to the servant. "Poppy, please return these dishes to the kitchen, then report the change in staff to Lady Egal."

Poppy put the empty bowl of custard and a half-empty mug of tea on the tray and swept past me. Something smelled wrong. Ever so faintly, but ever-so-certainly *wrong*. I caught Poppy by the shoulder. She gave me an odd look—as did Lady Sulat—but I ignored the prickling feeling and picked up the mug. I sniffed, then dipped my finger in the tea and tasted it.

"Do they not feed you in the kitchens?" Lady Sulat asked.

"No. I mean yes. What I mean to say, is, Lady Sulat, is that your early delivery shouldn't have happened. You were poisoned."

CHAPTER THIRTEEN

"Poisoned?"

"Usually this sweet cranberry tea would give you endurance-of-womb—encouraging a long and healthy pregnancy. But someone slipped soured red raspberry leaf in here. Raspberry leaf targets the womb so intensely I don't know any chef who'd give it to a healthy pregnant woman, just in case the cooking was off and it had an ill effect. It's best to use only in emergencies.

"The soured red raspberry leaf—strength-of-womb—was enough to start contractions. The endurance-of-womb effect from the cranberry guaranteed that those contractions continued until you delivered." I bit my lip. Had I said too much? I'd created an All-of-All today; analyzing a poison seemed inconsequential in comparison.

Lady Sulat studied me as she massaged the infant's back. How could she have such a piercing gaze, yet hold a child with such tenderness? "You're hiding something. But you didn't do this to us."

I didn't move. Not even to swallow.

"Poppy, you may continue taking those to the kitchens. Tell no one."

Poppy bowed and glided out the door. Lady Sulat turned her cold gaze back to me. "In the morning, you'll assume your duties as my poison-taster. For now, Suruc will show you to your room."

Poison taster. The king used one, but I didn't think anyone else in the palace did. The Master Chef tasted nearly everything himself and the servants who delivered meals were trusted members of the Royal Household. Who would risk condemning themselves to a cursed afterlife?

Not that Lady Sulat didn't have cause for concern. I bowed, not trusting my voice. Hopefully my palate wouldn't fail me.

My insides roiled. Food was for strengthening the body, for health and longevity. How could someone call themselves a chef, then stand in a kitchen and use their life-giving skills to attack a mother and child?

I followed Suruc—a man in a black uniform with shoulders a bear would envy—to a room so small it felt like an emptied closet. A single musty mattress lay inside.

Sleep didn't come. Not with Suruc breathing outside my door. Standing guard. I was a prisoner, but I didn't understand the rules of this jail.

Some time later, footsteps approached. "She's in there?" a male voice asked.

"Yes," Suruc replied.

"Good. Lady Egal was agreeable and registered the change in the archives. The Palace Guard probably won't try to take her now, but Lady Sulat wants this door guarded. Someone will relieve you at the next watch."

"Understood."

I wished I understood, but at least the brief exchange gave me something. Lady Sulat didn't want the Palace Guard to have me. That must be why she called me quickly, promoted me, and made the change official before anyone else learned about what happened. She'd dubbed me double-gifted. If she hadn't done all those things, I'd be sitting in a prison cell, awaiting a trial and execution.

The guard was for my safety, at least partly.

But *why* had she done all that? Lady Sulat had no reason to trust me, even if I'd saved her child.

I couldn't help but feel that clever Osem would have answers, if I could talk to her.

Someone left a black skirt, befitting of my station as Lady Sulat's servant, outside my door. I changed into it, then my guard escorted me to Lady Sulat's bedside. Next to her rested a tray of sour bone-marrow soup and grilled bean cakes drizzled with sweet cranberry syrup—all good for a recovering mother.

"Taste. Tell me if there's anything wrong with it," Lady Sulat commanded. The baby slept skin-to-skin in a wrap against her chest. Such a tiny infant needed his mother's warmth.

I tried the soup first. "Under salted."

Lady Sulat raised an eyebrow.

"But not poisoned." I hesitated, then tried the bean cakes and cranberries. The reconstituted berries were a shade too sweet, but nothing sinister accompanied them. "It's all safe."

"But you disapprove of the cranberries as well."

I replied diplomatically. "I think everyone will be happier when Hawak returns."

Lady Sulat's eyebrow quirked, as if she found my evasive answer amusing. She sipped the soup. "Can you stand quietly, without speaking?"

"Of course, Lady Sulat," I replied. I had no desire to draw more attention to myself.

Lady Sulat nodded. The baby woke and cried; a middle-aged nurse came and changed his soiled under things. After spending time with the Hungry Ghost, the tarry, black mess could have been roses. As the servant worked, Lady Sulat spoke to one of her six guards. I didn't know if she usually had so many, or if their number increased after yesterday. "I want to interview the kitchen staff. If you'd be so kind as to escort them here, one by one, and keep them on the far side of the room away from me and my child."

The soldier bowed and left; the servant handed back the infant.

Lady Sulat's face only broke its cool veneer when she gazed down at the tiny babe and rubbed his back. Despite his size, he seemed healthy—almost certainly thanks to his birthgift. For once, I didn't resent Dami for running off and forcing me into the palace. She couldn't have saved that child.

Tanoak came first. Even from her position sitting in her bed, Lady Sulat managed to stare coldly down her nose at him. "I am disappointed in the kitchen staff. A dish scrubber girl had to correct you. What would have happened if you didn't have a daughter from a real chef's house?"

Tanoak bowed, fidgeting with the hem of his shirt. "I... my most sincere apologies."

"Apologies are not enough. I want to know that you are competent. How would you treat a sore throat?"

He stammered, but managed to spit out, "Sweet and sour beet stems, Lady Sulat."

"And what if beet stems were unavailable?"

"Ah, spinach stems. But that comes into season with beets. If neither is available fresh, the best thing's pickled beet stems."

He'd gotten that much right; thick beets stems targeted the neck better than spinach stems, but fresh was stronger than pickled. Even if the sour-crisp beet stems tasted better.

"What if someone suffered from digestive issues?"

Lady Sulat kept up a barrage of questions until Tanoak was sweating like a diced onion over even heat. Then she asked, "How would you encourage labor?"

"A sour herbal infusion—cranberry would be best, but in a pinch, you could use red raspberry leaf if you were careful about it."

I stared in horror, but Tanoak didn't notice me. Lady Sulat asked a few more questions, then nodded demurely. "I'm satisfied. Thorn."

She turned to one of her guards. "Please return this man to his post and bring me another member of the kitchen staff."

They left. Lady Sulat daintily ate a few dried cranberries. "Dami. In the future, I ask you not to gape."

"I... apologize."

"Thrown in with so many other questions, Tanoak didn't notice. He is innocent. A guilty party would stumble, lie, or glance at you, wondering what you might have learned here. I would rather not remove you from the room."

"I will be still, Lady Sulat."

The next cooking apprentice came. Once again, Lady Sulat gestured at me and humiliated the young man. Then came the barrage of questions. He answered much like Tanoak, though his recommendation for incontinence would have exasperated the problem.

So it went with the rest of the apprentices. Once they'd all left, Lady Sulat addressed Poppy. "Do you know who handed you the tray with my infusion?"

"No. I fetched it from its normal spot."

She turned to me. "Did you see anything unusual in the kitchens?"

"Other than Hawak's absence?" I'd kept my head down as much as possible during the mad commotion. "I'm afraid the kitchen was... less than orderly. Any of the apprentices could have done it without being noticed. Or any servant waiting for a tray."

Lady Sulat nodded. "No one in this palace is stupid enough to poison me and do it *carelessly*. You'll speak of this to no one. All of you. I simply delivered early."

The guards bowed their heads. I did likewise.

Someone knocked on the lattice door. "My Lady Sulat, the Purple Heir Lord Valerian desires an audience."

"Enter," Lady Sulat called.

The heir to the throne, King Alder's son, dashed in—a twelve-year-old boy with fine cheekbones and a slender nose that made him seem four years younger. "Aunt Sulat! I just heard. Are you all right? Your little one?"

All the coldness washed from her face. She brushed Valerian's hair back from his eyes. "Yes, of course. But I can't let you hold your cousin yet. He needs to stay near me for warmth. Maybe in a month."

"I didn't come *just* to see the baby. I was terrified for *both* of you."

The boy spoke with such charming elocution, like he'd been raised on the polite talk of high-ranked lords and ladies. I blinked and remembered who this was—he *had* grown up in a palace.

Lady Sulat actually chuckled. "Well, I'm glad to report that we're well. This charming young lady cooked a marvelous meal for both of us."

The Heir of Rowak himself flicked me a smile. "That was lucky, with Hawak gone."

"Yes. Lucky." Lady Sulat's words stung like needles.

In all the rush, in all the chaos, it hadn't occurred to me until now. The poison showing up while Hawak was gone—that couldn't be a coincidence. I felt like an idiot. Fir had gotten rid of Hawak, which meant he almost certainly had a hand in trying to kill a *baby*. I felt ill. But he'd tried to kill me, too, hadn't he? Why should I think him above infanticide?

Lady Sulat continued in a more cheerful tone. "Tell me, how go your studies?"

"Marvelous! I finished *On the Governance of a People* and I wanted to tell you all these amazing things!"

Lady Sulat leaned against her pillows, smiling softly, while the Heir quoted bits of his book. I confess I couldn't stop listening. He had such ideas for improving roads and increasing trade. What a precocious child.

Lady Sulat occasionally asked a question, like how such a change would affect carters and farmers, or how he might garner political support for a new law.

Then his young forehead wrinkled. He excelled at extrapolating consequences but fumbled the political questions.

Halfway through one such question, Lady Sulat yawned.

"What am I thinking?" Purple Lord Valerian jumped to his feet. "You just had a baby. You must be exhausted. I'll go. Recover soon."

Lady Sulat drifted off almost as soon as Valerian left with his Palace Guards. I doubted I could sleep with people watching me, but perhaps she'd gotten used to it.

I chewed my lip. I still didn't understand why Lady Sulat had spared me. But perhaps I should simply trust her and tell her everything I knew about Fir. She'd housed Osem when her family perished and gave Bane a post. How many others had Lady Sulat helped?

The outside guard quietly passed a letter into Lady Sulat's room, but she woke with the whisper of sliding wood. The guard winced, but Lady Sulat didn't glare. She gestured for the envelope. Her child continued to sleep.

Lady Sulat pulled the paper from its brocade envelope and read it through. Then she turned to me. "Dami. Your trial for treason will commence two weeks from today."

I froze. "I'm standing trial?"

"In fourteen days. Thirteen, if you don't count today."

"I... I thought..."

"As a servant of the Royal House, you are assured a trial before the Purple-Blue Council and you are allotted two weeks to send for any witnesses you may need. Since you serve under me, I am responsible for you until then. I could relinquish that responsibility to the Palace Guard, but I will not.

"But if you flee, my soldiers will track you. When they find you, they will slice the tendons in your ankles, leaving you unable to walk, and drag you back here for trial. Understood?"

CHAPTER FOURTEEN

"No, I don't understand. I thought you were protecting me."

Lady Sulat regarded me coolly. "At the very least, you lied to the Royal House about your birthgift—you cooked a meal that created an All-of-All. Do you think I can make so many witnesses pretend it wasn't you? That I can bring back the whispers already circulating?"

Cold dread congealed in my gut.

"I stopped the Palace Guard from whisking you away to some torture hole to never be heard from again," Lady Sulat said. "My actions have guaranteed that you *will* have a trial, nothing more."

My head throbbed. "You said something about sending for witnesses. Must I bring any? Will King Alder summon my parents if I don't ask them to come?"

I didn't want them anywhere near this mess.

She raised a single eyebrow. "Not summoning your parents to defend you, in this case, is tantamount to admitting guilt. King Alder has no reason to send for them."

Good. If they came here and anyone learned they'd been complicit in my deception, they'd stand trial, too. "Thank you for explaining."

After that, Lady Sulat sent me to do some mending with Poppy.

Out of her mistress' gaze, Poppy relaxed her formalities. She cheerfully offered me her favorite porcupine needle. Then she helped me thread it and, after seeing my stitches, tactfully switched me from Lady Sulat's clothes to hem sheets. She asked polite questions and tried to engage me in conversation.

But all of her kindness washed over me, like so much oil on top of vinegar. I should be grateful, but why would Lady Sulat spare me from immediate arrest? Was this gratitude for saving her child's life? She didn't seem particularly thankful.

"Lady Sulat looks cold, but she's thoughtful when it matters," Poppy offered. "You'll get used to her."

"I have two weeks until I'm sent to trial. It's not a lot of time to get used to anything."

Poppy's brows furrowed, though her stitches continued in their tiny perfection without slowing. "You think you're guilty of something?"

The way she phrased it, *something* meant poisoning Lady Sulat.

Of course Lady Sulat spoke coldly to me. We couldn't find her poisoner. I had all the skill of a chef. I had access to the kitchens.

I tried to think like Osem would. If I were Lady Sulat's enemy, I hadn't acted alone. What had Lady Sulat said? *No one in this palace is stupid enough to poison me and do it carelessly.*

A dish scrubber had no reason to poison her at all. No, I'd be working for someone else. But if she suspected me, why not hand me to the Palace Guard? Maybe she was slighting them, given the rivalry between the Guard and the military.

"I've only tried to help Lady Sulat." True, though not a direct answer to the question. I stabbed myself with the needle again and swore. I'd never been good at sewing.

"Here." Poppy, ever helpful, repositioned my fabric and the way I held the needle. "Try again."

I did regular chores with Poppy for the rest of the day. After tasting Lady Sulat's supper, I asked if I could see the letter against me. I needed to know all the specifics.

She nodded for a guard to comply. "Unfortunately, they didn't accuse you of much."

My throat tightened. This woman wasn't my ally. I skimmed the short letter. It only charged me with lying to the Royal House about my birthgift. Which was more than enough to get me hanged.

"News of my poisoning is, alas, circulating. Rumor has it you're responsible."

How did Lady Sulat hear so much, laying in bed, recovering? I glanced at her soldiers, but of course none of them wore a sign saying *Master of Reconnaissance*.

"I petitioned the Ministry of Justice to also charge you with espionage, but as expected, the gesture was futile."

How generous of her. "I'm dead either way."

Lady Sulat shook her head. "Espionage would mark you as an enemy of the state. Instead of facing the Purple-Blue Council, you'd have a military tribunal, full of *my* officers. But the Minister of Justice is rather partial to having a vote in all trials and he was justified in turning down my request. There's no evidence you're a spy."

My throat burned. I'd never thought an accusation of spying would be desirable. "These ministers... do you know how they'll vote?"

"Ah, that is the right question. The Council decides guilt; the King allots punishment. The Council has become more cautious in their verdicts since the twelve apprentices hanged—they expected a mere dismissal—but King Alder's still influential and you're clearly guilty. I'd be surprised if you were condemned at anything less than an eight-to-two vote. For lying to the Royal House, the law prescribes anything from dismissal and fines to hanging."

The way she said *hanging* left me no doubt that would be King Alder's preference. "You're... the Minister of Military Affairs, right? You're part of the Purple-Blue Council."

"I am." She stared at me, adding nothing more. I still wasn't sure if she wanted to save me or kill me.

I dropped my eyes to the damning letter, futilely wishing the words would change.

The bottom paragraph snagged my gaze. It named the man who'd originally brought me to the attention of the Ministry of Justice. Yellow-ranked Fir of Askan-Wod.

Fir, as far as I knew, had no skills with poisons. And I couldn't imagine why he'd wish such harm to Lady Sulat or myself. But he was involved.

Perhaps if I could uncover his crimes—find evidence linking him to the poisoning—the King would grant me leniency for my lie. Maybe the Council would take pity and vote me innocent to spare me the King's wrath. Or maybe I'd hang.

But if I only had two weeks, I'd spend them trying to stop Fir from hurting anyone else.

ALL NIGHT, I thought about what Osem said yesterday—that perhaps Fir wasn't so much attacking me as trying to get the next girl on the servant waiting list into the Redwood Palace. Unfortunately, that was the only clue I had.

In the morning, I tasted Lady Sulat's breakfast—more marrow soup and sweet cranberry bean cakes—and managed not to critique the balance. Strangely, I missed scrubbing crocks. Watching the apprentices make their mistakes. Smelling their mistakes burnt onto pottery. Most of all I missed Osem. But I doubted anyone would let a rumored poisoner near the kitchens.

"L-Lady Sulat," I ventured.

She flicked me a glance.

"I was hoping for your permission to visit the Hall of Records."

"Go. Moss. Accompany her."

Moss was an older soldier, with gray hair and knotted hands. We cut through a budding flower garden, then the empty springball courts. Dew clung to the ground and my skirt. Moss clasped his hands behind his back and hummed—loudly and out-of-tune.

"You're cheerful."

"Why shouldn't I be?"

I frowned. "Aren't you worried I might try to run away? Make your life difficult?"

"Ah! I'm hoping you will." He pulled a bolas from his belt. "I made a bet with Suruc. If you run and I only trip you, I owe him five amber chips. If I break your legs, he owes me one."

Unnerving, to see him smile as he said it. "Why would he give you such odds?"

"Because he's an idiot!" He laughed. "It's been a long time since I tricked someone into less than ten to one. "

After that, I walked slowly. Just in case Moss had any idea that I might be trying to run.

The Hall of Records was its own building, with a broad porch and a row of those finely polished redwood pillars supporting the eaves. However elegant the structure, I flinched from the blue-clad guard before the door, remembering my trip to the aviary with Bane.

The Palace Guard sneered at us. Moss jogged up the steps. "Ah, thanks for decorating the door. Doesn't it feel nice, to be good for something?"

My lungs froze; was he that desperate to use his bolas today? But the bristling guard let us pass.

"What were you doing?" I hissed once we were inside.

Moss shrugged. "It'd be rude not to greet him, but what else can you say to a Palace Guard?"

Apparently the antagonism came from two directions. At least nothing had happened. I exhaled. Inside, elegantly carved shelves stretched from floor to ceiling—each full of slender, gleaming boxes. In the center rested several low, circular tables made from cross-sections of young redwoods, along with flat cushions for sitting. Perfect for hours of reading.

A pair of archivists greeted us. They were a matched set—wrinkled faces, slouched backs, blue-ranked sleeves, and smiles sweeter than honey. Something in the way they stood next to each other said they'd been married for a long time.

"I'm Kochan, the Chief Royal Archivist," the man said. "And my wife, Royal Archivist Linaan. How may we be of assistance?"

"I'd like to see the waiting list for servers in the palace."

Linaan grinned, disappeared into the stacks, and returned with one of those manuscript boxes. She set it on the table. "There you go!"

"Thank you." I rested the lid next to the box, laying each page face-down in it as I browsed. I finally found my sister's page, the same one she'd had Nisaat fetch when I first arrived. An elegant hand recorded her genealogy, birthgift, and the date of her application.

I flipped to the next page. Ilasa of Lillywhite. My pulse throbbed in my throat. "So... this is the girl next in line to serve in the palace?"

The girl Fir wanted to bring in. She was endurance-of-leg. Why would Fir need a runner?

"Well, now she is. The girl in front of her resigned a few days ago."

That couldn't be a coincidence. "Where's her page now?"

"With the Ministry of the Treasury. She has an awful lot of back-taxes to pay."

"And she's paying them?"

Linaan shrugged. "Something about getting married instead. Her family can afford the fine and I guess they spoil her."

"How common are resignations?"

"We haven't had one in two years."

This couldn't be a coincidence. Likely, this was the girl he'd been trying to get inside the palace, and he'd finally found another way to do it. One where having her name on the list would look odd or become a liability. I chewed my lip. Or he'd reached some kind of deadline, some crucial moment, and had to risk a more difficult route of entry?

When Dami put her name on the list, we thought she'd join the Redwood Palace in six months, not three years. Three years during which Fir pulled pranks and scared servants away, trying to hurry the list. And who better to do it? Everyone seemed to dismiss him as an inconsequential loafer living off Lady Egal's charity.

Fir became aggressive—robbing me, leaving the snake. The actions of a man running out of time.

"Do you know who the resigned girl is?"

"No." Linaan shook her head. "Someone from the Treasury came for her paper. I didn't look at the name."

"How do I see the records of the Ministry of the Treasury?" I asked.

Linaan laughed. "You become a Royal Auditor. Members of the Royal Household are welcome in the Hall of Records, but the Treasury's another matter."

OUTSIDE, Moss showed me the Office of the Treasury. With its dozen Palace Guards. No, I wasn't stealing those records anytime soon.

"Could Lady Sulat look at that record? Get the name?"

"The Treasury Minister has no great love for her. War plays havoc on ledgers."

"That's a no, then."

Moss laughed. "That's an it-would-take-longer-than-two-weeks, so-why-do-you-care?"

Even if he did have a robust, grandpa laugh, I didn't share his mirth.

"Why is this girl so important?"

"Don't worry about it." If Lady Sulat couldn't help, why explain? I still couldn't tell if she was my ally or not.

At least I knew one person who wasn't my enemy: Lady Egal. If she backed Fir's plots, she would have tossed me out of the palace instead of appointing me to the kitchens. As Matron of the Household, she'd approved this girl's application. And she might remember her name.

I paused. Nisaat had fetched my records. Perhaps she'd glimpsed the name beneath Dami's application?

I returned to Lady Sulat's quarters, tested her lunch, then headed out with Moss at my heels, like a faithful dog who'd like nothing more than to turn me into meat chunks for supper. Again, I walked slowly.

Nisaat sat on a bench under a cherry tree, near the gate. Pink and white blossoms trailed from the well-manicured branches. I didn't see any other servants, just Palace Guards. Nisaat's emerald green skirt with the bleached eagle was neat as always, her braided sandals well-oiled.

"Does Lady Egal often expect visitors?" I asked.

She smiled and gestured for me to sit next to her. "You look a sight better than when I first dragged you in. And it's not always visitors for her. As Matron of the Household, she's responsible to provide an escort for other guests, too."

"Ah."

"Besides," Nisaat lowered her voice, smiling, "she likes knowing everybody that goes in and out of that gate."

It seemed like everyone in this palace gathered secrets. Myself included. Moss stood some fifteen paces away, hands clasped behind his back.

"I have a question for you."

Nisaat's spine straightened and her eyes flashed. "Yes?"

"Did you happen to see the name of the girl's application under mine? When you fetched it for Lady Egal?"

Her shoulders slumped. "Oh. You're not here to ask about Bane. He's mortified it's been so long since he could call on you."

I shifted on the bench, my cheeks heating. Of course that's what she'd expected. I couldn't exactly explain that my double-life was the last thing Bane needed in a spouse.

"I know the trial delays things, but once your name is cleared of this slander..." she trailed off. Nisaat didn't realize it wasn't slander at all. "Did you enjoy touring the palace with him? He seemed to think so."

"Except for the part where he got attacked."

Nisaat shot the Palace Guards a dirty look, not that they were watching. "I'm afraid I didn't notice the name, but I could take you to the Hall of Records and help you find it."

"That's all right." I stood. "Thanks for talking with me."

TO LADY EGAL'S APARTMENTS, then. I breathed deeply, assuring myself as I climbed those porch steps that this woman wasn't Fir's ally, even if she disliked me.

A door servant admitted me into her sitting room; Moss waited outside.

Lady Egal still radiated regal beauty. Her slate-gray hair was sculpted into a dignified bun, her posture sang of poise, and her eyes seemed to flay the flesh from my bones. She laid her brush down on her desk.

"Yes?" Her monosyllabic greeting dripped with disdain.

"I had a question for you."

"Had? Did you lose it?" Sunlight streamed from the lattice-and-eagle window behind her, giving her a supernatural glow.

I swallowed my pride. "The girl on the serving list after me. Do you remember her name?"

"Lazy girl. Haven't you checked the Hall of Records?"

She dipped her brush in the well of the inkstone and wrote, ignoring me.

My knees knocked like hollow gourds, but I didn't have any other source of information to turn to. "She resigned. I'd hoped—"

"Then perhaps you should ask the Treasury." Her tone left no doubt that she knew they wouldn't help me.

"Please. It's one name."

She looked up again, her eyes sharp, predatory. "My Fir's told me about you. How you accosted him on the road, begging for money because you'd gambled your traveling funds away. No wonder you arrived so disheveled! Do you know why he journeyed to Meadowind?"

I gaped. He'd robbed *me*.

"He was paying respects to my late husband's family shrine. To our lasting dismay, he arrived too late to warn me about your coarse habits. If I'd known, I would have turned you out from your post."

I nearly choked. "Nonsense. Another one of Fir's pranks. He's apparently notorious for those."

"Fir is a good boy. A sweet boy. The only grandson of mine, regardless of rank, who's ever cared more about me and his ancestors than about fighting his way to a higher position in life."

My marrow turned to slush as she leaned forward.

"I am glad that your base nature has caught up with you. I've already put in my request to the Minister of Justice to witness as to your suspicious, disheveled arrival. I'll add today's odd behavior." She glared, her scorn slicing me like obsidian through soft dough. "Leave my grandson alone. Now get out, before I call the Palace Guard."

CHAPTER FIFTEEN

"I could have told you Lady Egal's fond of Fir. Brings her infusions for her joints regularly."

"Thanks, Moss," I muttered.

But the trip wasn't a complete waste. I'd confirmed Lady Egal wasn't behind Fir and that Fir wanted me out of the palace. If not for the downpour, he would have beaten me to Askan-Wod by cart and gotten me dismissed. I silently thanked my Ancestors for the rain that I'd cursed while I was walking through it.

For the rest of the day, I worked in Lady Sulat's apartments trying to make up the long absence she'd generously granted me. I polished chairs and tables with Poppy in the sitting room—all carved with low-relief chickadees and pine boughs that required slow, thorough work. Busy hands made for a busy mind, Mother always said. If she needed to think, she worked. Exercise increased circulation, after all.

Even with the aid of work, I couldn't puzzle it out. Fir couldn't be acting alone—he didn't have the skill to poison Lady Sulat so subtly. What did anyone stand to gain from hurting her? Did someone want her post as Minister of Military Affairs? Or were they trying to get rid of her influence on Heir Valerian?

I needed to understand the structure of the Royal Family better.

Poppy left for her half-day off, so I scrubbed the floorboards alone. By evening, my knees ached and I reeked of varnish. Sleep came slowly. With the guard breathing outside my door, I couldn't stop thinking about my trial. One day closer.

In the morning, I tasted Lady Sulat's breakfast, then asked leave to revisit the Hall of Records. Again, she consented. I thanked my Ancestors for small favors and headed back, Moss at my heels.

The room smelled as it had yesterday—of paper and time and sanded wood. Kochan, the crinkled Chief Royal Archivist, arranged some manuscript boxes on a shelf. I didn't see his wife. "Ah! Did you not find what you needed yesterday?"

"Yes, I did, thanks to your excellent help." I bowed. "But I'm hoping to look at something else. You have a copy of the royal genealogy, I presume?"

"We have several copies. I do love seeing young folks interested in our heritage." He winked at me and shuffled off into the stacks.

Moss dropped into a chair and polished the granite of his bolas. "This job would be a lot more interesting if you weren't so boring."

"I'm not sorry in the least to disappoint."

Kochan returned in a moment with the box—the title page read *The Genealogy of the Purple and Blue of Rowak*. Ranks determined what position a person could hold in the government. Only Kings and their ratified heir held Purple rank—the ability to sit in the throne. Those of Blue rank were related to the Royal Family, though only a blue-ranked father *and* mother passed that high rank to their children. The titles Lord and Lady were granted to children of present or former kings, regardless of their rank.

I carefully turned pages until I reached the end. Rowak currently had three men of Purple rank: the ailing King Former Fulsaan who'd abdicated; our current monarch, King Alder; and his son, Lord Valerian. King Former Fulsaan had two sisters: Lady Thrush, who died giving birth to Captain Gano, and Blue Lady Egal. Gano started life green-ranked, a highly honored citizen, but had been adopted into the Blue Rank to fill the position of Captain of the Palace Guard. Apparently, his skill merited this honor.

My eyes blurred over the charts of Blue-rank people. Nothing jumped out at me here—just long lists of families and genealogies.

So I focused on the current King. He had three siblings. I passed over Red Lord Ospren—he'd been the Purple Heir but was exiled some eight years ago for stealing from the Treasury. Stripped to the Red rank, he now lived in a remote cabin near Rowak's southern border with the Toskang Empire, forced to remain inside on pain of death.

Alder was next oldest, then Blue Lady Sulat, followed by Blue Lord Torut, who was only a few years older than me. Near Fir's age. Had they grown up together? I could imagine them becoming friends. Co-conspirators.

"Chief Archivist Kochan... might you answer a question for me?" I asked.

He shuffled to my side. "Yes?"

"The Purple-Blue Council... they decide the appointment of Ministers, don't they?" I asked.

Kochan knelt next to me. "The Purple-Blue convenes on all of the highest positions and makes a decision after hearing the advice of the Ministry of the Interior."

The Ministry of the Interior regulated the assignment of government posts. "If, for example, a new Minister of Military Affairs was needed... who would they chose to take the position?"

"Such talk!" Kochan shook his head, then tapped Blue Lord Torut's name. "But I'd place my wager here."

I bit my lip. "So he's an ambitious man?"

Kochan frowned, wrinkles cascading up his cheeks. Gingerly, he replaced the pages back into their box and settled the lid on top. "This is starting to reek of politics. You're a yellow-ranked servant. You should keep to your post."

Kochan turned to Moss, as if seeking approval.

"She's already condemned to die in… what do you have now, Dami? Eleven days to your trial?" Moss pitched in cheerfully.

Kochan coughed from deep in his throat. "Well, if that's the case…" he glanced around the still-empty Hall of Records and lowered his voice. "General Yuin is popular. He and Lady Sulat are a powerful pair—especially if he ever returns victorious from this accursed war. Lord Torut is anything but ambitious. He'd make an excellent puppet for the king, no? King Alder gave him the responsibility of delivering offerings to the Royal Shrine every evening, with the stated purpose of preparing him for a post."

Odd. "I've never seen Lord Torut in the kitchens."

"He has a servant fetch the offering."

"Oh." Wouldn't getting it himself be more respectful? "You think the Purple-Blue Council would approve Lord Torut's appointment?"

Kochan nodded slowly. "King Alder still controls the Council."

"Thank you. For all your help." After all the plots, a straightforward answer was refreshing.

"I wish you luck in your trial." He smiled, then disappeared into the racks with the royal genealogy.

I'd need more than luck. Despite the bright day and the lilac hedges in bloom, my stomach sank. If Fir was the King's man, and if King Alder held sway over the Council, uncovering Fir's crime would guarantee my hanging.

"I doubt His Majesty did it," Moss said. "If, you know, you'd like to stop looking for rain on a fine day."

"Why not? He wouldn't have to sneak someone in through the waiting list?"

"Oh, that's the perfect way to sneak someone in. If he's caught at anything, he can feign innocence. But poisoning's a bit blunt for him. Besides, he needs Lady Sulat and General Yuin if he wants a chance of winning this war."

"So he's not scared of her."

"No, he's smart enough to strike *after*." Moss laughed. "There's no great love between them. The King Former, their father? King Alder only lets Lady Sulat visit him once a week, under his close, personal supervision. I think he's worried they'd plot against him otherwise."

I peered at Moss, at his inconspicuous, middle-aged face. He spoke freely. Suspiciously so. The look he and Kochan exchange replayed in my mind. "Lady Sulat ordered you to be as helpful as possible to me, didn't she?"

"Oh, maybe."

Did Lady Sulat want me to succeed? I still couldn't tell. In any case, I didn't entirely trust Moss.

We strolled back toward Lady Sulat's apartments the long way, around the Royal Shrine—a stark building with a black peaked roof, black pillars, and white walls. Inside rested the heads of kings and queens, lords and ladies, protectors of Rowak. Beyond it stood the Royal Bear House—the king's residence, towering three stories high. Even its shingles shone bright red, signifying this was the true heart of all Rowak. Guards manned the wall—the only such wall inside the palace. If Lady Sulat could get in just once a week to see her father, I had no chance of investigating King Alder.

"Chief Archivist Kochan... he's loyal to Lady Sulat, isn't he?"

"Ah, you are getting a little smarter. Not that it's hard to see. Kochan's a brilliant archivist, but less brilliant on politics."

I chewed my lip. "You think he's wrong. About Lord Torut."

"Oh, spot-on. That one's not hard to see. But if you think that layabout Lord Torut planned this, you're grasping at straws."

Straws were all I had. "Do you know who the poisoner is?"

"Nope."

"Then don't mock me for looking."

I MENDED with Poppy until the midday meal. Then we beat rugs outside, the dust mushrooming out into the air.

Poppy intuitively understood my mood. She gave me a smile but let me think in silence. Was she perceptive-of-eye? Or just good with people? Either way, Poppy was an asset in her post. As Lady Egal had judged, scrubbing crocks suited my skills better than attending the Blue and Green ranks.

My brain felt dustier than the rugs. How could I spy on Blue Lord Torut? I had no such skills, no horde of willing soldiers, and precious little time.

"Dami!"

I turned. Bane jogged up the path. He looked as he had before: black hair sweeping low over his brown eyes, his military insignia tied in a lopsided, one-handed knot around his arm. Worry covered his face. "Dami... I heard what happened."

"With the trial." Thinking of it tightened my throat.

He fidgeted with the envelope in his hand. "I'm delivering this to Lady Sulat, but after that, it's my half-day off. Given your upcoming trial... maybe she'd give you the afternoon off as well. May I ask for you?"

Inwardly, I beamed. If he were a mercenary wife-hunter like Osem claimed, he wasn't a very good one. Who'd waste time courting a dead woman? Apparently I'd made a real friend that afternoon, sitting by the pond and skipping rocks. I'd been wrong to avoid him for so long.

"If you're sure you won't come to trouble for it. I've missed a good deal of work already today."

He nodded and headed up the steps to Lady Sulat's room.

It was nice that two people in the palace—Bane and Osem— would mourn me after the trial.

Bane returned shortly. "The ever-gracious Blue Lady Sulat granted my wish."

Poppy giggled, but I didn't mind. Talking to Bane might be more helpful than beating rugs. Moss didn't follow; apparently Lady Sulat trusted Bane to guard me.

We strolled together through the gardens. Bane watched my every step, like I was an ill-made crock poised to shatter. Like we were marching to my funeral.

"I hope... I hope the Council is fair to you," Bane said. I'm sure he meant that he hoped they'd pardon me, but unfortunately *fair* in this case meant hanging.

Time to change the conversation. "Did you ever do any spying? Out on the warfront?"

Bane's brow wrinkled. "Scouting. But it's not the same thing."

"Oh." I chewed my lip.

"Why the sudden interest? I won't believe you're a Shoreed spy no matter how hard you try to convince me."

I laughed, my unpracticed lungs creaking. "No. Nothing of the sort, Bane. That's the first thing you think of—me, a spy?"

"You can forage mushrooms and travel without an amber chip from Meadowind to Askan-Wod. Why should I think you incapable of anything? Two weeks from now, I expect to see you walking around happily on your own two feet, understand?" He said it in a mock-scolding tone, but concern shot through every syllable.

"Bane. Honestly, I don't know how to escape this trial."

"I'm going to keep hoping that saying so is all part of your master plan to escape." He walked a touch closer now, his buckwheat-brown eyes searching mine. He still smelled of juniper with a hint of smoke.

I considered him for a long moment. "If you're willing... I may need your help, Bane."

"Whatever you need." He said those words like he meant them. He halted and waited, silent, for orders—like a soldier before battle.

Somehow we'd ended up in the plum orchard again. Fallen blossoms speckled the grass and leave were unfurling on the trees. "Why are you so eager to help me?"

A warm smile spread across his broad face. "Why shouldn't I? I've sworn to protect Rowak. Every man, woman, and child inside these borders is Rowak. You are Rowak."

Quiet respect burned in me. I didn't know if Lady Sulat wanted me dead or alive, but she'd looked past Bane's missing arm, saw his dedication, and gave him a post. Somehow, that was reassuring.

"It'd be reckless to talk about this in an open garden," I said. We made our way to the springball courts, where we sat with an ivy-covered wall at our backs. We leaned close together as I whispered what I suspected about Fir and Blue Lord Torut.

A line creased between his eyes. "Why didn't you say you're twice-gifted in your application?"

I hadn't concocted an answer for that, yet.

"Have you sent for your parents? Could they help you with the trial?"

"No." I wished I could see their faces and talk to them. But what good would that do? They'd probably end up on trial themselves. If I couldn't invent anything better, I'd stick with the story about being a street urchin who stole Dami's papers for herself. I'd still hang and my parents would still owe back-taxes, but at least they'd keep on living.

Bane peered at me. "You're that embarrassed about being double-gifted?"

"Embarrassed..." I echoed. What an excellent lie—that I wanted to serve humbly, without drawing attention to myself. Bane was brilliant.

"When we skipped rocks, it seemed odd you accused me of being double-gifted, like that was a bad thing. Why would you be ashamed of starting life so well?"

"That wasn't it at all! What you did with those rocks looked surreal. I thought you must possess some other gift, because I couldn't imagine skipping a rock with a hundred years of practice."

Bane leaned his head back against the wall, staring up at the clear spring sky. "That was a nice afternoon."

"Yes." I leaned back too, soaking in the sky's color, that forget-me-not shade that only seemed to come this time of year. We ought to be sitting further apart, but I didn't want to move. I wished I had a century of clear afternoons like this before me, instead of eleven days. "Maybe the King will be lenient after the Council proclaims me guilty."

Bane gave me a pitying look. "Maybe you should tell me what you need help with, because appealing to the King's lenience won't be enough."

"I'm trying to find the poisoner—do you think that will work?" I asked.

He looked down at the grass where our hands rested a space apart. "I hope so. The Council might take pity and name you innocent, despite the evidence."

I exhaled. "What I need is a way to spy on Blue Lord Torut."

"Moss is right on this one. Lord Torut goes into Askan-Wod all the time to drink and gamble. He *likes* being unimportant."

"Or he's good at pretending." Just like Fir. I chewed my lip. "Do you know when, exactly, he goes into the city?"

"No, but Nisaat, my cousin, always watches the gate for Lady Egal. She could tell me the next time he leaves."

"Have her tell *me*. I won't let you get in trouble over this."

He looked so serious, despite the hair hanging over his eyes. "I told you I want to help."

"I'm going to have a trial anyway. I don't want you to risk one, too."

He pursed his lips, an argument in his eyes, but he didn't say anything. Bane sighed and nodded at the springball court. "Would you like to play?"

"Now?"

"Just sitting here isn't making you morose? Maybe a little relaxation will help us both think better. Besides, Blue Lord Torut never leaves before nightfall. I'll talk with Nisaat before then."

I looked down the length of the court, rimmed with an ankle-high wall of pale yellow bricks. Dami excelled at springball, not me. "There's only two of us."

Bane grinned. "While I'd love to play as partners, I'm willing to play person against person. You hardly seem at a disadvantage, Dami, strong-of-arm."

I wished Dami had been born nothing-of-nothing. But I couldn't dash Bane's smile. "Fine."

He fetched the equipment—the springball, a set of two acorn squash-sized sandbags, and four fist-sized balls in both yellow and green.

I took yellow so I wouldn't have to go first. Bane placed the springball in the center of the far side of the court, then jogged back to me. He stood behind the foul line and lofted a sandbag in a graceful arch, landing it near the springball. Having one arm didn't seem to affect his playing in the least. "Your turn."

I hefted a sandbag—it weighed about the same as a medium crock. Men usually played the bags and women rolled the balls. I glanced around once, but saw no other couple to join us.

I'd made a lie of omission and now Bane would know my lie of commission. I tossed the bag as hard as I could, hoping to get it at least half-way down the court.

It landed just out-of-bounds past the far end of the playing area.

Bane smiled. "That's often a problem with strong-of-arm players. Since you've never thrown bags before, I'd be happy to let you try again."

I mumbled a thank-you and Bane jogged to retrieve it before I could start down the court myself. I flexed my arms and wiggled my fingers while his back was turned.

More than a month of scrubbing crocks had made me stronger, even if I'd never lift a table one-handed like Dami. Maybe Bane was right. Maybe I could foil the courts and come out of this with my head.

My next throw fell short, but inside the legal playing area. Once we finished with the bags, we rolled the balls down the playing area, banking them off the walls. Bane placed his well enough, but I used my last roll to knock the springball into one of my bags.

"Shall we go score it?"

I strolled next to him. In the final evaluation, I had a sandbag and one of my balls closer to the springball than his best placement, so I scored two.

"How high do you want to play to? Ten?" Bane asked—a standard goal.

If I had to wait to spy, I couldn't think of a nicer way to pass the afternoon than playing springball with the perfume of columbines wafting in over the wall.

All said, I won, ten to eight. Bane graciously praised my skill as we put the equipment away. A little too graciously. I peered at him. "You let me win, didn't you?"

Bane rubbed his ear. "Hmm?"

I gave him the hard stare I usually reserved for children who wouldn't eat their food.

"Nisaat says I should always go easy on opponents on their first game, or there won't be a second. Honestly, I played very nearly at my best."

He looked adorably guilty. "Very nearly?" I asked, still using my chef voice. I wasn't about to let him off so easily.

"You'd never tossed before. It wasn't a fair match to begin with."

I raised a critical eyebrow.

Bane squirmed. "Are you going to argue that being strong-of-arm is a great advantage? I have the same birthgift, so it's hardly a difference between us, and it only made you overthrow your first toss. Really, in springball and in the military, being strong-of-arm isn't everything. In fact, when it comes to being a soldier, I'd rather be endurance-of-back."

He left that unusual statement hanging without explanation—a desperate attempt to change the topic of conversation. Given that his cheeks might set the rest of him on fire if he became any more flustered, I forgave him and followed his diversion. "Why endurance-of-back?"

Bane exhaled. He was no Lady Sulat—he wore his emotions too honestly on his face. "Let's say you've been marching all day with a pack pulling on you—your food, your weapons, your water. Maybe it's been raining, adding to the weight. And, without resting, you now have to ambush somebody. What gift would you rather have?"

"Strong-of-arm still seems like a good idea."

"Being strong only helps if you're not falling over. Endurance-of-back soldiers always fight fresh. You should have seen the way they moved. I wouldn't mind being agile-of-arm, either. Placing a strike just so... that's more important than pure force."

"You've thought about this a lot," I said, impressed.

He gave a modest shrug. "I always wanted to seem like an All-of-All, so I trained like I was one. I can't tell you how many times I loosed a bow as a boy, though I knew, given my birthgift, I'd be fighting with the spear."

And now he'd never nock an arrow again. "You wanted to be in the military that long?"

I wondered how long Dami wanted to join the military before she ran off. A day? Ten years? Wherever she was in this war, I hoped she was safe.

"I apologize. I'm getting carried away, rambling about personal things."

"No apology necessary. Go on," I encouraged him. "If you want to, that is. I'd like to listen."

He considered me for a moment. When he continued, his voice was soft. "I'm from a military family. My grandfather earned himself Yellow-rank for his heroism and we've all followed his legacy." He itched his stump with his good hand. "I woke before dawn to practice, even when I was little, so that when it came time to prove myself, I could earn Green-rank to honor him."

"I'm... sorry." I didn't know what to say.

"I'm getting used to having one arm... but I don't suppose you can imagine what it's like to train for something your whole life. To know your purpose, your destiny, and then have years of sweat and work snatched away from you in a single moment. I've spent the past three years trying to figure out who I am—just me—without a useful birthgift attached." He laughed at himself. "I sound half-crazy, don't I?"

My throat thickened. I looked down at the knife-scars on my hands—the result of uncounted hours in the kitchen. I ached to make a compote, a broth, anything. My voice came out husky. "You don't sound crazy at all."

A GARDEN HAD LAID siege to Lady Sulat's apartments. Flowers sat in vases on the floor. Flowers hung from the windows. Flowers trailed over the wooden dresser. But I saw no supper for me to taste.

Lady Sulat didn't look up. She held the newborn in one arm and a small girl, maybe three years old, against her other side. That would be her oldest—Blue-ranked Azalea—according to the genealogies I'd read today. The girl spoke quietly and touched her brother's toes. Lady Sulat's blank oval of a face softened into something motherly.

"What are all the flowers for?" I whispered to Moss.

"Congratulations on the birth, from her brave sons."

I peered at him. He wanted me to believe the premature infant picked these?

"Ah, from the soldiers. We're her brave sons." Adoration glowed in his voice as he glanced at Lady Sulat.

Maybe she was hard, but if the greenery was any evidence, her soldiers cared for her. Her daughter and Purple Lord Valerian adored her, too.

I stood in the corner watching the happy family. I saw no sign that Lady Sulat's and her newborn's lives had been endangered three days ago. No hint that the father wasn't around the corner, but on the frontlines.

I shifted on my feet. Should I leave and give them some privacy, since I had nothing to taste?

The door-guard let Poppy in. She bowed elegantly, keeping the tray in her hands level. "I apologize, Lady Sulat, for the lateness. A new chef has been called in for Hawak's absence. He just arrived and insisted on adjusting the seasoning of your dishes before they left the kitchens."

I strode forward. The simple soup of stinging nettles and green garlic was divine—a hint of sour from the parsley, a touch of sweet carrot in the broth, plus the bright spiciness of the garlic. Nettles targeted the breast and would help Lady Sulat's milk supply. Hard-boiled eggs with a nuanced dipping salt—flecked with juniper and maple sugar—accompanied it. There were buckwheat branches as well to soak in the soup, but that was standard, chewy apprentice fare. The new chef hadn't arrived in time to improve them. "It's all safe. The soup is quite good."

Poppy situated Lady Sulat with the nettle soup, then gave Azalea an egg and a branch. The girl cupped the egg in both hands and nibbled away, ignoring the dipping salt.

Lady Sulat took a few spoonfuls of soup, then a long sip of her tea. "Poppy. Who is the new chef?"

"You probably know his father, Green-ranked Yarrow, a former Master Chef, but this young man's name is Sorrel of Westbank."

CHAPTER SIXTEEN

Sorrel. He could cook as well as I'd dreamed he could. I choked back a sob.

Poppy's eyes widened and she snatched the branch back from Azalea. "You're ill?"

My cheeks heated. "No. The food's not poisoned. I…"

Lady Sulat stared at me, soaking up the details in my face. She knew Sorrel's name meant something to me, and that left me feeling naked.

My pulse fluttered wildly. I swallowed hard. "Might I be excused?"

Lady Sulat nodded, her cold eyes prickling the back of my neck as I hurried into the sitting room. Poppy had replaced the rugs we'd beaten clean that morning, but the furniture still lay out of place. Moss reclined on the most comfortable chair. I shuffled the other chairs and end tables back to their places, trying to think.

I couldn't simply burst into the kitchens on no particular errand. But I ached to. I needed to know his face. Hear his voice.

I wanted to tell him my real name.

"That vase is still off-center, you know," Moss said, jutting his chin at an end table.

I ignored him and chewed my lip, heart pounding. I gave up all pretense of moving chairs and paced. Sorrel. *Here.*

No, I couldn't risk telling Sorrel who I was. But maybe, given a chance to meet me, he'd want to marry me anyway. If I survived the trial, I could have my perfect life back.

Moss folded his hands behind his head and lounged in the chair. "I don't know why you bothered to clean the rugs if you're just going to wear holes in them."

I VOLUNTEERED to take Lady Sulat's tray back to the kitchens. Poppy happily conceded the task. Lady Sulat had fallen asleep, so I didn't have to endure her stare—though I had the nagging feeling she'd know about my excursion, anyway.

Moss followed, humming loudly and off-key. The bolas dangled from his belt, clacking.

I cracked the kitchen door and edged inside. The only person I didn't recognize stood with one of the apprentices over a bowl of rutabaga soup. He had to be Sorrel. He was of average height with a thin nose, but he held himself as confident as a king. In the kitchen, I supposed he was just that.

"You haven't tasted it since you poured it from the crock?" Sorrel asked the apprentice.

"I did, um, season it before it started cooking."

Sorrel grinned, dark eyes glittering like precious hematite. "Ah, but you must always taste again, after it's cooked. Do you know why?"

The man shook his head.

Sorrel spoke kindly, his words alive with passion. "Raw rutabagas aren't particularly sweet, but *cooked*... here, try a spoonful."

The apprentice took it. His eyes lit up. "You're right! The balance is off!"

"It's important to taste while you're cooking, or the dish might be unsalvageable. But always, always test a dish when it's finished, too."

The apprentice rubbed the back of his neck. "Chef Hawak said something like that, but I didn't understand why."

"Do you know how to fix it?"

Sour. I almost said it aloud.

"Not salt. That would be overpowering. Not spicy. So... sour?"

"Exactly right! Some parsley should do the trick."

My face flushed. My pulse raced. This man. I could have married this kind confectionary of a chef. I wanted to say something. Ancestors forgive me, I wanted to drop the tray, grasp his hand, and beg his forgiveness that I hadn't been a selfish daughter like the real Dami and abandoned my parents to pick up the pieces of her mistakes.

I wanted to ask him his theory on methods of broth-making. Or custards. Or if he preferred juniper or rosehip in his elk braises.

He turned toward me and *beamed*. I stopped breathing. He spoke. "Ah, my love. I'm so pleased to see you! Are you well?"

That's when I knew I'd already been executed. This was all a marvelous dream. A paradise where we'd spend the rest of eternity debating the proper way to make dumplings and feeding each other strawberries.

"Of course! I just miss you," said a voice behind me. I'd been too busy ogling Sorrel to notice her approach.

Her hair shone as lustrous as Dami's. Except, unlike Dami, she'd never fool anyone into thinking she was a boy, no matter how heavy the jacket. She flaunted her curves as she sauntered to him.

Sorrel embraced her tightly. One of the apprentices whistled. My innards turned to moldy leftovers. He ought to be holding me like that.

"She *is* my betrothed. Such a gesture hardly merits whistling," Sorrel said, one part embarrassed, one part grin.

How could he? Sorrel should be sobbing his heart out, after the way I tossed him aside.

The thrice-cursed young woman giggled. Sorrel, engaged. Not to me. He hadn't wasted any time.

"I spoke with Lady Egal," the vixen said. "Given that you're the Acting Master Chef, she insists on putting together our wedding. I told her we'd need to wait some time for your father."

"Nonsense! He doesn't want us to wait months until he can come. I'll talk to Lady Egal this evening. I'm sure we could arrange it in two weeks."

At least I'd be dead by then.

Sorrel finally noticed me. "Sorry. Did we keep you waiting?"

"N-no. I'm just delivering dishes." I dropped my eyes to the floor and shuffled past.

How could I say anything? I wasn't Plum. I was Dami, the rumored poisoner. Plum died the night Dami ran away.

If I'd been his betrothed, would he be as kind, as solicitous, to me? I couldn't believe otherwise.

I set the tray by Osem. She glanced up. "You look ill. Worried about the trial?"

Right. The trial.

"Sorrel's rearranged the schedule. I'll have a half-day off tomorrow. Think I could be of any help?" Osem asked.

"I'll meet you outside the kitchens, after I taste Lady Sulat's lunch."

Osem nodded and turned back to her crocks and plates. I had to cross the kitchen to get back to where Moss waited in the doorway. Between the hearths and crowded apprentices, I couldn't avoid walking past Sorrel.

I accidentally brushed his elbow. My breath hitched in my throat.

He didn't notice. His betrothed blathered about her dress while he mused about the menu. They monologued in tandem. Did that *count* as a conversation?

Moss leaned on the doorframe. "You're taking your time. Trying to poison someone?"

He chuckled at his own poorly-timed joke.

Sorrel's face hardened. "Poison?"

"Just a jibe," Moss said.

Tanoak frowned. "Not *just* a jibe. Most people think she did it."

"Get out!" Sorrel waved his hands at me, like he was shooing a crow from a garden.

I ached to explain, to defend myself, but I didn't have the words. I scurried away, Sorrel's scowl burning the back of my skull.

I WAITED on Lady Sulat's porch for Nisaat or Bane until the moon rose, but Blue Lord Torut must have stayed in tonight. By the time I retired to my dark closet, my mind had raced over my brief encounter with Sorrel a thousand times.

His hematite-brilliant eyes. His laugh. His kindness to his fiancée.

I wished I could kneel in the shrine at home, but kneeling on my mattress would have to do. I kept my voice low so the guard outside couldn't hear. "Dear Ancestors. If it's not too much to ask, could you plague Dami for me? Nothing that would harm her in battle. But maybe some boils on the backsides of her knees. Or under her arms. You know, uncomfortable places. Doesn't she deserve that much?"

I didn't feel anything in response. Perhaps the Ancestors weren't interested in handing out boils. I considered praying for warts or scabs, but collapsed onto my pillow instead.

I cried myself to sleep.

I WORKED with Poppy all morning, then met Osem in the afternoon as promised. Lady Sulat didn't seem to care where I spent my time. My eyes still ached from crying last night. I felt like someone had rammed a bucket of carrot peelings inside my ears in an effort to crack my skull open from the inside.

"You... look like you slept well," Osem said, giving me a look-over that meant the opposite.

I couldn't explain Sorrel, so I didn't. "The trial."

"You'll be a scapegoat for someone else's poisoning, even if that's not in the official charges."

"Exactly."

"Let's walk."

I strolled next to her, our skirts oddly mismatched—gray and black now. Osem led us to a small garden, a circular patch of lilies, not yet blooming. They'd unfurl spectacular, orange flowers when summer came. That's when Father and I picked and dried the bulbs, so we could all enjoy their peppery flavor through winter. I sighed. Sorrel probably picked lilies with his father, too. We could talk about so much, if only we could talk.

"Have you tried looking at the servant's waiting list?" Osem asked, jerking me from my thoughts.

"The girl Fir's trying to bring in resigned. Her record's trapped in the treasury now."

"Problematic."

Osem talked to me without a wisp of doubt as to my innocence. I wished I could make her candied hazelnuts. Reciprocate her kindness. But I didn't know how to tell her all that.

"I've searched elsewhere for answers," I said instead. "I think Lord Torut might be involved. If anything happened to Lady Sulat, he'd become the Minister of Military Affairs. He'd have more influence with Purple Lord Heir Valerian if his beloved aunt vanished, too."

"Maybe." Osem frowned. "But you can't hold coincidence against a man in court."

I explained how I'd sneak into Torut's quarters, once Nisaat told me he'd left for an evening of carousing.

Osem stared at me like I'd sneezed radishes. "How will you get in?"

"I hoped you'd have ideas. You have a good grasp on how the palace works."

Osem stood. "Let's go for a walk to admire the outside of the Royal Shrine." Only blue- and purple-ranked citizens could enter the Shrine itself. "That little excursion will take us past Lord Torut's apartments."

"Thanks!"

She snorted. "I'm not helping you, Dami. I'm showing you how stupid your plan is. You'll get caught."

"I'm already in trouble."

"But you're not locked up in a cell, surrounded by Palace Guards. It could be worse, Dami. Things can always get worse."

CRUSHED CLAM SHELLS lined the walkway to the Royal Shrine, white and glittering in the afternoon light. Massive log pillars, painted black, supported a black peaked roof over white walls—colors as stark as death itself.

A lilac hedge separated the Shrine from Torut's apartments—a low building of varnished redwood. A lawn spread before it, broken up with a pair of curly-barked madrone trees. Yarrow spread around their bases like white lace.

"It's easy to see into," I said. Not that we saw anyone besides the door servant.

"That's a bad thing. No cover for you."

"Oh. Is it better from the other side?"

Osem shook her head. "That puts you near Captain Gano's guardhouse. It's back there, along the wall of the Royal Bear House. You'd be spotted for sure."

I couldn't see the guardhouse, but a pair of guards stood above the wall gate to the Royal Bear House. No, I couldn't sneak in. I'd have to pretend to have some kind of business at Lord Torut's. I chewed my lip. The fabric-backed lattice windows of his apartments stared blankly back at me.

The wall guards looked fidgety, so we continued toward the Royal Shrine and sat on one of its garden benches.

Purple Heir Valerian strode up to the gates of the Royal Bear House, flanked by four guards. He looked like a miniature version of them, his face properly solemn instead of exuberant like at Lady Sulat's apartments. The guards on the wall let him in without pause.

"The Purple Heir... he's quite the intelligent child, isn't he?" My mind churned, watching those gates shut behind him.

Osem nodded. "Lady Sulat's proud of what a scholar he is."

"He seems to like puzzles. Finding things out. Curiosity for curiosity's sake." I chewed my lip. "Do you think... if I asked him..."

"You want to enlist Heir Valerian as your spy?" Osem stared at me.

I shrugged and stared down at the lawn. "I don't have access to the Royal Bear House. He does."

"Listen to yourself. You want him to spy on his *father*?" Osem shook her head. "I doubt he wants to—or is able to—keep secrets from him. You may as well paste a poster in the marketplace accusing the king."

Purple Heir Valerian did have difficulty navigating Lady Sulat's political questions. "You're right."

"Of course I'm right."

Osem stared up at the black, peaked roof of the shrine. The wind stirred. I needed an ally like Heir Valerian. Someone who could go places I couldn't.

"I'm not sure he'd help anyway. Why would he? He doesn't care about you personally. He owes you no debts. You have nothing to offer him."

She was right. The only people who cared about me here—Bane and Osem—were doing all they could.

"We should go," Osem said. "I hope you can see now how bad your plan is."

A deep, quiet voice behind us asked, "What's a bad plan?"

I jumped and turned. Five palace guards in blue, one the tallest man I'd ever seen, stood behind us. Before we could run, they surrounded us.

The tallest guard—he stood head and shoulders above me—wore a purple armband, elaborately embroidered with a bear. That had to be Gano, Captain of the Guards. His severely-trimmed mustache looked like a black gash over his lip. "I'll ask you once more—what are you planning?"

"Skinny dipping in the south pond at midnight," Osem replied before I could swallow. She shook her head. "Now all these men know, Dami! We'll never manage. I enjoy a swim, but I hate being ogled by shameless louts."

Osem was slick.

"My guards saw you loitering outside the Royal Bear House. I heard you speak of a plan. Suspicious, isn't it, considering one of you already faces a trial?" Captain Gano loomed over me. "Why are you here?"

"It's a public garden." The protest sounded childish even to me.

"And that isn't an answer."

"By my Ancestors!" Osem shook her head. "Are you that mad about missing the skinny dipping? I doubt your wife would approve."

One of the guards chuckled, but Gano didn't flinch. "Some questioning is in order. I'll take you both into custody now. Lady Sulat is too addled from childbirth to be responsible for accused criminals."

Osem hooked her arm through mine. "If it's all the same to you, given that our swimming plans are ruined, we must now make a detour to the bathhouse."

I ignored the knot in my throat and strode with her, elbowing past the guards.

Gano snapped his long fingers.

Something cracked against my ankle, flaring pain. I screamed. My foot buckled and I fell.

I rolled onto my back in time to see the butt of the guard's spear whir around to strike me again.

CHAPTER SEVENTEEN

With my good leg, I landed a kick straight on his kneecap. The guard grunted, shifted his stance back, and swung again with his spear butt. I rolled, knowing I wouldn't be fast enough.

Someone screamed. The spear dropped to the ground next to me. A bolas with cherry-sized weights entangled the guard's hands—his flesh welted red around it.

I scrambled to my feet. Moss stepped next to me, the granite bolas that usually dangled on his belt now in his hand. Where he'd pulled the smaller bolas from, or if he had more, I had no idea. I'd never been so happy to see him.

He glanced at me. "Dami, Lady Sulat needs your assistance. If you'll pardon us, Captain Gano." Moss bowed respectfully, but his eyes didn't leave Gano or his men.

Gano's lips formed a tight white line. He waved the guards back. I hobbled as fast as I could after Moss, with Osem's help.

"That could have been ugly." Osem glanced at my leg. "Uglier."

My ankle throbbed, burning from the inside out. I couldn't tell if it was broken or badly bruised. "It should've been worse. We were outnumbered."

"Captain Gano might be willing to pick a fight with two servants," Moss said, "but starting an actual skirmish between the Palace Guard and the Military? No. There's a reason I entangled the guard instead of breaking his wrists."

My pulse slowed and my brain started working as we neared Lady Sulat's apartments. Moss's presence couldn't be a coincidence. "You were spying on me."

"What do you think I was doing the *rest* of the time I followed you around?"

Of course. I cursed myself. Lady Sulat didn't know if I was guilty—but she did know that a poisoner wouldn't work alone. She gave me so much freedom to see what I did with it. Who I might report to. Then she'd have the name of her true enemy. "Did you stalk me when I talked with Bane, too?"

Moss whistled an innocent tune.

I missed Clamsriver, where the only cleverness required was a deft knowledge of vegetables. Vegetables, I could handle.

Moss and Osem helped me into Lady Sulat's sitting room. I lay on the floor and elevated my foot on a chair.

"You stay with her, Moss," Osem said. "I'll fetch the chef. He'll tell us if she needs a surgeon."

"I don't—" I began, but Osem had already left. I mumbled the rest to myself: "—need a surgeon." I sighed. "You're good with those bolas, Moss."

"Told you I was lucky to find someone silly enough to give me five-to-one odds." He eyed my foot. "I guess you won't be running, eh?"

I closed my eyes. Captain Gano probably confronted me simply because he wanted the prisoner Lady Sulat was keeping from him. But with how close he lived to Lord Torut, I wondered if they could be co-conspirators.

All my theories were as thin and insubstantial as spider webs.

The door guard admitted Osem. "I've brought the chef," she said.

I felt like an idiot for not remembering what that meant with Hawak gone. Sorrel stood next to me. Sorrel of Westbank. My pulse jumped, shooting more pain up my leg.

He frowned at me. "Aren't you the poisoner?"

"*Accused* poisoner," Moss chirped. "It's not the same thing, is it?"

Sorrel shook his head, but he knelt by my foot anyway. He was a chef, tasked with bringing health and longevity. It didn't matter that he thought I was a traitor to our profession.

"This is recent?" he demanded flatly.

"Yes," I said.

"Hmm. Can you wiggle your toes?"

I could dance on the moon, if it made him happy. I wiggled.

"Good. Now point your toes to the ceiling. Good. Now straight out, toward the wall."

I did so, trying not to wince.

"Well, it looks like this isn't so bad..." He trailed off, frowning. "I never did catch your name."

"Dami."

His frown deepened. "Dami? Why does that sound familiar? You don't happen to be from Clamsriver, do you?"

I couldn't say otherwise. Moss stood right there, spying for Lady Sulat. "Umm, yes."

"I knew it! Poisoners and heartbreaks! You have a sister named Plum, don't you?"

He'd called me a heartbreaker! I blushed and smiled. He'd wanted me.

Sorrel glared at me down his thin nose. "You think it's funny that she abandoned our engagement like that? I thought she wanted to *marry* me, not mock me."

My mouth felt like stale flour. I still wanted to marry him. I'd kiss him right now if he leaned a little closer. I could still envision us in a kitchen somewhere, chopping leeks and laughing at each other. "She..."

"She what?"

Osem and Moss both stood back, watching with amusement.

I clenched and unclenched my hands. What could I say? That I—no, that Plum—still wanted him? That there was hope for our marriage?

There wasn't. Not unless I lived. Not unless I could entrust him with the secrets that drove us apart—or my whole family would be executed for treason.

I couldn't risk that. Not yet. Not ever. Plum died the night Dami ran away.

"You wouldn't have liked her anyway," I mumbled. Saying those words felt like vomiting obsidian knives.

"Then she shouldn't have played with me! Tortured me!" he shouted, loud enough to be heard inside the building and out.

I kept my voice at a more reasonable level. "Torture? The engagement's broken not a whole month and you're cavorting with some other girl in the kitchens."

"You make it sound like a scandal. We're betrothed."

"I heard." I didn't bother hiding every ounce of hate I had for that twit.

His jaw clenched. I braced for another outburst, but he swallowed hard. "Not that I owe you any explanation, but Violet's the girl I was always supposed to marry. My father trained her father in the palace kitchens, and chose Palaw to be his successor. When Master Chef Palaw himself retired to see Red Lord Osem into exile, he asked my father to do the honor of picking the next Master Chef. They have the deepest respect for each other.

"But Violet has no love of cooking, so for years, I refused. I accepted Plum, a girl below my rank because I could imagine us together—chopping leeks in the kitchens and laughing. I wanted a wife who was my equal."

My chest felt like an egg shell under a block of granite. He'd imagined our future exactly as I had.

"But I was wrong to refuse Green-ranked Violet for so long. She may not have any talent as a chef, but she's *faithful* and I'll love her until the day I die. I'm glad I have her. That I wasn't left grieving for long."

From the bitterness in his tone, he still grieved.

"As soon as I can manage," Sorrel continued, "I'll be a married man. The mistake of trusting your fickle, yellow-ranked sister will be a distant memory. What's Plum's excuse?"

Acidic pain laced his every syllable. I wanted to ease his heart with the truth and cook him something sweet.

"How should I know what Plum was thinking?" However much it hurt, I shifted so I could stare him straight in the eye. "But I promise you, she's not off gallivanting with some young man. She was crying when I left for my post. Shame on you for fawning over someone else so soon."

Sorrel shook his head. "Shame on me? For doting on my betrothed? No." He dusted the front of his shirt. "Maybe I don't know Violet well. Maybe she isn't the accomplished chef I dreamed of marrying. But she'll be my wife and so I'm going to cherish her."

I TASTED Lady Sulat's food. The dish for my ankle came not long thereafter, around sunset—pickled garlic-stuffed cherries. Cherries targeted muscles, whole garlic targeted the foot, and the sour would diminish my pain. Bright, acidic flavors burst into my mouth, backed up by the fruit's sweetness and the garlic's spiciness. The sour coursed past my stomach and straight to my ankle. It wrapped itself around the injury, cooled it, limbered the flesh, and eased the pain. Sorrel was every bit a chef.

His words echoed in my head: *She'll be my wife and so I'm going to cherish her.*

We could have been so *happy* together. Instead, my brilliant chef settled for an unskilled girl who possessed nothing but a pretty smile. Why the Ancestors didn't see fit to scourge Dami with boils, I couldn't understand. Maybe I should have prayed longer.

As the pain eased, my head cleared. Why was I moping? Sorrel wasn't married yet.

I couldn't tell him the truth. I'd always be Dami to him. So I'd just have to make him love Dami.

And for that, I needed to prove my innocence—fast. He wouldn't glance at me while he thought me a poisoner. But once Fir was arrested, Sorrel and I would cook together. He'd see my skills. We'd laugh, like we'd both imagined. We'd argue over whether juniper berries or rosehips were better, and before his wedding, he'd cheerfully say goodbye to his curvy fiancée.

I silently prayed I'd find evidence against the guilty parties quickly. And that proving myself would be enough to save my life and my marriage.

"Moss," I said. "If you wanted to break into Lord Torut's apartments, how would you do it?"

Osem cut in. "Dami. You said you weren't going to try that."

"I'm going to try everything I can."

"You hurt your ankle!" She clenched her hands in her skirt, knuckles whitening.

I stood to prove I could and gritted my teeth. Sorrel had taken the edge off the pain, but the pressure made it throb. I kept my weight on my good foot and forced a smile. "I'm not going to sit here and wait for my trial."

"What did that cook feed you?" Osem demanded. "Some kind of crazy-of-mind recipe?"

Nisaat entered then, her emerald green skirt swishing elegantly. She paused and glanced nervously at the gathering. "Dami? Might I have a word alone?"

"We all know." Osem crossed her arms. "Lord Torut left, didn't he?"

Nisaat swallowed hard. She hadn't expected anyone else. "I... I came to give my cousin's regards, that's all."

She left as quickly as she'd come.

Osem turned to me, eyes hard. "This is idiocy. You don't have a real plan. You'll get yourself captured."

"Idiocy would be waiting for my execution. I don't have time to spare. The more avenues I investigate, the better my chance of finding something."

Moss leaned back in his chair, greatly entertained.

"At least execution is quick." Osem's hands quivered.

I'd never asked for the details of the attack that wiped out her family, but staring into her haunted eyes, I couldn't believe they'd joined their Ancestors in a painless fashion.

"Osem," I said softly. "I'll be careful. I promise."

"Being careful isn't the same as not being caught, and you can't promise that." Her voice cracked on the last word.

I sat back down, shifting in my seat. I had no gift for calming words—only calming food.

Moss polished his bolas on his shirt. "New pine boughs are coming in soon for the mattresses. To sneak into Lord Torut's, I'd gather myself a sackful of branches and pretend to have a delivery. There's a garden with some spruce trees."

I knew that wild garden well—it was near the kitchens' back door.

"Why are you encouraging her?!" Osem demanded.

Moss shrugged. "Maybe she'll find something interesting. And if not, and she's caught, she's right. What worse could happen?"

"The Palace Guard could haul her to her some horrible cell!"

"Ah, they'd have to give her up for the trial, or Lady Sulat will sue Captain Gano for interfering with justice."

"So the guard could *torture* her for a week and a half, *then* give her up to die." Osem turned to me, eyes fierce and protective. "Dami, I'll have no part in this."

"Then you should leave. Because I have to go." I didn't know how to convince her that the risk merited the reward.

Osem gaped at me as if I'd run her through with a spear. Tears rimmed her eyes. "Fine! Go get yourself mutilated!"

She ran out of the room.

"Osem!" I called, but she was gone.

CHAPTER EIGHTEEN

That evening, Moss gathered the boughs for me to spare my ankle. Did he want me to live, or was he just gathering information for Lady Sulat? I didn't know and it didn't matter. I snatched a purple skirt with a bleached-out bear to mark me as King Alder's servant. I'd tell Lord Torut's servants that His Majesty had extra boughs from the first shipment and told me to deliver them here. A tad convoluted, but I couldn't dress up as a servant of Lord Torut's—his real servants would know I wasn't one of them.

I clutched the spruce boughs and strolled straight across the cool, dark lawn. I tried not to limp on my tightly-bound ankle. *Act like you belong there*, Moss had told me. Actually accompanying me would look strange, so he sat praying nearby on a bench outside the Royal Shrine to the Fathers and Mothers of our nation—a perfectly respectable thing to do, whatever the hour might be.

My ankle flared as I worked my way up the stairs. The door servant, illuminated by a single torch in a sconce, said nothing.

"The first shipment of pine boughs arrived early. These are leftovers from—"

The young woman yawned and opened the door for me. "Lord Torut's room is through the carved lattice screen on the long wall of his front room."

I blinked. I'd half expected her to call the Palace Guard. Then I remembered myself and hurried inside. She kept the door open long enough for me to set the boughs down and light a lamp from the torch's flames.

I didn't see any other servants or guards. I guess when their master disappeared, they enjoyed an evening off, too. Or perhaps they attended him in Askan-Wod.

I dumped the boughs in Lord Torut's bedroom, then quickly searched his front room. The cabinet against the wall, carved with cougars and ferns, seemed promising, but the only unlocked drawer held liquor. Despite the cabinet's high polish, a fusty, weathered-wood smell clung to the interior. I checked under the liquor but found no hidden drawer. How long could I search before arousing the door servant's suspicions?

Trying to force the locks would make a ruckus. I moved to the writing desk but froze when I heard voices outside. I scurried into the bedroom, closed the door, and extinguished my lamp.

The front door creaked open as I hid behind the mattress and freshly-cut boughs. I bit my lip and cursed myself for panicking. I should have pretended to be at my task, lamp lit. Not that I could relight it now.

"Welcome home, Blue Lord Torut. Welcome, Purple Lord King Alder."

My marrow chilled. I carefully untied my skirt and stuffed it under the mattress. Better to be underdressed than dressed to my condemnation. The door closed again, and two bodies settled themselves in the front room. At least the lazy servant hadn't mentioned me.

"... dunno why we have t' stay in," said a slurred, raspy voice.

All right. Maybe the door servant realized her drunk master wouldn't care or remember if she mentioned me.

"I can't go traipsing about Askan-Wod with you, can I? It's not safe, or dignified, for a King. But I wouldn't mind sharing a drink."

"Have ten."

"It sounds like you already did." One of them rose and opened the cabinet. No servants. This was a private meeting.

"I wasn't just drinking," Lord Torut drawled. "There was a shadow play about a Vengeful Ghost. Very dramatic. Lots of death."

I exhaled and silently prayed. *Ancestors, please let them both pass out drunk. Please don't let them find me.*

But His Majesty didn't seem like a reckless drinker. I tried not to breathe.

"And plenty of pretty female puppeteers, I'm sure," King Alder muttered. I heard liquid and the scrape of cups. "Ah, plum wine. It's a pity you drink this like water."

"'S made for drinking," Blue Lord Torut said. "War still going poorly?"

King Alder sighed. "There shouldn't *be* a war. They used that land dispute as an excuse to invade. The only good thing about the war is how amazing it makes wine taste."

"Mmm."

"Now they're pushing up toward Napil and our obsidian mines. I'm carting obsidian to the capital as we speak, but if we lose our ability to make weapons... you're not listening to a word of this, are you?"

"Nope."

"If you weren't such a happy drunk, I'd slap you."

"Sometimes women slap me, when they don't know who I am."

His Majesty sighed. "If Mother weren't dead, one look at you would kill her all over again."

"Grandmother's the one who should rest with the ancestors... then we could have our chef back. Oww!"

I couldn't see what King Alder had done, but I imagined an ear-twisting.

"You may speak crudely of women in Askan-Wod, but never of our foremother. Understand?"

Lord Torut whimpered. "This family's full of dying people. Don't see what's wrong about pointing it out. Her and Father. He's not getting better, is he?"

"No."

My heart clenched at the weight of that one word.

"You really need to keep him up in your Royal Bear place all the time?"

"If I could, I'd place him in a room safe in the clouds, where no illness or age could ever strike him down. Where I could always have him nearby."

I bit my lip. These weren't the words I'd expected from the man who'd callously executed twelve apprentice chefs. Whatever else he'd done, this man loved his father.

"You should bring him liquor. Liquor makes everyone happy."

The king choked a bitter laugh. "And that's why you're no chef or physician. He's frail. Becoming delusional. I worry for him."

"Liquor cures *everything*," Torut mumbled.

"Why did I bother coming back with you? I should have ordered some strong-of-back guard to carry you to your room. Here. Stand up. I'm not so pampered I can't help you to your mattress."

I jerked toward the window. I could push the latticed shutters open, jump to the ground below... and be caught as soon as everyone heard the thump. I couldn't outrun anyone.

I ducked into the wardrobe instead, jamming myself behind fine mantles and shirts.

Someone thumped onto the mattress. "I'm not tired!"

"Just drunk," King Alder muttered. More shuffling—it sounded like cloth. A blanket? "Hmm. Pine boughs. I thought those came in tomorrow."

His footsteps receded.

Itches and aches volunteered themselves as I tried to hold still, balanced on my good foot. The wardrobe stank of mildew and stale alcohol—like it never quite washed out of Lord Torut's clothes.

He belched—loudly—and shuffled to his feet. "Hoity-toity... won't have a drink with me..."

I chewed my lip, waiting. Maybe he'd pass out soon. The lattice door opened, and he stumbled out into the front room. A drawer rattled, liquid splashed into a cup, and soon, raucous, off-key singing assailed my ears. The wardrobe muffled it, but not nearly enough.

The chorus gave a recipe for salmon roe—a food best known for targeting a problem my mother politely called a man with an unhappy wife.

Spicy, salty, sour, and sweet each got their own verse detailing the man's exploits after feasting on salmon roe so seasoned. But the only verse that mentioned a wife made it clear she was married to someone else; Lord Torut giggled wildly during that one.

I leaned my head against the wood, smelling it, my own sweat, and the wine-stained clothes. My ankle throbbed, begging for pickled garlic-stuffed cherries. Dread settled in my gut, as cold as three-day-old leftovers

I couldn't learn anything here. Either Lord Torut was an unequaled master of deception, or he was an unambitious lush, like Moss had said.

I exhaled, trying to calm myself. I couldn't afford to worry about anything but escape right now. Lord Torut would eventually go to sleep. Or pass out. But what story would the door servant believe? Perhaps it would be best to grab a heavy vase and knock her out.

I silently laughed at myself. Moss might try such a thing, but I had no experience rendering someone unconscious. She'd raise an alarm and I'd be caught.

All fell quiet. I waited until my legs screamed their aches. I creaked the wardrobe door open and eased myself along the wall, listening.

Beautiful snoring met my ears.

I slunk across the dark room, trying not to make the floorboards creak. I fetched my skirt, tied it on, and felt my way to the exit.

Lord Torut snored on—the deep, throat-rumbling sound only

liquor-lovers achieved. I'd tell the door servant Lord Torut detained me to pour his drinks. Surely that sounded reasonable.

I cracked the door and stepped outside into the crisp spring night, which thankfully smelled of yarrow and nothing like a musty wardrobe.

The door servant leaned against the wall, but she jerked awake as soon as I closed the door. She blinked at me, then smiled. "You hid, didn't you?"

"I—" All my lies ran out of my brain, like water in a sieve. She shouldn't sound hopeful that I'd deceived her master.

She frowned. "You *didn't* manage to hide?"

My palms turned sweaty. The truth was easier. "I panicked. I'm sorry."

"Don't be! Do you know how horrible Lord Torut is when he's drunk? He thinks everyone is his mistress. I worried about you, but I figured if he was singing, the two of you weren't... ahem."

My stomach clenched. The poor girl. "Does he try... with his servants?"

"Try? Of course. But we all know to offer him more wine. He'll *always* take that. Eventually, he passes out." She shrugged. "There are worse things. I could have been assigned to scrub crocks."

I'd rather scrub crocks until my bones broke than serve here. I gave her a nod and strode across the lawn, head high, like I belonged there.

CHAPTER NINETEEN

Moss caught up with me on the gravel path and let me put my arm around him for support on the hobble home.

Despite Moss' help and my splint, by morning my ankle looked like an over-packed sausage. After tasting Lady Sulat's breakfast, she glanced at my injury and informed me that I'd spend the morning helping Poppy arrange the many flowers from her brave sons.

However it grated, Lady Sulat was right. I couldn't make it down the porch steps. Poppy helped me sit down on the porch between a pair of those ubiquitous redwood pillars that supported the eaves.

At least last night wasn't a *complete* failure. I'd learned Lord Torut wasn't part of Fir's plots, either. He was simply a revolting human being. If I gathered enough such tidbits, wouldn't the whole picture fall into place?

Osem had been right to criticize my plan. I wanted to apologize for upsetting her, but that would have to wait until the day before my trial. No doubt I'd have to resort to more hasty, ill-conceived reconnaissance before then. I needed more time. And an uninjured ankle to go with it.

But where to look next?

Poppy kindly brought me a rock to prop my foot up on. "I heard about your fall, but I didn't realize it was that bad."

"Oh, she had a long night," Moss chipped in. He sat on the bottom porch step, whittling some pine. The curls of wood drifted in the breeze toward me, their scent sharp and bright.

Poppy's eyes widened in scandal. "You went to see Bane, didn't you?"

Frustration boiled in my chest. "No! Of course not!"

"That's a lot of protest," Poppy said as she added candyflowers and blue-eyed grass to her vase. "I suppose I wouldn't want to die an unloved woman either, but you should still make it proper. Have a rushed wedding without your family and without a formal engagement ceremony like the Acting Master Chef is. I thought Bane too conscientious to treat you otherwise."

"Bane is one of the best young men that I know! Nothing like that happened."

"So you are fond of him?" A smile crept onto Poppy's mouth.

My face burned. "I wasn't with him!"

"There's someone else?" Poppy asked, bright-eyed and eager for details.

Moss shook with silent laughter. I glared, but that made him laugh harder.

"Poppy." I exhaled and steadied my voice. "Would you be so kind as to request some pickled garlic-stuffed cherries from the kitchen for me? I can finish your vase for you, while you're gone."

She looked from her magnificently displayed blooms to my half-empty vase. "Keep working on what you're doing, all right?"

Arranging flowers. I should be following through on some plan to exonerate myself, but my mind felt like overcooked mush. The flowers stared at me. No answers here. I knew how to *cook* some of these, but not how to make them prettier.

"Y'know," Moss said, "I'm glad you didn't run away. I hate to admit it, but this may be better than knocking you down with bolas, no matter how much I like winning bets."

"Oh, stuff it," I grumbled, grabbing some wild roses.

He paused his whittling to put on a face of mock hurt. "Did I say anything untrue?"

I wanted to chuck the flowers in his face. My chest burned as badly as my foot—Moss was right. Nine days until the trial, and I was further from answers than when I started.

Poppy returned shortly. I ate the cherries, exhaling as its sour cooled and limbered my ankle. By the time we finished arranging and watering the flowers, I could put a bit of weight on it.

I tasted Lady Sulat's lunch and started the afternoon cleaning with Poppy. The more I tried to think of a solution, the madder I got at myself. Hard work, my mother said, made thoughts flow. But my hard work resulted in Poppy taking away the scrubbing brush and saying I needed to be nicer to the stairs. Thoughts wouldn't come.

I propped my foot up while Poppy fetched another bucket of water.

"Giving up?" Moss asked.

I wanted to slap him. I closed my eyes instead, sinking into the darkness of my own eyelids. "If you have any brilliant ideas, I would have liked to hear them hours ago."

"Nope. Not my job to be brilliant."

"Thanks," I snapped. He'd spent the afternoon playing with his bolas on the lawn. "I don't have the skills to solve this myself. For all I know, the answers are locked up behind a gate I can't pass. As for allies, well, I've got Osem and Bane."

"Ah, glad to see you're clever enough to know *I* don't work for you. But if it's any consolation, I hope you don't die."

It wasn't consoling at all.

"Anyone owe you a debt? Anyone you can offer something to for their help?" Moss asked, echoing Osem's earlier words.

"I don't hold any debts. And no one needs my help." The palace had respectable chefs *not* accused of poisoning.

I paused. That wasn't right. There was one person—just one—

who might do anything for my help. And no respectable chef, no chef with a future, would do anything to help them.

I TASTED Lady Sulat's supper. Azalea and the infant must be with the nurse, because I didn't see either of them. Just guards. Someone had brought a small desk in and Lady Sulat sat behind it, a manuscript box in front of her. She must be recovering from the labor well.

I set the bowl brimming with hotpot back on the tray. "It's fine."

She turned another page without looking at me. The handwriting and format on this one was different, report-like. Had she heard me? Would she listen if I asked permission to walk the palace grounds? Moss wasn't about to let me leave these apartments without permission.

"You can go," Lady Sulat said, turning another page.

The question tightened in my throat. "I... that is..."

Lady Sulat sighed. Then I noticed the fine circles rimming her eyes, the weariness weighing her hands. She'd just been poisoned. Just given birth. And still she oversaw the military. "Go wherever you need to. But return if your ankle swells. It makes you an easier target for the Palace Guard."

"Yes, Lady. Thank you, Lady." I bowed deeply, thankfully, and left her to her reports.

Moss followed me out into the cool, overcast evening. "Where are we headed?"

"To the kitchens." Shadows stretched long over the gardens. The sun would set within the hour. "I have a meeting with a ghost."

CHAPTER TWENTY

"You probably shouldn't say that aloud," Moss said. "Believing in ghosts is a dangerous business around here."

But he didn't try to dissuade me. He didn't laugh like the ghost didn't exist.

We sat in the spruce tree garden near the kitchens, where Moss had acquired the boughs for my expedition into Lord Torut's. The trees didn't look bad—more storm-weathered than mangled. With the ferns tumbling everywhere, the garden felt like a wild patch of deep, dark forest.

I caught a glimpse of Osem closing the back door and bit my lip. She'd hate this plan.

"You look serious," said Moss.

"Capital offense trials do that to a person."

Night engulfed the sun's last beet-red smear on the horizon. I stared at the kitchen's roof, at a lazy thread of smoke from the half-dead hearths, but nothing moved.

My backside and hands turned numb and stiff against the stone seat. The Hungry Ghost always came to the kitchens by now to whimper and beg. Why not tonight?

I shuffled toward the kitchen door, Moss trailing.

Long before I reached it, the stench struck. Like maggots bloated on sun-rotted meat. I pulled the neck of my dress over my nose and mouth, peering around for the ghost with watering eyes.

"Was that you?" Moss wrinkled his nose.

"Honestly," I muttered. "The ghost's here."

"You see it?"

"I *smell* it." I called softly toward the roof. "Come down. Come down and I'll talk with you."

Nothing but normal patches of darkness and pale moonlight.

"Maybe it's shy," I said.

"Shy?" Moss laughed.

"Has anyone *not* from the kitchens ever claimed to see it? Even before the apprentices were accused?"

Moss paused. "No."

Was it embarrassed about its state? "I think it wants to be exorcised quietly, privately. Could you go sit back at the garden?"

"And leave you all alone?"

"You can watch."

Moss' frown deepened. "I can barely see you from back there."

"I'll scream nice and loud if Captain Gano or his guards appear. I promise."

Reluctantly, Moss retreated, his footsteps almost silent in the grass.

I tightened my fist on my dress front, wishing I was chewing mint or spicy cress to off-set the stench. "Come. Please. Talk to me."

Darkness slunk off the roof, like overly-loose noodle dough stretching from counter to floor in a slow fall. On the ground, it heaped together into rolls of fat covered in black slime. Four puny limbs. A pin-prick mouth. And a pair of begging, pleading eyes.

I gagged and stepped back as the reek hit me. It felt like someone shoving gray-molded peas up my throat and down my nose.

The ghost whimpered.

"You need my help."

Its eyes widened.

"And I need yours."

It tilted its head to the side.

"I'm going to trial in nine days for lying to the King. Lady Sulat was poisoned, inducing early labor. I saved her and her child with cooking skills I said I didn't have. My only chance is to find the poisoner and hope that deed gains me the King's mercy."

It coiled back on the word *mercy*, like it didn't belong in the same sentence as *king*.

"I'm no great spy, but *you* are. You can hide on any roof—even on the Royal Bear House—and listen to what people say in secret."

It whined at me like a beaten dog.

"You help me and I'll try to exorcise you. Do we have an agreement?"

Sulkily, it nodded.

I took another step back, trying to control the nausea boiling in my gut. "I'll need to cook for you. Are you a ghost because your descendants aren't feeding you?"

It gave a slobbery, slime-dripping head shake.

"So you're a ghost because you lusted too much after this world?"

Nodding. At least we could communicate this much. I didn't need to discover its favorite food, then; I needed to discover what its faults were and craft an appropriate counter-dish.

Osem had mentioned that ghosts appeared at sunrise and sunset at the place of their death. "You died in the palace, didn't you?"

More nodding.

"Are you on the palace records?"

It whimpered, head still going up and down.

Perfect. I could look him or her up in the Hall of Records. "And you died this winter, right?"

The ghost rubbed its eyes, as if already frustrated with this talk, but again nodded.

"Good. I'll come back here in a day or two with a list of names.

You can tell me yes or no to all of those. It shouldn't be too hard to ask around for your vices once I have a name. Nothing in this palace seems to stay secret for long."

The ghost whined and lowered its head disapprovingly.

"Do you have a better plan?" I asked. The back of my throat tasted like vomit from breathing in its smell. "Can you write in the dirt?"

It tried, but its stubby arms weren't dexterous enough to draw any characters.

Instead, it pantomimed a basket and eating something out of it.

"The kitchen's locked up and you can't actually eat."

The ghost frowned, all its rolls of fat and the tilt of its tiny eyes shifting downward. It picked up a branch and pretended to eat it.

"Oh! Buckwheat branches. But... I already know those don't exorcise you."

Again, the ghost pantomimed the basket and eating branches out of it, then wiggled its fingers like everything turning to mush.

"I know food goes bad when you try to eat." Why was it so insistent about buckwheat branches? "I'm sorry I don't understand."

The ghost pantomimed a number of other things, but I couldn't figure out what they were. It slumped to the ground, looking for all the world like a puddle of dough.

I paused. If it couldn't tell me about itself, it couldn't tell me what it learned, either. I'd have to exorcise it *before* the trial to get its help.

"Part of exorcism is confession. When we get to that part... you'll be able to talk? To tell me about your spying, too?"

The ghost shrugged. It didn't know. And why should it? It had never been exorcised before.

The ghost slunk back onto the roof and disappeared into shadow.

"You didn't see it?" I asked Moss as we walked back to Lady Sulat's.

The gravel crunched under his boots. "Some shadows shifted, but that could have been the branches overhead."

Stealthy. Nearly invisible. The Hungry Ghost was the perfect spy. I'd have to be the perfect chef to match and cook up an exorcism —quickly.

CHAPTER TWENTY-ONE

Moss hooked his elbow through mine as we walked toward the Hall of Records the next morning. I limped, despite his help.

"If Bane were here, he could carry you," Moss said. "You'd have to hold him tight, seeing as he's got just one arm to support you."

"Can you stop that? It's silly of you to pretend Bane's interested in a condemned woman. He's not stupid."

Even if I weren't facing a trial, my whole life had revolved around cooking, and Bane wasn't a chef. He couldn't appreciate the best part of me—he couldn't possibly want me.

Despite the gray streaks in his hair, Moss grinned like a five-year-old. "You're not running away. I have to enjoy myself somehow. You're looking into your friend from last night?"

"Of course." I lowered my voice as we passed a butterfly garden, a half-dozen spring azures flitting between its blooms. "Archivist Kochan... you said he's loyal to Lady Sulat. Can I ask him about said friend?"

"Yes. He's got a pair of tight lips. But don't trust anyone else."

Moss helped me up the stairs and into the Hall. Inside, Kochan and Linaan sat next to each other at one of the round tables, their heads touching over a manuscript box. They muttered rapidly to each other, debating some point of text.

Nearby, a pair of clerks—from the Department of the Treasury by the sound of it—bickered over another manuscript. I'd have to wait until they left to ask about exorcisms.

Thankfully, I had other things to research.

Moss coughed loudly. Both of the archivists looked up, their wrinkled faces spreading into matching grins. "Ah, Dami," Linaan said. "A budding scholar. What would you like today?"

"Do you have records of deaths within the palace for the past year?"

"Feeling morbid? Or are you still curious about the palace staff?" Linaan asked as she stood.

I shrugged. "Curious... I guess."

"She's a right to be morbid." Archivist Kochan's old eyes filled with sympathy, like he could already see the noose around my neck.

Linaan handed me a manuscript box. In the year before the apprentices' executions, I found two names. Green-ranked Malin of Askan-Wod and Yellow-ranked Tol of Sandhead.

Since Moss was doing nothing more than polishing his bolas, I asked him over. "Do you know who either of these people are?"

"Green-ranked Malin perished from a bad winter fever. I believe she served as a gardener."

"And she died here, in the palace?"

Moss shook his head. "No. Her family's local. When she became ill, they saw to her private care in their own home."

"So it's Yellow-ranked Tol."

"That one was a palace guard assigned to watch Lord Torut on a visit into the city. Accepted Lord Torut's drinking challenge. Heart stopped when he drank too much. Or when a brawl left a knife in him. I can't remember which."

I bit the inside of my lip. The ghost claimed it died in the palace and that it was in the records. Had I misread its intentions? Or did my simple questions sound like gibberish to it?

The pair of clerks shuffled past me, out of the archives.

I couldn't believe that the ghost didn't understand me. Its eyes seemed so sincere, so pained. Had it *lied* to me? I traced the names on the page with a finger. It had to know I'd discover its deception.

And maybe that was the whole point. Liars could become Hungry Ghosts. Maybe that was his vice.

Endurance-of-tongue. Didn't honesty require long, consistent control over that tiny muscle? Sweet-grilled morels or molasses-braised duck tongues might exorcise the ghost. Or should it be strong-of-tongue? Or did it depend on the kind of lies? I hoped the library contained recommendations.

I put the manuscript box back and returned to the archivists. "Do you have anything describing the three steps for exorcising a Hungry Ghost? Or recommended dishes for the process?"

Linaan's smile vanished, replaced with a cold stare. Kochan's eyes widened in alarm. I blinked at the two of them, then turned to Moss. He'd said Archivist Kochan could be trusted.

"Dami," Moss said firmly. How odd to hear him sound anything other than flippant. "Your joke is in poor taste." He bowed to both of the archivists. "I'm sorry. She's young and new to the palace. Lady Sulat told Dami to satiate her morbidity, then scour the archives for any records of All-of-Alls, hoping that an appropriate name for her infant would surface."

Linaan's face softened, but the suspicion never left. Kochan beamed at Moss like he was brilliant. "We don't have a single such volume, but a perusal of genealogies, servant lists, and histories would prove quite fruitful. I can think of five manuscript boxes off the top of my head. Come, Linaan."

He pulled her away from the table, away from their manuscript. She moved slowly, always glancing over her shoulder.

I turned to Moss, confused. "What—"

His stern glare silenced the question in my mouth.

And so I wasted the rest of the day going through every

manuscript box that either Kochan or Linaan could find that might mention an All-of-All. By dusk, my head throbbed and my knees ached. The musty smell of paper gagged me.

All told, I'd found two records of All-of-Alls.

I managed to thank both the archivists profusely for their time, though I regretted ever sitting with Nana for reading lessons. The idea of manuscripts—recipe manuscripts—seemed so enticing back then.

Outside, the mercifully cool air washed over us, perfumed with columbines. "Moss, why did I waste a day wading through manuscript boxes?"

"Not for my enjoyment," he said, voice low as we crunched gravel back to Lady Sulat's. Clouds half-covered the emerging stars. "Didn't I tell you to be careful?"

"I waited until the clerks left."

"Was Kochan the only person in the room?" Moss demanded, incredulous.

He couldn't mean himself. "Linaan? She and Kochan are such a pair, I didn't consider... I assumed—"

"Ah, assumptions. I thought you were getting better at navigating the palace. I'd ridicule you all afternoon, but I'm guilty of assuming you understand simple sentences, like 'just trust Kochan.'" He shook his head. "Linaan's loyal to the throne. King Alder's grandfather encouraged her to marry the nation's brightest budding archivist so she could watch him. They may both love manuscript boxes, but that doesn't make them political allies."

I felt the blundering idiot. But I still couldn't imagine that those two happy, wrinkled faces belonged to political opponents.

"Don't you remember how King Former Fulsaan and his late wife always opposed each other?"

I remembered my parents saying something about the Queen fighting against Red Lord Ospren's exile. But I'd been a child and the Redwood Palace seemed distant. Irrelevant, even, compared to the cutting board and carrots in front of me. "You were right. I am young. I'm new to this place."

I'd gathered the anger and suspicion of Lady Egal, Fir, Captain Gano, and now Archivist Linaan. I wondered how many other servants could say the same after less than two months at the palace.

Moss shook his head. "If we're lucky, Linaan won't report what you said to His Majesty. If she does, well, it won't matter *what* you say at your trial."

I CONVINCED Moss to send another guard to the Askan-Wod market with my wages to buy morels, duck tongues, and a crock. Lady Sulat generously allowed me to cook the food over her bedroom brazier after I test-tasted her supper. My soul thrilled to cook again. And it was reassuring to know I hadn't lost my skills—I had all the guards drooling over the aroma.

I carried the dish like a bowl of precious garnets across the twilight gardens, Moss trailing like before. The meal itself couldn't exorcise the ghost—not without the other two steps—but if I'd guessed correctly, maybe it would be able to speak after eating this food.

Moss waited among the pines. I headed toward the door. If this went well, if I didn't have to do anything rash or dangerous after tonight to prove my innocence, I could knock on that door tomorrow and apologize to Osem. Talk and laugh with her again.

The ghost slunk down from the roof, foul as a urine-soaked tanner's workshop. I mostly managed not to gag.

"You're not on the list of palace deaths. I figured that made you a liar in life. These might help you."

I placed the dish down and stepped far back.

The Hungry Ghost wailed like a child being forced to eat something it didn't want. But it shuffled forward, like it couldn't help itself, and fell upon the food. The beautiful, fatty tongues melted into mush. The morels rotted away.

All the hope in my gut turned to ash.

"You weren't a liar."

It whined, like lying might have been part of its faults, but far from the whole picture.

I sighed. "You really *are* in the palace records, aren't you?"

It nodded eagerly.

"But you're not Green-ranked Malin of Askan-Wod or Yellow-ranked Tol of Sandhead." It shook its head. I bit my lip, trying to think of other possibilities. "The treasury."

Its head perked up.

"Were you killed in an attempt to rob the treasury? I mean, were you a thief?" Such a figure would show up in the records—just not the ones I'd looked at.

All its excitement sagged away, its head lowering to the ground.

"Someone trying to aide a thief? Help a thief escape?"

It tilted its head to the side.

"Was a theft in the treasury involved?"

It didn't move. I shook my head. "Have you learned anything, spying for me? I can ask you about people, one by one. If I live past my trial, I'll have more time to help you."

It shrugged, sending its rolls of fat rippling. Did it not care to give me an answer, or was it holding out for an exorcism?

"I promise I'm trying to help you. I *want* to help you."

The ghost whimpered and pantomimed eating buckwheat branches plucked from a basket.

CHAPTER TWENTY-TWO

I could try cooking every dish I could think of and hope *something* helped the ghost. Probably a futile gesture, but what else did I have? I only knew one thing for sure: Fir was connected to the poisoning.

Maybe I needed to focus on him.

The next morning, Lady Sulat's lattice-shutters opened to the fine spring air. I tasted her food. Perfect as always, thanks to Sorrel.

Then the door guard admitted Bane. He flushed when he saw me, then glanced between me and Lady Sulat. I peered at him. Was he embarrassed I'd failed at Lord Torut's?

Lady Sulat observed his fidgeting with her usual, placid face. "You wish to speak with me, Bane?"

"Yes, Lady." He bowed deeply. But no envelope occupied his hand.

Lady Sulat managed to sip her infusion and wave me out of the room at the same time. I frowned but did as she asked. I plunked down on the porch steps and gently stretched my ankle in preparation for shadowing Fir. However eager I was to get started, I could delay myself a moment or two for Bane. I should have found him yesterday and told him about Lord Torut's.

"Hoping to see Bane?" Moss asked.

Poppy joined us then, a basket of cloth on her hip. "Are you sure it's safe to talk about him right now? I saw him come into the apartments."

"Do you need help with anything, Poppy?" I asked, doing my best to ignore Moss.

She clutched the basket jealously to her hip. "Not with this fine cloth. It's my favorite to work with."

I sighed.

Bane strolled out, an excited smile on his face. "Good morning!" He said that like nothing could make it otherwise.

I stood, keeping my weight on my good foot. "Do you have a moment?"

Poppy giggled, but Bane didn't notice.

"If we can talk while walking to the main gate." He cheerfully waved the black envelope in his hand. Did he like his work that much? "I have a message for Lieutenant-General Behon at the city wall."

I hobbled alongside him. "That name sounds familiar."

"He's over Askan-Wod's defenses. You know, important and all that." Bane tucked the envelope under his amputated arm, then offered his elbow as a crutch for me. "Given the circumstance, and our chaperone, I think this is appropriate?"

He was always so careful to be respectful. Nana would have liked him. I put my arm through his muscular one, his juniper-and-smoke smell washing over me. Earthy, like the forest after rain. My cheeks warmed, though really, I had no reason to be embarrassed. I leaned into him, letting him take the weight. "Thank you."

"Let me know if we need to go slower," Bane said with one of his meltingly warm smiles.

Moss trailed behind us, snickering. Reacting would encourage him. Instead, I whispered to Bane about my failures at Blue Lord Torut's. Whispering was easy, walking so close together.

"Ah. That explains it," Bane said.

"Explains what?"

"Two mornings ago, Palace Guards found broken tree branches. One of them insisted that Bloodmarrow ghosts had vandalized the gardens, but then they heard about the fresh boughs in Lord Torut's apartments. The Justice Ministry fined him and Lady Egal demoted his door servant for allowing her master to act so unseemly. She's in the worst corner of the laundry, now—scrubbing diapers and mud stains."

I hated my layers of lies. I couldn't even apologize to her without singling myself out for suspicion. Poor girl. She'd *liked* being Lord Torut's door servant.

"She got off easy, without a dismissal. Her father's important enough not to insult lightly." Despite everything, he sounded as chipper as if we'd discussed an early harvest of pears. "Don't look so sad. I won't let anyone hurt you."

As if he could stop the Purple-Blue Council from proclaiming me guilty or the King from ordering my death. We passed the pond; a breeze rolled off it, carrying a whiff of turtles and reeds.

"I'm going to start following Fir. Hope something turns up. I know it's not much of a plan, but..." I sighed. I always seemed to be following not-much-of-a-plan.

"I saw him, on my way here."

I jerked to a stop. "Really?"

"Entering the men's bathhouse. He might still be there, if you think eavesdropping would help."

I halted and beamed at him. "Bane. You're amazing. Thank you."

Oddly, he glanced down at the gravel, embarrassed. Then he looked up, those brown eyes searching mine. He opened his mouth, closed it, stared back at his feet, then hurried off without making eye contact again.

Moss strode up from behind. "Poppy's not entirely off the mark. He'll be crushed when King Alder leaves you dangling from the city wall."

"Of course he'll be sad." He was a good man. A kind man.

"Ah. You missed my tone. I meant the kind of sadness that drives a perfectly sane man to write terrible poetry about unrequited love."

I sighed and shook my head. Given that seven days stood between me and a trial, I was the worst prospect for a wife in all of Askan-Wod. Bane knew that. I wouldn't insult his intelligence by imagining otherwise.

Even without the trial, we were as poorly matched as Violet and Sorrel. Bane wasn't a chef. He couldn't love the best part of me. "You shouldn't talk like that. You'll put ideas into his head, and then he *will* be crushed. Bane's just a soldier helping a citizen. He said as much."

One last quest for the soldier who'd never see the front lines again. I was grateful for his help.

"Yup. Soldiers are well-known for constantly blushing and then running off without warning. I'm not sure if you're blind, Dami, or if you're too polite to admit you find him attractive."

"I do not!"

"Mm-hmm." Moss breathed on his bolas and polished them on his tunic. "We heading to the bathhouse, then?"

I PRESSED my ear against the wooden wall of the men's bathhouse while Moss pretended to nap behind the bushes. At least, I think he was pretending.

A muffled, male voice reverberated through the wood. "You could join the army, you know."

"With the current casualty rate?" Fir snorted.

The other man—I didn't recognize his voice—slapped the top of the water. "That's unpatriotic. I know you have no birthgift, but plenty of young men serve with gifts that aren't ideal for combat. Your brothers all went."

"I want an end to this war as much as you do," Fir said. The usual honey-and-oil of his voice shifted into something raw and honest. Odd. I didn't think Fir cared a whit about the war. I stretched my bad ankle out on the lawn, trying to get comfortable. My short walk had it throbbing again.

"What are you doing here, then? If you enlisted, you might earn yourself some *respect* and, Ancestors willing, Green rank. Do you like loafing and doting on dear Grandmamma Egal?"

I doubted he'd earn himself a rank for a military feat with no marvelous birthgift to assist him.

"One day, she'll be in the Ancestral Realm, looking over me and spinning souls for her descendants. I could do worse things than honor her in life."

That shut the other man up. I listened to the gentle sounds of water, the occasional splash. Other people conversed on the other end of the bathhouse, but I only caught murmurs, soft and sleepy. Moss snored.

"They could use you, you know, on the front," the man said, tone almost apologetic.

Fir responded, "I'm needed here."

"The Shoreed took Baylet. Word says they'll spearhead northward and take Napil next."

My stomach churned. King Alder mentioned that too—that we could lose our obsidian mines.

"When they march on Askan-Wod, I'll enlist," Fir said.

"You'll need plenty of time to shape up your scrawny arms. I'd start now."

"Thank you for your flattering opinion."

More splashing. Somebody leaving. Shoreed had to be fighting like mad. Was Dami on the front lines now? Had she been discovered?

At least the army traveled with good chefs. That would keep the soldiers strong. Let them heal. Save them from infections.

"Odd to see you here," Fir said. I silently cursed and jerked to my feet. Ignoring the protests of my bad ankle, I started to leave.

Fir placed one hand on the wall behind me, blocking me. His damp shirt clung to the muscles of his chest. Not so scrawny. His voice rumbled dangerously low. "What are you doing here, Dami?"

"Umm." What would Osem say? "Waiting for my guard to finish his bath. I can't stand to be next to him anymore—he stinks."

Fir frowned and glanced around the garden. "Where is your guard? Are you trying to slip away from him?"

I could just see Moss behind the shrubbery, but I knew where to look. "Me? No. Of course not," I rambled, trying to sound guilty. "Why would I do that?"

He grinned. "Ah. If you're unencumbered by him, my friends, the Palace Guards, would love to have a friendly chat with you. They have the most charming accommodations."

"Perhaps I'm better off with the smelly old man."

Fir's expression turned wolfish. "You shouldn't have tried to oppose me. Now the council will take care of you for me. Too bad your trial isn't sooner."

"And you'll walk free of your crimes, is that it?" I tried to sound big, but my voice squeaked in my throat. I couldn't run. Right now, how hard would it be to separate me from Moss and give me to the Palace Guards?

"Crimes? I didn't commit any crimes."

"You poisoned Lady Sulat."

"Me?" He placed his remaining hand on the wall near the other side on my head. I choked on the stench of too-strong pine soap. Water from his hair dripped in my face. "I hold no ill will against Lady Sulat. Why would I do such a thing?"

That was the question. "I'll find out why."

"By sulking around bathhouses. I'm terrified, Dami. Just terrified. You should have gone home when I stole your amber."

"You admit to that much, then." My breath trembled in my lungs. Fir could break my nose with one quick jab.

"It's no grand confession—who would believe you? I'd pay you back... but given your trial, it seems like a waste." His handsome grin mocked me. I hated that grin.

"But you're good at wasting things," I said. "You live by loafing on your grandmother's good will. Your only talent is picking on servants. You're yellow-ranked, an honored citizen, yet you sulk and do *nothing* with that position. You don't even have the courage to defend your country. By the King's own forbearers, keep the money. Perhaps polishing it will give you something *useful* to do."

My head spun like I'd been in the heat too long. But, Ancestors forgive me, it felt good to say.

"I am *not* useless," he growled, all traces of handsome washed from his face.

I'd found a sore spot. I hit it as hard as I could. "Do you think being giftless gives you an excuse? You're the same rank as Bane. The war half-destroyed his gift, but he found a way to move forward, to serve as a messenger. Bad circumstances couldn't stop him from making an honorable life for himself. You? Your name fits you perfectly. You're a fir tree in a grove of redwoods. You might talk about being as strong and grand as the giants around you, but you'll never reach their heights. All the luckiest circumstances in the world couldn't change you into a better person. You're nothing, Fir. And you always will be."

On the last word I tried to shove his arms away, but Fir caught my wrists, digging his fingernails into my skin. He stepped closer, pinning me chest-to-chest against the bathhouse wall. My bad leg buckled. Fir refused to let me fall. He leaned in, mouth so close to the side of my face he could bite my jugular out like a wolf.

He whispered, breath hot on my skin. "I could break your wrists right now."

"But you won't," I managed. "Hurting me will make you look suspicious."

"I won't hurt you *if I don't have to*. Try to wait patiently for your hanging, like a good little girl. I'd hate to have this talk with you again."

Fir released me and stepped back. I crumpled against the wall. He straightened his shirt and donned a smile of perfect civility. "I'm sorry you turned down my offer to go find some palace guards. Good day, Dami. Enjoy days while you still have them."

CHAPTER
TWENTY-THREE

After I caught my breath and shook Moss awake, I headed off to stalk Fir. No sign of him on the nearby paths. I searched everywhere. I even hid behind a bush near Lady Egal's apartments for two hours, hoping to catch him coming or going.

Had he left the palace? I hobbled to the gate, but Nisaat hadn't seen him.

I returned to Lady Sulat's and tasted her lunch, mind tumbling over new ideas for finding Fir. Maybe I should have stayed outside Lady Egal's longer.

But one glance at my awkward gait, and Lady Sulat ordered me to stay put until tomorrow morning. No more tracking Fir today. No expedition to feed the Hungry Ghost tonight.

Poppy left for her half-day off, so I scrubbed the muddy porch steps alone. Except for Moss.

"I can't believe you fell asleep." My wrists still ached from where Fir had grabbed them, an unwelcome counterpoint to the ankle. "Aren't you supposed to guard me?"

"I'm also spying on you." Moss sat on the lawn, nonchalantly braiding grass. "Didn't we cover this already? You don't get to be indignant about it twice."

"How are you supposed to spy if you're asleep?"

"I'm talented like that."

I wanted to whack him upside the head with the brush. I scrubbed harder instead.

"Do you think Fir would've talked so much if he knew I was there?" Moss asked.

I blinked. No, he wouldn't have.

Moss' voice turned soft and serious for once. "I'm sorry Fir was rough with you. I didn't expect that in broad daylight. Are you all right?"

"A bit of soreness is the least of my worries right now."

Moss sighed. "I hope that snake has to answer for all of his crimes one day."

"Me too." I dipped my brush back into the water bucket.

"Well, now you know there's a lovely secluded spot behind the bathhouse," Moss said cheerfully, the seriousness gone as if it had never existed. "Maybe you should show it to Bane sometime."

"So he can spy on Fir?"

"So he can give a detailed report the next time another messenger asks him if young ladies who are perceptive-of-tongue really are amazing kissers."

"Moss!"

My guard showed no hint of shame. He just jutted his chin at the bottom stair. "Looks like you missed a spot."

BANE WASN'T A CHEF. He couldn't want me. But as I weeded Lady Sulat's flowerbeds, it occurred to me Sorrel was perceptive-of-tongue, too. It was all too easy to imagine his exquisitely trained mouth filling me with equally exquisite kisses.

Cursed wedding. Cursed trial. Cursed war. I yanked the little weeds out with vengeance, leaving the azaleas—white and pink with a delicate yellow center.

Who did Fir trust? Who might he work for?

"Having fun murdering those plants?" Moss asked.

"I'll bet you, with one-to-ten odds, that you can't stay quiet until sunset."

Moss laughed. "Oh, I'd love to take you up on that one."

"Please go away."

"I am leaving; that's what I was about to tell you."

Confused, I sat back on my good ankle and wiped the sweat from my face. Moss nodded to the soldier behind him, a stoic young man in black. "This is Resin. Lady Sulat's given me until tomorrow evening off for my granddaughter's first birthday."

"Oh, congratulations!" A child surviving infanthood was something to celebrate. "You'll be presenting her to your ancestors, then?"

Moss nodded. "I'm afraid my family's from Hawkfern, so we only have plaques in our shrine. But it will still be a fine evening."

"I didn't know you had grandchildren," I apologized. I'd never asked him about himself.

"Well, we've already covered that there are plenty of things you don't know, Dami. It seems to be a downfall of yours."

"Then make me a little less ignorant and tell me about your descendants."

He smiled. " I've got six living children and the one granddaughter—though by winter, I'll be the grandfather of three."

I could picture him rolling on the floor and chasing grandchildren through the forest. Except children in Askan-Wod probably did something other than play in the woods.

Moss bowed and left. Resin just stared at me, face perfectly impassive. Unnerving.

I returned to the weeds, trying to forget Resin existed. Perhaps I hadn't located Fir"s master because he served someone too powerful to be caught—like King Alder. A man who could love his father and worry over his nation, yet send twelve of his innocent citizens to hang.

But it didn't matter. Whether I could save myself or not, I wanted the peace of knowing I'd done everything I could to stop Fir's plots.

THE NEXT MORNING, Poppy fetched more garlic-stuffed pickled cherries for me. Lady Sulat still didn't allow me to leave until midday. Maybe if I was lucky, I could find Fir coming or going from Lady Egal's quarters today.

As Resin and I headed down the path, Violet walked toward us, that sickly-sweet smile plastered on her face, her dress accentuating her curves.

After years of living with the real Dami—gorgeous, town-beauty Dami—I thought I was content to be the one people called clever, or skilled, or well-mannered. But how would Sorrel ever see me when he was busy looking at all of her?

"Hello, sir!" Violet called to Resin. "Might you direct me to Dami?"

Resin nodded at me, nearly as lifeless as the gravel under his feet.

It took more self-control that I'd like to admit not to snap at him. Reluctantly, I admitted, "I'm Dami."

"I'm Violet. Didn't I see you in the kitchens once? It's *wonderful* to meet you!" She gave a quick bow.

Given that she was allowing my heartbroken Sorrel to doom himself to a loveless marriage to a woman who didn't understand his art, I didn't return her sentiment.

Violet coughed awkwardly. "I haven't seen the grounds of the palace yet. I asked Lady Egal, Matron of the Household, for a tour, but she and her servants are busy. She said you're the newest servant, so you have time to help me."

Of course Lady Egal would recommend me for extra work. She loathed me.

"I trust I'm no inconvenience to you?"

I'd rather scoop my own eyeballs out with spoons, pickle them, and eat them for supper than spend an afternoon helping my replacement. "I'm busy."

Or I would be, as soon as I found Fir.

"Lady Sulat told me to accompany you wherever you wished to go," Resin said—the first words I'd heard out of him. How helpful. "She said not to worry about tasks."

Violet clapped her hands together. "Splendid!"

My ankle decided to spite me, too—after a morning of rest and the cherries, it barely twinged. I diverted our tour to places I thought Fir might be first. No luck. After that, I took Violet through the gardens as systematically and quickly as I could. Despite my flat monotone, she clasped her hands and praised everything with overly sweet, high-pitched words that, I'm sure, explained the lack of birds in our vicinity. She lingered in the plum orchard, wandering between trees, lips pursed.

I stood at the edge of the path, not hiding my impatience.

Eventually, Violet gave a dramatic sigh. "No. Let's move on. This place isn't grand enough."

I'd take plum trees putting out leaves over fancy flowers any day. We continued, rounding the gravel path until we overlooked the pond where Bane and I had skipped rocks.

"Oooh! How delightful!" Violet cooed. Was she incapable of speaking in a normal voice? She ran down the sloped lawn to the white-pebble shore. She flicked a rock in and giggled. Amateur. "It's perfect, isn't it?"

She swayed back and forth, hands clasped in front of her, beaming at me and Resin. If she expected an answer, she'd be disappointed.

"Are you afraid of water?" Violet asked, tilting her head to the side.

I actually missed Moss. If he were here, we could bet over whether or not he could get Violet with his bolas from this far away.

She meandered back up the lawn, looking right, then left, as if inspecting the place. She stopped in front of me. "You don't... say much. Are you not feeling well?"

"Horrid."

"Well, come to the kitchens! My Sorrel, he's very busy, being the Acting Master Chef and all, but if I asked him *nicely*, I'm sure he'd cook something that would make you feel better!"

If I had to watch her ask him *nicely*, I'd vomit on my sandals. "No. That's fine."

"You can't be shy! Sorrel's nice. I promise. We're getting married, you know." She sighed wistfully. "Our wedding will be so special."

I smoothed my black skirt. Certainly that was better than screaming at her. Sorrel was *my* betrothed. He deserved better than this saccharine bride. We should be cooking and arguing over junipers and rosehips together.

The throb in my ankle returned; I shifted awkwardly, trying to favor my other foot.

"You poor thing. We'll take you right back to Lady Sulat's. Are you sure I can't fetch you anything?" Violet asked.

Maybe I was too harsh on her. Kindness wasn't a virtue to sneer at, even if it came with silliness in Violet's case. More pickled garlic-stuffed cherries certainly wouldn't hurt.

But I still didn't want to be indebted to her. "I'm fine."

"Well then, I suppose I'll let you head back to Lady Sulat's on your own. Thank you for the tour. This lawn will be the *perfect* place for our wedding. You'll come, won't you?"

My cheeks burned—how could she trick me into helping her with her wedding? "I'm afraid I'll be quite busy next week."

"Oh!" Violet pulled up short. "Didn't you hear? My Sorrel, he's so very eager to have this wedding as soon as possible. He asked Lady Egal to move it up."

Nervousness flickered in her eyes, but she smiled through it.

"Tell him to slow down if you're uncomfortable," I urged, meaning every word. Telling Sorrel to call it off would be even better.

She laughed and waved her hand, voice a half-octave higher than usual. "Don't be silly. I want my Sorrel to be happy. Besides, Lady Egal's a wonder and she's already arranged everything for tomorrow! Won't that be lovely?"

Tomorrow. I stared at her, blinking and dizzy like I'd been concussed. I could think of nothing original to say and dully echoed her last word. "Lovely."

CHAPTER
TWENTY-FOUR

Resin refused to send someone to the marketplace to buy me ingredients without Lady Sulat's explicit permission. By the time she had a moment to see us, the markets had closed. I couldn't try anything for the Hungry Ghost tomorrow, either—the kitchens would be bustling for the wedding.

My embroidery needle wandered through the cloth. Poppy, sitting next to me, lined up neat stitch after neat stitch. "Are you feeling well?"

"Yes." I managed that one word without my voice cracking. Wedding. Tomorrow. This wasn't what I'd planned. I couldn't prove my innocence and win Sorrel's affections in one day.

Moss returned late that evening and soaked in the congratulations of the other soldiers. I tried to match their celebratory smiles. Lady

Sulat gave Moss a bolt of cheery, yellow brocade for his granddaughter, then admonished everyone to get some rest.

Finally left to the solitude of my closet-room, I collapsed to my knees. I clenched my hands together. My heart raced as fast as my thoughts.

"Ancestors, why won't you listen?" I whispered, voice hoarse with emotion. "Haven't I sacrificed enough for you? Or do you consider me already dead, with the upcoming trial? I'm not dead. *I'm here.*"

I waited for calm reassurances, for a clear mind and clear thoughts, but nothing came. My legs tingled, numb from kneeling so long. Didn't my ancestors care if I died young, without descendants? Moss' joy in his granddaughter hung fresh in my mind. I imagined his wife and daughter-in-law marveling over the yellow brocade, debating whether they should make whole dresses from it or use it, bit by bit over the years, to trim the girl's clothes. I'd never have such a debate. I'd never stand over a tiny, sleeping form and whisper silent promises of peace, safety, and love.

"I'm Plum. Remember?" I wished for the luxury of kneeling in our family shrine, or in a redwood circle. But even if I was in a strange closet, Nana couldn't forget me—she'd held me on the day I was born and loved me every day after. "Why won't you hear me? I need help. Direction. Don't you still love me?"

Nothing. My chest clenched so hard I didn't have air for crying. The darkness pressed tight about me in my tiny closet.

I managed to breathe in and breathe out. Sorrel loved me before he met me simply because of my reputation as a chef. We would have spent our days harvesting greenhouse vegetable together in the morning and reading recipe manuscripts in his father's library in the afternoons. My future had been beautiful. "Nana, won't you hear your granddaughter? I'm about to lose everything I've ever wanted."

Something pricked at my chest. For a moment, I thought Nana knelt with me. I smelled her honey-scented skin. Then it decayed into the overpowering rot of a Hungry Ghost.

I gagged, but then the smells vanished.

My hands shook, so I hugged myself tight. Yes, I wanted something else more than Sorrel—I wanted to prevent Nana from becoming a Hungry Ghost. I wanted my parents' safety. My sister's, too. I decided that the day I tore up Sorrel's letter.

"Oh, Nana. I didn't think I'd have to meet him. To know everything I'd miss." My eyes stung and my throat felt raw. "And I didn't think I'd have to meet *her*. My replacement. Why didn't you stop Dami from leaving in the first place?"

Fainter now, I smelled honey. Warmth washed through my chest. *I love you always, little blossom*, the warmth seemed to say.

I burst into sobs.

I missed her. I missed her like I missed cooking. I felt like someone had split open my ribcage. "Nana, I want there to be some world where you're rocking my baby while Sorrel and I cook breakfast for all of us. I hurt all over just thinking of it."

Hush, hush, little blossom.

The warmth seemed to stroke my cheek. I found myself laying down, my tears running into my pillow. "But you're not coming back, and Nana... Nana, is there any way to win Sorrel over?"

Hush, hush, little blossom.

I cried. I don't know for how long, but I didn't want to stop because I could smell her. I could feel her near. I didn't want to sleep. I told Nana everything—about Dami and Fir, Sorrel and Violet, Osem and Bane. About trying to exorcise the Hungry Ghost. I could *feel* her listening, even if I couldn't see her.

Nana stayed with me, as patient as she'd been when I was a four-year-old protesting I wasn't tired. I fell asleep with her warmth next to me.

In the morning, my hands were cold, my room empty.

A STEADY SPRING drizzle dampened the morning. If it turned into a vicious lightning storm, Violet would have to postpone her ill-matched wedding.

I tasted Lady Sulat's breakfast in the sitting room, then Poppy took it inside—our Lady was in the middle of an important meeting. As soon as Poppy disappeared, Moss caught my shoulder.

I tried to hide my puffy eyes, but he didn't comment on my face. Instead, he handed me a crumpled, folded piece of paper. "This came for you. In the middle of the night."

Sorrel. Somehow he'd felt that we were meant to be together. That our mutual love of cooking would grow into a happy lifetime of loving each other.

I retreated into the corner and opened the paper. The hasty script read:

THREE STEPS TO exorcise a Hungry Ghost created by their own lust for this world. First, a meal, perfectly prepared—one that off-sets their ill habits. Second, the true remorse of the ghost. Third, their confession. A Hungry Ghost created by neglect requires similar things—their favorite food, the true regret of those living where it died, and a formal apology from them.

A LIST of dates and times followed, with Linaan's name crossed out at the bottom. Times when Linaan wouldn't be in the library—times when I could research what to cook for an adulterer or a glutton or a liar. The earliest was tomorrow afternoon. I'd cook everything the manuscripts recommended. Surely *something* would work. Silently, I thanked Archivist Kochan and tucked the paper into the waist of my skirt.

If it worked, I'd have three remaining days to use whatever information the Hungry Ghost had for me.

But I'd still be at least a day too late to win Sorrel back.

Surely they'd postpone the wedding due to the rain? Surely I'd get a fair chance to reconcile with him?

Poppy returned, sighing. "Lady Sulat's speaking with Lieutenant-General Behon, but she said not to leave her apartments—she wants to see you afterwards."

Odd. Outside of confirming that her food was safe to eat, Lady Sulat hardly talked to me.

Poppy began checking the windows for leaks, so I joined her. "The tents they're setting up are magnificent."

"Tents?" I asked.

"For the wedding!" Poppy sighed romantically. "Huge and white, like clouds."

The lump in my throat swelled to the size of an onion. "They're... setting up? Despite the rain?"

"Um, that's what the tents are for." Poppy paused. "Are you well?"

I stared at the windows, running my finger—slow as if I were swimming in molasses—over the seams, feeling for wet spots. My feet ached to run to the kitchens. Now. To tell Sorrel everything. Now. But I had my parents, Nana, and Dami to think of. I swallowed hard. I couldn't continue this conversation with Poppy. I abruptly turned to Moss. "Who's Lieutenant-General Behon?"

He sounded familiar.

"The man in charge of Askan-Wod's defenses. Double-gifted. Agile-of-face and agile-of-hand. The first lends itself to his superb speeches; the second to outstanding archery."

"Ah."

The door to the bedroom opened.

Lieutenant-General Behon strode out. He looked like a hundred other men—middle aged, bald, about my height—but he had *presence*. With a tiny slant of his eyebrow, he made me feel like street refuse. "Blue Lady Sulat is ready to see you."

He turned and bowed to her. His expression changed completely —a hint of warmth around the mouth, downturned eyes, a relaxed brow. He radiated gentle respect. Agile-of-face indeed. My scowls and smiles weren't half as expressive.

He left through the sitting room. I strode in and Moss closed the door behind me. The room held me, Lady Sulat, her infant, and her two guards standing in the corner like a pair of potted trees.

Today, Lady Sulat rested in her chair, her long crimson skirt covering her feet. The tiny bundle of a child rested against her chest, breathing steadily in sleep. Between the scores of flowers from her soldiers and the drawn windows, I felt like I'd entered a midnight garden. Rain plinked on the roof.

Lady Sulat's voice was soft. "I spoke with Moss yesterday."

I clasped my hands in front of me and stared at the floor. I wished I could make my face as peaceful as Lieutenant-General Behon's, but I knew nervousness pinched my expression.

"Fir might play at being your enemy to make me trust you, but you've never mentioned who stole your money on your journey."

I swallowed hard, the delicate scent of the azaleas and forget-me-nots drowning my thoughts.

"I now believe, with some confidence, that you are in fact innocent in these plots."

I looked up. Her face remained composed and elegant, but something had softened. "Thank you, Dami, for acting quickly and saving the life of my child."

I bowed shakily. "You're welcome."

"You would have been safer to leave us alone. Creating an All-of-All... there is no way to pretend you're not perceptive-of-taste-and-smell. You placed yourself in danger. Why?"

The tiny child shifted, peeped a tiny sound. Lady Sulat rubbed his back. She held a precious, innocent life.

My throat felt too small, like I'd tried to swallow a radish. "I couldn't let a baby die."

"You have no relation to me. No reason to care about the fate of this child."

"None? He's... he's a child. And I could save him. Do I need any other reason?"

Lady Sulat actually smiled in that dimly-lit room. "You have a soldier's heart."

I tilted my head to the side. "I... don't understand."

"Being a soldier is about sacrifice. All of them give up comfort. Some will give up an arm. Some will give their life. They never know when they begin what their sacrifice will be. But there are people—a nation—to protect. You chose to save this child without knowing what consequences would follow."

"Ah. Thank you, then." It sounded a lot like the reasons Bane chose to help me. But Fir's brothers went to war hoping to earn rank. Dami wanted to be important. Not all soldiers fought out of a desire to protect. I supposed whatever their reasons, they still all sacrificed.

I wanted to think that Lady Sulat, with all her loyal soldiers, did what she did for the right reasons. She sipped her mint-and-nettle tea from her glazed cup and studied me.

I glanced at her, then away. At my feet, then at her guards. Still, she said nothing. My palms turned clammy. "You want to know why I didn't say I'm perceptive-of-taste-and-smell on my application, don't you?"

"Of course."

I bit my lip. After the things she'd done for Osem and Bane, after what she'd done for *me*, I believed her a good person. But a good person who knew the truth would hang me and my whole family.

"But," Lady Sulat continued, "I haven't asked. If I did, would you give me the untainted truth?"

I looked down. "No."

"Then I won't ask." She set her teacup aside. "I don't like to have lies between me and those on my staff."

"You'd rather have secrets?" I frowned, confused.

"Everyone has secrets." The way she said it, it sounded like she knew most of them, too. Her eyes remained calm. If she wanted to know the truth of my past, how long would it take her to figure out?

"Someone poisoned me," she continued. "There are always plots in the Redwood Palace and in the capital, but they are usually of a less direct nature. I, unfortunately, do not know who orchestrated this."

"I don't either."

She inclined her head. "I noticed. If you had some notion, your reconnaissance would have been more focused."

Was she criticizing my spying abilities? It wasn't like I came from a family that encouraged slipping around corners and eavesdropping.

"Tell me what you know."

I recounted Fir's theft, the snake, and how Fir arranged for Hawak to be sent away. Oh, and the girl who'd taken her name off the list. Then I paused.

Lady Sulat stared expectantly at me. "Do go on."

My tongue stuck to the roof of my mouth, like sauce burnt onto a crock. What else did I know? I'd learned so little. "Lady Egal didn't dismiss me, so I don't think she's involved."

Lady Sulat nodded. She'd already put that together.

"Umm. And I didn't find anything in Blue Lord Torut's apartments."

"My brother's a useless drunk," Lady Sulat stated, with the same emotion of someone noting that grass is green.

What else had I learned? "I think I can exorcise the Hungry Ghost. Maybe. I've... employed it as my spy."

"Yes. Admittedly the cleverest thing you've done," Lady Sulat said. And still she stared at me.

My ankle throbbed dully from Captain Gano's attack. So much work, so much running about, and I'd learned so little. Lady Sulat was right. I had no great skill in reconnaissance. "I... I don't have anything else."

"Yes, we do."

I bit my lip. Moss must have noticed something I overlooked.

"We have you."

"M-me?"

Lady Sulat nodded, one hand on her son's back. "Yes, you. Fir knows you suspect him. You've made him nervous. He won't neglect to report your conversation to whomever he serves."

"I don't see how that helps us," I admitted.

Lady Sulat didn't ridicule me—she seemed to appreciate plain speech. "Tonight, there will be a wedding for Acting Master Chef Sorrel. I assume you've heard about that?"

She may as well have thrown vinegar in my eyes. I managed a curt nod.

"Given that he's holding an honored spot in the palace, the

Purple, Blue, and a good portion of the Green rank within the palace will attend. You will also come to the wedding. I'll keep Moss nearby, of course. Plus a few other guards on the fringes. I want to see how others react to you. Fir's master may give himself away."

Go to the wedding? I might as well disembowel myself and grill the offal. "You think whoever dared to have you poisoned will be careless enough to say something to me?"

"Ah. Has no one told you? I'm perceptive-of-eye, like my husband. He uses it to survey battlefields. I use it to read people. Tiny twitches. Pulse in the throat. Pupil dilation. You, for example, have no desire to go to the wedding—but a blind man could see that from your tone. You're coming anyway."

CHAPTER
TWENTY-FIVE

I volunteered to take Lady Sulat's tea tray back to the kitchens. Moss and I hurried through the gardens, but the rain soaked us through anyway. I should have grabbed my mantle before we left.

The kitchens were hot, muggy, and almost as busy as the night Lady Sulat was poisoned. The apprentices bustled and swore as they burned their fingers or as their crocks boiled over. In the only clean, unhurried corner of the kitchens, three servants I didn't recognize scrubbed crocks.

"Where's Osem?" I asked them. Half of me wanted to see her and the other half dreaded apologizing for doing dangerous things I intended to keep doing.

"Getting more firewood, but it's slower work with the rain," said the oldest girl. "We're here temporarily—Lady Egal wants the kitchen running smoothly for the wedding."

I nodded and turned. Unlike everyone else, Sorrel stood still. He leaned over the menu slate, muttering to himself, that line between his brows. So serious. So focused.

I wouldn't see him again before the wedding. I bit my lip. Why couldn't I have proved my innocence first? Why didn't I have a week with him in the kitchen, cooking, to convince him to adore me? Fear burned my throat, but today was my only opportunity.

I strode behind him and read over his shoulder. The wedding menu.

"Did you come to the kitchens to poison something, or is your ankle acting up?" he asked, turning around.

"My ankle's doing much better, thank you."

"So you're here to poison me? Please come back later. I'm busy today." He rubbed his neck, then stretched it from side to side. Wedding feasts required five courses—turning all that food into a harmonious, balancing meal was no small feat. As the Acting Master Chef, everyone would judge his skill on this dinner. No wonder he looked stressed.

"If you change the soup course from parsnips to beet greens, that will balance out the sweet problem with the honey-acorn custard in the fourth course."

He stared at me, then his chalk board, then back at me. "I... I do believe you're right. That's perfect. Thank you."

Surprise and—better yet—respect showed in his eyes. "I don't suppose you have any miraculous suggestions for the main course?"

"What's the problem?" The skewered, spiced meat he proposed would be perfect.

"Rain. If we bring them out on large platters, they'll cool. If we cover the platters, they'll lose their crust in the steam. Covers aren't a problem for anything else, but this..."

I chewed my lip. Sorrel wanted perfection. He wanted to prove himself. "Skewers cook quickly."

"I know."

"In the summer, back at home, sometimes we'd dig a long, thin trench and fill it with coals. Everyone could come with their individual skewers, turning them as we talked, eating them hot as they finished. Most of the village turned out."

Sorrel shook his head. "It's still raining. We can't all sit on the grass."

"So you make the trench across the table." I took his slate and chalk and sketched a narrow brick trough, lined with sand, then coals. "If you do it right, you won't burn the table. Fire at eye level. It will look spectacular, and you can ensure the skewers all turn out perfect."

Sorrel peered at my drawing, looking at it from one side, then the other. He erased it, then redrew it with the bricks arranged slightly differently. "Dami, you're brilliant. This will work."

Tanoak, on his way to the cellar, glanced at it. "Huh. That is clever, Dami."

"Clever indeed. Thank you." Sorrel beamed at me. His eyes glittered when he did that. He smelled of well-oiled maple cutting boards and coriander. Smells I could sink into forever.

My stomach felt like a white-hot coal. Maybe I couldn't explain who I was. Maybe I didn't have time to win him over slowly, cooking together in the kitchens, but I wouldn't lose this fantastic chef of a man because cowardice tied my tongue.

"I love you," I whispered.

He jerked back, all the warmth in his face snuffed into confusion. "This is my wedding menu you helped with, remember?"

"Which is why I had to tell you now." My mouth tasted like sand and salt. This was the part where his smile would return. Where he'd take both my hands and everything would be fine again.

Rage simmered behind his eyes, but he kept his voice down. "Are you trying to gain my affections so you can humiliate me like your sister did? Or is throwing me off-balance part of another poisoning plot of yours?"

"Sorrel, I'm not playing games with you. I mean it. You're amazing."

He brusquely chalked in beet green soup for the second course. My innards felt like someone was making forcemeat out of them. But I couldn't convince my feet to move. He could still smile. He could still take my hand. His cold anger could turn into something warm— shouldn't he know that he loved me, once?

Sorrel didn't look up. "Get out of my kitchen."

"THAT WENT WELL!" Moss said cheerfully, one step behind me as we returned to Lady Sulat's rooms. "I'm sure it will give the apprentices something to gossip about for a solid week. Maybe two."

"Not helping, Moss," I muttered. We passed under a covered walkway, but I didn't try to shake out my wet hair. Other servants wore mantles tucked over their heads, but the marrow-numbing spring chill matched my mood. My arms hung limp at my side. If I'd had a little more time. A few days.

Ancestors, why did his wedding have to be today?

I felt nothing in response to my silent prayer—just the bitter hollowness in my chest.

"Didn't you expect him to reject you? I mean, if Sorrel *had* called off his wedding, then you couldn't stand before the guests. And that'd ruin our Lady's plans, hmm?"

Moss was chiding me, but I was too empty to respond. I wanted to crawl under the porch and spend the rest of my life with worms.

THE WEDDING WAS, for lack of a better word, splendid. The rain dimmed to a mist and the sun, low in the western sky, shone through it—creating a warm haze around each of the five white pavilions. They shone like ethereal pearls in a lighting no mortal hand could orchestrate.

Lanterns flickered along the walkway. I followed a half-step behind Lady Sulat to the pavilion for the first course. Weddings always had five courses—one focusing on sour, spicy, salty, and sweet, then a final morsel served in a small spoon that harmoniously combined all four flavors. The actual wedding was the fifth course, with the bride and groom feeding each other the final, perfect bite. Usually the oldest person in the family performed the wedding, but King Alder took precedence here, as the father of our nation.

I sat next to Lady Sulat on a cushion around the low table. She'd left her son with his nurse. Even though I could tell she was still sore from birth, she seated herself gracefully.

Others filled in around us. Blue Lord Torut listed tipsily to one side. Captain Gano of the Palace Guard towered over everyone in the rear of the tent, his hair and severe mustache immaculately combed and waxed. King Alder sat at the largest table, with Sorrel on his right and Violet on his left. The honored couple.

I couldn't bring myself to look at Sorrel, but Violet was radiant, her skirt a mixture of yellow, green, red, and white—each color representing a different taste. She'd tied it tightly to accentuate her curves. Spring flowers trailed through her crowns of braids.

I stared down at my hands in my lap. Plain hands, calloused from scrubbing pots and nicked by a handful of old knife wounds and burns. If I looked as lovely as Violet, would Sorrel have considered my words this morning, noted my skill, and remembered that he'd first dreamed of marrying a chef?

Servers brought the first course in tiny bowls—vinegar-marinated mushrooms garnished with green garlic and crushed, candied hazelnuts. I tasted Lady Sulat's, then ate my own bowl. Sour dominated, as it was supposed to, but notes of salty, sweet, and spicy played in the background. Elegant. Lovely. And it settled like ash in the pit of my stomach.

Purple Lord Heir Valerian arrived and squeezed in next to Lady Sulat. As a servant scurried off to fetch him a bowl, Valerian explained to his aunt how he'd gotten caught up in the most fascinating manuscript on the proper construction of bathhouses—then regaled her with the details.

Lady Egal sat, stately as ever, at the table next to ours. Relatives and officials surrounded her, including Fir. He had the gall to wink at me. I clenched my hands in my skirt and refused to look his way after that. Nearby, Lord Torut slurped down his mushrooms without chewing, eyes bloodshot from wine.

Valerian finished his story and tasted the food. "Mmm. We haven't eaten like this since Hawak left. Is he due back soon?"

"Your great-grandmother is very old, Valerian. Hawak will probably return after she passes. Returning to health at her age... it's unlikely."

"Oh." That dampened his mood considerably. "But... Grandfather. He'll get better, right?"

Given the way King Alder fretted over him? Well-treated illnesses that lingered for months like this usually meant a long, slow end. I doubted King Former Fulsaan would escape that fate.

Lady Sulat rested a hand on Valerian's shoulder. "I hope so. You should pray in the Royal Shrine for him."

Valerian smiled at her, as if her word alone had power to heal.

We finished the course and moved to the next tent, making way for another wave of guests to enter the first pavilion. Most were lesser officials; servants would come last. As we settled in the second tent, Lady Egal sneered down her nose at me. She addressed Lady Sulat. "I can't fathom why you'd bring an accused poisoner to feast with you."

I wanted to defend myself, but Lady Egal wouldn't believe my innocence no matter what I said.

Lady Sulat remained glassy calm as she sat. "Accused, yes. I have also accused her of saving my life and that of my child. Do tell, should we revile or honor her?"

Lady Egal turned back to her own companions without another word. She loathed me, but I already knew why. I tried to read the other faces. Valerian laughed as the servers placed the beet greens soup before us. Lord Torut recited poetry to the unfortunate woman next to him. King Alder smiled, but his eyes held the same sadness I'd heard in his voice the other night when he talked about his father and this war.

I tasted Lady Sulat's dish, then my own. The ribbons of greens floated in a broth well-spiced with hotradish. Once again, Sorrel showed perfect execution.

At the first and largest table, Violet giggled. "Oh, Sorrel, you're so talented. This is wonderful!"

He smiled, flustered by her praise. I resolved to stare at the tablecloth.

"Have you heard that the Shoreed are nearing Napil?" asked a gray-bearded man of the Blue Rank. I thought I heard someone call him the Minister of the Interior.

"We can't let them have the mines," said the woman next to him. She looked half his age and had his nose—probably his daughter. "What is General Yuin doing about it?"

King Alder interrupted. "Enough." That one word rumbled through the tent. "This is a wedding, not a war chamber. We'll not talk of such sad things tonight. Onto the next course."

We left half-finished soup bowls behind. How must it be, to sit as king while your nation warred? Families suffered individual tragedies, but he reigned as Father of our nation. Every death was his own tragedy.

But if he felt the loss so deeply, how could he hang twelve apprentices? He could have dismissed them instead or investigated the truth.

Maple charcoal scented the air as soon as Captain Gano stooped and pulled back the tent flap for His Majesty to enter the third pavilion. Guests gasped in delight.

Per my suggestion, a shallow trench of bricks blazed on each table. Servers handed skewers of quartered rabbits, glittering with salt, to each guest. Some stared at them, confused, but Sorrel explained.

"This meat cooks quickly, so it seemed a shame to do it anywhere but here. Lay it across the coals." He demonstrated. "And turn it frequently. When you smell char, it is complete."

"I'm impressed," King Alder said, laying down his own skewer. "How did you come up with such an idea?"

"My beautiful bride inspired me."

No. Chefs didn't claim other chefs' inventions. "Liar."

The accusation jumped from my mouth before I could catch myself, but I had no desire to take it back. This was a matter of professional integrity now. I stared defiantly at him, face hard.

"Did you call me a liar?" Sorrel demanded.

Most of the guests glanced between us. It wasn't my place to comment. But Lady Sulat gestured for me to speak, her face as unreadable as always.

"I did. Apprentice Tanoak heard our conversation. I'm surprised your pride has run away with you. I suggested this."

Sorrel's face twisted. "I decided where to lay each brick."

"True. But I'm the one who suggested a trench of bricks in the first place. You can't claim this is your invention, or that Violet sparked it."

The line between his eyebrow tightened, then relaxed. He smiled. "Are you that jealous? Alas," Sorrel said to the table at large, "I don't think Dami's sound in the head. She professed her feelings for me this morning. And now this? Publicly insulting me on my wedding day?"

If he didn't want to credit me in front of the King or his bride, he should have given an off-hand answer: *some servant suggested it* or *I'm just glad it looks so lovely.*

I stood, planning to snatch a skewer and say something devastating like, *Then let us fetch Tanoak and prove your hubris!*

Instead, my foot caught on the tablecloth. I knocked into the table, hard. Two of the bricks fell out of place, sending coals rolling across the table, flames licking up the fabric in their wake. I gaped in mute horror.

Some quick-witted server tossed a pitcher of chilled rosehip tea over the whole thing. Sodden ashes, steam, and blackened cloth remained.

Everyone stared at me. Some sneered, some laughed, some gaped, some shook their heads in pity. Servers, lords, ladies, and lesser guests alike.

My throat pinched off. My chest tightened.

"Not sound in the head, indeed," Lady Egal muttered, loud enough for all to hear. Fir snickered.

I ran out of the tent. Up the hill, into the bushes framing the lawn around the pond. I sank onto the rain-soaked ground, buried my head in my knees, and wished I had the strength left to cry.

CHAPTER
TWENTY-SIX

I didn't know how long I'd sat there when a broad, gentle hand touched my shoulder. "Dami?"

I blinked up. Bane. In his black uniform, he practically melted into the bushes.

Elegant as always, I wiped my nose on my sleeve. "What are you doing here?"

"One of the servers told Nisaat, then she ran to tell me."

So glad to know rumors about this wouldn't spread fast. The sun had set completely and the clouds had cleared, leaving the stars and lanterns competing for attention.

"I saw Osem yesterday, too," Bane continued. "She called you a rash idiot."

"I know she's mad at me."

"She's mostly upset that you're avoiding her. She's worried."

"Oh." I'd thought it would be easier for her not to talk to me. At least while I was still investigating.

"Are you all right?" Bane asked.

Below, the wedding party moved out of the fourth tent. Since the rain had stopped, they gathered on the lawn. Under the sky, where the ancestors could watch—that was the best place for the final morsel. King Alder spoke, Sorrel and Violet before him, though I couldn't hear the words.

Sorrel was a good chef. He was kind to his betrothed on principle. And he only hated me because he thought I'd poisoned Lady Sulat. If we'd met like we'd planned—as Plum and Sorrel—we would have been happy. As soon as he tasted my cooking, he would have loved me. And I would have loved and appreciated him better than Violet ever could.

"No more brooding over what to do," I mumbled. Sorrel despised me. And he belonged to someone else. That didn't make it any easier to forget the joyous vision of gardens, libraries, and a lifetime with someone who loved what I loved. Who might love *me*.

A pair of servers waited behind the king, each with a tiny bowl containing a masterpiece that combined elements from the four courses into one, harmonious bite—the fifth course.

"Maybe you won't lose the trial."

"Oh. Right." The trial. My life. That seemed like eons from now.

Violet beamed and said something—agreement to marry Sorrel.

Then the King turned to Sorrel.

I felt like I was drowning in rocks. *Run. Leave. Say no.*

But Sorrel beamed. The King said a few more words, officially marrying them. They fed each other the perfectly balanced bites.

Sorrel was a married man.

"Romantic, isn't it?" Bane asked.

"No." I wanted to throw up. I wished I was the real Dami—the girl who broke hearts and noses and laughed because she didn't care about anyone. Not even her family. If she'd been at this wedding, she would have just enjoyed the free food.

Bane leaned back, shocked. "Nisaat said something about you and him... but I thought she exaggerated."

"Exaggerated? I only set a table on fire tonight! How quickly do you think rumors inflate?"

"Do you actually care about him?"

A cool wind whipped up from the pond, ruffling Bane's hair. If this young man did have intentions toward me, as Moss and Osem kept claiming, blunt honesty was the kindest thing I could offer him. Let him despise me and forget about me before he did something as embarrassing as I just had. "Yes. Yes I do. I wish I stood across from him instead of Violet—I'd cut off my right ear to have him."

Already, Sorrel led Violet away from the party toward their quarters. The high-ranked guests waved politely; a number of servers whooped and called inappropriate things. I ought to be his bride, blushing next to him. And now it was too late.

"Oh," Bane said. That single syllable was as round and hollow as an empty crock.

Dread crept up my gut. Ancestors preserve me, Osem and Moss were right. I was a naïve country girl. But Bane knew I was going to hang. He wasn't that stupid.

His brown eyes met mine—wide and vulnerable and yearning. His whole body leaned toward me. Yes, he was that stupid.

My pulse thundered in my throat. If I weren't Plum, if I weren't a chef, I might have leaned toward him. I might have inhaled his juniper-and-smoke scent, brushed the hair from his eyes, and figured out just how warm his broad mouth was.

But I was Plum. I was a chef. I wasn't strong-of-arm, like him. Nana had loved me unconditionally simply because I was her granddaughter, but I'd have to earn a husband's adoration. Bane wasn't perceptive of taste-and-smell. He couldn't appreciate the best part of me. We had no happy future together.

I swallowed, my throat still dry. Suddenly, being blunt seemed cruel. How to explain gently, without hurting him? "I'm... I'm a chef. That's been my whole life until now—cooking for my family, for the people of Clamsriver. It's who I am." It felt good to give him even a sliver of the truth—like peeling off the corner of a scab. "It's what I'll always be. Who besides a chef could love me today, tomorrow, forever?"

He studied me for a long moment, his features soft in the moonlight. When he spoke, pity tinged his voice. "You're more than a birthgift, Dami. You're a *person*."

A person who had lied to him. A person who was about to hang. Bane deserved better than my pale imitation of my sister. I rested my chin on my knees and stared at my toes.

"I can't watch you sit and mope like this. Over him." Bane stood. "Can I come see you tomorrow? When you've had a chance to think?"

"Of course!" I nearly reached out and clung to his hand. Just because we would make a poor match didn't mean that I wanted to lose one of the only friendly faces I knew in the palace.

Bane nodded. "Tomorrow then."

It seemed like that conversation had gone as well as it could have, but as Bane walked away over the lawn, I couldn't help but feel like all the warmth in my body went with him.

I was helping Poppy change the linens when Lady Sulat returned from the wedding. She hobbled stiffly, flanked by two soldiers. All the moving and sitting must have tired her.

Gingerly, she crawled between the fresh sheets. Her pallor was off—a good whole stock would help. But her voice remained hard and smooth as river stones. "If you'd *planned* to make a scene, Dami, I might congratulate your ingenuity. A guarded man may still show his face when surprised. But you didn't plan that incident, did you?"

"No, my Lady." I stared at the floor, shame burning my face.

"I didn't think so. But I'm too tired to chastise you for your lack of discretion right now. Your spat gave me exactly what I needed."

I jerked upright. "You noticed something?"

She nodded.

Hope bloomed in my gut. "Who? Who's behind this?"

Poppy pulled the blanket over Lady Sulat, then slipped out to retrieve her infant.

Lady Sulat closed her eyes. "I'm not positive, of course. It's merely a hint. A direction to pursue. Perhaps, once you've learned a little discretion, I'll disclose the name. You're dismissed."

NEEDLESS TO SAY, I didn't sleep well. Over and over my half-awake nightmares replayed that gut-sinking moment when the table burst on fire. But I couldn't forget Lady Sulat's words, either. She had a hint. A clue. Might I still live?

Even if I'd be living without Sorrel.

I woke, back aching, stomach feeling like a sackful of rocks. Resin was watching my door again—Lady Sulat must have given Moss the evening off while we attended the wedding. I glanced outside. False dawn lit the sky. Lady Sulat wouldn't need me for some time.

Osem would be up, though. And I had amends to make. Even if I couldn't win Sorrel or help Lady Sulat with my own trial, I could do that. I should have done it days ago.

Resin followed me without comment. We passed through a handful of gardens and lawns, dew clinging to my sandals. I hugged my arms to my chest.

I caught Osem on her way to the firewood shed. "Care for an extra set of hands?"

"Looks like you've brought two." She glanced at Resin. He remained stoic and silent, as always.

"He's ornamental. Osem, I'm sorry about our disagreement earlier."

"You mean you're sorry I disagreed with you. You still went."

Dew clung to my sandals, chilling my feet. I fumbled for the right words, the right explanation.

Osem sighed. "I understand why you're being reckless. There's not much time. It's... it's hard to watch, though."

That haunted look flickered across her eyes.

"Can I walk with you?" I asked.

She nodded. We linked elbows and headed down the dark lawn together.

"You're... planning something else, aren't you?"

"It's not stupid though." I glanced back at Resin. Given that Lady Sulat assigned him to guard me, he probably wouldn't cause trouble. But I side-stepped the damning details of acknowledging the Hungry Ghost. "Do you think I could use the kitchen hearths to cook tonight?"

"I'll leave the door cracked. Just don't let in any ghosts or snakes."

"I hope that won't be a problem." I fully intended to feed the ghost out on the lawn. "Let me cook for you, too."

Candied hazelnuts. How long had I wanted to make that for her?

"No stealing from the kitchens," Osem said, raising a half-mocking eyebrow.

"I'll pay someone to buy ingredients in the marketplace. No worries there."

We stacked wood into our sacks and headed back to the kitchens. "This afternoon I need to go to the Hall of Records," I said, "but I could help you scrub crocks this morning. You must be working longer days, now that I'm gone."

She gave me a sad, crooked smile. "Some other time, Dami. Sorrel will be in soon."

"The morning after his wedding?" My stomach sank. I couldn't stay. Not with him here.

"He told Tanoak not to arrange the menu without him." She peered at me. "The rumors are true, then. Why Sorrel? Does Bane know?"

"Umm..." I didn't know how to explain. We stepped into the warmth of the kitchen. The familiar smells of polished granite and warm crocks washed over me. I'd missed this place. I'd missed Osem.

"Tonight, you'll tell me all about it?" she asked.

"Of course."

We went back for one more load of wood. I'd taken half a step inside to drop off my sack when I spotted Sorrel. I rushed back out. Pressed my back against the wall. I didn't need another confrontation with him.

One step outside the door, I could still hear his voice.

"What would my beautiful bride like for breakfast?" he asked.

Violet giggled. "I'm happy just being with you!"

Her voice cut me like knives—but at least they hadn't seen me.

"My darling must keep up her strength. Smoked trout?"

"That sounds amazing!"

Violet's chipper voice made me gag. I imagined the two of them, standing close, hands on each other's cheeks.

Osem finished stacking her bag of wood and came for mine. "You should go."

I nodded. Nothing good could come of staying.

"I'm so glad, so glad," Sorrel said, "that you accepted my proposal. And then Fir, talking to Father about recommending me for this post... our Ancestors truly smile on us."

I nearly tripped. Fir brought them here?

Violet. Violet was the woman Fir desperately needed to place in the palace. After Sorrel proposed, he'd gotten rid of Hawak. So he could bring in Sorrel—and *her*. The fiancée. Fir couldn't leave her on the servant's list, not if he was sneaking her in as someone's betrothed.

"I'm going to go talk with that crazy woman from yesterday," Violet said. "I don't want any more problems."

"Oh, pumpkin, there won't be."

"Don't you worry about me. I'll be back before you have our breakfast ready."

My pulse pounded. I shouldn't confront Violet. Taking this information to Lady Sulat was smarter. Surely Violet expected me to be in her apartments? Would she grow suspicious if I wasn't?

Poppy's voice rang from the kitchens. "Lady Sulat's tray?"

"Oh, that's over here," Violet said. "May I walk back with you to Lady Sulat's?"

I ran, taking a roundabout route so Violet wouldn't spot me from behind. Resin followed gamely, our sandals churning gravel. Sweat beaded down the back of my neck. But when I turned the hedge to Lady Sulat's apartments, Violet already stood by the door. Apparently neither she nor Poppy wasted time appreciating the gardens. Poppy and the tray disappeared into the sitting room while the door soldier informed Violet I wasn't present.

Violet turned and spotted me. Her frown bloomed into a sickly-sweet smile. "Ah! Dear Dami. I wanted a word with you."

She dug her nails into my wrists and pulled me back around the hedge. Resin frowned, but he didn't stop her.

"I'm quite embarrassed by you. I thought we made friends the other day."

I jerked my hand away and rubbed it ruefully.

Violet peered at me. "Why were you out so early?"

Her frivolousness melted away, leaving a calculating stare behind. She *was* plotting with Fir. Sorrel wasn't mine, but I still wanted him to be happy. And he'd married a lie, a façade.

Half of me ached to accuse her right here, but I swallowed it. I'd tell Lady Sulat. She'd use the information better than I could.

"Well?" Violet demanded.

I couldn't tell her I'd been with Osem; I'd approached Lady Sulat's apartments from the other direction. But why should I answer at all? If I wanted her suspicions to drop, I should show her nothing more than an angry, spurned woman. "You're a skunk."

"Excuse me?"

"You're right. Skunks are adorable from a distance. I don't know what to call you. What's the saying? *A rushed wedding is followed by an early birth?*"

She clenched her fists and glared, little wrinkles puckering at the corners of her eyes. "He was *grieving* over a broken engagement. *He* insisted on a fast marriage."

"Ah. I'm sure his bed felt cold and lonely after he got bored of Plum," I lied, straight-faced.

"Sorrel is the image of virtue! He'd never—"

I laughed. Loud and hard and with all the bitterness knotted tight in my gut. "Maybe you should have insisted on slowing down the wedding. Getting to know his *reputation*. Maybe if you're lucky, none of his other lovers will show up. Or did he tell you that you're special? That he *really* loves you, that he'll always be faithful?"

Resin actually blinked. I'm not sure if he was entertained or just shocked.

Somewhere logical in the back of my head, I knew all my vitriol had a goal—presenting myself as oblivious to Violet and Fir. But the cutting lies spilled out with uncanny ease. How could she work with Fir—Fir who'd tried to have a baby killed?

"Plum's my sister, you know. He whispered plenty of pretty things to her," I continued. "She disappeared to stay with family right after I came here. Do you know why?"

Violet's fist shook at her side.

"She's expecting Sorrel's child. If she tried to name him as the father, Sorrel promised he'd deny everything. And who would believe Plum? They met in the woods between Westbank and Clamsriver with no witnesses. Sorrel didn't rush your wedding because he's heartsick, Violet. He's been worried, terrified, that someone will discover the truth of his sordid ways and make him marry a yellow-ranked girl. Take responsibility."

Violet narrowed her eyes. "That's not right. He told me all about your declaration of love—he's very honest."

"No, I said *she* loved him. I said he should stop this wedding. Plum's my sister and he betrayed her. Abandoned her!"

Of course I'd never met him before, never touched him. Of course he was justified in marrying someone else—I'd broken the engagement. But it still felt like a betrayal. The best lies are half-truths. I let the raw emotions flood my words.

Violet would have little trouble dismissing me as angry and oblivious after this. "Are you the reason he abandoned her and her child? A better-ranked woman, a more advantageous match?"

Violet spluttered.

"Plum will never marry now. Who would take her? All her chances for a good future are *erased*." That last bit, at least, was true.

"I don't believe you," Violet said, spine stiffening.

"Fine. Just be careful to keep your eyes half-closed, so you can keep believing me. Enjoy your marriage. I'm sure it will be full of mistresses."

Violet sneered back. "At least I'll live long enough to see. How many days until your trial? Enjoy your grave, Dami."

As soon as Violet swept off, my hands shook. Had I said too much? Been too cruel? It seemed like she suspected nothing now, but maybe she hid her expressions well.

Resin followed me up the porch. The door guard silently admitted us.

Lady Sulat occupied one of the chairs in the sitting room. She nursed her child, her breakfast tray growing cold, untouched beside her. A military officer in black sat across from her, clutching an envelope.

"You're late," Lady Sulat said, voice edged.

I bowed, anxiety turning the back of my throat bitter. I whispered, "I have something to report."

"It will wait. Taste, then leave," she snapped.

I flinched. Where was her cool composure? She'd never shown anger to me before. I tasted the cranberry-drizzled buckwheat and the tea, but not even the over-sweetened drink could wash the bitter from my mouth. "It's safe. Blue Lady Sulat—"

She cut me off with a knife-like sweep of her hand, eyes never wavering from the envelope.

I slunk outside, trying to swallow. I addressed the door guard, voice low. "How long will she be occupied?"

"The messenger is from the front, with a letter from General Yuin," he said.

News from her husband—now I understood her exposed anxiety. I pursed my lips. "That doesn't tell me how long."

He scowled at me. "She'll have the messenger read it, question him, then draft a response. Some time."

"Ah. Umm. Thank you." I shifted down the stairs. If I just sat here, I'd go mad.

Maybe I could gather more information about Violet in the

meantime. Nothing direct, nothing dangerous. I couldn't afford to waste what time I had. Maybe I'd even learn something that impressed Lady Sulat.

The Hall of Records wouldn't have anything. But Nisaat, sitting by the gate day after day—she might have heard something. Seen something.

I hurried over the gravel paths, past the butterfly gardens and the plum trees. Resin frowned, as if concerned I was trying to escape. But he followed, silent.

I spotted Nisaat on her stone bench, patiently spinning, waiting for anyone who might need an escort. As soon as she saw me, she wound the thread and stuck it in a pouch laying next to her. She clasped her hands, cold and business-like, over her emerald green skirt. "Dami. How may I help you?"

I strode to her side and whispered, "Listen. Do you know anything about Violet?" I paused. "I don't even know what her birthgift is."

That might give me a hint as to what Fir wanted her to do.

"They're already married," Nisaat growled.

I flinched. Of course she'd be upset for Bane's sake. "It's not like that. Do you know anything about Violet or don't you? Please? I need help."

"If Bane weren't so keen on helping you, I'd slap you and leave you to your misery."

I hadn't expected so much anger from her. "I'm about to die, Nisaat. In the long run, he's better off without me."

She pursed her lips. "Fine. Violet's perceptive-of-taste-and-smell, like her father, former Master Chef Palaw. Did you want to hear about him, too?"

Sorrel already told me about him — how he'd retired to see the exiled Red Lord Ospren settled in his mountain prison and let Sorrel's father pick the next Master Chef. But her birthgift... my mouth still tasted bitter. Fir couldn't be the poisoner; he didn't have the skills. But Violet, perceptive-of-taste-and-smell... Violet, who Fir got into the palace...

Sorrel mentioned that she had no love of cooking; I'd thought she possessed some other gift, not that she wanted others to dismiss her gift to keep suspicions low. How could she use her life-giving skills to attack and kill?

I chewed my lip. Violet couldn't be the poisoner. Sorrel didn't arrive until after Lady Sulat gave birth. Fir needed her here for a different task.

"Something wrong?" Nisaat demanded. "Or does your provincial bumpkin brain just work that slow?"

Part of me admired her familial loyalty. I didn't rise to the insult. "I thought I'd figured something out... but Violet and Sorrel came from Westbank too late for that."

"They didn't both come from Westbank."

I peered at her.

"*Sorrel* came down from Westbank. *Violet* came up from Napil, where she's been living with her grandmother. She arrived some time before him. I remember escorting her to Lady Egal's, then showing her to a guest apartment."

My pulse thudded so loud, I worried Violet could hear it wherever she was. "When? What day?"

Nisaat frowned and smoothed her skirt. "I think... yes, it had to be. Bane's errands were delayed, so we played springball together that evening. Violet arrived the day before Lady Sulat gave birth."

Violet was the poisoner.

CHAPTER
TWENTY-SEVEN

I returned to Lady Sulat's apartments, desperate to tell her what I'd learned. But the previous night and the letter had left her drained; she'd retired to her bed, with instructions not to be bothered.

"It's urgent," I pleaded with the door guard.

He glowered at me, one hand steady on his spear. Scrubbing crocks had strengthened my arms, but I couldn't knock a guard down. I doubted Lady Sulat would sleep long.

I tried to help Poppy with her current task—stitching more doll-sized diapers for the infant—but after my twitching hands marred a length of fabric, she sent me outside. I sat on the front step of the porch, leg bouncing, unable to sit still.

The poisoner. At last. I *knew*. I could bring an important prisoner to my trial, then beg the Council for lenience.

Moss relieved Resin of his watch. He tilted his head to the side, examining me. "Trying to break the step?"

"I need to report to Lady Sulat."

"You managed something useful, didn't you?" Astonishment dripped from his words.

"Yes, Moss. That *is* possible." I folded my hands over my knees, trying to sit still. "I know who Fir wanted to bring into the palace. She's our poisoner."

Moss frowned and sat by me. "If she was on the servant waiting list, someone's been planning this for a long time. Before Lady Sulat was pregnant."

"She tailored the poison to fit the situation. I don't know if they want Lady Sulat grieving and distracted, or if they hoped she'd die in a complicated, early birth. But it was *subtle*, Moss. If I hadn't been there, no one would know to suspect a poison. No crime means no criminal."

"That's... a good point."

"Would you stop sounding so surprised about that?" I snapped.

He shrugged. "Old habits."

"Can you talk to the guard? Convince him to let us in?" My stomach felt like a crock about to over boil. Finally, finally I'd figured something out. Lady Sulat would know how to proceed.

Moss shrugged. "It can probably wait until she wakes up. Lady Sulat can't think if she never sleeps. Besides, it looks like you have company."

He nodded down the gravel path. Bane strode toward us, buttercups and pink shooting stars clenched in his hand. His uniform seemed extra-clean and he must have gotten someone else to tie his armband for him. Instead of a lopsided, one-handed knot, it looked elegant. Perfect.

He cleared his throat. His voice sounded unusually deep. "Yellow-ranked Dami of Clamsriver. Could you spare a moment to speak with me?"

Were those flowers... for me? He shifted nervously on his feet. Ancestors above, the flowers were for me.

The tang of my sweat mixed with the perfume of Bane's flowers. Why was he making me turn him down again? This time, he'd have an audience in Moss. No. I wouldn't do that to him. I'd have to keep the conversation away from us. Thankfully, I had big news. "I figured out who Fir brought in."

"That's great!" He came closer and lowered his voice. "Who is it? Has she been arrested?"

"Not yet. I'm waiting to see Lady Sulat. It's Violet. She's the poisoner."

Bane jerked back from me. He didn't bother whispering. "Violet? I can't believe you're that desperate... to accuse his wife?"

"What?"

"You're jealous. So jealous and mad about losing Sorrel, you'd resort to false accusations." Bane gawked at me with hurt, hollow eyes. "Are you going mad, or are you not who I thought you were?"

Of course I wasn't who he thought I was. He didn't even know my name. But the look on his face still made me feel like I'd drunk a whole jar of vinegar.

"Resin heard everything." I turned, but of course Resin left long ago. "Listen. Fir arranged for her and Sorrel to come here. Violet arrived the day Lady Sulat was poisoned. She's perceptive-of-taste-and-smell, too."

Bane's amputated arm twinged, like it suddenly itched. "You're in the palace. You were in the kitchens when Lady Sulat was poisoned. You have the same gift! That's not evidence. That's *coincidence.*"

Moss leaned back on the stairs, thoughtful. "An awful lot of coincidence."

"You too?" Bane glared at him. "Dami. I don't understand why you cared so much about Sorrel in the first place, but if you can't forget him, you won't survive your trial."

"I'm trying to survive my trial! This isn't about him. I *heard* Sorrel say that Fir invited them here. It's her. Violet."

Bane barked a dry, bitter laugh. "So you saw him. Morning of his wedding and you still can't step away."

"It wasn't like that," I said, standing. "Osem—"

Bane threw his flowers at my feet. "Stop making excuses and just say you'll never have me. I've heard it before."

He stormed away.

The flowers lay in the gravel, their delicate yellow and pink petals already marred by the dust. I glanced up at Bane's receding back, then down again. "I don't understand him, Moss."

"I noticed. Quite entertaining."

I sighed and I tried to salvage the flowers, but most of their petals fell to the ground. "Flowers. Flowers right after I told him not to court me."

I felt daft for only seeing what I'd wanted to in Bane—a friend and an ally.

"He wasn't just courting. He was proposing."

"Ha ha," I said dryly, not in the mood for teasing. But Moss wasn't smiling. My stomach dropped. "You're serious, aren't you?"

"Lady Sulat spoke to him of it two days ago, after she noticed his interest. As a soldier's wife, you'd get a military trial as soon as Lady Sulat named Bane complicit. Instead of facing the Purple-Blue Council, you'd *both* face a military tribunal. King Alder could choose to preside, but a military tribunal would pardon both of you, denying the King a chance to pass punishment."

"W-why didn't anyone said so?" I spluttered. After I made an idiot of myself in the Hall of Records, Bane had been oddly insistent that I'd live. Now it made sense. He thought he could save me.

"Bane's a romantic. He wanted to formally propose. Lady Sulat agreed." Moss nodded at the bruised flowers. "Too bad he wasted his time picking those."

Marriage to Bane. My chest twisted. No kitchen. No recipe manuscripts. Just Bane. If we married, would he learn my secrets? Would he have me and my family hanged? If I managed to keep all my secrets, would I ever hear him say my real name?

"He's a good young man," Moss said.

All the more reason to reject him. Bane deserved a wife as genuine as himself. If I married him to use him, I was no better than Violet. "That doesn't mean I should wed him."

"Of course not. It means there's a decent way to save your neck." Moss picked something out of his teeth. "Except you stomped the boy's heart all over the ground. Don't think he still wants you."

He shouldn't want me. He knew a pale imitation of Dami, not Plum. Not the chef.

"I didn't mean to hurt him—I didn't know he was proposing."

"Obviously."

I shook my head. "Moss, I know what I saw. Violet *is* behind this." I sat back down on the porch next to him. "I... I didn't really sound crazy-jealous, did I?"

"If I answer that honestly, you're going to glare at me."

I SPREAD the remnants of Bane's flowers around the ferns and bleeding hearts planted outside Lady Sulat's apartments. It felt like scattering someone's ashes. Bane's offering would have looked better next to the blooms Lady Sulat's brave sons gathered for her. My mouth tasted as bitter as it had when she dismissed me.

I glanced at the door guard. He glowered at me. So I waited outside in the clean, spring air. Part of me wanted to curl up in my closet and sleep until Lady Sulat called me. My thoughts moved sluggishly. Violet, Bane... I had too much to think about. My hands felt clammy.

Was I that jealous? Had I imagined Sorrel's words?

No. No, I'd heard it. Just because I didn't like Violet didn't mean she couldn't be guilty. Whatever Bane thought, this wasn't about Sorrel.

Thinking of Bane made me nauseous. Would he ever talk to me again after this? It probably wasn't fair to ask him to. If I'd known he wanted to propose, I could have gently told him no. Written a letter. Or—my head throbbed—said yes? Was the risk to my family worth saving myself from a civil trial?

I could imagine Bane marrying the real Dami, the two of them wandering the woods together or playing springball. I'd be proud to call him my brother-in-law. But this proposal seemed like one more ill product of all my lies. If we'd met as just Plum and Bane, as chef and soldier, I couldn't imagine him offering to tie his life to mine. I wasn't the adventurous young woman he thought I was.

I yawned, the exhaustion growling in my skull getting the better of me. "Moss. You're married, right?"

"For twenty-eight years now."

"Do you have any idea why Bane would want to marry me?"

Moss grinned. "I bet he's asking himself that right about now."

"That's not a real answer," I grumbled. I blinked the cobwebs from my eyes, trying to stay awake.

How could we play springball now? Or skip rocks together? I'd miss that terribly. And some small, bitter part of me blamed him for ruining it.

"Is it so hard to believe that he admired you? That he liked the idea of marrying you?"

What was there to admire? I was only good at—only passionate about—one thing. Over a letter, I could believe Sorrel wanted me. Could *love* me. He already knew everything I loved about myself.

But Bane? To him, I was some strong-of-arm girl caught in a tight place. I didn't want to *be* that girl. Why would he want to *marry* her?

"I suppose it is." My eyelids felt as heavy as granite. I rubbed them, trying to stay awake. Sometime soon, I should find Bane. Apologize. Explain to him all the reasons he should be happy I wasn't his.

"He told Lady Sulat that he wanted to meet you as soon as he heard the story of how you traveled alone to Askan-Wod," Moss said. "He thought a woman with such strength and courage might look at a man with one arm and see *him*—not just the difficulties such a union would bring you. He's only grown fonder of you since."

Bane saw all that in me? I let my head rest against the porch railing. I wasn't strong. Or brave. I just did what was necessary.

"Dami? Are you feeling well?"

"Just tired." The bitterness, that nervous bitterness, stained my throat.

"You need to take better care of yourself or you won't make it to your trial. Are you not sleeping well, or is running around on that injured ankle catching up to you?"

He sounded like my father. "Probably both, Moss."

But I didn't have time to rest or baby my foot. If I'd hurried a little faster to taste Lady Sulat's breakfast this morning, maybe I could have spoken with her already. My ears felt full of water and my mind blurred toward sleep. Bitter blossomed in my mouth.

Why had I been late? That question nagged me. Important.

Violet. Violet had been in the kitchens. She'd walked with Poppy. Then delayed me. I'd tested Lady Sulat's food late. A less cautious person, maybe, would have eaten without waiting?

Violet was the poisoner. Bitter had been in my mouth before I tasted the food. I hadn't been paying attention. Hadn't thought it strange that the cloying honey didn't wash it away.

Bittersleep leaf. It was toxic, avoided even by deer. It had no odor. Just a faint bitter aftertaste, easily concealed from the average tongue with an ample helping of sweetness. Children sometimes mistook it for cress. I'd helped Father treat such carelessness before. But this bittersleep hadn't hit me with instant, nauseating weakness like it should have.

What flavor had the tea been? Yarrow. Yarrow would direct the toxin to the veins. And the sweet, the endurance—that ensured a gradual decline. The kind of weariness that felt like mere exhaustion, not sudden poison. That encouraged a morning nap.

In a sufficient dose, the bittersleep paralyzed the veins, until the victim's pulse stopped entirely.

I jerked to my feet. My brain swirled in my skull. I clutched the railing so I didn't pitch over. Dizziness screamed in my ears, pressing down on my knees.

"Moss!" I barked, blinking hard, trying to focus. "Lady Sulat's been poisoned."

CHAPTER TWENTY-EIGHT

Moss tore past me. The door guard must have heard my cry, because he stepped out of the way. I stumbled after, each step like swimming through over-thickened sauce. Accidentally, I kicked a vase. Water, petals, and broken pottery swam around my sandals.

Inside the bedroom, Moss spoke to Lady Sulat's still form. Then took her hand. Then tried to sit her up. Her eyes stayed closed, her arms hung limp at her sides. Poppy followed Moss, eyes wide, horrified.

I shuffled forward, past all of them, to press a finger to her throat. A pulse, sluggish and faint. She'd ingested much more than me, but she wasn't dead.

Her veins had already been targeted by the yarrow. Targeting them directly might result in complications. I had to target her heart.

A sweet-and-sour rabbit's heart would give her the strength she needed to live. Or strawberries macerated in tangy blackberry molasses—surely the greenhouses had strawberries by now. But I didn't have time to butcher a rabbit or macerate strawberries. And she couldn't chew.

Tea could be ready quickly. "I need hot water. And celeriac. And parsley." Celeriac for the heart; parsley for sour. Strength, to rise out of the danger. We'd worry about full recovery later.

Soldiers sprinted from the room. Moss steadied me with an arm. "Do you know what you're doing?"

"Yes." I'd practiced my whole life.

The door guard scowled at me. He opened his mouth to protest or suggest some other course of action, but a soldier brought me a glazed, ceramic bowl of water from the bedroom—one meant for washing, but the vessel looked as clean and sturdy as any kitchen crock. I restarted the fire in Lady Sulat's brazier and nestled the bowl in the coals.

Then two other soldiers burst in, one of them holding a half-grown celeriac ripped right out of some palace garden. Black dirt trickled from it onto the rugs.

"Take that outside," I ordered, words slurring. Raising my eyelids after a blink felt harder than hefting fifty-pound sacks of beans. "Peel it. With your spears, if need be. No dirt!"

They nodded, military-sharp, and sprinted outside. Someone brought a handful of baby parsley next. I tossed it in. The guards returned with the celeriac—now a clean, cream-colored cube—and handed it to me. I used one of their spears to shave bits off. Oh, it would have been better as a soup. Tastier. More helpful. But she needed something now.

I dribbled the crude tea into her mouth, then checked her pulse again. No discernable improvement. But no decline, either.

"She needs a spoonful of this. Every half-minute. Meanwhile, someone should—" I set the bowl on the end table as the world swirled about me. "Should fetch—"

The floor swayed under my feet and I fell, striking my head against something hard. Pain bloomed at my temple, but I couldn't open my eyes. My arms felt heavy as fallen logs, unmovable.

"—fetch a chef," I mumbled.

I DON'T KNOW if I slept. The world seemed a hazy array of shapes and noises I couldn't place. Words that didn't sound like my own language. For a moment, I thought I'd become the real Dami—lying with my skull cracked open on a battlefield while others counted the dead.

By the time I felt the wood grain under my fingers and remembered where I was, my mouth tasted faintly of celery and parsley. My head pounded.

"Dami should recover soon; she didn't digest enough to ever be in danger of dying. Lady Sulat's stable, but she'll need constant care and it might take her a week or more to wake up. She was already frail from delivery."

Such a sweet voice. It sent a thrill through my heart. What did I love so much about it? Sorrel. Ah, Sorrel the amazing chef, Sorrel who had greenhouses and a library at home. Sorrel—

—who'd already chosen and married someone else.

I groaned and opened my eyes. Soldiers crammed the room. Sorrel sat by Lady Sulat's bed, glaring at me. I still laid on the floor, staring up at rafters and soldier's beards. Odd, that I'd never noticed the rafters were as clean and polished as everything else in these apartments.

One of the soldiers knelt next to me, dripping parsley-flavored celeriac broth into my mouth. Sorrel must have cooked this version; a hint of green onion and sweet carrot backed the mild sour.

A soldier spoon-fed Lady Sulat as well. Her chest rose up and down in long, shallow breaths. Alive. I'd kept her alive.

I brushed my fingers over the pounding part of my skull, but only found a lump. I'd be fine, too.

"Is it wise to keep *that* person here?" Sorrel jutted his chin at me, like I was a stain on the floor. "The poisoner belongs in a cell where she can't do more harm."

I spluttered, trying to defend myself, sending warm broth trickling down my neck and into my dress.

"Before she warned us about Lady Sulat and subsequently *saved her life*," Moss said, "she named someone else the poisoner."

Sorrel kept glaring at me, as if that could erase me from this world. Yesterday I'd prayed that he'd notice me, look at me. But I hadn't imagined hate glinting in those dark, hematite eyes. "She tasted Lady Sulat's food. You can't believe she's innocent."

"You think Dami poisoned herself?"

"She's alive, isn't she?" Sorrel snapped.

The doors slid open and Lieutenant-General Behon strode into the bedroom. His skin glistened from exertion, but his agile face showed nothing of fatigue—only cold inquiry. "It's true. Lady Sulat's poisoned. How did this happen?"

"She did this!" Sorrel ranted. "She's a hateful, spiteful—"

Lieutenant-General Behon silenced him with a masterfully raised eyebrow that seemed to reach to the top of his bald crown. "Lieutenant Yellow-ranked Moss. Your explanation, please."

Moss bowed, then summarized.

Lieutenant-General Behon pinned me with his stare, the condescending curve of his mouth screaming his loathing. "The poison taster failed to warn her mistress. Suspicious, indeed."

All the syllables in *suspicious* sounded like rope hissing against rope, a noose being tied.

"I don't know why she isn't already locked up," Sorrel agreed.

The wood floor dug into my shoulders and back. With a single step, either of them could crush my face underfoot. "It was bitter-sleep. I didn't notice it beneath the sweet. I tasted poorly today, but I didn't attack her."

"Lieutenant-General Behon, we needn't rely on accusations." Moss stood in a military-stiff posture. It didn't suit him. "As soon as Lady Sulat's poisoning was confirmed, I sent a squad of soldiers to search both the rooms Dami has lived in and the room of the woman Dami accused—a Green-ranked Violet of Napil."

Moss had believed me, had trusted my word. When I could sit up again, I'd make him a honeyed fruit compote.

"You didn't wait for my commands." Lieutenant-General Behon

stabbed Moss with narrowed eyes and a tightened mouth, the picture of condemnation.

Moss barked a laugh. "You only now arrived! If I'd waited for the messenger to fetch you from the walls, it might have given the poisoner time to cover her tracks."

"You say that like you found something." Lieutenant-General Behon's face returned to a disciplined neutral. "You have evidence of Dami's guilt?"

Moss turned to the lattice door. "Suruc! Bring it in."

Suruc carried a redwood box, the varnish making the red even richer. Low-relief carvings of buttercups and bees decorated the corners. The top panel consisted of a lattice of interlocking squares, contrasted against a pale white-pine backing.

"That's my Violet's! How dare you take it?" Sorrel snapped.

Lieutenant-General Behon graced him with a flat, incredulous stare.

Suruc knelt. He emptied the contents one by one—a small manuscript box and a number of letters. Then he snapped a false bottom out of place. Suruc's broad shoulders blocked my view, but Lieutenant-General Behon peered closer and Sorrel blanched.

"All these vials, with their liquids and dried herbs... it seemed rather suspicious," Moss said. "I had Suruc consult with Tanoak, an apprentice in the kitchens, as to their natures. They are all poisons."

I exhaled, not sure if I was shaking or imagining it. Silently, I whispered a prayer of thanks to my Ancestors for this proof that I wasn't crazy-jealous or a would-be-murderer.

Sorrel's pallor greened. "Dami planted those. She must have..."

"Somehow crafted a false bottom to a box in Violet's possession?" Moss asked. "I didn't know Dami possessed such fine carpentry skills. We've wasted her talents here."

Sorrel's hands clenched and unclenched at his side. Under his hateful glare, I felt like a bear hanging in the butcher's room with my innards already scooped out.

What had I expected—that Sorrel would be pleased I'd disposed of his new wife? The woman he doted on?

"Somehow, she did it. To frame Violet." Sorrel's hoarse voice sounded like sand scrubbed against a crock wall.

"Dami's been under the military's watchful eye since the first poisoning. When would she have done this?"

"You're right, Moss," Lieutenant-General Behon said, expression neutral. As he turned to Lady Sulat, his face softened in concern. "The evidence against Violet is undeniable."

Moss bowed. "Violet is in a military prison." He handed Lieutenant-General Behon a slip of paper. "This location. You can interrogate her at your convenience."

"I will."

The other soldiers in the room nodded gruffly. No one here had love or sympathy for the woman who'd poisoned their Minister of Military Affairs.

Except for Sorrel. I wanted to stand, to run my hands over the lines carving his face into hateful chunks and apologize. I'd hurt him once by abandoning our engagement. And now I'd hurt him by revealing Violet's duplicity. He needed candied beets or honeyed hazelnuts or ripe, sweet blackberries for his heartsickness. I ached to cook for him, to be in the kitchen with a crock humming merrily next to us.

Maybe if I convinced the Council to pardon my lies, we could spend the rest of our lives in the kitchens. We could both be happy, like we'd planned. "I didn't mean to hurt you, Sorrel."

"I'll prove you're guilty somehow, poisoner." He spat on my face, then stomped past the soldiers and out of the room.

CHAPTER
TWENTY-NINE

I stared at the bedroom ceiling while Moss, Lieutenant-General Behon, and a few others discussed their next action in the sitting room. That left Lady Sulat, more soldiers, Poppy, and the wet nurse in the same room with me. But I couldn't focus on any of them. My head buzzed.

However much I loathed Violet, it still seemed surreal. She'd tried to kill Lady Sulat. She'd tried to kill this infant. Poor Sorrel loved her. I couldn't imagine that kind of betrayal. Dami had abandoned me, but she hadn't tried to murder anyone.

Sooner than I expected, Moss knelt next to me.

"Meeting over?" I asked, head still pounding, vision still swimming.

He nodded. "We're sending Azalea, Lady Sulat's daughter, east to stay with her paternal grandmother. Lady Sulat and the infant will go to a safehouse. You're to come with us and nurse our Lady back to health. Can you do that?"

To cook again. My heart thrilled. "Yes."

I'M NOT sure where we went. Moss told me to let the poison-induced sleep come, and I obeyed. I woke in a dim room with rough wood paneling. It smelled like spruce, with something earthy behind it. A lantern in the corner trailed smoke up to a vent in the ceiling.

"We're underground, aren't we?"

Moss sat next to my rolled-out mattress, whittling. "Didn't know you had eyes."

"This is the safehouse?"

"Three bedrooms including this one, a cellar, and the main room with the hearth. It's not fancy, but it's secure."

"The... Palace Guards. King Alder. They don't know where this place is, do they?"

"Did you not understand what *safehouse* means? There are a handful of people here, all highly trusted."

I sat up slowly. Despite feeling well-rested, my skull ached like someone had slammed it against a wall. "Can I stay here?"

"You are staying here." Moss gave me an odd look.

Hope twisted my innards. "Can I hide here during my trial? Someone else could tell them Violet's the poisoner, and maybe they'll pardon me."

"You're hoping they'll let you go because Violet's done worse?"

"I caught her."

Moss exhaled slowly. "That's no guarantee you'll escape judgment. You lied. There's every justification to hang you."

"I know. That's why I'm asking to stay. Here. Safe."

Moss leaned back in his chair. "I could ask—Lieutenant-General Behon is the highest-ranking officer in Askan-Wod now—but it won't happen. Lady Sulat vouched for you. If you don't appear, the Palace Guards would have a right to search all Lady Sulat's buildings, including military facilities. We can't have that."

My lungs felt like they'd collapsed, but I tried to keep my breathing steady. "This safehouse is under a military facility, isn't it?"

"Looks like you're growing a brain."

"Thanks, Moss."

"Always here to help."

I sighed. "Is there a second safehouse? One the guards wouldn't find if they searched?"

"Oh, they wouldn't find this one. That's not the problem. But would you let the Palace Guard crawl over every building under your command? They have no love for the military. What they could find isn't half as dangerous as false evidence they might plant."

I stilled. The spruce smell was suddenly suffocating. "I'm not as useful as they are dangerous. That's what it is, isn't it?"

"Dami, Lady Sulat doesn't want to see you hang. She gave you a way out."

Bane. If I was Dami, why wouldn't I agree to his proposal? Would he hate me, once he uncovered my lies?

"I know young people are prone to romantic fits and ideas of love, but you'll have plenty of time to develop love later."

Going to trial only risked my life. Not Dami's. Not my parents. Who'd keep Nana from becoming a Hungry Ghost if my family disappeared? I'd already lost Nana once. I wasn't going to lose her again.

Besides, I couldn't treat Bane the way Violet treated Sorrel. I couldn't use him, trick him into marrying an imitation of Dami. "Is there any way to know what the Council will decide beforehand?"

Moss tsked. "You're that disgusted by his missing arm?"

"No!" Guilt burned in my chest. Is that why Bane thought I rejected him?

"I know it's rushed. No formal engagement ceremony, no courtship, but what choice do you have?" Moss asked. "I didn't meet my wife until our wedding day. Batting eyelashes beforehand might be pleasant, but it doesn't make a good marriage. It's a good deal more about compromise and taking care of each other. Bane's not a selfish man. You could be happy together."

My heart clenched like over-kneaded dough. Maybe Bane could be happy with me. Maybe he wouldn't regret my lies or betray my family—I'd never told him why I'd lied to the Royal House and he'd still proposed.

But *I* was selfish. I wanted more from my marriage than a kind man. I wanted a kindred spirit. I wanted a chef. I wanted to wake up next to someone who adored me so much that I didn't wake up wondering why Nana wasn't humming in the next room over. Why Nana wasn't singing good morning in my doorway. Why Nana wasn't sitting in the corner of the kitchen, spinning and chatting while I put on the buckwheat for breakfast.

I wanted my new life to be so full of love that I could look fondly back at my memories of Nana without hurting anymore.

Moss continued, voice soft. "I can run a message to him this evening. Lady Sulat won't command Bane to marry you, but now that we know Violet's guilty, he might be willing to take your acceptance."

Bane deserved someone as unselfish as him. "I..."

My words clumped together.

Moss peered at me. "I don't understand you. Are you scared of the wedding night? Because having an unselfish husband is advantageous in that regard, too. You needn't worry."

"That's not what I was thinking about!" My cheeks burned like freshly-raked coals. "How soon do I have to choose?"

"Before the trial," Moss muttered, frowning.

"So, if we get married the day before?" Four days to the trial. Three days to decide. To gamble on whether or not the Purple-Blue Council would acquit me.

He sighed, exasperated. "Yes. That would do. I guess I'm not running him any messages. Trying to avoid this marriage until the last hour... that'd probably crush him all over again."

But Bane would heal. He couldn't have cared that deeply about me to begin with. Hopefully I'd find my own way out of this trial. Hopefully Bane would enjoy long, happy years with an honest and unselfish wife.

I bit my lip. "I... think I'm getting closer with the Hungry Ghost. Can I go back to the kitchens tonight and cook?"

"Cook what?"

I stared down at my hands. I needed to cook something. Anything. "Archivist Linaan won't be at the Hall of Records this afternoon. I could research with Archivist Kochan."

"I'm not going to risk dropping you into the arms of an upset Palace Guard without a better plan that that. They have every reason to suspect you of poison and you have no conscious Lady Sulat to dissuade them."

I TOOK stock of the safehouse pantry. Lots of beans, buckwheat, and peas. Jars of salt fish, rabbit jerky, dried plum, apricots, and cherries. Crates of turnips, pumpkin, and parsley root. Blackberry molasses, maple syrup, salt, an array of vinegars and wines. Crocks of whole pickled cabbages, pickled hotradish, and pickled herbs. Cords of wood. I'd be cooking like it was the middle of winter, with only storable ingredients, but the variety impressed me. And the quantity. With six guards, Lady Sulat, myself, and the nurse down here, we could live off the cellar for six months.

I grabbed some dried peas, dried mushrooms, assorted vegetables, and celeriac before jogging upstairs. I made Lady's Sulat's celeriac infusion, then prepped a midday meal for everyone else. My hands fell into their old rhythms. I smelled and tasted, stirred and simmered. Immersed in this kitchen, my soul felt centered. For a moment, I could forget ghosts and trials and focus on vegetables and hotpots.

"Everything meets your approval?" Moss asked. He sat on the floor, a pace away from the low table, his head leaned back against the wall.

I nodded. "She'd benefit from a broth made with heart. Bear or elk is best, though duck or rabbit would suffice. Could we get that down here?"

"We're not trapped. You tell us what she needs and we'll deliver," Moss said.

I didn't see Lieutenant-General Behon anywhere. The other

guard sat on the floor, on top of a trap door, playing a game of stones. I frowned. If we were underground, we'd have to go down and come back up to leave. I supposed the room was more defensible this way.

I laid out bowls of the pea stew, made savory and bright by the dried chanterelles. "These are for you. I'll go feed Lady Sulat."

I entered the room. A wet-nurse already sat there, humming to the infant. Except for the slight movement of her chest, Lady Sulat looked like a corpse. "There's food for you by the hearth."

The wet-nurse nodded and left. Moss followed me and watched me dribble lukewarm broth into Lady Sulat's mouth. Maybe the military still didn't trust me. If I gained that trust, would they risk hiding me?

The knot in my stomach said no. Not when I could easily save myself without giving power to the Palace Guard.

I spent the rest of the day preparing food. On principle, I started a crock of buckwheat so we'd have branches on hand to munch. Then I steeped some salted fish to make a stock and sliced some vegetables for tonight's hotpot: thin rounds of beets, carrots, and parsnips.

The fruit compote I'd silently promised Moss came next. I set the steaming bowl in front of him, interrupting his turn in the game of stones. He blinked up at me.

"Thanks," I said. "For believing what I said about Violet."

His soft quarter-grin lacked his usual sarcasm. "You're welcome."

I gave a grateful bow, left him to the treat, and descended into the pantry once more. I rummaged until I found a lipped plate suitable for sprouting. Bean sprouts weren't my favorite—zesty hotradish sprouts tasted better—but dull fresh greens were better than no fresh greens. In this cool pantry, beans would take six or seven days to sprout, but I doubted Lady Sulat would be recovered by then.

My stomach clenched. I set the empty plate down. Four days—my trial was in four days. I wouldn't be around to finish growing these.

THE NEXT DAY, mid-afternoon, someone knocked on the trap door in a distinctive pattern. My hands were sticky with buckwheat from half-formed branches, but I glanced over my shoulder at our guest.

"Osem?"

She held a lidded, glazed bowl. "I brought you a present."

"How…" I stared at her, then at the trap door. None of the guards moved to throw her out.

Osem crossed the room and pressed the bowl into my hands. "Open it."

I cleaned my hands on a rag, then cracked the lid. A few freshly-butchered slices of bear heart rested inside. Just what Lady Sulat needed. I spluttered. "How did you know?"

"Oh, I'm thoughtful like that." She grinned. "Moss asked me to bring it in, actually."

My heart sank. "I'm sorry you're tangled up in all of this."

"All of what?"

I gestured around the room and sighed. "Whoever's targeting Lady Sulat could come after you, too."

We'd gotten Violet by following Fir, after all. But Osem shrugged, unconcerned.

I gave Moss a stern look. "I thought you'd buy some, not endanger her."

"We did buy some. Osem's less conspicuous than a guard in the market. Besides, it's no great additional threat to her. Anyone with half a brain in the palace already knows that Osem is Lady Sulat's person."

I bit my lip. Apparently I didn't have half a brain. I glanced at Osem.

She sighed. "Great, Moss. Now you've hurt her feelings."

The way she said it made me feel like a sheltered child. But I didn't want to sound like one, too, so I busied myself banking coals against a crock of water.

"Lady Sulat took me in." Osem's soft tone conjured up her siblings, parents, and husband who'd died in Shoreed's first strike. "She's as wise as she is kind. So, yes, she has my loyalty. I'm her eyes and ears in the kitchens."

"You're a spy. Like Moss." My words felt distant, surreal.

Osem laughed. "Ha! Like Moss? I'd say I'm far *better* at it than him."

"Arrogant youth," Moss muttered. "I was her guard, Osem. It's not as if I had much opportunity for subtlety."

My mouth tasted like chalk. "On our days off—you always came in so late at night. You were reporting on me. Weren't you?"

"You and everyone else. Don't take it personally. *Then* I took lessons on reading from an officer's wife in the city. Like I said, Lady Sulat cares for her own."

I pinned my eyes on Moss. "Did Lady Sulat send Bane, too?"

"What? No. That boy's perfectly addle-headed on his own."

Did I trust Moss?

"Dami, don't be upset. I *do* enjoy your company," Osem said. "My report to Lady Sulat is part of the reason she trusted you weren't the poisoner. She originally wanted me in the kitchens to look into the Hungry Ghost."

I peered at her. "You always scare it away."

"I'm no chef. I can't exorcise it. I merely funneled information to Lady Sulat. Some of Hawak's research, mostly the ghost's behavior. Once I tried to follow it into Askan-Wod, but that black lump of fat can run faster than the wind. After the hangings, Lady Sulat told me to stop. Better to have ears in the kitchens than another execution."

"You knew the exorcism steps," I said, hurt. "You knew and wouldn't tell me." And then I'd foolishly alerted Archivist Linaan to my intent.

"Believe that if you like, but I didn't know. Before the hangings, Hawak didn't share that particular tidbit with the kitchens because he didn't want the apprentices trying anything by themselves. Now he says nothing about ghosts at all."

A perfectly cooked meal, the ghost's true regret, and a confession of the ills it had committed. I searched Osem's familiar face, the face of a spy, and couldn't decide if I believed those honest brown eyes or not. Across the room, the soldier's game of stones clinked on.

"Why would I need to know how to exorcise a ghost? I'm no cook.

Lady Sulat was arranging to sneak a trusted chef into the palace to deal with it." Osem tilted her head to the side. "Hmm. If you survive this, she'll probably use you. You're already here."

Moss gave her a sharp look. "That's enough details."

"After our duplicity, doesn't she deserve a show of trust?"

"Lady Sulat hasn't asked for her loyalty yet," Moss muttered.

I faced the hearth, turning my back to Moss and Osem. Not to scorn them, but to hide my face. Would Lady Sulat ask for my loyalty?

Lady Sulat had saved me from the Palace Guards already. She had compassion on people like Bane and Osem. But I'd also seen how well she put people to use. Under her protection, I could try to cook an exorcism. Perhaps she'd send me to heal others that served her.

I could be a chef. I could be *Plum* again.

To the crock of hot water I added slices of heart and a number of herbs. When Lady Sulat woke up, I'd talk to her. I'd ask her what plans she held for me. And if it matched what I imagined, I'd swear my allegiance to her.

For the first time since I tore up Sorrel's letter, I was excited about my future.

Maybe I shouldn't be too hard on Osem and Moss. They weren't entirely insincere with me. Not even Osem could fake that haunted terror in her eyes whenever I placed myself in danger.

"Are you managing in the kitchens without me?" I asked.

Osem blinked, surprised at my shift in tone. She grinned. "Sorrel's making the apprentices take shifts scrubbing, like they did before you came. The dishes are getting clean."

"Glad to know I was helpful," I joked.

"Oh, you'd be plenty of help *cooking* if we let you back in. Old King Fulsaan has been asking for basket after basket of branches every day. Then he mashes them up, pisses in them, and sends them back to the kitchens all foul. Can't even use it as fodder for ducks. If he weren't purple-ranked, I'd scold him for wasting all that beautiful, glossy buckwheat."

My heart stopped.

"Dami? Are you all right?" Osem jogged to my side and laid a hand on my shoulder.

The basket of branches. The Hungry Ghost had tried to devour them, turned them to foul slime, then pointed at the basket. Every time we met since, he'd pantomimed it.

Now Old King Fulsaan did the same—baskets of branches, desecrated as if by a Hungry Ghost.

The Ghost wasn't demanding branches to eat. He'd been sending a message, trying to point me to Old King Fulsaan. Had the ghost not noticed my absence from the kitchens, or had it hoped I'd hear about Fulsaan's strange behavior anyway?

The palace records held no answers for me. But Old King Fulsaan could tell me about this ghost's past, how it had died, and perhaps even what vices the exorcism needed to target.

"I have to talk to Old King Fulsaan."

CHAPTER THIRTY

Moss gave me an odd look. "You can't visit King Former Fulsaan. King Alder barely lets Lady Sulat visit—and that's once a week, under his personal watchful eye. The King is paranoid about his father's health."

The other guards in the room gave us uncomfortable glances, but kept playing their game of stones. Their conversation shifted to someone's wedding.

I salted the broth. "The King Former has lived in the palace so long, in such a position of power—it makes sense he knows who the Hungry Ghost is. And somehow, he can communicate with it."

"That's ridiculous. Why would the King Former converse with ghosts?" Osem asked.

"Maybe he's lonely." He had to be, confined in that room. I continued, explaining all about the branches.

Moss leaned back in his chair. With only the hearth light in this room, his face seemed lined, older. "Hmm. I don't see how we could sneak you in, though."

"Moss!" Osem snapped.

Either Osem was a brilliant spy, or she did care about me. Her anger cheered me immensely. "I'm the perfect person to go," I said. "If I'm caught, well, I'm already going to trial. And if I'm sneaking into the King Former's room, couldn't you all claim I'm a Shoreed spy? Maybe I could have a military trial after all."

Osem scowled, face lined, eyes haunted. "The Palace Guard does its best to never give up prisoners. Hoping we'll get you is a gamble—one dependent on the Ministry of Justice. He did us no favors setting up your trial. Why would you risk this?"

"She has a point," Moss said. "If you're captured, especially with Lady Sulat incapacitated, you're not likely to come back. And who will care for Lady Sulat?"

"And who arranged for Lady Sulat to be poisoned in the first place?" I demanded. "Who commands Fir and Violet? Our enemies are still out there. Besides, after my trial you'll need someone else to care for Lady Sulat anyway. I'll make a few batches of stock beforehand."

"That's morbid," Osem muttered, arms crossed.

Morbid, but true. "Isn't it odd that that the King Former sees no one? Maybe he's not as sick as King Alder says. Maybe he's locked up his father to keep the man silent about some plot between the ghost and the King. His Majesty did, after all, approve of sending Hawak away. And I've heard both of you talk about how he fears the military's growing political power."

Moss and Osem both frowned deeply; so did the other guards, though they didn't turn from their game. I wasn't the first person to suspect the king.

"Treasonous words," Osem muttered.

"As if the King doesn't have enough justification to kill me already! Don't you think Lady Sulat would want me to try?"

"Our Lady's *clever*, not idiotic," Osem said. "She doesn't throw lives away."

"My life is a short-lived asset."

Moss scratched his nose. "It's a calculated risk. I'd ask Lieutenant-

General Behon's permission to proceed, except there's no good way to get you in to King Former Fulsaan."

My insides fluttered. "I have a plan for that, actually."

MOSS LEFT to speak with Lieutenant-General Behon. My bones felt like overcooked noodles, waiting for his return. Perhaps tonight, I'd sneak out of the safe house. Converse with the King Former. Learn how to exorcise the Hungry Ghost and gain its knowledge.

"Do you have a death wish?" Osem demanded. She sat in the corner, legs stretched before her.

I scrubbed parsley root for tonight's hotpot, utilizing the best light from the hearth. "I do hope to come out of this alive."

"Then why haven't you married Bane yet?"

My throat squeezed. Did everyone in the Redwood Palace know about his proposal? "You're going to tell me it's a perfect match too, aren't you? That I should be so pleased."

"There's no such a thing as a perfect match."

I paused, rag dangling from my hand. "You... didn't get along with your husband?"

"He didn't live long enough for me to find out."

My marrow ached for her. "I'm sorry. I thought you'd been married half a year, before..."

"We were. Marriage is an adjustment, Dami."

I peered at her. Osem shrugged. "At first, we fought constantly. But I learned that he pinched the bridge of his nose when he was tired, not upset at me. He learned I'm easier to talk to after meals, when I'm not hungry." She gave a self-deprecating smile. "We still fought. A lot. But we were making it work. Maybe even creating something good."

Had Moss' marriage started like that? I bit my lip, trying to find the right condolences, but words failed me. I left the parsley root and fetched some hazelnuts from the cellar. I toasted them while I boiled honey, maple sugar, and a splash of ginger tea together. I tested the sugar mixture in a cool cup of water—it solidified like a crack of lightning. Then I tossed in the hazelnuts, a pinch of salt, a few drops of blackberry molasses for a bit of acidity, and then poured the whole thing onto a slab of granite. The candy cooled quickly, leaving each nut glowing like an amber star. I passed them all to Osem.

She peered at them. "What...?"

"I'm sorry. About what happened." Candied hazelnuts. Endurance-to-the-soul.

Her eyes widened with the first bite. She nibbled slowly, savoring the sweet with those hints of salt, sour, and spice. As she ate, her whole body relaxed, shoulders to toe.

That is, until Moss returned, face lined. No smiles today.

"What happened?" Osem demanded.

"Nothing," Moss muttered. "Dami, Lieutenant-General Behon approved your plan. He figures that we need all the information we can get. But if you're caught, we had nothing to do with any of this. Deny everything. Lieutenant-General Behon made it clear he won't risk men in some ill-conceived rescue attempt just to send you to trial a day later."

"Of course. But why do you look so horrible?"

He shook his head, then fetched himself a bowl of hotpot. He didn't seem worried about me; he seemed exhausted.

"Are you going to tell me what happened?"

"Lieutenant-General Behon personally oversaw Violet's interrogation. As he should have, given her crimes. But his interrogator's used to dealing with enemy soldiers, not young women." The words sounded blank, hollow. Moss dumped my carefully-sliced vegetables and fish in his mouth, his arm moving by rote.

My stomach clenched. "She's badly hurt, isn't she?"

"She's *dead*."

The words rang through the room, ushering in silence.

I stared. She was supposed to have a trial. Fairness. Justice.

One of the guards asked, "Did we learn who she served first?"

"No, more's the pity. If Lady Sulat were awake, she'd give Lieutenant-General Behon a tongue lashing to turn his hide blue."

The guards muttered curses under their breaths. One snorted. "Can't say I blame the interrogator. Not after what she'd done."

Whatever she'd done, she deserved a trial. The law decided guilt, not angry soldiers.

"What's going to happen to the interrogator?" My voice felt no louder than a squeak. I half-feared the soldiers might berate me, but they kept mumbling.

Moss shrugged. "Nothing. These things happen."

"Often?" I felt ill.

"Now and then."

Osem glared at Moss. "This is *exactly* why Dami shouldn't be chasing ghosts. Prisons aren't safe. If a guard is bored, or if someone thinks you have information..."

"After this incident, the interrogators will be more careful," Moss rebutted.

Not exactly a comforting thought.

Should I have told Violet to flee, then accused her? I felt like I'd licked a Hungry Ghost. She was a traitor, a poisoner. She'd defiled her precious birthgift, meant for healing, by attacking a baby and nearly killing Lady Sulat. Violet deserved whatever judgment the courts gave. But she didn't deserve this. "How... did she die?"

"She cracked her head on the lip of the room's hearth."

I didn't ask why the interrogation chamber had a hearth; I didn't want to know. "That killed her?"

"Her brain bled out from the inside. They didn't notice until too late." Moss said, monotone. He slurped his broth.

The lump near my temple throbbed. Recipes raced through my brain. Fiddlehead ferns—no, those were out of season already. Dried hen-of-the-woods or spinach, then, to target the head. Yarrow or bone marrow to further target the blood in the head. She'd need sour to get past the immediate danger, then sweet acorns to heal any cracks to her skull.

If I'd been there, could I have saved her?

"You'll stay now, of course." That old terror lingered in Osem's eyes. She understood human cruelty better than I did.

I swallowed and turned to Moss. "You said the Palace Guard would be more careful with me? After this incident?"

"I'm sure. They'd never pass up an opportunity to rub something in the military's face. Keeping you alive would let them do just that."

Osem glared at him. "Careful! Careful doesn't mean they won't burn and break her hands!"

"I'm sorry, Osem." My innards felt stabbed with a thousand obsidian blades. "But I'm still going."

MOSS BLINDFOLDED me and led me out of the safehouse. He took the cloth off in the basement of a noodle shop, jammed with crates of dried food, then led me through the cramped, twisted backstreets of Askan-Wod. Osem strolled silently with us, the words of the argument dropped, the pain in her eyes remaining.

We had no issue getting through the palace gate. When we reached the kitchens—now empty and glowing with dimmed hearths—she disappeared into what had been our room, shoulders tight with anger.

I wanted to call out. To apologize again. But it seemed insincere, given that I wasn't abandoning my plan.

"I'll be in the spruce trees. Good luck." Moss nodded and walked away.

I sat in the open doorway, the smells of the day's dishes washing over me: smoked venison, long-simmered pumpkin, freshly-shredded ramps. A fruity scent beneath it all—cherries? They'd still have plenty of dried cherries stored from last autumn.

I passed the time listing dishes that made good use of cherries. Stewed mixed fruit, tossed into a hotpot or salad for sweetness. I shivered in the darkness. What if a Palace Guard found me first?

I smelled the ghost before I saw it—the mold of vegetables left in the ground to rot, the stench of flies on spoiled meat. I took Moss' blindfold and tied it around my mouth and nose, but it barely helped.

I stepped outside and closed the door behind me as the Hungry

Ghost dropped from the roof onto the lawn. Its face pinched like a starved dog's as it stared at the door. Its distended, enormous stomach growled.

"I want to help you. The Old King knows your secrets, doesn't he?"

It tilted its head to the side. The whimpering ceased.

"I can't walk through the halls to him. But you, you could walk over the roofs and bring me to his window."

The ghost didn't move. I frowned. Did it not understand? "I need—"

It laid down flat on the lawn, the layers of fat rolling across the grass, inviting me to mount.

CHAPTER
THIRTY-ONE

I tried to climb up the ghost, but my foot slipped on the patina of slug-like slime that covered every corpulent roll of its flesh. The stench reached its foul hand down my throat and threatened to squeeze my stomach empty.

"One moment," I whispered, trying not to gag. I turned back to the kitchen. Mint? Cress? Those weren't strong enough by half to block the smell, not with my perceptive nose. The last thing I needed was to vomit and fall off while the Hungry Ghost scaled the roofs.

I grabbed a hotradish from the pantry and sliced a few rounds off. I popped one into my mouth, tucked the remainder in my skirt's waist, and bit down. The heat burned up my sinuses and down my throat. I couldn't smell anything else. I couldn't see particularly well, either, with my eyes watering, but I'd make do.

This time, I managed to mount. So close to the ghost, I could smell the rot, like must and mildew under a rug. The hotradish kept the worst of it away. I tightened my legs around its side and clung to a roll of fat with both my hands.

"I'm ready."

Or, at least, I thought so. It jerked upright and scrambled up a wall. I tightened my legs and dug my nails into its flesh, but my hands slipped on the slime.

It flattened onto the roof. I grabbed at a roll of fat further up and yanked myself closer to its shoulders just as it sprinted across the sloped shingles.

The stench of it knotted my throat. I bit down on the hotradish again, burning myself with new heat. Tears blurred the rooftops, the curve of the trees, but I kept chewing, trying to keep the stink out. Droplets of slime, picked up by the wind, splattered my face. Why had I tucked the rest of the hotradish in my skirt's waist? I couldn't pause to reach it, not here. My thighs numbed from the cold of its slime.

Oddly, the Hungry Ghost hardly made a noise. Maybe its limbs were too small. Maybe its fat padded the sound.

The cloth over my face pulled free and fluttered away in the breeze. I tried to sit up straighter, away from the reek, but my stiff legs wobbled.

I lay flat, face pressed next to the slime of its skin and sobbed as spicy vomit welled in my throat and spewed out my nose, streaming back onto my face and neck.

The Hungry Ghost jerked to a stop, then lowered me through an open window with its tiny hands. I collapsed on the floor. My legs ached from clinging. I could barely uncurl my fingers. I turned my head to the side so I didn't drown in my own vomit.

The ghost's enormous bulk shouldn't have fit through the window, but it squeezed through like noodle dough in a press. Behind it, the window showed only stars and tree tops—we weren't on ground level.

The Hungry Ghost apologetically nosed the recent contents of my stomach, coming close enough to engulf me again in the miasma of its stench.

"Just..." My throat burned like someone had seared it on white coals. "... go. Please."

It whimpered, then climbed up the wall, leaving the way it had come in.

I shivered. The roomed still smelled foul, but not unbearably so. I lay, trying to compose myself. The raw hotradish, being the opposite of a well-prepared meal, dampened my sense. Sight, hearing, touch, and—mercifully—smell all fuzzed around the edges. I managed to sit up.

Polished redwood composed the floors, walls, and ceiling. An antechamber with open curtains lay on the far side, but the opulent lacquered bed inside held nothing but wrinkled blankets. A number of beautiful things adorned the room—vases, calligraphy posters, an elegantly carved wardrobe and a pink-granite washbasin—but no King Former Fulsaan. No sign of life other than a lantern glowing softly on a low table.

But the King Former never left. I dragged myself to a window as the ill effects of the hotradish ebbed. I spotted a wall a good distance below encircling the building. This had to be the third floor of the Royal Bear House. The Hungry Ghost perched on a nearby roof, looking like a greasy shadow. It lowered its head, plaintive, and gestured with one stubby arm for me to stay inside. To wait?

I made a wide gesture at the room, then held up my arms in question.

It nodded, like it knew no one was inside. I gestured for it to come get me, to take me to King Former Fulsaan, but it shook its head and held out its hand. *Wait.*

I eyed the steeply peaked roof and contemplated climbing out. But if the fall didn't kill me, breaking both my legs ensured the Palace Guard would catch me. I peered under the door and saw the heels of two guards. No escape that way, either.

My chest knotted. The Hungry Ghost wanted my help. It hadn't brought me here as a taunt.

Wherever King Alder had taken his father to, they'd probably return soon. When they did, I didn't want King Alder to glimpse any trace of me.

Quietly, so the guards wouldn't have more to think about, I

stripped my foul clothes off, poured a pitcher of water into the basin, and scrubbed myself liberally with the parsley soap. Then I upended the basin over the floor and used my clothes to mop it all up. I stuffed the whole wet mess under the dresser. By then, goose bumps riddled my skin, but at least the world smelled like soap and stench instead of just stench.

Impertinent as it was, I helped myself to one of the long shirts and soft pants inside the king's wardrobe. I'd already been bold enough in coming here; borrowing clothes seemed like a small crime next to that. The sleeves tumbled over my fingertips, impeding movement, and the pants bunched and rubbed between my knees.

I hid myself behind the bed, where I couldn't be seen from the doorway. Hopefully King Alder wouldn't notice the lingering, acrid taste in the air, or that the floor shone a little too brightly.

My body protested the stiffness of the position, but I didn't dare wait somewhere more comfortable. Cheek pressed against the redwood, I inhaled the crisp smell of the forest and the musk of oil. There were worse smells. Worse places to be. Where was Dami right now? Sleeping in a tent, with a dozen other unwashed soldiers? Marching through the rain? Fighting hand to hand on some battlefield I'd never see, reeking with the tang of blood?

I dozed off, thinking of her—of her long braid and all the people she'd left behind.

When I woke, the lamp had burned out. By the false dawn outside, I made out the Hungry Ghost's silhouette in the window. It dropped down onto the floor.

I scrambled to pull my neckline over my mouth, but oddly, I didn't smell anything foul.

The rolls of fat boiled inward. The ghost's filth wicked off the floor, back into its body. Its limbs rounded and its belly shrank. The head domed into something more human-shape. A nose grew. The mouth widened and sprouted lips. Hair stubbled its scalp, then poured down its shoulders. Black slime turned into wrinkled skin.

A ray of real sunlight glanced across the window top and I found myself staring at an old, pudgy, naked man.

As a chef, I was no stranger to anatomy, but I closed my eyes, then covered them with a hand.

"Kitchen girl," he called softly, his voice higher than I'd expected after seeing him as a massive ghost. "You're still here, aren't you?"

"Yes."

He yawned. "I have no desire to search for you, but I do want to talk with you. Come out."

"Ah. Are you dressed now?" I hadn't heard him take so much as a step.

"Clothes. Curse it," he mumbled. I heard the wardrobe open. "If it's warm, I usually don't bother. My only daily visitor is my son. I'm not about to exert myself for his comfort."

His words tumbled together in my skull. My chest knotted. "You're King Former Fulsaan."

"Of course. Didn't you get the message with the branches? Ripping them up was exhausting. You can come out."

Our own past monarch, a Hungry Ghost. The Father of our nation. Shame for all of Rowak welled in my chest. I stepped out from behind the bed, my stiff muscles groaning. Purple Fulsaan sat on the floor. He'd pulled on a pair of trousers and a tunic, but hadn't bothered to tie a belt or comb his hair.

"You're dead."

"I noticed." He rubbed his eyes. "I'd like to be exorcised."

"Why didn't you ask your son? The King could—"

Fulsaan waved a hand. "Who do you think keeps me in here? He knows."

"But why—" I didn't finish before my insides frosted. "King Alder *knew* the apprentices weren't lying?"

"Of course."

"He had them all hanged!"

Sadness rimmed his eyes. "How could he hide me, with such rumors flying?"

I shifted half a step back. This man, however pitiful he looked, didn't become a ghost through neglect. "You knowingly put me at risk of the king's wrath."

"I did hope, separated from the Royal Bear House, that you'd be clever enough to escape the King's notice. I gave up asking my guards for help after Alder killed the third set. The fourth set's deaf now."

Did he mean they'd always been deaf, or that the King had punctured their eardrums? The King had seemed so sad about the war, about his father's failing health. So... human. I wanted to believe he felt justified in the apprentices' deaths. That he wasn't a murderer. That, maybe, he'd listen to my pleas for a merciful punishment at the trial.

"So the King keeps you imprisoned here to protect himself."

"Oh, no. The smart thing to do would be to bring in a good chef, exorcise me, and then cremate the chef. Do you know what happens if it's found out I'm a Hungry Ghost?"

I frowned, uncertain.

"I'd be struck from the records as a king and my descendants all demoted to red-ranked. Alder, Sulat, Torut. Alder would be dethroned and Valerian disinherited. The upheaval would give the Shoreed the perfect opportunity to attack and end Rowak all together." Fulsaan shook his head. "Alder should have ended me a long time ago. I wish he had. All this sneaking about and trying to get exorcised without Alder slaughtering the whole palace is incredibly tiring."

"Who would succeed if Alder was demoted?" I demanded. This stank of a plot.

"Hmm. I have no brothers. Lady Thrush is my oldest sister—long deceased — but it would be her oldest living descendent, Blue-ranked Captain Gano of the Palace Guard."

Captain Gano. Did Fir work for him? My adrenaline cooled and my brain began working. But why would Captain Gano poison Lady Sulat if he could disinherit her?

"Why doesn't King Alder exorcise you?" I asked.

He shrugged. "I'm his father. However rude and obstinate I am during our visits, he wants to keep me around."

Alder's words from that night I spied on Lord Torut played through my mind: *If I could, I'd place him in a room safe in the clouds, where no illness or age could ever strike him down. Where I could always have him nearby.*

Is that what he thought of having his father turn into a Hungry Ghost? How could he be so callous to other people's sons when he cherished his father so? Not that he followed his father's wishes for an exorcism.

I sat on the floor, several paces back from Fulsaan. King Alder would show no mercy to a girl from the kitchens who'd asked questions about Hungry Ghosts in the archives. I'd have to count on the Council to acquit me.

In the meantime, I should finish what I'd started. "You still want me to exorcise you, right?"

"Yes." He sighed. "Are you going to hold me to that whole spying-for-you thing?"

I frowned. "Did you not even look?"

"I did. A little." Fulsaan rested his elbows on his knees. "Lieu-tenant-General Behon, the man in charge of Askan-Wod's defenses, is sending secret messenger-birds at night. But for all I know he's writing a mistress."

My shoulders dropped. With such an ideal spy, I'd hoped for more. "Your son isn't behind the poisoning?"

"He seems genuinely disturbed by it. Using two poison-tasters now."

Was the king just trying to look innocence?

"So. Back to my exorcism..."

A lump of disappointment pressed against my ribs. He'd failed me, but as a chef, I still wanted to help him. "First I need to know what vices tie you to this world."

Fulsaan sighed, jowls drooping.

"Don't you want me to help you?" I asked, firm-but-kind. Almost like talking to a child.

"I do. It's just such a long story. Fetch me a cup of huckleberry wine. Bottom drawer of the wardrobe."

I poured Fulsaan his drink, which he slurped down before speaking. "Ahh. Tell me what you know about my oldest son, Ospren."

"He used talk about tax reformation to cover his thefts from the treasury. For those thefts, he was exiled eight years ago to a cabin on the southern border, under heavy guard."

Fulsaan nodded. "The bit about the treasury's all lies, of course."

I peered at him.

Fulsaan scratched the back of his neck. "Well, I suppose he did want to reform taxes. Right now, the governor of every province collects taxes, then sends the throne their portion. Birdie wanted royal tax collectors who'd bring everything to the capital, then redistribute it to the cities. The Blue-Green councils of the provinces have little ability to check the governors in regards to taxes—Birdie thought handing the whole matter over to the Royal House was the best way to stem corruption."

"Birdie?"

"That's what we called Ospren when he was little."

"Ah."

"It wasn't a popular motion, taking power from the governors and giving it to the Royal House. He also had some strange ideas about improving roads. In any case, Alder came to me with a plot to exile Birdie."

"And you agreed?" I asked, incredulous. Speaking with Fulsaan seemed surreal—I didn't think to keep my tone polite.

But Fulsaan didn't seem to mind. He shrugged. "Easier than dealing with upset magistrates and their machinations. Or assassination attempts."

"You... weren't a very good king, were you?"

"I was an excellent king!" He tried to take another drink, then waved at me to refill his cup. "I didn't rule like a tyrant. I kept enough control that people considered me malleable, but not a mere puppet to be dethroned."

I handed him the wine. Is this where Lord Torut picked up his habits?

"You didn't want to make Rowak... better?" I asked.

"I was just a king." He sipped. "I wanted to eat and sleep and have excellent baths. You sound like my wife."

I frowned. I didn't know much about the late queen.

"*She* had ambition. Edged out I don't know how many other women to marry me. Ospren, with all his plans... he was her joy. I'm afraid she rubbed off on Alder and Sulat as well."

"She died of a fever, correct?"

"Oh, I don't know if she's even dead." He finished his drink and set it on the floor. "She disappeared after Alder and I framed and exiled Birdie. But there's no sign of her at Birdie's cabin. So we said she died. Staged a funeral. Much easier than trying to explain a missing person."

I rubbed the side of my skull, head aching. "Haven't you tried to find her?"

"Not particularly. She hated me. Me and my banquets and my pretty serving girls."

My stomach fell. "You weren't faithful to her, were you?"

"Ancestors above! Of course I was. Usually. Do you know how much effort's involved in keeping mistresses? Let alone keeping them secret? Besides, late-night tumbling leaves me sweaty. I detest sweating. And then there's cleaning up and getting dressed again! Bah."

I'd frozen, ears burning as surely as if someone had lit my hair on fire. Given his earlier transformation, I could unfortunately craft an accurate image of a naked, sweaty Fulsaan.

"Oh. I apologize. Being dead does make one rather cavalier. You're not married, are you?"

"No."

"Ah, you're so lucky. Well, now that you know what my crimes are, you can exorcise me, right? I can't tell you how bothersome it is to be a ghost all night, compelled to run and run searching for scraps. There aren't enough naps in a day to make up for it."

"*That's* what you find bothersome? Running?"

He blinked at me, eyes wide atop his round cheeks. "You say *running* like it's not an evil word! Part of my brain is my own, but I can't stop my search for food. I can't even lounge in this room—closed doors or windows keep me from entering any space *inside* a building, but they don't keep me from going *outdoors*. Alder tried boarding up the window, but I could still squeeze through. It's horrid! Every moment, I'm perfectly aware that my soft, warm bed lies empty and unappreciated, my pillow deprived of the creases of a happy dreamer's head."

He rudely slapped one hand into the other to emphasize his point.

I don't know who I'd expected to meet in this third-story room, but I certainly hadn't imagined a lackadaisical king who considered getting dressed a bother. "You're..." the words lumped in my throat, but I kneaded them out. "You're *lazy*."

"Well put! Usually my advisors tried to be polite about it."

I scowled. "And you want me to exorcise you, because you're too lazy to bother being a ghost?"

"Yes! Exactly!" He sighed and shook his head. "I'm sorry for what I let happen to my son. And my wife, if that's my fault—it probably is. And that I didn't find out more for you and your trial. But I'm dead now and ready to rest for eternity. The running's horrible. And I have to start every sunrise and sunset in this exact same spot where I died. If I'm not here, I'm *ripped* back, all pins and needles. Found *that* out when Alder tried to stash me in an internal room with no windows. Rather uncomfortable. Would you fetch me another cup?"

Lazy. What kind of food did I make to exorcise a lazy ghost? And would it work? Exorcism also required the true remorse of the ghost and King Fulsaan didn't seem remotely ashamed.

At least I could report this all to Lady Sulat. I sighed. I'd expected this to somehow be tied to Fir, to the poisonings... but why would anyone poison her if they could disinherit her with far greater ease?

Besides, Violet had been on the waiting list for three years—long before Fulsaan died.

"King Former Fulsaan, I will try to help you. Ghosts should find their rest. But it won't be easy. And given your particular nature, you might have to do something to achieve it."

He frowned, letting the empty wine cup fall to his side. "*Do something* sounds a great deal like work. I don't suppose I could nap for this instead? I am exceptionally good at napping."

The door opened. I'd been so busy focusing on Fulsaan, I hadn't heard the footsteps.

Purple King Alder stared at both of us, along with his four personal guards. The pair of deaf guards turned to see what everyone else was staring at.

My breath tangled as King Alder's wide-eyed surprise narrowed into hate. "Arrest her!"

CHAPTER
THIRTY-TWO

I dashed for the window. Boots thundered behind me. I swung one of my legs over the ledge and hoisted myself up.

Someone grabbed my ankle. I punched him in the nose. He let go and I pitched forward onto the steeply sloped roof.

My feet skittered against the shingles as I slid downward. I splayed my limbs and dug in with my fingers. I halted, my feet a handspan from the lip of the roof.

I wasn't Dami. I wasn't strong-of-arm. I wasn't agile-of-anything. My breath shook. I tried to shuffle sideways but slipped another inch. Three stories to fall. I wouldn't survive that.

Someone skidded toward me. A guard in blue. I shrieked and tried to push him away, but I couldn't do that and keep my balance. He deftly looped a rope over my hand, then grabbed my other hand and tied it, too.

He yanked, and I fell on my side. I slithered up the roof, belly grating on the wooden shingles as he pulled me back up. Thrashing only added scrapes to my elbows. I glanced up at the guard. He stared back, face serene. A purple band encircled his arm, embossed with amber bears. Why had I thought I could outrun a high-ranking palace guard?

He hauled me through the window and dropped me onto the floor like a sack of beans. The soldier I'd punched stood in the corner, nose dripping blood, receiving a hushed, sharp lecture from his superior.

"Lieutenant Bracken, haul her away," King Alder commanded.

Fulsaan sat where I'd left him. He hadn't so much as stood up to help me. As the four guards hauled me to my feet, he stretched, yawned, and then reclined back on the floor, his double-chin resting against his neck.

"Why," Fulsaan drawled, "is she being arrested?"

"She's an invader," King Alder snapped.

"She's my guest. Unless you're suggesting that I'm a prisoner, who has no right to visitors I wish to see?"

The guards straightened, ears prickling. One of the four turned to Fulsaan with questioning pity in his eyes. The deaf guards still stood outside, spears ready for anyone who might come up the hall.

"She risked your health by coming here," Alder said.

"I invited her. I risked my own health. Shall we arrest these Palace Guards as well for entering?"

The guards betrayed no fear on their faces, though more than one neck tensed.

The King considered me, gaze prickling my skin like vinegar. "I would have your name."

I swallowed, hard. Part of me ached to make up something wild, but I doubted such subterfuge could last. "I am Yellow-ranked Dami of Clamsriver, a servant of the Royal House."

"Dami…" he mumbled my name, eyes sharp. He turned to Fulsaan. "Father, I'm surprised you chose to entertain an accused criminal as your guest. Or did you not know she has a trial set?"

Fulsaan leaned back and raised an eyebrow. "Then she should reach that trial alive, don't you think?"

"I'll have the Palace Guard lock her up, like any other prisoner."

"Ah, but she's not any other prisoner. She's a servant of the Royal House and my friend." He turned to the guards. "Lieutenant Bracken. Make sure nothing ill happens to her. If it does, I want a full investigation."

Lieutenant Bracken glanced from King Alder to Fulsaan. Alder's face and shoulders tightened.

Last autumn, the Palace Guard answered to Fulsaan. I swallowed hard. If King Alder killed me outright, would these men remain loyal to their current master, or would they spread rumors that Fulsaan was trapped, his throne usurped?

"You may agree," King Alder said to the guards, voice void of emotion. Apparently he didn't know who they'd choose, either. Lieutenant Bracken bowed.

King Alder stared at me, eyes burning in his otherwise impassive face. Had this man sent Violet to murder his sister? He was cold enough to do it. Either way, it wouldn't matter that I'd revealed Violet as the poisoner. When my trial came, he'd see me dead, just for finding me here. If not for Fulsaan, I didn't doubt he'd kill me today.

"Lock her up in a spare room of the Royal Bear House. If my father insists she is treated like a guest, she will have every luxury."

The guards bowed low, then grabbed me by the elbows and escorted me down the stairs.

THE ROOM KING Alder provided oozed ostentation. My bed—a standing bed—rested in its own curtained alcove, the fabric rich with stylized embroidery of hawks and salmon. The main room boasted a rug I could sink my fingers into up to the second knuckle. The high, narrow lattice window on the west face repeated the hawks and salmon in low-relief. I had three chairs, likewise carved, a lacquered wardrobe, and a table inlaid with shell and stone. All of it smelled of fine, ginger-scented wood polish.

If King Alder put me in here to intimidate me with his wealth, it was working.

Four women entered, their purple skirts decorated with a bleached-out bear, denoting them as servants of King Alder. They carried a wooden washtub between them and pitchers of water.

They gracefully set the tub down, then nudged me into it.

"Ah," I began. "What, is, umm..."

They kept their eyes lowered, as if I were some great person. Did King Alder tell them to act like that to mock me, or did they think me a real guest? I'd seen the guards positioned outside the door when the women entered.

"His Majesty desires his guest to be comfortable and clean," one of them said. Then they deftly stripped me naked and scrubbed me like a particularly muddy radish. After they toweled me off and wrestled my hair into smooth locks, they brought me a dress from the wardrobe. How odd, to see a dress of Yellow-rank width made with fabric as light and smooth as whipped egg whites, delicately dyed a forget-me-not-blue. A pale yellow skirt followed, delicately embroidered with streaks of amber and pink, reminiscent of a sunrise. Or, in my case, sunset.

The servants braided and twirled all my hair into a pile on top of my head, then adorned the braids with tinkling shell ornaments.

I felt off balance, as frail as a forget-me-not poking through the snow of early spring. The King had stated his wealth with the room and his power over me with the servants—he decided when I bathed, what I wore.

The women left as quietly as they came. I glimpsed the guards again, spears at their sides. I couldn't escape that way.

I ran my hand over the embroidered skirt. So lovely. My chest ached. This was exactly the kind of dress I would have wanted to meet Sorrel in. I might look half as beautiful as the real Dami, now.

"Oh, Nana. Whether it's poisonous snakes or gilded dresses, I can't navigate this palace. What's the realm of the Ancestors like? I hope it's peaceful."

I didn't feel anything except my own roiling stomach. I couldn't stay here. My trial was the day after tomorrow. King Former Fulsaan had bought me precious little time.

Walking carefully in the dress, I crossed to the high, narrow window. I was on the second story, opposite of Fulsaan's room, facing west.

The door opened. I startled. King Alder stood there, clothed in blood-dark violet brocade. The wide cut of fabric draped around him, his sleeves tumbling to his fingertips in another display of wealth. I swallowed and stepped away from the window.

"Sit." He gestured at the chairs. The door thudded closed behind him. He'd left his guards outside. Did he not want them listening? "Are your accommodations sufficiently comfortable?"

"Yes. Thank you." I sat, the hairs on my arms prickling. At least he couldn't see that. I tried to mirror his face. Impassive. Unreadable.

The King kept his voice low. "You have not been in the palace long. How did you become my father's friend so quickly?"

I didn't doubt that he'd kill me if I told the truth. He'd hanged twelve apprentices for seeing the Ghost—and I knew its secrets.

"He sent me a note."

"A note."

"I found it scrubbing his dishes. He said he needed someone to come to his chambers."

"Scrubbing dishes," he echoed, tone unchanging.

I swallowed hard. "Yes."

"What did he want?"

"He said it was urgent. But when I came, he asked me to fluff his pillows. For more comfortable naps."

Alder leaned back. "He went to the trouble of sending you a note for that?"

"Has he not asked you for a servant, to do these things for him?"

Alder's face darkened. Fulsaan had asked, but Alder apparently didn't trust anyone enough for the task.

"He seemed very ill, Your Majesty." I dropped my eyes to my lap. "He couldn't even fetch a cup of wine for himself."

"And for this small service, he names you a great friend?"

"He seems to take his naps seriously. He's a kind old man. May his Ancestors smile on him and send him a swift recovery."

I kept my eyes down, not daring to look up, lest Alder see the lie in my face.

"How did you get into his room? The guards won't admit anyone without my physical presence. I deliver all his food, take away all his dishes."

I spread my fingers over my embroidered skirt, trying not to clench them. Did I have a reasonable answer? "I'm strong-of-arm. I scaled the wall and he let me through the window."

"Very well." King Alder spoke a touch softer than before. I couldn't tell if I'd fooled him, or if I'd left him satisfied that I needed to die.

He swept out of the room, leaving me alone in oppressive luxury, with my hands clutched in the soft fabric of my skirt, my heart pounding in my throat.

CHAPTER
THIRTY-THREE

My midday meal consisted of simple buckwheat branches. Grain targeted no part of the body and the preparation held no hint of spicy, salty, sour, or sweet. King Alder wanted me to have no advantage. At least they weren't poisoned.

For drinking, he sent rhubarb wine. No water. Did he want to intoxicate me, loosen my tongue? I sipped only enough to quench my thirst after the dry branches.

My door opened again. Captain Gano of the Palace Guard ducked under the lintel, the purple band on his arm bright in the afternoon light. A pair of guards in blue flanked him.

"Good afternoon, Dami." He didn't hide his emotions as well as King Alder; loathing twisted his face, turning his softly-spoken greeting insincere. His severe mustache looked sharp as obsidian.

If I stayed standing, I'd start to pace and fidget. I sat in one of the chairs, even though looking up at the tall man would put a crick in my neck. My information could make this man a king. I had a way to bargain for my own freedom and protection.

But telling him about the Hungry Ghost betrayed Lady Sulat as well. And the Shoreed would use such an upheaval to strike. My life wasn't worth Rowak's sovereignty.

"Good afternoon, Captain Gano. Did His Majesty send you to question me?"

"A number of people are petitioning to visit you. The King merely approved my request." He sat across from me and folded his manicured hands in his lap. So different from Bane's calloused one. "You've become quite an interesting person, Dami."

I didn't know how to respond, so I said nothing.

Captain Gano tensed in the silence. Good. I wanted him as off-kilter as I felt.

"You found Lady Sulat's poisoner. A remarkable feat."

"Thank you." Was he testing my connection to Lady Sulat, then?

"How did you uncover Violet's plot? I have yet to hear that story."

My throat prickled. The truth—that Fir pointed me to them—would hand him information that I'd rather keep close. "She tried to delay me from tasting Lady Sulat's food. I'm afraid her clumsy maneuvers were obvious."

"Ah. Lady Sulat must be pleased with your efforts," he said, nibbling at my loyalties again.

I didn't agree or disagree with his statement. "My efforts were humble."

"You seem to attract attention everywhere you go. Old King Fulsaan truly named you his friend?"

"Yes."

"How did you earn his trust so quickly? You've not been in the palace long. More importantly, how did you get past my guards?" His ridiculous mustache twitched in annoyance.

Of course he resented me. I'd made him look foolish.

The moment for bargaining had come. But I couldn't offer him the throne for my freedom.

I paused. Why had King Alder even allowed this man to speak with me?

The truth struck me like a rock in the gut. Lady Sulat had already taught me about giving someone enough freedom to allow them to expose their loyalties. Of course I wouldn't tell the King that I knew about the Hungry Ghost. But I might tell this man, his biggest threat. I peered at the ceiling, then the walls. Was there a peep-hole? Or a trusted, perceptive-of-ear spy nearby?

The real danger here was still the King. If I'd spoken, I doubted either me or Captain Gano would see sunset. Dealing with the repercussions in the Purple-Blue Council would be simpler than drawing the truth back in once revealed.

"You look unwell. Does my question trouble you?"

"It's merely exasperating. Surely you have already heard it from King Alder."

Captain Gano glared flatly. "Humor me."

"No."

"That's pert." He leaned back and laid his hands lightly on the armrest, a subtle reminder of the guards at his sides. "I came for a peaceable visit and this is how you treat me, a blue-ranked man of the palace?"

"Peaceable?" I let the frustration in my gut uncoil into my voice. "You attacked me less than a week ago! My ankle is still bruised. Why should I waste my breath repeating myself to a man who's already declared himself my enemy?"

Maybe I'd gone over-the-top. Maybe whoever was listening would say as much to King Alder.

Gano narrowed his eyes. "You call Violet clumsy, yet you allow yourself tantrums. I am the Captain of the Palace Guard. I could make your life longer, if you proved... interesting."

I remained silent, insides writhing despite my best attempts at smooth breathing.

"You need time to consider this, when your trial is the day after tomorrow?"

"No. I fell silent for fear of saying anything you'd find interesting."

He stood, hooked a foot around my chair leg, and yanked. I fell backwards, head smacking onto the soft rug. Nowhere near hard enough for my brain to bleed out from the inside. He wouldn't have

been so gentle if we sat in a prison instead of the Royal Bear House—
I could see it in his eyes.

Gano towered over me, his boot next to my throat. "I look forward
to your execution."

He left with his men.

I exhaled. Limbs shaking, I straightened the chair, then laid down
in my bed. Whoever was listening would tell King Alder that I wasn't
Captain Gano's person. Maybe I belonged to Lady Sulat, but she'd be
disinherited, too, if Fulsaan's ghostly nature came to light. I wasn't a
threat. His Majesty could let me live.

A deluded hope. Why let a liability live, when he could dispose of
me so effortlessly?

"Thanks, Fulsaan, for these two days," I muttered to myself, "but I
don't think they're doing me any good."

I'd spent one of them sitting there, interrogated by King and
Captain alike. What good was dying with Fulsaan's secrets? King
Alder didn't deserve to rule, but Lady Sulat made the palace a better
place. With her teaching Purple Lord Valerian, we'd have a good king
one day—if no one revealed Fulsaan and stripped him to Red rank.

For all my efforts, I hadn't uncovered who'd threatened Lady
Sulat in the first place. I'd only got myself trapped and prodded at.

I felt like a tadpole cupped in a child's hand. Here, I had nowhere
to swim and the water was all dribbling away.

CHAPTER
THIRTY-FOUR

When night fell, I thought I was done with visitors. I sat on that beautiful bed in the dark alcove, nibbling my last buckwheat branch. The apprentices had charred it, leaving my mouth parched and ashy.

Maybe I should have cautiously stayed at Lady Sulat's side until the trial. My venture here meant nothing if the information died with me.

The stench of rotting peas tumbled through my high, narrow window. Then that lovely lattice shutter of hawks and salmon rattled.

I'd never been so happy to smell the Hungry Ghost before.

Dropping my branch, I ran to the window. I tossed the frame open. Fulsaan waited for me, his massive rolls of fat perched just below the window—perfect for mounting.

His reek twisted down my throat, gagging me, but I still tried to throw a leg up onto the sill. Too high. I grabbed a chair. This time, my foot easily cleared it. I wriggled my shoulder through the window, but my head clunked against the frame.

It was too narrow.

I twisted, grinding my head against the wood. I felt like buckwheat between a pair of millstones. Scrapes decorated my cheeks and the wood bit at my ears, but I made no progress.

Of course King Alder wouldn't put me in a room where I might slip out the window.

"Can you eat wood? Can you melt my prison?"

He whimpered. I lowered myself back onto the chair.

"Please try. I can't get out otherwise."

The ghost licked the wood with his tiny pin-prick mouth. Ooze from his body coated it like a rotten-egg tar, but the wood remained. I pried at it with my fingers, then tried to use chair legs as a lever. Nothing budged.

Fulsaan whimpered again, then disappeared, his massive bulk lost in the darkness of night.

I closed the shutter. Not that it did anything to block the lingering stench.

No one came to interrogate me the next morning. Unable to sit still, I paced my lovely room. It would take longer than I had to live to wear holes in this rug.

Mid-afternoon, the door slid open. My shoulders tensed and I tried to make my face unreadable. Somehow, I had to work these interrogations to my advantage. How, I didn't know. I wished I could ask Moss for advice.

Sorrel stepped inside. He stared at me with bloodshot eyes, his hair and clothes disheveled, reeking of cheap mead.

I ought to be cooking for him, apologizing, *something*. He'd gone through so much in so short a time. But there wasn't a kitchen here.

He jabbed my shoulder with a finger. I stumbled back a half-step, more startled than anything.

"You're a monster," he snarled.

"Sorrel..."

He pushed me with one hand. "Don't try to defend yourself."

"I'm not—"

He shoved me hard—both hands. I stumbled on the rug, barely keeping my feet. I'd seen him angry before, when he shouted about the broken engagement, when he kicked me out of the kitchens after I professed my feelings. But something grimmer, colder, had taken hold of his expression.

"I never wanted to hurt you," I whispered.

He swung his fist. Pain flared in my jaw and I sprawled to the floor, hip smacking onto hard wood.

"You *killed* her," he hissed over me.

I prodded my tender face. Sorrel had actually hit me. "I didn't mean for... for that..."

His foot cracked into my ribs. I shrieked and rolled, then pulled myself to my feet. But the guards didn't come. Weren't they supposed to protect me? Or had they been told not to intervene?

"Didn't mean!" Sorrel screamed. "She's dead!"

The words cut through me like freshly flintknapped spears. "Why did you come here, if you hate me?"

"You're going to die soon, too. And I wanted you to know that I'll be cheering when your neck snaps in the noose. Murderer. Liar."

"I didn't lie." Not about Violet.

He stepped forward to strike me, but I dodged. He tried again, but I ducked. Intoxication dulled his aim.

"I hope you wander the world as a Hungry Ghost for a thousand years. I hope you smell as rotten as your soul is, so everyone knows what you are."

He strung some choice obscenities after that. When all his punches failed, he threw a chair at me. I tried to dodge, but it hit my leg and I fell. Pain shot through my thigh and on my elbow where I'd caught myself.

I made it halfway to my feet before Sorrel kicked me in the gut. My eyes blurred as I lay crumpled on the floor, trying to catch my breath. I didn't see the next kick—just felt it crash into my side.

Sorrel spat on my face. "Stay on the floor, traitor. Poisoner."

He stumbled out of the room, leaving me alone in silence, on the floor next to the maltreated chair.

I fingered my side where he'd kicked me. Nothing broken. But I'd be bruised. Probably on my face as well.

Sorrel still didn't know my name. How for a day, we'd been destined for each other. I'd already grieved losing him on his wedding night.

So why did this feel like a betrayal?

My mouth tasted of blood and acid. I couldn't stop thinking that he'd petitioned King Alder to see me, solely for the chance to beat me before I died.

I traced my cheek again, feeling the welling bruise. He acted out of rage for his deceased wife. Part of me understood that and pitied him.

But there are no words to take back a bruise. He couldn't take away the throb in my ribs by calling it a misunderstanding or by saying he didn't know who I was. Worse still, he was a chef, tasked with caring for the health of all around him.

Even if everything he said were true, he had no right to hit me.

I FLINCHED the next time the door opened. Then I saw who it was.

"Osem!"

She crossed the room and hugged me. "Dami, Dami. How do you get yourself in these messes?"

"It's a gift."

She stepped back and peered at my cheek. "King Alder said the soldiers would leave you alone."

"Soldiers didn't do this."

Osem raised an eyebrow in question. I sighed. If a guard was eavesdropping, he'd already heard Sorrel's visit. I briefly explained.

"That's horrid!"

Her indignation was oddly comforting. "Thanks."

Osem sighed. "I wish I could take you with me when we leave. Did the King Former—"

I cut her off with a sharp gesture, then tugged my ear and gestured to the room instead.

Osem nodded, then gestured at the door and pantomimed holding a spear. One of the door guards was perceptive-of-ear, then. She already knew.

"The King Former?" I prompted, making a crown-like gesture around my head to establish a symbol for him. Finally, I had a chance to tell someone what I'd learned.

"Did he arrange for this room? It's lovely."

"Yes." I paused, thinking of the words I needed. "He is very kind."

On *is*, I made my hand into a fist.

"This is much better than our small room," Osem prattled. She didn't sound much like herself, making small talk for the benefit of the guard.

I made the crown gesture, clenched my fist, then pantomimed a huge belly and plugged my nose.

Osem frowned. "I bet you're never hungry in here?"

On *hungry* she made the huge-belly gesture. I nodded, confirming: *Fulsaan is the Hungry Ghost.*

Her eyes widened. Coming here hadn't been a selfish waste— Osem knew. Relief ran through me, undoing all my tensed muscles. I felt weary enough for a ten-year nap.

True, I couldn't pantomime the whole story about Red Lord Ospren's unjust exile, and I had no idea how to relate Lieutenant-General Behon's suspicious messenger birds, but Osem could relay this one important fact to Lady Sulat. Once Lady Sulat recovered, she'd make good use of the information.

"How is..." I trailed off. If I said Lady Sulat, the King would know where Osem's loyalties lay. But he probably already knew.

"Bane?" Osem grinned mischievously. "He applied to see you, too, but was rejected. I doubt the Palace Guard would let a military man through, anyway."

While she spoke, she pantomimed sipping soup and sleeping, then smiled. Lady Sulat was recovering, then. Good.

I hugged Osem again. "Thank you for coming. You should probably go, though."

Before I messed up and said something that got Osem in trouble with the guards.

"I know." She frowned, sad, solemn. "Dami, if I had a way to help you…"

"You'd do it."

She didn't nag me about how she'd been right or bemoan that I hadn't married Bane when I had the chance. Osem squeezed my shoulder. "I keep losing people in this war. I hope you make it somehow, Dami, but if you don't… will you send my love to my family? My husband's name is Cress of Fawn Hill. He can point you to my parents."

"Of course."

THAT EVENING, I laid in bed, staring at the ceiling.

Didn't I have much to be grateful for? I'd sent a message with Osem—a true friend. If I hanged tomorrow, I'd die knowing that I could do Osem one last favor in bringing a message to her family. In the short time I'd served in the Redwood Palace, I'd saved Lady Sulat and protected Dami. My parents would still owe horrible back-taxes, but perhaps Lady Sulat would help them with those—it seemed like the kind of thing she'd do.

I should have felt bitter or scared, but calmness filled me, vast and still as a mountain lake before dawn. Soon, I'd be living with Nana again. I'd had seventeen years filled with plum blossoms and simmering crocks and Nana's honey-scented hugs. Seventeen good years. Plenty of young soldiers suffering gruesome deaths left this world with less.

In the morning, guards escorted me out of the Royal Bear House and toward my trial. The sky shone that clear spring blue. Soon, soon, I wouldn't live in this world. I'd done all I could. I felt detached, apart.

What else could this world do to hurt me, after all?

CHAPTER
THIRTY-FIVE

I f my chamber was intended to unnerve me, the Hall of Moral Law was designed to paralyzed me. Wolves—a symbol of justice —decorated the high lattice windows. The whole-log pillars of the circular room shone white, but the floor glinted blood-red, as if stained with thousands of innocent lives. Whorls of red crawled up the white pillars, like the voices of victims crying for vengeance.

Between each of the ten pillars sat the members of the Purple-Blue Council. Palace guards flanked nine of these seats for security, but a pair of soldiers in black watched over the seat for the Minister of Military Affairs. Lieutenant-General Behon sat there.

So Lady Sulat still slept. Lieutenant-General Behon stared openly at me, one corner of his mouth curled in disgust, his eyes narrow. How could he look at me like that, when he was responsible for Violet's death? She should have had a trial, too.

King Alder sat in the middle of the pillars on a throne carved with amber-eyed bears; advisors and officials stood outside the pillars, behind the Purple-Blue Council. Lady Egal was among them, sneering elegantly, ready to make good on her promise to testify against me. No Fir, though. I recognized a few of Lady Egal's friends from Sorrel's wedding, with likewise unkind expressions.

I was escorted into the empty space before the king. A court official followed, standing several paces away from me. "Yellow-ranked Dami of Clamsriver, servant of the Royal House," he said. "You have been brought to trial this day on charges of lying to the sovereign of Rowak, Purple King Alder. You are accused of hiding your double-gifted state, being both strong-of-arm and perceptive-of-taste-and-smell. Do you confess to these charges?"

"I do not." I held myself tall and straight as a redwood. "I am not double-gifted."

The King's finger twitched with annoyance. "I don't have time for a dawdling trial."

Oddly, he wore traveling boots, not the soft, embroidered slippers he'd worn in Fulsaan's quarters.

The official bowed. "All pardons to your grandmother's health, King Alder, but we must listen to Dami's witnesses."

Had the king's grandmother died, or was Alder rushing to see her before she passed? In any case, I'd never intended to draw out the trial. "I didn't bring any witnesses."

The official blinked, startled. "You had sufficient time. Were they delayed?"

"My parents do important work in Clamsriver. I saw no reason to inconvenience them or the good people of that town for my own behalf."

The king glared. "A yellow-ranked girl seeks to exonerate herself based solely on her own word? You're guilty, and you're wasting precious time."

"I didn't claim innocence."

All heads snapped toward me. I let the silence hang for a moment and stared at the king. He glared, ready to combat anything I might say about his father. *I am harmless*, I tried to say in that look. *Let me live.*

"It is true that I am perceptive-of-taste-and-smell. I used this ability to save the king's sister twice. The second time allowed me to identify the poisoner, Green-ranked Violet of Napil. But I am not double-gifted. I am not strong-of-arm."

Murmurs rippled through the hall. Lieutenant-General Behon's agile face became carefully neutral. Confusion sprawled over the king's features—and everyone else's.

I knelt, then bowed myself flat before the king. "I admit my guilt in lying. I plead for mercy."

I sat up, waiting on my knees for an answer. But I only needed one glance at King Alder to know that my hopes were as feeble as I'd feared. He would not so much as ask *why* I lied. He simply wanted me dead.

The official asked for all the advisors to witness they'd heard my confession. Each chimed, one after another, like a flute pinging a vast range of notes. None made any protests or comments on my behalf.

"As she has admitted guilt, there is no need to lengthen this trial with witnesses. The Purple-Blue Council will now vote."

The official brought a tray around, onto which each councilor laid a red or white stick. Justice or mercy. Death and life. When the last piece of wood clinked to the tray, I dared to look.

Red. All red. Even Lieutenant-General Behon voted against me.

"It seems that Council is unanimous." King Alder allowed himself a dry smile. "Death by hanging. At sunrise tomorrow. As custom dictates, the Master Chef will deliver her last meal tonight."

Before I could rise, he swept past me, intent on his journey.

THE GUARDS RETURNED me to that beautiful room. Mid-morning sun shone through the lattice of hawks and salmon. Three-quarters of a day left.

I decided to spend it gazing out the window at the king's private pond and the bleeding hearts and foxgloves encircling it. Lovely.

But I didn't have long to admire the floral-scented wind or the rippling water. Three Palace Guards pulled an elegant passenger cart through the gate to the front of the Royal Bear House. Its purple window drapes brought out the deep scarlet of the varnish. Neatly-packed traveling supplies filled the chest-like endboard.

Another pair of Palace Guards held open the cart door. King Alder strode inside and seated himself on the cushioned bench, followed by Purple Lord Valerian.

A pair of guards dragged Fulsaan after. The old man struggled half-heartedly as the guards tossed him inside. I clenched my hands against the window sill. Something was wrong.

King Alder jumped out the other side of the cart, scowling and shouting. He slapped a guard across the face. Of course he didn't want Fulsaan to come along; at sunset, Fulsaan would turn into a ghost and be ripped back to the room where he died.

The slapped guard jammed his spear butt into King Alder's gut.

I gasped. I had no love for that man, but one doesn't strike the King.

Guards gagged King Alder and shoved him unceremoniously into the cart with Fulsaan. The doors shut. Guards pulled the cart forward.

This couldn't be good for Rowak—not in the middle of a war.

"Stop! Help! They're kidnapping the k—"

A rough hand clamped around my throat. A guard from outside. "Calm down."

My blood turned to ice. These guards were in on the plot. I should have stayed silent. I should have *thought* before I shouted.

"They're going to visit the king's grandmother." He spoke to me as one would a frightened animal. "His Majesty got word this morning from Hawak that she won't recover, so they must go now if they want to see her."

Had Hawak sent it, or had... this plot... arranged for it?

"The King's not here to complain if we slit her throat," the second guard muttered.

"I'm not killing anyone without Captain Gano's permission. And someone's coming."

The guards swiftly resumed their posts, locking the door behind them and leaving me with my breathe lodged in my throat.

Captain Gano had removed everyone of purple rank. But I doubted he knew about the Hungry Ghost. Otherwise, why wouldn't he keep Old King Fulsaan here, in the open, to display at dusk?

But the Purple-Blue Council might appoint him as a regent if Lady Sulat had died and the three royals disappeared. From regent, he could angle for king. But Lady Sulat wasn't dead. She'd be awake in a few days.

My swallowed. I couldn't reason out Captain Gano's plans, but kidnapping a king meant one thing. A coup. A coup in the middle of a war—did Gano not care about his country? His people? This could give the Shoreed an opening to destroy us.

Sorrel strode into the room, his face hollow, but sober. "I'm here for your request for your last meal, murderer."

"Sorrel, listen," I began, then paused. If I told Sorrel, the guards would lock him up. How to sneak a message out? "Umm. Can you bring it right away? I'm hungry."

"You'll eat your last meal at nightfall and not a moment sooner."

Better to send a delayed message than none at all. "Noodles. Lots of noodles, please."

I could arrange those into characters to tell him what I'd learned. No one would suspect anything for days otherwise. I hoped my plan proved as clever as whatever Lady Sulat would do in my place.

"I'll make them on the sweet side, with some beet stems. Maybe a bit of endurance-of-neck will let you suffer in the noose."

I gritted my teeth. Our nation was in danger. He could mock me when I was dead. "Just bring the noodles."

"Noodles. You deserve poison."

"That was Violet's specialty, not mine!"

He punched me across the jaw. Completely sober. The inside of my cheek slashed open against my teeth. I coughed, dribbling viscous blood and saliva down my chin. I raised a hand to my mouth and gaped at him.

Why was I shocked? Sober or drunk, it didn't matter—he'd

sought solace by beating his pain into another's flesh. How had I thought I could love him? Whatever his cooking tasted like, Sorrel was a poor excuse for a chef.

"You have no right to say her name," Sorrel spat. "Come tomorrow, you won't be able to."

VIOLET DIDN'T DESERVE to die in that prison. She should have stood trial. And I should have realized that turning her in would, eventually, lead to her end. Every time pity or guilt rose in me, I remembered Lady Sulat's tiny, mewling baby. Of the child she tried to murder, of the child who might still die young from complications of his early birth. No, turning her into the military... I'd acted correctly. What they did afterwards made me sick. But I wasn't responsible for that, was I?

I exhaled. I didn't want to hang tomorrow with regrets.

I'd rather not hang at all.

All the calm I'd pooled inside ran out, like water in a cracked crock. My knees turned into wobbly custard. Tomorrow.

I knelt on my bed in the alcove and pulled the curtain tight.

Ancestors, I thought I was ready for this, but I'm not. I want to live. And I need to tell someone about the king.

More than anything, I wanted to tell Lady Sulat. She'd know what to do.

Maybe I should pray to the monarchs who rested in the Royal Shrine. Ancestors watched their descendants, but Kings and Queens, the Fathers and Mothers of our nation, watched over all Rowak.

Kings and Queens, please take care of us, I pleaded. But they felt so distant. I was just a yellow-ranked girl they'd never met.

I again directed my prayers at Nana. She'd hear me, no matter how many walls stood between us. *If you could send Osem back, I could tell her. Somehow. Once that's done, I think... I think I can go quietly tomorrow. But I can't leave with something undone here.*

Softer than falling plum blossoms, I felt a voice in my marrow: *Isn't something always undone on Earth?*

I bit my lip, the reservoir of emotion piling up. If I had more time, I'd want to check on Dami. My parents. Skip rocks with Bane again—Bane who had kind eyes, even if he didn't have a library or a greenhouse. I wanted to serve as a chef for Lady Sulat and learn how to exorcise a ghost. I wanted to *do* a hundred things. I wanted to make a thousand hotpots and knead ten thousand noodles. *I can't think about that.* I prayed. *It hurts too much.*

Thinking about it ending *hurts. Your hopes for the future—those are bright and lovely, little blossom.*

I closed my eyes and imagined petals on the wind like Nana and I used to chase. One day, I wanted to be that old woman, with a grandchild at my side. I wanted to hold a small, warm hand in my wrinkled one.

I curled my legs to my chest and pressed my forehead into my knees. I shouldn't have prayed. I'd been so calm. So peaceful. I didn't know how to get that back.

Wanting to live wouldn't change tomorrow. I'd only succeeded in making my last day miserable.

CHAPTER
THIRTY-SIX

I hoped against reason that someone would come. That Osem would want a final good-bye.

No one came.

No one except Sorrel. I heard him long before he entered, chatting softly with the guards. Laughing a bit. Letting my last meal get cold. Did he have to go to such lengths to spite me? I stood behind a chair, giving myself some scant defense. Somehow, I had to make him listen.

He slid the door shut behind himself and gently set my bowl on the table. I'd expected him to slam it down or throw it at me. Sprigs of spicy cress topped a pile of buckwheat noodles. He'd brought a vinegar dipping sauce, too. Odd—why not the sweet beet stems he'd promised?

He stepped close to me and whispered, "Dami —"

"Thank you for the noodles," I interrupted loudly. "They look delicious."

I pantomimed a spear, then gestured out from my ear. Every

muscle in my body felt taunt and my stomach churned. Sorrel wasn't the ally I needed.

Oddly, he didn't snap at me. He nodded patiently, understanding, as if he hadn't made me bleed just hours earlier. His eyes looked puffy —but not with liquor. Had he been crying?

"I'll wait until you're done to take back the dishes," Sorrel said.

He sat, shifting his weight impatiently in the chair. Why wasn't he gloating about my death? I pulled a long noodle from the bowl and tediously shaped it into the character for *king*.

Sorrel held up a hand and shook his head. He arranged the noodle into *wait*. "You should eat. It will grow cold if you savor it."

Why wait? I supposed I didn't need the whole meal to spell messages. I ate. The noodles had a lovely, toasted flavor, perfectly contrasted by the bright, acidic sauce. I hadn't expected the small kindness of well-cooked food from him.

I'd eaten half—all I planned on eating—when Sorrel stood and pressed his ear to the door. He cracked it, then closed it.

"It's safe to whisper," he said at my side.

"He's perceptive of ear. Didn't I make that clear?"

"He's gone. Dami... I thought you wanted to destroy my country, that you'd destroyed my wife, that..." He dropped his hands to his side, defeated. "I hated you more than I knew I *could* hate anyone. It didn't help that you're Plum's sister. But... but I misdirected all my loathing."

I blinked. That was the last thing I'd expected him to say.

"I have Violet's things now." His voice cracked on her name. "The investigators returned them after the military left."

My heart slowed and my skin frosted. "Excuse me? The military *left*?"

"Oh. I suppose you haven't heard." Sorrel sat in the chair closest to mine. "Shoreed's besieging Napil. Lieutenant-General Behon sent most of Askan-Wod's soldiers as reinforcements."

With Lady Sulat incapacitated, Lieutenant-General Behon commanded the local army. Fulsaan mentioned him sending suspicious messenger birds. And he'd been interrogating Violet when she died, taking the secret of who she served with her.

Sending reinforcements to the obsidian mines sounded reasonable, but I felt nauseous.

"I've been reading through Violet's things." Guilt laced Sorrel's words and crumpled his posture. "She'd started a letter asking about a recipe, but it was odd. Wrong. Her poison box had a sheet of paper with a list of culinary substitutions that made no sense, either. I used the substitution list like a cipher. I guess the military didn't know enough about cooking to put it together. I think she worked for Shoreed."

His voice wavered with shame. "I'm sorry I doubted you."

Those brilliant hematite eyes filled with admiration and apology. How long had I waited for him to look at me like that? How many times had I imagined my marrow melting at the welcomed sight?

Oddly, I felt nothing. No, not nothing—a blankness, a sour hollowness. My gaze drifted to his anxiously clasped hands. It didn't matter how he looked at me, because I'd never be able to forget what he'd done—first with liquor to aid him, then out of simple hate.

If we'd met like we were supposed to, as chefs, would we have been happy? I wasn't sure anymore. Bane was right—I wasn't just my birthgift. I was a person. A library of recipes and a greenhouse garden alone wouldn't make me happy. Once, I'd found happiness in chatting with Nana every morning while I prepared a simple breakfast. Or in working alongside my father to make healing food from humble ingredients for the people of Clamsriver. Here, at the palace, I'd found it in scrubbing crocks with a friend. In saving a defenseless infant. And in a lazy afternoon of skipping rocks and listening to the stories of a remarkable young veteran.

I didn't acknowledge Sorrel's apology, because I found I didn't need or want it. "What did the letter say?"

"Here."

The paper he handed me had all the ingredients crossed-out and replaced with new words. "These edits, those are what the substitution list called for?"

"Yes."

I read it, then read it again.

FATHER, I've removed the spiced blueberry from the stock. The obsidian knife is waiting for the pickled parsnips, and we've nearly removed the purple nasturtiums from the stock. I know you can return the birdie to the stock with the oysters, but I worry over the technique. You are a better chef than me—the very blood and marrow of knowledge. Love, Violet.

"SHE DIDN'T HAVE a chance to send it before the soldiers took her," Sorrel said, voice soft.

I nodded. "Spiced blueberry—perceptive-of-eye. That's Lady Sulat."

"And pickled parsnips are strong-of-arm... but I'm not sure who that matches," Sorrel said.

My stomach sank. It was all too clear. "Parsnips. Plural. It means soldiers. They've all gone to Napil—the place of obsidian. Just as Lieutenant-General Behon directed. The purple nasturtiums are easy, too. Those of purple rank. Captain Gano arranged their kidnapping. I guess that makes the stock Askan-Wod or the palace."

Sorrel's eyes widened.

"That's what I wanted to tell you with the noodles. Most of the remaining Palace Guards appear loyal to Captain Gano."

"Oh."

I tapped the paper. "Blood and marrow of knowledge. Do you think that's important?"

"Bloodmarrows?" Sorrel suggested.

I frowned. Bloodmarrows were supposed to be Vengeful Ghosts who worked for Shoreed—Osem had dismissed them as nothing but superstition. I'd seen Violet during the day and the night. She was no ghost. But she was dangerous, secretive, and working in league with Shoreed. The name fit her well.

Had she and her father taken the name from the stories, or were they responsible for the stories? Violet connected *bloodmarrow* to *chef*. The thought of a group of chefs using their skills to hurt others turned my stomach. "Maybe she's just making a play on words. Making fun of the whole idea of Bloodmarrows."

"It doesn't sound like that at all."

I hated that he was right. I hated this war. I hated that people could take food that looked nourishing and comforting and turn it into a weapon. "Do you have any ideas about this last part? Birds and oysters? It doesn't make sense."

"Oysters are the national dish of Shoreed. That one, I understood."

I blinked at him, surprised. "How do you know that?"

"Violet's father traveled after he retired—he brought my father several manuscript boxes from Shoreed before the war broke out. I always hated *substituting* clams." He said *substituting* like a bad word. Sorrel sighed. "You seemed to know what was happening earlier. I hoped with this, you could tell me what to do. I don't want my nation to fall to Shoreed."

"I don't either," I murmured. "But I don't know what to make of the bird."

"It's so generic. Why not a duck or grouse or goose? And why such a childish spelling?"

Birdie. I gasped. "It's Red Lord Ospren."

"What?"

"He's the Birdie."

Sorrel chewed his lip. "That... makes sense."

"No, it doesn't!" I said, forgetting to keep my voice low. "He's in exile on the southern border!"

"Dami, if the Palace Guards are loyal to Captain Gano, why should we expect the guards around Ospren's cabin to be different? Violet's father was close to Lord Ospren... what if seeing him settled in exile really meant helping him sneak into Shoreed's capital?"

After my time in the palace, it sounded all-too-plausible.

Sorrel nodded. "Shoreed has military strength. Red Lord Ospren still has a few allies in the palace. Why wouldn't Shoreed form an alliance with Red Lord Ospren to conquer Rowak together?"

"If Shoreed puts Ospren on the throne, it'll be a vassal throne." We'd lose our independence as surely as if we'd surrendered. My pulse pounded. These weren't the answers I wanted. "Why wouldn't Lord Ospren announce it? Tell everyone? Wouldn't that have caused confusion, made this war a lot shorter?"

"Lord Ospren wasn't exactly popular as the Purple Heir. Keeping himself hidden allows his supporters to move without suspicion."

Supporters like Captain Gano and his Palace Guards. Fir. Violet and her father. And almost certainly that agile-of-face Lieutenant-General Behon. I swallowed the sticky lump in my throat. "I need you to bring Osem here. I have to talk with her."

She could bring all this information to the safehouse. If Lady Sulat still slept, at least Osem could tell Moss. Alder might be a horrible king, but I didn't want to see Rowak lose its sovereignty.

Sorrel flicked his eyes downward. "Osem's missing."

"Missing? I saw her yesterday!"

"She never came back from her audience with you."

I swore under my breath. I'd been so careful not to say anything incriminating! The guards must have noticed our halted speech. And now she was, what? Hidden away in some cell? Already dead? There suddenly wasn't enough air in the room. My lungs burned.

"Do you know where Moss is?"

"Who?"

I ground my teeth. "Bane, then."

"Bane...?"

"He's the military messenger with one arm."

Sorrel's eyes lit with recognition. "I passed him on the way here. He's playing springball with Nisaat."

"I need you tell him what we've figured out about this coup." I prayed Bane knew where the safehouse was. Or Moss. They could form a plan together.

"I intended on taking you with me."

"My guards, remember?" I paused, dread creeping up my breastbone. Even if the perceptive-of-ear guard had left, shouldn't the remaining guard wonder what was taking so long? He'd probably have ropes and gags waiting for Sorrel as soon as he stepped outside.

But Sorrel smiled. He opened the door. Both my guards lay slumped on the floor, a jug toppled on its side between them. Sweet plum wine dribbled from its lip, staining the carpet red.

"W-what did you do to them?"

"I did have Violet's poisons. I lightly dosed that with bittersleep. It slowed their muscles until they dozed off. They'll wake up stiff tomorrow, nothing more. I offered it as a friendly drink." He yawned. "Unfortunately, they made me share a few sips, too."

I stared at him. "How could you taint a drink like that? If any other guards had walked by—"

"There aren't many guards inside the King's Quarters, not without a king to protect. All the guards are on the lower floor, watching the entrances."

"How am I supposed to leave, then?"

"Do they know your face?" Sorrel asked. "I'll pretend you're from the kitchens. It was true, once."

I bit my lip. "Leave me here; I have a better plan. And tell Bane I'll know where King Alder is by nightfall. Have him meet me outside the kitchens with Moss and any soldiers they trust. Make sure they don't let Captain Gano or Lieutenant-General Behon know."

"But how will you escape? You know where King Alder is?"

I glanced at the window. Daylight was fading fast. "Too long to explain. Just get Bane!"

CHAPTER
THIRTY-SEVEN

Nana was right. I'd told someone what I knew, but my anxiety hadn't departed. There was too much left undone. There would always be something left undone.

Sorrel disappeared down the hallway, heading out to find Bane. I pulled my unconscious guards inside my room, then peered out the window. Color seeped from the sky. If Sorrel was right about the guards at ground level, I'd be safer making my way to Fulsaan's room than waiting here and hoping no one noticed the absence of guards or the wine stain.

With no torchlight and sporadic windows, the hallways all looked different. I scrambled up a flight of steps. Had it been this first hall? No. I paused at the next. It looked familiar, though I couldn't see very far down it.

I'd taken a handful steps down it when a man spoke, somewhere nearby. "I told you no one's on this side of the building."

"I heard footsteps. I know I did."

Warm torchlight rounded the corner and with it, five Palace Guards.

"Who are you?" the first demanded, spear lowered.

I ran. Down the pitch-black corridor, one hand on the wall. Maybe I could bar myself inside Fulsaan's room. Or hide on the roof. Once he came, I'd be safe.

Orange light licked around me. The torch—and guards—were closing. There it was. Fulsaan's door. Carved, heavy redwood.

A hand clapped down on my shoulder, yanking me to a halt. I twisted, but the guard expertly whipped both hands behind my back.

"You're under arrest for trespassing."

Something groaned behind the door and I smelled rot. Night had fallen—Old King Fulsaan had been ripped from wherever the kidnappers took him, back to the place he died.

But he couldn't open that door. I swallowed hard. "I'm not trespassing. I'm investigating King Former Fulsaan's room."

"Spying," one of them muttered.

"Don't you hear it?" I asked.

The guards paused. The whimpering unmistakably came from behind Fulsaan's door.

"Open it," my guard ordered. "No one should be up here."

The other guards obeyed. Darkness swallowed the room, except where moonlight gleamed in arcs off rolls of fat.

The guard's fingernails dug into my shoulder, as if that could ground him to reality and make the ghost disappear. "Retreat! We'll come back with more men and better lights!"

He pulled me with them. I dropped my weight, stumbling to stay, but the man had to be strong-of-arm. He didn't let go or slow down.

"Help!" I shouted.

Fulsaan whined, a high note that reverberated through the wood. He squeezed through the open door and reached for me with a spindly hand.

The guard holding me shoved me toward the ghost. I hit my shoulder against the wall but kept my feet. My lungs filled with the smell of over-boiled cabbage and sickly-sweet decay.

Down the hall, boots retreated.

I yanked my neckline over my mouth. "They'll be back. We need to go, now."

Ghost-Fulsaan laid on the floor and whined. Pinprick wounds riddled his layers of fat—like he said would happen if he wasn't here at sunrise or sunset. They oozed clotted slime.

"You know where the cart is, don't you? With your son and grandson?"

He flopped his head in a weak imitation of a nod.

"There are people who want to help us. They'll meet us outside the kitchens."

He closed his eyes.

"The lives of your descendants and the sovereignty of your nation is at stake!"

He groaned and rolled over. This was like trying to wake up Dami in the morning, except more than Mother's back would suffer if I failed.

I dropped my tone, soft. Maybe I could goad him into helping. "You don't belong in the Ancestor's realm."

Ghost-Fulsaan stared at me with hurt welling in its beady eyes.

"Ancestors watch over their descendants. They weave souls for new babies. You're still here—you have a great chance to help your descendants—and you'd rather roll in your own filth."

Ghost-Fulsaan whimpered.

"I know it's hard. But right now, that doesn't matter. Your descendants and your nation need their father."

His tiny mouth quivered, as if wishing to offer a counter argument.

I was wasting time. This lump wouldn't help. "Fine. Did the kidknappers take them east?"

Shake of the head.

"West?"

Nod.

"On the road to Napil?"

He shook his head again.

"On the Old North Path?"

He nodded.

Hardly anyone used that winding track through the woods, not with a straight road to Napil. Abandoned and surrounded by forest, they ran little chance of being spotted.

"Perhaps you should spend all night praying for my return so I can keep my promise and exorcise you."

Fulsaan whined as I swung my feet over the window ledge, but I didn't look back. I splayed myself over the shingles. The low moon did little to show me the steeply sloped roof and nothing to illuminate the dark haze of the ground gaping below. I dragged myself sideways, scraping my forearms as I went. A cool, spring breeze prickled my skin. At this rate, I'd make it to the kitchens by tomorrow afternoon.

Ghost-Fulsaan crept out the window and perched near the sill. He whimpered, asking me to come back inside.

"No." I kept moving, trying not to look at him.

He shuffled over the shingles until he stood below me. Shame quivered in his fat. He lowered himself, offering me a chance to mount again.

The reek nearly sent me tumbling off the roof. "Only if you're taking me where I need to go."

He dipped his head once.

I pulled my neckline over my face, masking the scent slightly. I stepped toward him and tripped. The fabric jerked off my face as I fell.

Ghost-Fulsaan shifted his weight, uncannily graceful, and caught me against his side. Drops of his ooze splattered into my mouth.

I threw up. All those lovely noodles, all over the roof.

Breathing shallowly, I situated myself on his back and replaced my neckline over my mouth and nose.

Light as a spider, Ghost-Fulsaan slunk over the rooftops, down to the garden, and toward the kitchens.

ONLY BANE and Sorrel waited for me. I slipped off Fulsaan but opening my mouth to ask questions sent me gagging. All dry heaves; my stomach was long-emptied. Fulsaan huddled against the wall and waited.

Bane brought me some water, those brown eyes still kind under his dark, low-sweeping hair. Ancestors, I didn't deserve any kindness from him. I wanted to thank him for showing me kindness anyway; I wanted to reconcile, but we didn't have time right now to talk about any of that.

"Why..." My throat burned, raw. "Why isn't Moss here? More military?"

Sorrel blinked slowly, his drugged eyes showing no comprehension.

Bane's broad shoulders tightened. "There's practically no military in the palace. Moss isn't here—I'm guessing he's at the safehouse. I could talk to people at the walls, but Lieutenant-General Behon's in charge there. You said not to trust him or the Palace Guards."

"Then let's go to the safehouse." I rubbed the side of my skull, trying not to think about how much I craved a hot bath.

"I, um, don't know where it is."

The pit of my stomach sank. "What?"

"It's not much of a *safehouse* if everyone knows about it."

I swigged more water, but it didn't do anything to press back the panic rising in my gut. Sorrel slumped against the floor, right in the doorway.

"Sorrel?"

Bane cleared his throat. "He's not going to be any help."

"Didn't he cook something to help himself recover?" I asked.

Bane itched his stump. "Well, he did start cooking. I'm no chef, but I'm fairly sure drinking honey mixed with maple syrup wouldn't help. I took it away from him."

Straight sweetness like that, unbalanced and misused, would exhaust him instead of increase his endurance. "I don't know if we have time for me to cook him something proper and wait for him to wake up."

Fulsaan quivered like an undercooked custard in his spot against the wall.

"We don't." Bane's mouth formed a grim line.

"Did something new happen while I was coming?"

"No, but the message Sorrel told me about—they're returning Red Lord Ospren to Askan-Wod. Napil's besieged, but the Shoreed aren't actually attacking yet. Don't you see?"

I was no soldier. I blinked at him.

Bane sighed. "The siege is a lie. The Shoreed can leave a few men to maintain the appearance of a camping army, then circle up to Askan-Wod. With most of our men in Napil, it's an easy target. Lieutenant-General Behon will probably open the city gates to welcome him. Under normal circumstances, it would still be crazy to take Askan-Wod—they'll be pinched between Napil and the east half of Rowak with no supply lines. But many won't want to fight with a Rowak Lord on the throne, especially with King Alder gone. Our leadership will be in chaos. Shoreed will destroy us."

"If Shoreed gives Rowak to Lord Ospren, it'll be a vassal throne."

"I know."

I exhaled. Rowak couldn't afford to lose its monarch or its capital. I wiped my hands on a part of my skirt that wasn't covered in tarry ghost slime. "We have to alert the army to Shoreed's maneuvers, then rescue King Alder and Purple Lord Heir Valerian. Do you know where the army is? We'll need a squad of men to get King Alder away from the Palace Guards. He's somewhere on the Old North Path."

Ghost-Fulsaan cut in, whining.

"What's wrong with that plan?" I asked.

"Dami," Bane said, "if the cart is headed east across the Old North Path, that's probably the direction the Shoreed army is coming. It circles from Napil to Askan-Wod through terrain with plenty of cover."

Fulsaan bobbed his head.

Ancestors watch over us. "If they get King Alder to the Shoreed army..."

"If he's that well-guarded, we've lost him," Bane said. "The

Shoreed would slit his throat before they let us take him. Keeping Rowak kingless will go a long way to putting Ospren on the throne."

"So we have to be stealthy and fast."

Bane sketched a quick map in the dirt—two lines that bowed out from each other, nearly touching at the ends. "Askan-Wod," Bane said, pointing to one dot. "And Napil in the west. Rowak's army camps here, on the main road, outside of Deben." He marked the spot with an *X*. "Ghost, can you tell me where you think the passenger cart is on the Old North Path?"

Fulsaan's arms couldn't manage to write on the map, so Bane slowly traced the road until the ghost squeaked, then marked another *X*. They were roughly the same distance west as the army—I supposed the cart had headed east toward Sandhead at first, to avoid suspicion.

"How far apart are the two roads?" I asked.

"Over two hours, at a decent pace."

Not particularly close, then. Fulsaan whined and shuffled toward the map.

"Do you know where the Shoreed army is, as well?" I asked, stepping back a few paces. Even so, my throat had that about-to-gag thickness from his stench. Bane looked queasy, too, but he did a good job of hiding it.

Fulsaan nodded and cupped his hand up near where his ear would have been. He'd overhead his captors? Or ghosts had exceptional hearing? I didn't know.

Bane moved the stick again until Ghost-Fulsaan whined for him to stop. "There's a spot about there where a river runs close to the path. Is this the Shoreed's camp, or a moving force?"

Fulsaan gurgled unhappily. The question was too long for his limited ability to communicate.

"Is it a camp?" I asked. Fulsaan nodded.

Bane frowned at the map. "We still can't make it."

"Our ghost friend is fast. Incredibly fast."

"It wouldn't matter even if we already stood in the Rowak camp with a squad of soldiers ready to run north through the woods. The cart would still reach the Shoreed before we got to them." He stared at his map for a moment more, then turned to Fulsaan. "Does that sound right to you?"

Fulsaan keened sadly.

What to do? Sorrel snored softly—part of me wished I could change places with him.

"Fulsaan, could you get us to the cart before it reaches the Shoreed?" I asked.

He nodded. Bane stared at me like I was mad. "The two of us can't take out the guards. Can your ghost fight?"

"He could probably hold one or two down, but other guards would run ahead and sound the alarm. Or kill King Alder. "That's not what I have in mind. We need to overwhelm them all at once, like you said."

"Three of us can't manage that," Bane said.

"I know."

I stepped over Sorrel and packed an empty buckwheat sack. Wood, tinder, a crock. Parsnips, carrots, a knife. Osem's clean, spare dress. It was the wrong rank for me, but I'd comitted worse crimes than dressing outside my rank.

"What are you doing?" Bane asked, following me into the kitchens.

"You're right. I'm not just a birthgift." I didn't have to marry a man who was perceptive-of-taste-and-smell. I cared about more than cooking—I cared about my nana, my family, my nation. I could barter with ghosts, track down poisoners, and escape from jails. "But I've spent years honing my skills, Bane. I'm a good chef. I'm going to cook."

CHAPTER
THIRTY-EIGHT

Alarm drums pounded from the direction of the Royal Bear House. I cursed and stuffed a jar of lamp oil and another fistful of herbs into my bag. "We have to go."

"Sorrel?" Bane asked.

I glanced at him. His head flopped back at an awkward angle and drool glistened on his chin. "He stays. If the guards find him, he can rightly claim he was poisoned, too. Let's put him in my old room."

They'd look for him in his quarters or the kitchen proper, after all. Bane shrugged and helped me drag him onto one of the musty mattresses.

I grabbed two rags and a few slices of hotradish.

"What are those for?" Bane asked.

I tied a rag around my face, then his. I handed him some hotradish. "Put this in your mouth. Chew as needed. It'll dull all your senses a little—straight hotradish is definitely not a balanced dish. But that's something of a mercy right now. We're going to ride a Hungry Ghost."

Bane blinked at me but followed me back outside.

I bit down on the radish, burning my mouth and nasal passages. The reek reduced to an unpleasant undercurrent, masked by spiciness and muted by the effects of straight hotradish. The horizon blurred, everything sounded a touch muffled, and my fingers tingled like they'd fallen asleep. "Bane, I'll hold onto Fulsaan. You hold onto me. Here. I'll tie my pack around your back."

"Fulsaan's here?"

I gestured at the black blob of ghost whining on the grass, then secured the pack.

Bane stared, but he didn't comment. I climbed on first, wedging myself between two oozing rolls of fat that nearly engulfed my legs. Bane followed. His good arm slid around my waist; his stump rested against my side. In other circumstances, I might have been embarrassed at his closeness, but simple gratitude flooded me. I needed Bane—real, warm, and solid against this strange and cold night.

Without hesitation, he'd climbed up on a ghost with me. I wanted to say something, but I didn't have time to find the right words for Bane. I swallowed the burning hotradish juices streaming down my throat. "Fulsaan, take us to the cart. You'll have to move fast."

Fulsaan groaned and rose up on his tiny limbs.

"Run, Fulsaan. Run like all the food in the world is waiting ahead of you, one step out of reach."

Ghost-Fulsaan ran. I clenched my arms around him, gut soaring into my throat as he leapt across rooftops. I glimpsed bits of shingles, streets, a barking dog. Wind whipped my hair back—I murmured a silent apology to Bane for that.

My legs ached. My arms ached. Buildings gave way to knobcones, firs, and then redwoods. A hint of their cool, evergreen scent made it through the spiciness and stink. We skimmed the forest like an angry black cloud. The moon shone brightly overhead, a queen among a sea of stars. Everything below blurred—either Fulsaan had sped up, or the hotradish was taking its toll.

Bane's grip tightened on me.

I tucked the chunk of hotradish to one side of my mouth and

spoke, knowing that the wind would whip my words away. Perhaps I could say it because I knew he couldn't hear. "I'm sorry I hurt you. And I'm so grateful for all your help. I wish we'd met as Plum and Bane. Maybe then I wouldn't have told myself that I only enjoyed your company because Dami would have. That you only cared for me because I was a pale imitation of her. If we survive this, I want to start over. With no more lies. Though somehow, I think I lied to myself better than I ever lied to you."

It felt right to say, even if I had to chew down on the hotradish after opening my mouth.

A moment later, Ghost-Fulsaan jerked to a stop. The treetops swayed, creaking ominously. He gestured downward with his puny arm.

The passenger cart. The encroaching ferns brushed its wheels, but the guards still traveled at a good pace down the Old North Path.

To the south on the main road, smoke curled up into the sky, maybe two hours' walk away. That would be Rowak's army, camping for the night on their way to reinforce Napil against the decoy siege. I swayed, dizzy, but Bane held me fast.

"Fulsaan, how far is the Shoreed camp? Can you tap the hours with your hand?"

Once, twice he hit the branch under us. Bane was right—even if we could alert the Rowak army this instant, they wouldn't arrive in time to snatch the king and his heir before they rejoined the Shoreed army—but that's why I'd come prepared.

"Fulsaan," I whispered. "Take us another hour down the road. You're going to leave me there and take Bane to the Rowak army camp on the main road. I'll stall the kidnappers until Bane returns with a troop of soldiers. If the cart reaches the Shoreed army, we've lost them. Bane, you've got to tell the army what the Shoreed are planning, too. Otherwise we'll get King Alder back to Askan-Wod just to watch it fall."

Bane shook his head. "Dami, you can't—"

But I never heard the end of the sentence. Ghost-Fulsaan

sprinted, nearly jerking me from his back. We soared, faster than a hawk, trees blurring beneath us.

Fulsaan slowed, then spiraled down a redwood tree with thick, burled roots. "My bag?" I asked.

Bane fumbled with it. "I'll stay with you. Fulsaan can fetch the army."

I smiled sadly at him. "He can't talk. They're as likely to attack him as to try and listen to him." I straightened the insignia around Bane's sleeve. "You're a military messenger. Go deliver the message."

Bane must have been a good soldier. Determination solidified his expression—he saw this was necessary. He bowed as if I were his officer. "I accept your command." Softer, he whispered, "Try to stay alive until we come for you."

He mounted Fulsaan, situated himself, then disappeared up the trees.

Woozy from the ride and the hotradish, I struggled to open my bag with half-numb fingers. I got it eventually, but I cursed that it had cost me precious extra seconds. I pulled out the wood—dry wood that wouldn't smoke and bring the Shoreed army—then dumped the lamp oil all over it and sparked a fire. *Watch over my efforts, please, Nana.*

While the fire burned, I ditched my ghost-soiled dress deep in the woods and pulled on Osem's fresh one. No one would want to eat with that stink around. I folded the dress sleeves on top of my shoulders, so the wrongness of the length wouldn't distract me. The cool night air prickled my arms and filled my nose with the rich smells of pine and loam—the ill-effects of the hotradish were wearing off.

I jogged back to my fire. If I made a perfect meal, a perfectly enticing aroma, the passenger cart would stop. They'd eat. And hopefully that delay would give Bane enough time to bring the Rowak soldiers.

I exhaled. Spicy, salty, sour, sweet. I'd saved a child's life before with a perfect dish. Now I needed to save a nation.

I started by making sure my crock was clean.

AFTER HIKING through the woods in the dark, the kidnappers would be exhausted. Endurance-of-limb and soul; that would entice them to stop, to eat. I diced my parsnips, carrots, and beets in equal amounts. That would target the arms, legs, and navel. I sweated them in the bottom of the crock with a little salt.

I rummaged through my bag for my waterskin of stock. More wood, herbs... there was the waterskin. I opened it, but something seemed off. I sniffed.

This was plain water, not stock.

My throat dried. I'd grabbed the wrong waterskin in the hurry to leave.

I exhaled. Panicking wouldn't help. I had half an hour until the cart appeared and a few moments until the carrots burned.

I shifted the crock a little further off the coals to give the vegetables more time to cook. Well-caramelized carrots, parsnips, and beets could still give me the depth of flavor I needed for this dish. I stirred carefully, waiting until they turned dark brown, then tossed in the water. It hissed and steamed, sending the rich flavors into the air.

I shoved white coals around the already-hot crock and seasoned the dish—a bit of grated hotradish; chopped parsley for its balancing, sour quality; and a touch of maple syrup, to play up the smoky-sweet vegetables. I made a slurry of white bean flour to thicken and unify the soup, which added additional, nutty layers of flavor.

Warm and bubbling, thick and aromatic. A touch on the sweet side, to grant endurance. I put the lid on. Now it just needed to simmer.

A cold obsidian knife pressed against my throat. "Stand up."

I did so slowly, trying not to swallow the lump in my throat shaking against the blade. I hadn't even heard him approach. The man turned me around.

He wore the uniform of a Palace Guard.

"I—"

"Not another word or I slit your throat."

He pressed the knife against my flesh, forcing me to stand on tip-toe.

Then we waited. He had the cold patience of a snake.

My ankles both ached and tingled by the time the cart and its dozen Palace Guards rattled up the road. Fir walked in front, all white teeth and dashing smile. He raised a fist and the cart stopped. "Hello, Dami."

"You know her?" asked the oldest guard—a tall man with dignified gray hair.

"She's the girl I tried to get rid of to bring Violet into the palace."

My ankles quivered from the strain.

"Is she a spy?" the old guard asked—I think his armband gave him the rank of commander. I wasn't sure if he'd interrogate me or kill me if Fir answered yes.

Fir pursed his lips, studying me. "She's not one of ours, if she is."

"Why are you out here?" the commander demanded of me.

Fir waved a hand and my guard stepped back. Finally I could let my heels drop. My calves burned. "I... I'm condemned."

"To death. At first light," Fir tossed in. "For lying to the Royal House."

Behind Fir and the commander, the guards' posture shifted as the aroma of my dish filled the narrow path. Their shoulders turned subtly; they glanced at my simmering crock. It did smell good—of warmth and rest and renewal, properly seasoned.

The commander took a step forward. "The king sentenced you to death?"

"Yes. For lying."

"It sounds like you need a new master." He flicked a meaningful look at Fir.

Fir raised an eyebrow, asking a silent question I couldn't discern. The commander shrugged, then nodded at me again. Fir studied me, as if seeing me for the first time.

My hands shook. I didn't try to hide it. Let them see me as weak. As anything but a threat. "I just want to live."

"You might live, depending on your answers." Fir stepped closer. "Why did you lie to the king about your gift?"

A thousand excuses ran through my head. I could pretend to be the street waif who stole Dami's identity. I could describe a simple misunderstanding. But I didn't know if I could lie well enough for that. So I said the words I'd wanted to scream since I first entered the Redwood Palace. "My name isn't Dami."

The commander's eyes narrowed. Fir stared at me; the guards stared at my cooking.

"My sister is Dami. Strong-of-arm. She ran away from home because she didn't want to work in the Redwood Palace." Even though I doubted these traitors could do anything to hurt Dami, I glossed over where she'd gone. Let them think she'd run off to extended family, or a beau, or simply vanished in the woods. "My family couldn't afford the back-taxes if we forfeited her post at the palace. So I pretended to be her. My real name is Plum."

Fir sucked a sharp breath between his teeth. "You. Pining after Sorrel. That makes *sense* now."

The commander didn't say anything.

"You've always been a traitor to King Alder," Fir said. "And now you're a fugitive. Let's see if our army has any use for you."

The commander was oddly deferential, watching as Fir pulled a spoon from the supplies on the endboard of the cart, took the lid off my crock, and eyed it eagerly. But he brought the spoonful to me. "You first."

I ate it.

"Not poisoned. Good." He smiled, then got himself a bite. His shoulders softened. His face eased. The weariness melted from his limbs and his soul.

"Fir?" the commander asked when he didn't turn around.

"We'll keep her."

Another guard wet his lips. "Sir... may we have some?"

The commander glanced at Fir; Fir nodded. "We've earned a short break. Take shifts. This half," the commander waved at the guards, "watch the cart. The rest of you may eat. There's enough here for *one* person's generous supper, so you will take small bites instead of gorging yourself, leaving plenty for your companions to sample. Understood?"

They saluted. Soon a half-dozen guards sat around my cooking. They dipped their spoons in and licked them slowly, savoring every glistening bite.

Fir stayed next to me, but he sheathed his knife. "How did you learn to cook like that?"

"My father taught me," I said. I couldn't read Fir's face.

"You possess a strong birthgift, no doubt. Your skill is superb."

I raised an eyebrow. "I didn't know you had an interest in cooking."

Outside of poisoning people.

"I wanted to be a chef when I was little." He gave me a half-smile, no malice in it. That unnerved me more than any cruel thing he could have done. "Cooking seemed so enticing—the hearths and crocks and the bubbling smells."

I glanced at the obsidian knife gleaming in his belt, delicate black whorls reflecting orange firelight. Would he stab me once I relaxed? The commander kept a sharp eye on both of us.

"What changed?" I asked. The longer we talked, the longer the cart stood still.

Fir shrugged. "My mother indulged me in cooking lessons, but I gave it up myself. I could become a decent cook with enough effort and practice, but I'd never be a true professional. Not in cooking or any other traditional occupation—not with my lack of birthgift. So I placed my efforts elsewhere."

"Ah."

"The palace wasted your skills," Fir continued. "Having you scrub crocks instead of cook."

"Thank you." I stared at the ground, then at the soldiers licking spoons. The aroma of caramelized carrots hung thick in the air. What else could I say to Fir? A conversation with a stranger would have been easier.

"You don't trust me," Fir said.

"You just held a knife to my throat."

Fir shrugged. "A moment ago, you were Lady Sulat's person, loyal to Rowak. Now you're a traitor with no one to turn to but Shoreed and Red Lord Ospren."

"Red Lord Ospren?" I feigned ignorance.

"He's going to sit on the throne." Fir glanced at me. "Does that bother you?"

I fervently shook my head. "Not if it means I live."

Fir's relaxed smile almost made him seem amicable. "You'll need someone to watch out for you in this new monarchy. Keep you safe. Find you work."

The commander ordered the guards to switch their posts so the other half could sample my cooking.

But Fir didn't move. His words turned in my head. "You want me to become *your* person."

"Of course. You're talented. Everyone with a high post in the government needs loyal followers. And in Lord Ospren's new government, I *will* be someone, Plum. He's promised me no meager position for my help."

I stared at him. Fir wasn't fiercely loyal to Lord Ospren on principle. He was ambitious. Cruelly ambitious. He'd put deadly snakes in my crock. Got Hawak out of the palace, brought the Bloodmarrow Violet in, and nearly killed Lady Sulat's infant.

I couldn't imagine Lady Sulat resorting to such means. She was calm, justified, careful.

But the commander still watched us and I had to keep stalling. I leaned against the tree behind me, twining my fingers into the curling, fern-like moss growing up its trunk. "Don't you hate me?" I asked. "I ruined your plans. I uncovered Violet."

Regret touched Fir's eyes, but not for long. "You made a good opponent. Now you can oppose my enemies. I'll help you find a new life in Lord Ospren's Rowak. I'll see you have fine ingredients, imported recipes, and access to the royal greenhouses. What more could you want?"

Once, that was exactly what I thought I wanted. But nothing

about Fir's offer tempted me. Bane admired me without tasting my cooking—he'd seen a soldier in me. That part of my soul was just as strong as the part that loved clean crocks and fresh vegetables.

"Life isn't just about cooking." I'd happily serve Lady Sulat for the opportunity to be a chef, but not Fir.

"Ah. You want a post." Fir nodded as if he'd expected it. "The Redwood Palace may need a new Master Chef. I can't make promises, but I'll certainly try to maneuver you into that position. Red Lord Ospren rewards those who follow him."

The highest chef in Rowak. For all my ambition, I'd never dreamed that high. And I didn't want to. In Clamsriver, the war had seemed distant. Even now, I'd only seen the smallest part of it—the veterans heading home on their carts, Bane's lost arm, Osem's lost family—but I'd rather haul firewood for the rest of my life than prolong its ruin on my country.

"Oh." I said, stalling. "I don't think I deserve such an office."

"You made an All-of-All. No one could argue you're unqualified."

The commander frowned and strode up to us. I made a horrible actress. He stood on the other side of me, flanking me against Fir. "You're scared, aren't you?"

Of course I was scared. How did I answer that?

"It's a lot to take in," he said. "A new monarch for Rowak. But Fir makes no small claims here. He's worked diligently for Lord Ospren, and they're kin. Fir can care for us."

Us. Fir nodded benevolently at the commander, who bowed politely in turn. The young man really was building himself up a network of followers.

"You can be part of this, Plum," Fir said.

The commander patted my shoulder and smiled. He looked almost like Moss when he did that—the grandfatherly Moss, not the sarcastic one. "You seem like a nice young lady with hard times behind. But now you have this great opportunity to benefit yourself and your family in our new Rowak. Your luck has finally come in."

The commander toppled onto me. I shrieked and pushed him away, trying to spot his knife hand.

He thudded to the ground, an arrow sticking from his neck. His blood soaked my hands, my dress, the ground.

Fir protectively threw himself on top of me, tackled me. We crashed hard onto the ground. He tugged on me, trying to get me to crawl into the ferns with him. Better cover. A chance of escape. When I didn't move, he left me there, laying in the dirt, ribs aching from the fall.

Half of the Palace Guards around me yelled and brandished their spears. One whipped out a bow. The rest lay dying on the ground from arrow wounds.

"Drop your weapons, or you will also die," called a voice in the treetops.

Three of the guards, including the archer, sank to their knees and placed their shaking hands on their heads.

The remaining three guards charged. They all fell, dark-fletched arrows sticking out of their chests.

My throat pinched closed. How could there be corpses where men once stood? How could the sympathetic commander be slumped over so unnaturally, his face in the dirt? I didn't even know his name. The sticky blood on my hands and dress shone black in the pale moonlight. It felt far too thick to be beet juice.

Ancestors, I hated this war.

Bane ran to my side. He gawked at the blood. "Dami, are you injured?"

"No."

He beamed at me. How could he smile so easily, when corpses stared up at us? "The Rowak army sent me with twenty of their fastest runners. The ghost plowed ahead of us, blazing a trail straight to you. I'm glad we made it so fast. You led us to victory today."

I couldn't even stand back far enough on this swath of road to see all the carnage at once. "They're dead."

"They were traitors."

I knew that. I did. Our country was safer without them. But lying on the ground, they just looked like men. Surely their mothers, fathers, wives, and children would curse this day.

"We won," I mumbled. The words tasted acrid on my tongue. My marrow felt cold.

The chef part of me itched to tend all their wounds, but dead men's mouths can't swallow curing food. Bane's soldiers flushed out Fir, then tied him up with the three surviving Palace Guards.

I should be cheering that dark, blood-soaked ground, the blood of traitors, but my marrow gave out. I imagined all the battlefields so much worse than this. I imagined Dami among them—among bodies and blood and life growing cold—and I collapsed to my knees and wept.

Ghost-Fulsaan edged out of the trees, whimpering. He scooted to the nearly-empty crock, throwing me plaintive looks.

I wiped my eyes with my sleeves. "Go ahead, Fulsaan. I know your nature makes it hard to resist."

It seemed fitting that the meal that cost these men their lives should turn to ghost-fouled mush. Fulsaan picked up the crock with his stubby arms and slurped.

Oddly, those beautifully cooked vegetables didn't turn to slime. His mouth widened. His fat rolls shrunk, his legs strengthened.

"Fulsaan?" I asked, rising from my knees.

I caught a glimpse of a human face, of a grateful smile, before Fulsaan dissipated into smoke. The crock fell to the ground and broke, empty and clean inside.

I tilted my head back and watched that smoke curl and wheel, like a rejoicing eagle, up above the trees. It disappeared into the stars.

Exorcising a ghost requires three things. A meal perfectly cooked. True regret from the ghost. And a confession.

He'd confessed to me that morning in his room—had it only been three days ago? He'd displayed true regret by rejecting laziness tonight. And the meal he'd just eaten—endurance to the limbs and the soul. Isn't that what a lazy man needed? The ability to keep going, to persevere, to not give up?

I peered upward through the trees, imagining that I could still catch a wisp of him as he ascended to his ancestors.

The ground around me stretched ugly and cold, but gazing up at the stars and the glorious moon, I smiled. "May you rest with your ancestors in peace, Purple-ranked Fulsaan of Askan-Wod. And say hello to my nana for me. You owe me, you lazy old man," I said fondly. "Make sure she's all right."

Somehow, I knew he would.

CHAPTER
THIRTY-NINE

Bane's soldiers opened the passenger cart, helped King Alder and Purple Lord Heir Valerian outside, then cut their bonds and gags.

The captain of the soldiers frowned. "Where's King Former Fulsaan? I understood he was taken as well."

His subordinate turned to me. "She called the Hungry Ghost that."

Alder's face tightened in rage. I wasn't leaving this clearing alive.

"That was a Vengeful Ghost, not a Hungry Ghost," I said quickly. "The traitor guards killed King Former Fulsaan on the road. Since we were friends in life, he asked for my help to avenge his murder and save his descendants. Now that you great soldiers have rescued his son and grandson, he is at rest."

I bowed to King Alder first, then the guards. Alder's face stayed hard. Unreadable.

The captain's eyes widened in wonder. "Your Majesty, where is

Purple-ranked Fulsaan's body? I'll send some of these men to recover the late Purple-ranked Fulsaan."

"It disappeared. When he changed into a ghost of vengeance. We'll have to set a plaque for him in the Royal Shrine," King Alder said, voice flat.

He couldn't denounce my lie and order my execution on the spot without disinheriting himself. My lie was as good as any—filled with half-truths—but Alder's eyes showed no truce.

The troop's captain sent a pair of messengers to run ahead to the Rowak army. The remaining soldiers hid the dead bodies and the cart off the overgrown road.

We all walked through the forest then—me, Bane, prisoners, soldiers, King Alder, and Lord Valerian. Dark, wet ferns brushed my leg. Just dew, not blood.

All of my adrenaline sank into a cold, tired pit in my gut. Bane's mouth tightened with worry, but he stayed a step back. I was grateful. Forming words seemed an insurmountable task. I plodded one foot in front of the other. Fulsaan was free. The king wouldn't kill me this instant. I'd stopped a coup. And now Rowak's armies knew the location and plans of the Shoreed forces. They'd deal with defending the capital.

When we reached the army, an escort group from General Yuin awaited us. Since traitors filled Askan-Wod, he wanted the Royal Family safely in Napil. Soldiers emptied out two supply carts, giving one to the purple-ranked, and one to me, Bane, and the prisoners.

I ended up sitting directly across from Fir.

Bane snored softly, but despite the exhaustion sinking into my marrow, I couldn't doze. Not with traitors here, not with the smell of mud and drying blood and a lingering hint of my aromatic carrots, parsnips, and beets.

"Are you going to gloat?" Fir asked in an oddly mild, conversational tone. The muddled sky above us diffused the starlight into blackness.

"Why would I gloat?"

"Because I was *somebody,* somebody important, and you overthrew me."

The cart jostled over the uneven road. "I wasn't fighting you. I fought against a vassal Rowak."

"I don't know why you're more loyal to King Alder than Red Lord Ospren. Only one of those men condemned you to hang."

"King Alder won't be king forever," I said. "But after he passes, Rowak will still be free—if we weather this war."

"If." Fir smirked. Then he leaned toward me and lowered his voice. "When Red Lord Ospren takes the throne, my offer still stands."

I hugged my arms to my chest, trying to ward off the chill. "You tried to sell the sovereignty of your nation for a post. Why would I serve that?"

"You're still such a country girl. Why should we care if Rowak is sovereign or not? We'll never rule this country. What matters is how many people you control. I suppose you're perfectly happy with the way things are. Lady Sulat is a powerful woman to serve."

I shifted away. Cold, stiff blood plastered my dress to my skin. I didn't serve Lady Sulat because she was powerful; I served her because she made honorable choices and supported those under her. People like Osem, left without family. People like Bane, left without a limb. Given a chance, I'm sure she could put even Fir to good use. "You're Lady Egal's grandson. That wasn't enough?"

"A doting grandmother bestows little respect or power. Especially on a giftless child."

I shook my head. "There are plenty of people with little or no gift who live honest lives."

"But not remarkable ones."

I stiffened. "Everything Bane did tonight—that wasn't remarkable? His impaired birthgift never came into play." I thought of Osem, too—her birthgift wasn't to thank for her skills as an informant, or her loyalty and kindness as a friend. "Out of pride, you almost destroyed Rowak."

Just like Dami had almost destroyed my family. Why couldn't Fir see what a tragedy it would be if Rowak fell?

Oddly, Fir smiled. "See? You should gloat about defeating me. I made myself into someone of consequence."

IN NAPIL, I was given my own room in the governor's house, one with a soft mattress in a curtained alcove. I slept.

The morning light displayed the handsomeness of the room—gleaming redwood window lattices with cut-outs of leaping trout and thick rugs depicting pink foxgloves. But the inside air felt too dusty, too close.

As soon as I stepped from the alcove, a servant girl appeared. She asked me if I'd like breakfast or a bath. I opted for the later. My stomach didn't feel ready for food.

Afterwards, clean and dry in a soft, straw-colored dress with appropriately yellow-ranked sleeves, I asked for directions to the gardens, then for solitude. She bowed and obliged.

The dirt path felt oddly quiet under my feet, but I found the garden easily. I sat on a stone bench by a small pond, near a plum tree. A few old petals still scattered the ground, and broad green leaves spread above me. I tossed a rock into the water and watched the concentric ripples. Somehow, that was soothing.

Bane strolled up and sat next to me, mixing his juniper scent with the cool smells of morning dew and awakening flowers. At first, he said nothing. Then the ripples faded and the pond returned to its glassy smoothness, reflecting the sky.

"Last night, riding Fulsaan into the army camp... I prayed to my Ancestors for you. I thought the sun might rise on a world where you and Rowak were both things of the past. And here you sit, drenched in sunlight."

The day might be clear, but I felt like I'd left half of myself at the ambush in the woods. "How fares Rowak?"

Bane smiled. "Last night, General Yuin took half of Napil's forces and all the soldiers sent from Askan-Wod onto the Old North Path. They flanked and ambushed the Shoreed. We took the victory."

He still said *we*, even though he was a messenger now, not one of the combatants. I tried to cling to that bit of solidarity instead of imagining the dead littering the forest floor.

"The survivors scattered," Bane continued. "Some must have made it to the Shoreed's pretend siege camp, because they're all retreating now. They'll sit in the forts they've already taken from us and lick their wounds. The rest of Rowak will be safe for a while. Now we'll retake the capital from the traitors."

"More deaths." I didn't want to see the palace gardens strewn with bodies instead of flowers.

"Not many. General Yuin believes most of the military remains loyal. I doubt the small Palace Guard will give our army any trouble."

Because they'd surrender, or because the soldiers would squash them? I tossed another rock in the pond. "There are probably guards who didn't know what was happening."

Bane nodded. "They'll all have their trials."

And how many of them would live through that? Or even live until their trials started? I shivered.

"The coup leaders will be executed, but any innocent Palace Guard will simply be sent to reinforce the front lines. The king will need a new Palace Guard—one he can trust."

So neat. So thought out. "You're well informed."

"Ah." His cheeks heated with modest pride. "I got to report to General Yuin in person this morning. About what happened last night. You were sleeping. He asked me to invite you to eat lunch with him. You've saved his wife twice and his country once. You're a national hero."

Bane beamed at me.

I was grateful to have someone real and trustworthy and alive sitting next to me after the horrors of last night. But his joy caused no pride to burn in me. I turned my hands over in my lap, staring at them. Despite my trip to the bathhouse, my nose still picked up a tang of blood on my skin.

Bane's postured softened. "You've never seen a dead man before, have you? It's normal to be unsettled. Perfectly normal."

I exhaled, but my throat remained tight. "I've seen people die, Bane. I've seen them die of fever and accidents and childbirth and old age. I've never seen anyone *killed* before."

"I'm sorry. If we could have taken them out without you seeing..."

I squeezed my eyes shut. That's not what I meant. I didn't want to be so engrossed in cooking that I never noticed this war or what it cost our country. I didn't want to be blissful because other people suffered and left me clean from the hard, dirty tasks. I wanted my life to be peaceful because the world was actually at peace.

"Dami... it gets better. I promise. I was like this after my first skirmish, too."

I didn't want it to get better—to pretend I'd been blind since I left Clamsriver. I wanted to hate killings in ten years as much as I did right now. What had that commander left undone? Surely he had a list as long as my own.

I tossed another rock in the pond. I stared at the ripples, back tense, neck aching. "My name isn't Dami."

Bane blinked at me.

I was tired of hearing my sister's name. Tired of so many things. "It's Plum."

The silence stretched, eerie between us. Riding on Ghost-Fulsaan, with the wind whipping away my words, it had been easy to say more. Here, in the calm of morning, I didn't feel like I could manage anything besides than that six-word confession.

But Bane didn't ask me to explain. He tossed a rock into the pond, too. "Plum. That suits you."

GENERAL YUIN HELD lunch in the gardens around a circular redwood table. Servants delivered elegant fare: roast trout smothered in a scallion sauce, white bean cakes with hazelnuts, and a kale salad garnished with sun-colored nasturtium flowers. The governor must have a greenhouse—nasturtiums weren't quite in season, yet. From the aroma alone, I knew this was well-seasoned. A pair of soldiers flanked the general, their faces as unreadable as furniture.

But the General himself smiled, warm crinkles in the corners of his eyes. "Please, sit."

"Thank you."

He sat after I did. I nibbled around the trout, hoping the bean cakes would settle my stomach before I tried the richer fare. They didn't have quite enough hotradish, though the salt level was perfect.

"So you are the girl who undermined the coup. And saved my wife and son." He managed to watch me and eat heartily at the same time. Maybe that was a soldier's habit?

"I... suppose so."

"Tell me what happened."

I fidgeted with my spoon. Was General Yuin an ally of Lady Sulat's? I hadn't heard her say, directly. He seemed trustworthy and that made me cautious. Especially after my blunder with Archivists Kochan and Linaan.

I tried the salad. Over spiced, with those nasturtium petals. I mixed it in with the bean cakes to balance the flavors.

"If you don't wish to talk about yourself, will you tell me about my son? I've yet to see him, you know."

My insides melted at that. Yes, I could speak of the infant. I told him about too-tiny hands and feet and how he spent his days wrapped to Lady Sulat or the nurse to keep him warm.

General Yuin nodded, pleased. "Bane told me about his birth and his birthgift."

My words dammed up again, embarrassment heating my cheeks.

"You must have worked hard, for such skill."

I bowed my head. Dami always said I was lucky or gifted—but the General gave the compliment I was proud to hear. "Thank you."

"I spoke with King Alder." His crinkle-cornered eyes turned serious. "He informed me that you're condemned to die and he expects me to keep you safely imprisoned."

The warmth in my face sank into icy dread. Why had I thought my sentence would disappear? The king had a simple way to dispose of me—of course he'd use it.

"Dami, I didn't mean to alarm you. Do you think Lady Sulat would let someone like you perish? You have the heart of a soldier, do you know that?"

I did. Bane taught me that. But it seemed flippant to say as much to Rowak's general. "I'm a chef, not a soldier. I wouldn't know."

General Yuin smiled. "Perhaps I should have said I'm grateful for all the soldiers who have the heart of a chef, then. Eat up. We march for the Redwood Palace in an hour."

We marched halfway to Askan-Wod, camped for the night, then marched the rest of the way by midday. Retaking the capital went nearly as well as Bane predicted. Lieutenant-General Behon put up a brief skirmish trying to escape, but General Yuin surrounded him. Sixteen men died.

Half the Palace Guard stood outside the palace gates, tearing off their office armbands in shame and surrender. The guards remaining inside the palace resisted, but General Yuin quickly overwhelmed them. Another three deaths.

I heard all of this from the back ranks, surrounded by my four guards. I think General Yuin selected them personally; they treated me respectfully and left my wrists unbound. My guards grinned at the reports as they came by. "Only nineteen dead; General Yuin works so smoothly!"

I didn't know how he could call nineteen deaths a smooth affair.

With the Redwood Palace secured, the soldiers escorted me to my old room in the Royal Bear House. Stuffy opulence surrounded me once more—redwood reeking of polish, the heavy curtain of embroidered hawks and salmon hiding the bed in the alcove.

A single bowl of plain buckwheat porridge waited for me, the condemned, on the carved table. No visitors followed. Just hollow silence, muffled by the too-thick, ornate rug.

The sun set, red as a roasted beet through the window. I curled up on the soft bed in the alcove. Could Lady Sulat save me?

I'd left so many things undone. I wanted to know if anyone had found Osem. I wanted to talk to Hawak about exorcisms—did he know the steps didn't have to go in order or occur on the same day? I wanted to see Dami return safely home.

At least, on the other side of the Royal Bear House, Fulsaan's room lay empty. That wasn't left undone. And whatever happened to me and my family here, he'd take care of my nana.

I slept uneasily, thoughts of what my life could be rattling in my skull.

TWO DAYS PASSED. More porridge was delivered. Plain. It never so much had a pinch of salt or a drizzle of blackberry molasses. I paced my beautiful room. Why should I feel restless? Shouldn't I be grateful for extra days to live—even days alone?

When I couldn't pace any more, I crept into my alcove and asked my Ancestors to watch over Dami.

Night fell again. Maybe I'd live in this room forever, locked up and half-forgotten like Fulsaan.

THE NEXT MORNING, three soldiers stepped into my room.

One of them was Moss.

"You're here!" I ran and stopped short of throwing my arms around him. "I'm so glad to see you."

"Good to see you too. I wish I could say I'm here to free you." He gave me a crooked smile. "But I'm under orders to escort you to the Hall of Moral Law. Lady Sulat's made a very good argument that you need a second hearing, since there was a traitor on the last one. The Purple-Blue Council is waiting for you."

CHAPTER FORTY

Morning light poured through the high windows of the Hall of Moral Law, backlighting the elegant wolves cut into the screen. The blood-red floor and white pillars gleamed. This place smelled of old wood and oil.

The same ten people sat between the whole log pillars as last time, except Lady Sulat replaced Lieutenant-General Behon. Her hair and skin radiated a healthy glow, and her infant slept soundly, strapped to her chest. A knot in the back of my neck loosened. My patient had recovered.

Unfortunately, the other nine councilmembers here had already marked me for death.

King Alder sat on his throne before me. The carved bears decorating the back and arms seemed to stare at me, amber eyes filled with as much hatred as their master's. I could almost taste the snarl in King Alder's too-tight face.

This man wanted me dead. I'd saved his life, his country, and set his father free. But I was a liability.

I glanced to Lady Sulat, but she stood without looking at me. Apparently the opening formalities had already occurred, because King Alder gestured for her to speak.

Her regal voice echoed against the pillars. "I lament the circumstances that prevented me from being present at the previous trial and I thank you all, members of the Purple-Blue Council, for allowing this hearing today. Here, we will decide the fate of a patriot of Rowak."

From the curiosity on the councilor's faces and the frustration on the king's, the Council chose to see me against King Alder's wishes.

"You have all heard how this woman before you was instrumental in saving our nation from the Shoreed. She rescued Purple King Alder and Purple Lord Heir Valerian. Alas that the kidnappers murdered my frail father—may he rest in peace with our Ancestors."

Lady Sulat spoke with measured calm, her face placid, but when she finished that sentence, she stared up at Alder. Did she know the truth, then? Maybe Osem had escaped and delivered my message after all. I hoped so.

I paused. Bane knew about Fulsaan, too. He could have told her just as easily.

"Yet she lied to the king," Lady Sulat continued. "Why? Why would one capable of noble deeds stoop to such a base act as lying to the Royal House?"

The councilors shifted forward, studying at me. That's exactly why they'd agreed to this hearing—they wanted to know. Lady Sulat let the question hang in the air. Had she spread the story of what I'd done, or had the councilors heard it on their own?

My insides felt like an over-boiling hotpot. Silence ached in the air.

"There is a simple answer," Lady Sulat said at last. "I asked her to."

I bit down on my lip and kept my eyes on the floor, trying to hide my surprise. She'd done no such thing. The councilors muttered to themselves.

Why would Lady Sulat risk herself like this? Rowak needed her more than it needed me.

"I am the Head of Military Affairs. I gathered intelligence that the Shoreed might attempt to place a poisoner inside the Redwood Palace to tip the balance of the war. To protect King Alder, I needed to place my own, trusted person in the kitchens to watch for such a spy. Yellow-ranked Dami of Clamsriver, a young woman strong-of-arm, was next on the list to join the rank of palace servants. But Dami had an older sister. An accomplished chef who could trade places and watch for poison."

I didn't dare look up from that condemningly red floor. How could she *know* that? Had she somehow gotten it from Fir?

Lady Sulat sounded all-too calm for a woman incriminating herself.

"Yellow-ranked Dami graciously stepped down and allowed her sister to secretly replace her. The name of the woman before you is Plum. While the enemy proved more ambitious than I anticipated, my faithful agent still managed to quell the coup."

I glanced up. Awe and fear tinged the faces of the councilors as they gazed at me and Lady Sulat. And why shouldn't they stare? She had such knowledge, such foresight. I tried not to choke on my own tongue. She'd nearly lost her life and her country, but she could spin all of that into a story where she'd never been in the dark about anything.

But I don't think King Alder believed a word of it. Either that, or he didn't care. His eyes tightened. His back stiffened, painfully straight.

Lady Sulat bowed gracefully, her wide sleeves sweeping to her sides. "This Council has already condemned Yellow-Ranked Plum, but that trial was held in error. I am her superior. She obeyed her orders with exactness. Any crimes she may have committed rests solely on my own head. My fellow Council members, I submissively await your judgment."

She stood, folding her arms calmly in front of her infant. I wanted to shout at her—she couldn't let herself be executed!—but perhaps that was the kind of risk Lady Sulat took for her people.

Gratitude and awe showed in the councilor's faces. No, there was no risk here. King Alder scowled, but with a defeated slump. He wouldn't—or couldn't—kill his sister.

"We vote," King Alder said, voice hard.

The official made his rounds once more. White token after white token dropped onto the tray. He presented this to the King.

"The vote is unanimous. A full acquittal," King Alder announced.

Acquittal. Such a beautiful word.

Lady Sulat bowed deeply, one hand supporting her child's back. "Thank you, Purple-Blue Council, for your wise judgment. Plum is a hero. In accordance with her exceptional service to Rowak, I nominate her for the Green rank."

King Alder glowered at Sulat, but a murmur of approval rose from the council. An official collected the vote. King Alder could do nothing to protest the all-white tokens presented on the tray. He tried to look pleased —I doubted he wanted to display his true feelings when the councilors so obviously approved—but he still looked like he'd swallowed vinegar.

Moss walked forward from somewhere behind the pillars, carrying a gray servant's dress wide enough to cover my elbows. The clothing of a green-ranked woman. He laid it gently in my arms, grinning.

"Congratulations," he whispered.

Green-ranked Plum of Clamsriver. How odd.

Lady Sulat swept out of the hall. Moss nabbed my elbow and pulled me after. I nearly tripped over my feet, but he kept me steady.

Shortly, we came to Lady Sulat's sitting room. Osem sat in one of the chairs—Osem! I ran and hugged her, then stepped back and frowned at the bruise across her jaw. "Oh, Osem."

"My interrogator had more important things to worry about than getting information for a king he was dethroning. That's my only injury, and it's healing well."

"I'm so sorry."

"You didn't do this to me," she said stubbornly. "Let's figure out a sign language so we're never in that kind of a tight spot again."

"Good idea."

"You should change, Plum," Lady Sulat said, a hint of a smile around her serene mouth. She relaxed into one of the sitting room chairs. "Feel free to use my room."

"Thank you." I meant those words in so many ways. I reluctantly stepped away from Osem, into the next room, and put on the dress.

The smooth cloth tumbled to my elbows. How surreal to have fabric there. I tied my black skirt on and adjusted the more-voluminous drape of the dress. Tonight, I could write my parents and tell them I'd not only been acquitted, but honored.

When I stepped back into the main room, General Yuin had joined us. He sat by his wife, eyes crinkled in amusement. "I take it that your hearing went well, Plum?"

"Yes, sir."

With her husband in the room, Lady Sulat's countenance softened. She even smiled a fraction.

The general turned to his wife, laying one of his calloused hands on the back of his infant's sling. "I've sent a squad to fetch Azalea. In a few days, we'll all be together again."

I didn't want to invade their familial conversation, so I excused myself, then rejoined Osem on the other side of the room. "No dishes to scrub today?"

"Ah. I got lonely down there, working by myself." She smiled teasingly. "Y'know, now that I don't have a ghost to keep me company."

She sounded like herself; I couldn't help but smile in turn.

"Sorrel kindly gave me today off. The apprentices don't approve; they're taking turns scrubbing right now."

So Sorrel had survived. I had no desire to speak to him again, but I was grateful there wasn't more news of bloodshed and cruelty. There'd been far too much of that already.

Moss strode up, arms crossed. "So. I guess I'm not going to get to use these bolas on you."

"Nope." I shook my head, watching Lady Sulat and General Yuin fuss over their child. "How did she do it, Moss? How did she know about me?"

He smirked. "Plum, the *first* rule of navigating the palace is knowing what everyone's birthgift is."

"She's perceptive of eye," I said, frowning. That let her see my face—not my soul.

Moss tugged one of his ears. "You never learned what I am, though."

I paused. No, I hadn't. "You're perceptive-of-ear?"

"I heard your prayers. Lady Sulat has known your real name—and why you came to the palace—for some time. The prayers might have been a lie to make yourself look innocent, but time proved otherwise."

The door guards let Bane into the sitting room. The morning sun shone like amber in his hair, and a broad smile lit the rest of his face. Now everyone I cared about in the palace had gathered into this one happy, bright spot.

"You're free," Bane said, in one great exhale.

"Yes."

General Yuin smiled at him. Bane looked like he might faint from the attention. "Did you doubt she would be?"

"Ah, no sir." Bane bowed, then stood straight like a soldier, then fidgeted, as if unsure how to act around the famous general.

Yuin dismissed him with a wave of his hand. "Go see her."

Bane crossed the room. His whole body seemed to lean against that two-foot gap of air between us that propriety demanded. I leaned against it, too.

"I'm glad you're safe. Plum."

I loved hearing my name, my real name. I loved not hiding who I was. Though maybe I'd never really hidden from Bane. He'd always seen me.

His posture, his smile—it was all an invitation. I was a free person of the Green Rank now, with no trial hanging over me. I could accept, or I could walk away.

Already I could smell his skin—woodsy, like juniper and smoke.

His hair hung low over those mesmerizing brown eyes. I remembered his warmth on my back as we rode the Hungry Ghost together. Bane was solid. Dependable. Charming. Brave.

I slipped my hand into Bane's, intertwining my fingers with his. I didn't know yet, if he was my man. But now I had a chance to find out —as Bane and Plum, without any lies between us.

Bane held my hand like he never wanted to let go. I didn't want to let go, either.

"Do you want to play springball?" I asked. "Me and you against Osem and Moss. Proper pairs."

He smiled, as brilliant as a summer sunrise. Warmth curled through me—this was exactly where I wanted to be.

"I'd love to," he said.

Osem and Moss grinned at the two of us—like they both thought Bane and I would make very entertaining company right now.

I turned to Lady Sulat. "Unless you need us for something else?"

"Go. All of you. Enjoy yourselves," our Lady said. "You deserve it."

EPILOGUE

Mid-morning the next day, Lady Sulat requested I travel with her back to the safehouse. She didn't explain until we stood at the bottom of the ladder in the main room.

"I've transferred an injured soldier here," she said

"One of your officers?"

"No. A new recruit. But this soldier, I've learned, saved my husband's life during the battle in the woods between here and Napil. One of the Shoreed tried to shoot him from behind. This soldier tackled Yuin out of the way, taking an arrow in the ribs."

"Admirable."

"Indeed," she said. "Until now, the soldier had been too unstable to transport, and rested at Napil. I want you to personally watch over and cook food for the recovery."

Chef—Lady Sulat's chef. Quiet pride simmered in my chest. I wasn't just cooking—I was cooking for someone who deserved my loyalty.

Lady Sulat gestured toward one of the rough wooden doors. I entered first, Lady Sulat following. Her guards remained behind.

Bandages covered the patient from collarbone to the midriff, outlining a feminine shape. But I only needed one glance at her ashen face to know this was no man.

Her eyelids sluggishly opened under those wisps of poorly-cropped hair. My throat tightened like I'd swallowed a disk of hotradish. She was alive.

"Hey, sis," the real Dami croaked, her voice little more than a scratch. She tried to smile. "Fancy finding you here."

I dropped by the bedside and took her hand. I squeezed it and discreetly checked her pulse at the same time. Dami was weak, but in no danger of dying. Silently, I thanked our Ancestors. I swallowed hard. "You too."

But the weight of her hand tempered my joy. Dami lived. But her secret was dead.

I looked up to Lady Sulat. "What's... what's to happen with her?"

"She broke the law." Lady Sulat said, her face that unnerving calm.

"So did I. She saved your husband's life," I pleaded.

Lady Sulat nodded. She'd already thought this through. "Given the king's displeasure with you," she flicked me a meaningful glance, "if Dami's behavior becomes public knowledge, he'll ensure the full measure of the law is followed. And he'll use that trial to defame you as well."

Dami snorted. I stared at her—didn't she know who stood next to us?—but that was just like Dami. Reassuringly so.

Lady Sulat kept speaking as if she hadn't heard. "I can't keep you safe from King Alder indefinitely if you remain in the Redwood Palace, Plum. But if your sister recovers well and if she's willing to be of service... I believe I have a task for both of you."

I exhaled. Away from the palace? But I didn't need to think about that yet. Dami was here, alive, delivered into the hands of my allies as neatly as if the Ancestors themselves had arranged it. And I had work to do. Pickled celery. Dami needed that first, to dull the pain and help her ribs heal. Then sweet marrow soup to improve her circulation and pallor.

I hadn't expected both of us to survive. "Thank you."

I wasn't sure if I was speaking to Lady Sulat or our Ancestors, but I thought they'd both understand.

Lady Sulat raised an eyebrow. "Perhaps you should wait to hand out thanks until after you hear what I have in mind.

ACKNOWLEDGMENTS

Thank you Matt Brown, John Hutchins, Ailsa Lillywhite, Kindal and Emily Debenham, Aneeka Richins, Kate Heartfield, Carolyn Duede, Michelle Cowart, Brinton Berg, and Michelle Walker for your insightful comments. This book would not be the same without you.

I've been delighted to meet such great people through Immortal Works. Thank you, Beth Buck, Holli Anderson, Benjamin Kocher, and Clare Dugmore for your expertise. It was lovely to have my manuscript in your capable hands.

I'm grateful to all the supportive friends and family in my life—including uncles. Many of my family members have also been excellent historians, preserving old photographs and stories. Thank you for giving me an opportunity to connect with the remarkable people who went before me.

ABOUT THE AUTHOR

M.K. Hutchins regularly draws on her background in archaeology when writing fiction. Her YA fantasy novel Drift was both a Junior Library Guild Selection and a VOYA Top Shelf Honoree. Her short fiction appears in Podcastle, Strange Horizons, Fireside, and elsewhere. A long-time Idahoan, she now lives in Utah with her husband and four children. Find her at www.mkhutchins.com.

This has been an
Immortal Production

9 781733 908542